Yasmina Khadra is the pen name of award-winning Algerian author Mohammed Moulessehoul. His novels include *The African Equation* and *The Dictator's Last Night*. In 2011 Yasmina Khadra was awarded the prestigious Grand prix de littérature Henri Gal by the Académie française.

Howard Curtis's many translations from French and Italian include works by Balzac, Flaubert, Pirandello, Jean-Claude Izzo, Marek Halter and Gianrico Carofiglio. He previously translated *The African Equation* by Yasmina Khadra.

Also by Yasmina Khadra

# THE ANGELS DIE

GALLIC

# THE ANGELS DIE

Yasmina Khadra

Translated from the French
by Howard Curtis

Gallic Books
London

A Gallic Book

First published in France as *Les anges meurent de nos blessures*
by Éditions Julliard, 2013
Copyright © Éditions Julliard, 2013
English translation copyright © Gallic Books 2016

First published in Great Britain in 2016 by Gallic Books,
59 Ebury Street, London, SW1W 0NZ

A CIP record for this book is available from the British Library
ISBN 978-1-908313-91-1

Typeset in Fournier MT by Gallic Books
Printed in the UK by CPI (CR0 4TD)

2 4 6 8 10 9 7 5 3 1

My name is Turambo and they'll be coming to get me at dawn.

'You won't feel a thing,' Chief Borselli reassures me.

How would he know anyway? His brain's the size of a pea.

I feel like yelling at him to shut up, to forget about me for once, but I'm at the end of my tether. His nasal voice is as terrifying as the minutes eating away at what's left of my life.

Chief Borselli is embarrassed. He can't find the words to comfort me. His whole repertoire comes down to a few nasty set phrases that he punctuates with blows of his truncheon. *I'm going to smash your face like a mirror*, he likes to boast. *That way, whenever you look at your own reflection, you'll get seven years of bad luck* ... Pity there's no mirror in my cell, and when you're on death row a stay of execution isn't calculated in years.

Tonight, Chief Borselli is forced to hold back his venom and that throws him off balance. He's having to improvise some kind of friendly behaviour, instead of just being a brute, and it doesn't suit him; in fact it distorts who he is. He comes across as pathetic, disappointing, as annoying as a bad cold. He's not used to waiting hand and foot on a jailbird he'd rather be beating up so as not to lose his touch. Only two days ago, he stood me up against the wall and rammed my face into the stone – I still have the mark on my forehead. *I'm going to tear your eyes out and stick them up your arse*, he bellowed so that everyone could hear. *That way you'll have four balls and you'll be able to look at me without winding me up* ... An idiot with a truncheon and permission to

7

use it as he pleases. A cockerel made out of clay. Even if he rose to his full height, he wouldn't come up to my waist, but I suppose you don't need a stool when you've got a club in your hand to knock giants down to size.

Chief Borselli hasn't been feeling well since he moved his chair to sit outside my cell. He keeps mopping himself with a little handkerchief and spouting theories that are beyond his mental powers. It's obvious he'd rather be somewhere else: in the arms of a drunken whore, or maybe in a stadium, surrounded by a jubilant crowd screaming their heads off to keep the troubles of the world away, in fact anywhere that's a million miles from this foul-smelling corridor, sitting opposite a poor devil who doesn't know where to put his head until it's time to return it to its rightful owner.

I think he feels sorry for me. After all, what is a prison guard but the man on the other side of the bars, one step away from remorse? Chief Borselli probably regrets his overly harsh treatment of me now that the scaffold is being erected in the deathly silence of the courtyard.

I don't think I've hated him more than I should. The poor bastard's only doing the lousy job he's been given. Without his uniform, which makes him a bit more solid, he'd be eaten alive quicker than a monkey in a swamp filled with piranhas. But prison's like a circus: on one side, there are the animals in their cages and, on the other, the tamers with their whips. The boundaries are clear, and anyone who ignores them has only himself to blame.

When I'd finished eating, I lay down on my mat. I looked at the ceiling, the walls defaced with obscene drawings, the rays of the setting sun fading on the bars, and got no answers to any of my questions. What answers? And what questions? There's been nothing up for debate since the day the judge, in a booming voice, read out what my fate was to be. The flies, I remember, had broken off their dance in the gloomy room and all eyes turned to me, like so many shovelfuls of earth thrown on a corpse.

All I can do now is wait for the will of men to be done.

I try to recall my past, but all I can feel is my heart beating to the relentless rhythm of the passing, echoless moments that are taking me, step by step, to my executioner.

I asked for a cigarette and Chief Borselli was eager to oblige. He'd have handed me the moon on a platter. Could it be that human beings simply adjust to circumstances, with the wolf and the lamb taking it in turns to ensure balance?

I smoked until I burnt my fingers, then watched the cigarette end cast out its final demons in tiny grey curls of smoke. Just like my life. Soon, night will fall in my head, but I'm not thinking of going to sleep. I'll hold on to every second as stubbornly as a castaway clinging to wreckage.

I keep telling myself that there'll be a sudden turnaround and I'll get out of here. As if that's going to happen! The die is well and truly cast, there's not much hope left. Hope? That's one big swindle! There are two kinds of hope. The hope that comes from ambition and the hope that makes us expect a miracle. The first can always keep going and the second can always wait: neither of them is an end in itself, only death is that.

And Chief Borselli is still talking nonsense! What's *he* hoping for? My forgiveness? I don't hold a grudge against anyone. So, for God's sake, shut up, Chief Borselli, and leave me to my silences. I'm just an empty shell, and my mind is a vacuum.

I pretend to take an interest in the bugs running around the cell, in the scratches on the rough floor, in anything that can get me away from my guard's babble. But it's no use.

When I woke up this morning, I found an albino cockroach under my shirt, the first I'd ever seen. It was as smooth and shiny as a jewel, and I told myself it was probably a good omen. In the afternoon, I heard *the* truck sputter into the courtyard, and Chief Borselli, who *knew*, gave me a furtive glance. I climbed onto my bed and hauled myself up to the skylight, but all I could see was a disused wing of the prison and two guards twiddling their thumbs. I can't imagine a more deafening silence. Most of the time, there have been jailbirds yelling and knocking their plates against the bars, when they weren't being beaten up by the military police. This afternoon, not a single sound disturbed my anxious thoughts. The guards have disappeared. You don't hear their grunting or their footsteps in the corridors. It's as though the prison has lost its soul. I'm alone, face to face with my ghost, and I find it hard to figure out which of us is flesh and which smoke.

In the courtyard, they tested the blade. Three times. Thud! ... Thud! ... Thud! ... Each time, my heart leapt in my chest like a frightened jerboa.

My fingers linger over the purple bruise on my forehead. Chief Borselli shifts on his chair. *I'm not a bad man in civilian life*, he says, referring to my bump. *I'm only doing my job. I mean, I've got kids, d'you see?* He's not telling me anything new. *I don't like to see people die,* he goes on. *It puts me off life. I'm going to be ill all week and for weeks to come* ... I wish he'd keep quiet. His words are worse than the blows from his truncheon.

I try and think of something. My mind is a blank. I'm only twenty-seven, and this month, June 1937, with the midsummer heat giving me a taste of the hell that's waiting for me, I feel as old as a ruin. I'd like to be afraid, to shake like a leaf, to dread the minutes ticking away one by one into the abyss, in other words to prove to myself that I'm not yet ready for the gravedigger – but there's nothing, not a flicker of emotion. My body is like wood, my breathing a diversion. I scour my memory in the hope of getting something out of it: a figure, a face, a voice to keep me company. It's pointless. My past has shrunk away, my career has cast me adrift, my history has disowned me.

Chief Borselli is now silent.

The silence is holding the prison in suspense. I know nobody's asleep in the cells, that the guards are close by, that *my hour* is stamping with impatience at the end of the corridor ...

Suddenly, a door squeaks in the hushed tranquillity of the stones and muffled footsteps move along the floor.

Chief Borselli almost knocks his chair over as he stands to attention. In the anaemic light of the corridor, shadows ooze onto the floor like trails of ink.

Far, far away, as if from a confused dream, the call of the muezzin echoes.

'*Rabbi m'āak*,' cries one of the inmates.

My guts are in a tangle, like snakes writhing inside a pot. Something takes hold of me that I can't explain. *The hour* has come. Nobody can escape his destiny. Destiny? Only exceptional people have one. Common mortals just have fate ... The muezzin's call sweeps over me like a gust of wind, shattering my senses in a swirl of panic. As my fear reaches its height, I dream about walking through the wall and running out into the open without turning back. To escape what? To go where? I'm trapped like a rat. Even if my legs won't carry me, the guards will make sure they hand me over in due form to the executioner.

The clenching of my bowels threatens my underpants. My mouth fills with the stench of soil; in it, I detect a foretaste of the grave that's getting ready to digest me until I turn to dust ... It's stupid to end up like this at the age of twenty-seven. Did I even have time to live? And what kind of life? ... *You're going to make a mess of things again, and I don't feel like cleaning up after you any more,* Gino used to warn me ... What's done is done; no remorse can cushion the fall. Luck is like youth. Everybody has his share. Some grab it on the wing, others let it slip through their fingers, and others are still waiting for it when it's long past … What did I do with mine?

I was born to flashes of lightning. On a stormy, windy night. With fists for hitting and a mouth for biting. I took my first steps surrounded by birdshit and grabbed hold of thorns to lift myself up.

Alone.

I grew up in a hellish shanty town outside Sidi Bel Abbès. In a yard where the mice were the size of puppies. Rags and hunger were my body and soul. Up before dawn at an age when I should have been carefree, I was already hard at work. Come rain or shine, I had to find a grain of corn to put in my mouth so that I could slave away again the following day without passing out. I worked without a break, often for peanuts, and by the time I got home in the evening I was dead beat. I didn't complain. That's just the way it was. Apart from the kids squabbling naked in the dust and the tramps you saw rotting under the bridges, their veins ravaged by cheap wine, everybody between the ages of seven and seventy-seven who could stand on their own two feet was expected to work themselves to death.

The place I worked at was a shop bang in the middle of a dangerous area, the haunt of thugs and lowlifes. It wasn't really a shop, more like a disused, worm-eaten dugout, where Zane, who was the worst kind of crook, squatted. My job wasn't hard: I tidied the shelves, swept the floor, delivered baskets twice my own weight, or kept a lookout whenever a widow up to her eyes in debt agreed to lift her dress at the back of the shop in return for a piece of sugar.

It was a strange time.

I saw prophets walking on water, living people who were more lifeless than corpses, riffraff sunk so low that neither demons nor the Angel of Death dared look for them there.

Even though Zane was raking it in, he never stopped complaining in order to protect himself from the evil eye, with the excuse that business was bad, that people were too broke even to have money for a rope to hang themselves with, that his creditors were shamelessly bleeding him dry, and I'd take his complaints as holy writ and feel sorry for him. Of course, to save face, he'd sometimes, either by chance or by mistake, slip a coin into my hand, but the day I was so exhausted that I asked for my back pay, he kicked me up the backside and sent me back to my mother with nothing but a promise to give me a hiding if he ever caught me hanging round the area again.

Before I reached puberty, I felt as if I'd come full circle, convinced I'd seen everything, experienced everything, endured everything.

As they say, I was immune.

I was eleven years old, and for me that was equivalent to eleven life sentences. A complete nonentity, as anonymous as a shadow, turning round and round like an endless screw. The reason I couldn't see the light at the end of the tunnel was because there wasn't one: I was simply travelling through an endless darkness ...

Chief Borselli fiddles with the lock of my cell, removes the padlock, opens the door with an almighty creak and stands aside to let in the 'committee'. The prison warden, my lawyer, two officials in suits and ties, a pale-faced barber with a bag at his side and the imam all advance towards me, flanked by two guards who look as if they've been carved out of granite.

Their formality makes my blood run cold.

Chief Borselli pushes his chair towards me and motions me to sit down. I don't move. I can't move. Someone says something to me. I don't hear. All I see is lips moving. The two guards help me up and put me on the chair. In the silence, my heartbeat echoes like a mournful drum roll.

The barber slips behind me. His ratlike fingers ease my shirt collar away from my neck. My eyes focus on the shiny, freshly polished shoes around me. By now, fear has taken hold of my whole being. The *end* has started! *It was written*, except that I'm illiterate.

If I'd suspected for a single second that the curtain would come down like this, I'd never have waited for the last act: I'd have shot straight ahead like a meteorite; I'd have become one with nothingness and thrown God Himself off my trail. Unfortunately, none of these 'if's lead anywhere; the proof is that they always arrive too late. Every mortal man has his moment of truth, a moment designed to catch him unawares, that's the rule. Mine took me by surprise. It seems to me like a distortion of my prayers, a non-negotiable aberration, a miscarriage of justice: whatever shape it takes, it always has the last word, and there's no appeal.

The barber starts cutting the collar off my shirt. Every snip of his scissors cuts a void in my flesh.

In extraordinarily precise flashes, memories come back to me. I see myself as a child, wearing a hessian sack instead of a gandoura, running barefoot along dusty paths. *After all*, as my mother used to say, *when nature, in its infinite goodness, gives us a thick layer of dirt on our feet, we can easily do without sandals.* My mother wasn't far wrong. Neither nettles nor brambles slowed down my frantic running. What exactly was I running after? ... My brain echos with the rants of Chawala, a kind of turbaned madman who, winter and summer, wore a flea-ridden cloak and a gutter-cleaner's boots. Tall, with a voluminous beard and yellow eyes painted with kohl, he liked to get up in the square, point his finger at people and predict the horrible things in store for them. I'd spend hours following him from one platform to another, so impressed I thought he was a prophet ... I see Gino, my friend Gino, my dear friend Gino, his incredulous eyes wide open in the darkness of that damned stairwell as his mother's voice rings out over the thunder: *Promise me you'll take care of him, Turambo. Promise me. I'd like to go in peace* ... And Nora, damn it! Nora. I thought she was mine, but nothing belonged to me. Funny how a helping hand could have changed the course of my life. I wasn't asking for the moon, only for my share of luck, otherwise how can you believe there's any kind of justice in this world? ... The images become muddled in my head before giving in to the clicking of the scissors. In the cosmic deafness of the prison, the sound seems to suck out the air and time.

The barber puts his equipment back into his bag. He's in a hurry to leave, only too happy not to be forced to stay for the main attraction.

The imam places a noble hand on my shoulder. I couldn't feel more crushed if a wall had fallen on me. He asks me if there's a particular surah I'd like to hear. With a lump in my throat, I tell him I have no preference. He chooses the Surah ar-Rahman for me. His voice penetrates into the depths of my being and, by some strange alchemy, I find the strength to stand up.

The two guards order me to follow them.

We walk out into the corridor, followed by the committee. The clanking of my chains scraping the floor turns my shivers to razor cuts. The imam continues his chanting. His gentle voice is doing me good. I'm no longer afraid to walk in the dark, the Lord is with me. '*Mout waguef!*', an inmate says to me in a Kabyle accent. '*Ilik dh'arguez!*', 'Goodbye, Turambo,' cries Bad-Luck Gégé, who's only just out of solitary. 'Hang on, brother. We're coming ...' Other voices are raised, escorting me to my

15

martyrdom. I stumble, but don't fall. Fifty more metres, thirty … I must hang on till the end. Not just for myself but for the others. However reluctantly, I must set an example. Only the way I die can redeem a failed life. I'd like those who live on after me to talk about me with respect, to say that I left with my head held high.

My head held high?

At the bottom of a basket!

*The only people who die with dignity are those who've fucked like rabbits, eaten like pigs, and blown all their money*, Sid Roho used to say.

*And what about those who are broke?*

*They don't die, they just disappear.*

The two guards are walking in front of me, quite impassive. The imam keeps on reciting his surah. My chains weigh a ton. The corridor hems me in on either side and I have to follow its confines.

The outside door is opened.

The cool air burns my lungs. The way the first gulp of air burns a baby's lungs …

And there she is.

In a corner of the courtyard.

Tightly wrapped in cold and horror.

Like a praying mantis awaiting her feast.

I see her at last: Lady Guillotine. Stiff in her costume of iron and wood. With a lopsided grin. As repulsive as she's fascinating. There she is, the porthole at the end of the world, the river of no return, the trap for souls in torment. Sophisticated and basic at one and the same time. In turn, a mistress of ceremonies and a street-corner whore. Whichever she is, she's going to make sure you lose your head.

All at once, everything around me fades away. The prison

walls disappear, the men and their shadows, the air stands still, the sky blurs. All that's left is my heart pounding erratically and the Lady with the blade, the two of us alone, face to face, on a patch of courtyard suspended in the void.

I feel as if I'm about to faint, to fall apart and be scattered like a handful of sand in the wind. I'm grabbed by sturdy hands and put back together. I come to, fibre by fibre, shudder by shudder. There are constant flashes in my head. I see the village where I was born, ugly enough to repel both evil genies and manna from heaven, a huge enclosure haunted by beggars with glassy eyes and lips as disturbing as scars. Turambo! A godforsaken hole given over to goats and brats defecating in the open air and laughing at the strident salvoes from their emaciated rumps ... I see Oran, like a splendid waterlily overhanging the sea, the lively trams, the souks and the fairs, the neon signs over the doors of nightclubs, girls as beautiful and unlikely as promises, whorehouses overrun with sailors as drunk as their boats ... I see Irène on her horse, galloping across the ridges, Gino gushing blood on the staircase, two boxers beating the hell out of each other in the ring in front of a clamouring crowd, the Village Nègre and its inspired street performers, the shoeshine boys of Sidi Bel Abbès, my childhood friends Ramdane, Gomri, the Billy Goat ... I see a young boy running barefoot over brambles, my mother putting her hands on her thighs in despair ... Discordant voices crowd the black and white film, merging in a commotion that fills my head like scalding hail ...

I'm pushed towards the guillotine.

I try and resist, but none of my muscles obey me. I walk to the guillotine as if levitating. I can't feel the ground beneath my feet. I can't feel anything. I think I'm already dead. A blinding white light has just seized me and flung me far, far back in time.

# I
# Nora

# 1

I owe my nickname to the shopkeeper in Graba.

The first time he saw me enter his lair, he looked me up and down, shocked by the state I was in and the way I smelt, and asked me if I came from the earth or the night. I was in bad shape, half dead from diarrhoea and exhaustion as a result of a long forced march across scrubland.

'I'm from Turambo, sir.'

The shopkeeper smacked his lips, which were as thick as a buffalo frog's. The name of my village meant nothing to him. 'Turambo? Which side of hell is that on?'

'I don't know, sir. I need half a douro's worth of yeast and I'm in a hurry.'

The shopkeeper turned to his half-empty shelves and, holding his chin between his thumb and index finger, repeated, 'Turambo? Turambo? Never heard of it.'

From that day on, whenever I passed his shop, he'd cry out, 'Hey, Turambo! Which side of hell is your village on?' His voice carried such a long way that gradually everyone started calling me Turambo.

My village had been wiped off the map by a landslide a week earlier. It was like the end of the world. Wild lightning flashes streaked the darkness, and the thunder seemed to be trying to smash the mountains to pieces. You couldn't tell men from animals any more; they were all tearing in every direction, screaming like creatures possessed. In a few hours, the torrents of rain had swept away our hovels, our goats and donkeys, our cries and prayers, and all our landmarks.

By morning, apart from the survivors shivering on the mud-covered rocks, nothing remained of the village. My father had vanished into thin air. We managed to dredge up a few bodies, but there was no trace of the broken face that had survived the deluge of fire and steel in the Great War. We followed the ravages of the flood as far as the plain, searched bushes and ravines, lifted the trunks of uprooted trees, but all in vain.

An old man prayed that the victims might be at rest, my mother shed a tear in memory of her husband, and that was it.

We considered putting everything back that had been scattered by the storm, but we didn't have the means, or the strength to believe it was possible. Our animals were dead, our meagre crops were ruined, our zinc shelters and our zaribas were beyond repair. Where the village had been, there was nothing but a mudslide on the side of the mountain, like a huge stream of vomit.

After assessing the damage, my mother said to us, 'Mortal man has only one fixed abode: the grave. As long as he lives, there's nothing he can take for granted, neither home nor country.'

We bundled up the few things the disaster had deigned to leave us and set off for Graba, a ghetto area of Sidi Bel Abbès where wretches thrown off their lands by typhus or the greed of the powerful arrived by the score.

With my father gone, my young uncle Mekki, who wasn't very far into his teens, declared himself the head of the family. He had a legitimate claim, being the eldest male.

There were five of us in a shack wedged between a military dumping ground and a scraggy orchard. There was my mother, a sturdy Berber with a tattooed forehead, not very beautiful but solid; my aunt Rokaya, whose pedlar husband had walked out on her over a decade earlier; her daughter Nora, who was more or less the same age as me; my fifteen-year-old uncle Mekki, and me, four years his junior.

Since we didn't know anyone, we had only ourselves to rely on.

I missed my father.

Strangely, I don't remember ever seeing him up close. Ever since he'd come back from the war, his face shattered by a piece of shrapnel, he'd kept his distance, sitting all day long in the shade of a solitary tree. When my cousin Nora took him his meals, she'd approach him on tiptoe, as if she was feeding a wild animal. I waited for him to return to earth, but he refused to come down from his cloud of depression. After a while, I ended up confusing him with someone I may once have seen and eventually ignored him completely. His disappearance merely confirmed his absence.

And yet in Graba, I couldn't help thinking about him every day.

Mekki promised we wouldn't stay long in this shanty town if we worked hard and made enough money to rebuild our lives somewhere else. My mother and my aunt decided to start making biscuits, which my uncle would sell to cheap restaurants. I wanted to lend a hand – kids a lot weaker than me were working as porters, donkey drivers and soup vendors, and doing well – but my uncle refused to hire me. I was bright, he had to admit that, I just wasn't bright enough to handle rascals capable of beating the devil himself at his own game. He was particularly afraid I'd be skinned alive by the first little runt I came across.

And so I was left to my own devices.

In Turambo, my mother had told me about dubious shanty

towns inhabited by creatures so monstrous I had bad dreams about them, but I'd never imagined I'd end up in one of them one day. And now here I was, slap bang in the middle of one, but this was no bedtime story. Graba was like an open-air asylum. It was as if a tidal wave had swept across the hinterland and tons of human flotsam and jetsam had somehow been tossed here. Labourers and beasts of burden jostled each other in the same narrow alleys. The rumbling of carts and the barking of dogs created a din that made your head spin. The place swarmed with crippled veterans and unemployed ex-convicts, and as for beggars, they could moan until their voices gave out, they'd never get a grain of corn to put in their mouths. The only thing people had to share was bad luck.

Everywhere amid the rickety shacks, where every alley was an ordeal to walk down, snotty-nosed kids engaged in fierce organised battles. Even though they barely came up to your knee, they already had to fend for themselves, and the future they could look forward to was no brighter than their early years. The birthright automatically went to the one who hit hardest, and devotion to your parents meant nothing once you'd given your allegiance to a gang leader.

I wasn't scared of these street urchins; I was scared of becoming like them. In Turambo, nobody swore, nobody looked their elders directly in the face; people showed respect, and if ever a kid got a bit carried away, you just had to clear your throat and he'd behave himself. But in this hellhole that stank of piss, every laugh, every greeting, every sentence came wrapped in obscenity.

It was in Graba that I first heard adults speak crudely.

The shopkeeper was getting some air outside his shack, his belly hanging down over his knees. A carter said, 'So, fatty, when's the baby due?'

'God knows.'

'Boy or girl?'

'A baby elephant,' said the shopkeeper, putting his hand on his flies. 'Want me to show you its trunk?'

I was shocked.

You couldn't hear yourself breathe until the sun went down. Then the ghetto would wrap itself around its troubles and, soothed by the echoes of its foul acts, allow itself to fade into the darkness.

In Graba, night didn't come, didn't fall, but, rather, poured down as though from a huge cauldron of fresh tar; it cascaded from the sky, thick and elastic, engulfing hills and forests, pushing its blackness deep into our minds. For a few moments, like hikers caught unawares by an avalanche, people would fall abruptly silent. Not a sound, not a rustle in the bushes. Then, little by little, you would hear the crack of a strap, the clatter of a gate, the cry of a baby, kids squabbling. Life would slowly resume and, like termites nibbling at the shadows, the anxieties of the night would come to the surface. And just as you blew out the candle to go to sleep, you'd hear drunks yelling and screaming in the most terrifying way; anyone lingering on the streets had to hurry home if they didn't want their bodies to be found lying in pools of blood early the following morning.

'When are we going back to Turambo?' I kept asking Mekki.

'When the sea gives back to the land what it took away,' he would answer with a sigh.

We had a neighbour in the shack opposite ours, a young widow of about thirty who would have been beautiful if only she'd taken a little care of herself. Always in an old dress, her hair in a mess, she'd sometimes buy bread from us on credit. She'd rush in, mutter an excuse, snatch her order from my mother's hands and go back home as quickly as she'd come.

We thought she was strange; my aunt was sure the poor woman was possessed by a jinn.

This widow had a little boy who was also strange. In the morning, she'd take him outside and order him to sit at the foot of the wall and not move for any reason. The boy was obedient. He could stay in that blazing heat for hours, sweating and blinking his eyes, salivating over a crust of bread, with a vague smile on his face. Seeing him sitting in the same spot, nibbling at his mouldy piece of bread, made me so uneasy that I'd recite a verse to ward off the evil spirits that seemed to keep him company. Then, unexpectedly, he started following me from a distance. Whether I went to the scrub or the military dumping ground, every time I turned round I saw him right behind me, a walking scarecrow, his crust in his mouth. I'd try to chase him away, threatening him, even throwing stones at him, but he'd just retreat for a few moments then, at a bend in the path, reappear behind me, always keeping at a safe distance.

I went to see his mother and asked her to keep her kid tied up because I was tired of him always following me. She listened without interrupting, then told me he had lost his father and so he needed company. I told her I already found it hard to bear my own shadow. 'It's your choice,' she sighed. I expected her to lose her temper like the other women in the neighbourhood whenever they disagreed with something, but she just went back to her chores as though nothing had happened. Her resignation made me feel sorry for her. I took the boy under my wing. He was older than me, but judging by the naive grin on his face, his brain must have been smaller than a pinhead. And he never spoke. I'd take him to the woods to pick jujubes or up the hill to look down at the railway tracks glittering among the stones. In the distance, you

26

could see goatherds surrounded by their emaciated flocks and hear the little bells teasing the lethargic silence. Below the hill, there was a gypsy encampment, recognisable by its dilapidated caravans.

At night, the gypsies would light fires and pluck their guitars until dawn. Even though they mostly twiddled their thumbs the lids of their cooking pots were constantly clattering. I think their God must have been quite a good one. True, he didn't exactly shower them with his benevolence, but at least he made sure they always had enough to eat.

We met Pedro the gypsy in the scrub. He was pretty much the same age as us and knew all the burrows where game went to hide. Once his basket was filled, he'd take out a sandwich and share it with us. We became friends. One day, he invited us to the camp. That's how I learnt to take a close look at these tricksters whose food fell from the skies.

In spite of a quick temper, Pedro's mother was basically good-natured. She was a fat redhead with a moustache, a lively temperament, and breasts so large you couldn't tell where they stopped. She never wore anything under her dress, so when she sat on the ground you could see her pubic hair. Her husband was a broken-down septuagenarian who used an ear trumpet to hear and spent his time sucking at a pipe as old as the hills. He'd laugh whenever you looked at him, and open his mouth to reveal a single rotten tooth that made his gums look all the more repulsive. And yet in the evening, when the sun went down behind the mountains, the old man would wedge his violin under his chin and draw from the strings of his instrument laments that were the colour of the sunset and filled us with sweet melancholy. I'd never again hear anyone play the violin better than he did.

Pedro had lots of talents. He could wrap his feet round the back of his neck and stand on his hands, he could juggle with torches; his great ambition was to join a circus. He'd describe it to me: a big tent with corridors and a ring where people went to cheer wild animals that could do amazing things and acrobats who performed dangerous stunts ten metres above the ground. Pedro would gush, telling me how they would also exhibit human monsters, dwarfs, animals with two heads and women with bodies you could only dream about. 'They're like us,' he'd say. 'They're always travelling, except that they have bears, lions and boa constrictors with them.'

I thought he was making it all up. I found it hard to picture a bear riding a bicycle, or men with painted faces and shoes half a metre long. But Pedro was good at presenting things, and even when the world he raved about was far beyond my understanding, I happily went along with his crazy stories. Besides, everybody in the camp let their imagination run riot. You'd think you were at an academy for the greatest storytellers on earth. There was old Gonsho, a little man with tattoos from his thighs up to his neck, who claimed he'd been killed in an ambush. 'I was dead for a week,' he'd say. 'No angel came to play me a lullaby on his harp, and no demon stuck his pitchfork up my arse. All I did was drift from sky to sky. Believe it or not, I didn't see any Garden of Eden or any Gehenna.'

'That makes sense,' said Pepe, the elder of the group, who was as ancient as a museum piece. 'First, everybody in the world would have to be dead. Then there'll be the Last Judgement, and only then will some be moved to heaven and others to hell.'

'You're not going to tell me that people who kicked the bucket thousands of years ago are going to have to wait for there to be nobody left on earth before they're judged by the Lord?'

'I've explained it to you before, Gonsho,' Pepe replied condescendingly. 'Forty days after they die, people become eligible for reincarnation. The Lord can't judge us on one life alone. So he brings us back wealthy, then poor, then as kings, then as tramps, as believers, as brigands, and so on, to see how we behave. He isn't going to create someone who's in the shit and then condemn him without giving him a chance to redeem himself. In order to be fair, he makes us wear all kinds of hats, then he takes an overall look at all our different lives, so that he can decide on our fate.'

'If what you say is true, why is it I've come back with the same face and in the same body?'

And Pepe, like an infinitely patient teacher, replied, 'You were dead for only a week. It takes forty days to pass on. And besides, gypsies are the only ones who have the privilege to be reborn as gypsies. Because we have a mission. We're constantly travelling in order to explore the paths of destiny. We've been given the task of seeking the Truth. That's why since the dawn of time, we've never stayed in one place.'

Making a circular movement with his finger at his temple, Pepe encouraged Gonsho to think for a few moments about what he'd just told him.

The debate could have gone on indefinitely without either of them agreeing with the other. For gypsies, arguing wasn't about what you believed, it was about being stubborn. When you had an opinion, you held on to it at all costs because the worst way to lose face was to abandon your point of view.

Gypsies were colourful, fascinating, crazy characters, and they all had a religious sense of responsibility towards their families. They could disagree, yell at one another, and even come to blows, but they all deferred to the Mama, who kept an eye on everything.

Ah, the Mama! She'd given me her blessing the moment she'd seen me. She was a kind of impoverished dowager, lounging on her embroidered cushions at the far end of her caravan, which was piled high with gifts and relics; the tribe worshipped her like a sacred cow. I'd have liked to throw myself into her arms and sink into her flesh.

I felt comfortable among the gypsies. My days were filled with fun and surprises. They gave me food and let me enjoy myself as I wished ... Then, one morning, the caravans were gone. All that was left of the camp was a few traces of their stay: rutted tracks, a few shoes with holes in them, a shawl hanging from a bush, dog mess. Never had a place seemed to me as ruined as this patch abandoned by the gypsies and returned to its bleak former state. For weeks I went back, conjuring up memories in the hope of hearing an echo, a laugh, a voice, but there was no answer, not even the sound of a violin to act as an excuse for my sorrow. With the gypsies gone, I was back to a grim future, to dull, endless days that went round in circles like a wild animal in a cage.

The days passed but didn't advance, monotonous, blind, empty; it was as if they were walking over my body.

At home, I was an extra burden. 'Go back to the street; may the earth swallow you. Can't you see we're working?'

I was scared of the street.

You couldn't go to the military dumping ground any more since the numbers of scavengers had increased, and woe betide anyone who dared fight them over a piece of rubbish.

I fell back on the railway and spent my time watching out for the train and picturing myself on it. I ended up jumping on. The local train had broken down and was stuck on the rails, like a huge caterpillar about to give up the ghost. Two mechanics were fussing around the locomotive. I approached the last carriage. The door was open. I hoisted myself on board with my partner in misfortune, sat down on an empty sack, and gazed up at the sky through the slits in the roof. I imagined myself travelling across green countryside, bridges and farms, fleeing the ghetto where nothing good ever happened. Suddenly, the carriage started moving. The boy staggered and clung to the wall. The locomotive whistle made me leap to my feet. Outside, the countryside began slowly rolling by. I jumped off first, almost breaking my ankle on the ballast. But the boy wouldn't let go of the wall. *Jump off, I'll catch you*, I shouted. He was paralysed and wouldn't jump. The more the train gathered speed, the more I panicked. *Jump, jump* ... I started running, the ballast cutting into my feet like broken bottles. The boy was crying. His moaning rose above the din of the livestock carriages. I realised he wasn't going to jump. It was up to me to get him. As usual. I ran and ran, my chest burning, my feet bleeding. I was two fingers away from gaining a handhold, three fingers, four, ten, thirty ... It wasn't because I was slowing down; the iron monster was growing bolder as the locomotive increased its output of smoke. At the end of a frantic run, I stopped, my legs cut to pieces. All I could do was watch the train get further away until it vanished in the dust.

I followed the track for many miles, limping under a blazing sun ... I caught sight of a figure and rushed towards it, thinking it was the boy. It wasn't him.

The sun was starting to go down. I was already a long way from Graba. I had to get home before nightfall, or I might get lost too.

The widow was at our house, pale with worry. When she saw me on my own, she rushed out into the street and turned even paler than before.

'What have you done with my baby?' She shook me angrily. 'Where's my child? He was with you. You were supposed to look after him.'

'The train —'

'What train?'

I felt a tightness in my throat. I couldn't swallow.

'What about the train? Say something!'

'It took him away.'

Silence.

The widow didn't seem to understand. She furrowed her brow. I felt her fingers go limp on my shoulders. Against all expectations, she gave a little laugh and turned pensive. I thought she'd bounce back, sink her claws into me, break up our shack and us with it, but she leant against the wall and slid down to the ground. She stayed like that, with her elbows on her knees and her head in her hands, a dark look in her eyes. A tear ran down her cheek; she didn't wipe it away. 'Whatever God decides, we must accept,' she sighed in a muted voice. 'Everything that happens in this world happens according to His will.'

My mother tried to put a sympathetic hand on her shoulder. She shook it off with a gesture of disgust. 'Don't touch me. I don't want your pity. Pity never fed anyone. I don't need anybody any more. Now that my son's gone, I can go too. I've been wanting to put an end to this lousy life for years. But my son wasn't right in the head. I couldn't see him surviving among people who are worse than wolves … I can't wait to have a word with the One who created me just to make me suffer.'

'Are you mad? What are you talking about? It's a sin to kill yourself.'

'I don't think there could possibly be a hell worse than mine, either in the sky or anywhere else.'

She looked up at me and it was as if the distress of the whole of humanity was concentrated in her eyes.

'Torn to pieces by a train! My God! How can I do away with a child like that after putting him through so much?'

I was speechless, upset by her ranting.

She pressed down on the palms of her hands and got unsteadily to her feet. 'Show me where my baby is. Is there anything left of him for me to bury?'

'He isn't dead!' I cried.

She shuddered. Her eyes struck me with the ferocity of lightning. 'What? Did you leave my son bleeding on the railway tracks?'

'He wasn't run over by the train. We got on it, and when the train started, I jumped off and he stayed on. I shouted to him to jump but he didn't dare. I ran after the train and walked along the rails, but he didn't get off anywhere.'

The widow put her head in her hands. Once again, she didn't seem to understand. Suddenly, she stiffened. I saw her facial expression go from confusion to relief, then from relief to panic, and then from panic to hysteria. 'Oh, God! My son is lost! They'll eat him alive. He doesn't even know how to hold out his hand. Oh, my God! Where's my baby?'

She took me by the throat and started to shake me, almost dislocating my neck. My mother and aunt tried to get me away from her; she pushed them back with a kick and, totally losing her mind, started screaming and spinning like a tornado, knocking down everything in her path. Suddenly, she howled and collapsed, her eyes rolled back, her body convulsed.

My mother got up. She had scratches all over. With amazing calm, she fetched a large jailer's key and slipped it into the widow's fist – a common practice with people who fainted from dizziness or shock.

Dumbfounded, my aunt ordered her daughter to go and fetch Mekki before the madwoman returned to her senses.

Mekki didn't beat about the bush. Nora had told him everything. He was all fired up and didn't want to hear any more. In our family, you hit first, and then you talked. *You bastard, I'm going to kill you*. He rushed at me and started beating me up. I thought he'd never stop.

My mother didn't intervene.

It was men's business.

Having beaten me thoroughly, my uncle ordered me to take him to the railway track and show him the direction the train had gone in. I could barely stand. The ballast had injured my feet, and the beating had finished me off.

'How am I supposed to look for him in the dark?' Mekki cursed, leaving the shack.

At dawn, Mekki wasn't back. The widow came to ask for news every five minutes, in a state of mental collapse.

Three days passed and still there was nothing on the horizon. After a week, we began to fear the worst. My aunt was constantly on her knees, praying. My mother kept going round in circles in the one room that made up our house. 'I suppose you're proud of yourself,' she grunted, resisting the impulse to hit me. 'You see where your mischief has landed us? It's all your fault. For all we know, the jackals have long since chewed your uncle's bones. What will become of us without him?'

Just when we were beginning to lose hope, we heard the widow cry out. It was about four in the afternoon. We ran out of the shack. Mekki could barely stand up, his face was dark, and he was covered in dirt. The widow was hugging her child tightly to her, pulling up his gaiters to see if he was hurt, feeling his scalp for any bumps or injuries; the boy showed the effects of wandering and hunger, but was safe and sound. He was staring at me dull-eyed, and pointing his finger at me the way you point at a culprit.

## 2

Ogres are nothing but hallucinations born of our superstitions, and an excuse for them, which is why we are no better than they are, because, as both false witnesses and stern judges, we often condemn before deliberating.

The ogre known as Graba wasn't as monstrous as all that.

From the hill that served as my vantage point, I had seen its people as plague victims and its slums as deadly traps. I was wrong. Seen from close up, the ghetto was simply living as best it could. It might have seemed like purgatory, but it wasn't. In Graba, people weren't paying for their crimes or their sins, they were just poor, that was all.

Driven by boredom and idleness, I started venturing further and further into the ghetto. I was just beginning to feel part of it when I had my baptism of fire. Which of course I'd been expecting.

A carter offered me a douro to help him load about a hundred bundles of wood onto his cart. Once the job was done, he paid me half the promised sum, swearing on his children's heads that it was all he had on him. He seemed sincere. I was watching him walk away when a voice behind me cried out, 'Are you trying to muscle in on my territory?'

It was the Daho brothers. They were barring my way.

I sensed things were about to go downhill. Peerless street

fighters, they reigned supreme over the local kids. Whenever a boy came running through the crowd, his face reduced to a pulp, it meant the Dahos weren't far away. They were only twelve or thirteen, but talked through the sides of their mouths like old lags. Behind them, their bodyguards rubbed their hands at the prospect of a thrashing. The Daho brothers couldn't just go on their way. Wherever they stopped, blood had to flow. It was the rule. Kings hate truces, and the twins didn't believe in taking a well-earned rest. Squat and faun-like, their faces so identical you felt you were seeing the same disaster twice, they were as fast as whips and just as sharp. Adults nicknamed them Gog and Magog, two irredeemable little pests bound to end up on the scaffold as surely as ageing virgins were destined to marry their halfwit cousins. There was no getting away from them and I was angry with myself for having crossed their path.

'I don't want to fight,' I said.

This spontaneous surrender was greeted with sardonic laughter.

'Hand over what you've got in your pocket.'

I took out the coin the carter had given me and held it out. My hand was steady. I wasn't looking for trouble. I wanted to get home in one piece.

'You have to be nuts to be content with this,' Daho One said, weighing my earnings contemptuously in his hand. 'You don't move a cartload of stuff for half a douro, you little toerag. Any idiot would have asked for three times this much.'

'I didn't know,' I said apologetically.

'Turn out your pockets, now.'

'I've already given you everything I have.'

'Liar.'

I could see in their eyes that confiscating my pay was just the start and that what mattered was the thrashing. I immediately went on the defensive, determined to give as good as I got. The Daho brothers always hit first, without warning, hoping to take their victim by surprise. They would strike simultaneously, in a perfectly synchronised movement, with a headbutt to the nose and a kick between the legs to disconcert their prey. The rest was just a formality.

'Aren't you ashamed of yourselves?' a providential voice rang out. 'A whole bunch of you picking on a little kid?'

The voice belonged to a shopkeeper standing in the doorway of his establishment with his hands on his hips. His tarboosh was tilted at a rakish angle over one eye and his moustache was turned up at the ends. He moved his fat carcass to adjust his Turkish sirwal and, advancing into the sunlight, looked around at the gang before letting his keen eyes fall on the twins.

'If you want to take him on, do it one at a time.'

I'd been expecting the shopkeeper to come to my rescue, but all he was doing was organising my beating in a more conventional way, which wasn't exactly a lucky break for me.

Daho One accepted the challenge. Sneering, his eyes shining with wicked glee, he rolled up his sleeves.

'Move back,' the shopkeeper ordered the rest of the gang, 'and don't even think of joining in.'

A wave of anticipation went through the gang as they formed a circle around us. Daho One's snarl increased as he looked me up and down. He feinted to the left and tried to punch me but only brushed my temple. He didn't get a second chance because my fist shot out in retaliation and, much to my surprise, hit its target. The scourge of the local kids flopped like a puppet and collapsed in the dust, his arms outstretched. The gang gasped in outraged amazement. The other twin stood there stunned for a few moments, unable to understand or admit what his eyes were telling him, then, in a rage, he ordered his brother to get up. But his brother didn't get up. He was sleeping the sleep of the just.

Sensing the turn things seemed to be taking, the shopkeeper came and stood beside me and we both looked at the gang picking up their martyr, who was deep in an impenetrable dream filled with bells and birdsong.

'You didn't play fair,' cried a frizzy-haired little runt with legs like a wading bird. 'You tricked him. You'll pay for that.'

'We'll be back for you,' Daho Two vowed, wiping his snotty nose with the back of his hand.

The shopkeeper was a little disappointed by my rapid victory. He had been hoping for a more substantial show, full of falls and suspense and dodges and devastating punches, thus getting a decent slice of entertainment for free. Reluctantly he admitted to me that, all things considered, he was delighted that someone had succeeded in soundly thrashing that lowlife, who blighted the ghetto and thought he could get away with anything because there was nobody to take him on.

'You're really quick,' he said, flatteringly. 'Where did you learn to hit like that?'

'That's the first time I was ever in a fight, sir.'

'Wow, such promise! How would you like to work for me? It isn't difficult. All you have to do is keep guard when I'm not there and handle a few little things.'

I took the bait without even asking about my wages, only too happy to be able to earn my crust and make a contribution to the family's war chest.

'When do I start, sir?'

'Right away,' he said, pointing reverently at his dilapidated shop.

I had no way of knowing that when charitable people intervene to save your skin, they don't necessarily plan to leave any of it on your back.

The shopkeeper was called Zane, and it was he who taught me that the devil had a name.

What Zane referred to as little things were more like the labours of Hercules. No sooner had I finished one task than I was given another. I wasn't allowed a lunch break or even a moment to catch my breath. I was told to tidy the shambles that was the premises (a veritable Ali Baba's cave), stack the shelves, polish the bric-a-brac, dislodge the spiders, a bucket of water in one hand and a ceiling brush in the other, and deal with deliveries. Before giving me a trial, Zane subjected me to 'loyalty' tests, leaving money and other bait lying around to see how honest I was; I didn't touch a thing.

Within a few months, I learnt more about human nature than an old soldier. Zane was like a first-class school, and the people he came into contact with provided wonderful lessons in life. The most curious characters would creep into his shop, some with suspect packages, others with futile projects. Zane – smuggler, blackmailer, fence, snitch and pimp – controlled his circle with an iron fist, and he had a finger in every pie; there wasn't a single deal, even the most insignificant, carried out in Graba that he didn't get a cut from. He would buy for next to nothing and sell at exorbitant prices, and wouldn't take no for an answer. Everyone in Graba owed him something. People would go down on their knees to him, prepared to do any dirty work to merit his generosity. Zane had no qualms. For a can of food or a trifling bit of credit, he would ask for the moon. He shamelessly exploited every opportunity and took every advantage he could of people's misfortunes. He was a pawnbroker too. When the item was something of value, a decent piece of jewellery for example, he would make the excuse that he didn't have enough money available and ask the customer to come back the following day, which gave him time to arrange a trap. The next day, the customer would reappear, deposit his jewel, count his money and leave … only to come back ten minutes later, his face covered in blood and his clothes torn to shreds as if he'd just been in a fight with a bear. 'I was attacked and robbed not far from here.' To which Zane would reply imperturbably, 'What's that to me? Am I supposed to give my customers an escort to make sure they get home safely?' And with this he would dismiss the poor devil. It was perfectly obvious that the ambush had been set up by my employer. He had henchmen who just waited for a sign from him to pounce. Zane wasn't content with these practices, which weren't all that unusual; he also boasted of having policemen under his thumb and claimed he could have anyone sent to jail just by clicking his fingers. He was widely feared and nobody haggled with him. Often, humble women draped from head to foot in filthy veils, with just a tiny opening at the front to see where they were going, would come into the shop. They were usually at the end of their tether and were prepared to make any sacrifice for a piece of sugar or a small coin. Zane would push them into the back room, pin them up against a big table cluttered with all kinds of implements, pull their dresses up over their naked buttocks and possess them unceremoniously. He loved humiliating them and making them suffer before throwing them out like dishcloths. I think he was mad. You had to be mad to put down roots in Graba when you could afford a house in the city; you had to be completely demented to flaunt your fortune in front of people so broke they'd think a bit of spittle was cash; and you had to be suicidal to rape mothers, sisters and aunts, one after the other, when you knew that in that deadly place no secret could be kept for very long, public condemnation was swift, and a knife was as sharp as it was accurate. Zane didn't give a hoot, convinced he could cross a minefield with his eyes closed. He carried with him amulets stronger than spells and curses combined. He had been born under a cast-iron star and feared neither gods nor men.

According to a marabout, when Zane finally gave up the ghost, with his sins intact, he wouldn't go to either heaven or hell because the good Lord would deny he'd ever created him.

For the first few weeks, the Daho brothers would come by and remind me that they had a debt to settle with me. They would stand at the corner of the alley to avoid confronting my formidable employer and yell challenges at me as if casting a spell. They would make obscene gestures and mime cutting my throat. I kept calm, sitting on the steps in front of the shop ... In the evening, my uncle Mekki would come to fetch me, carrying a nail-studded club over his shoulder.

A jack of all trades gets to go everywhere. With all my deliveries and errands, I broadened my field of activities and before long made a number of new acquaintances. The first was Ramdane, a puny kid who was always in two places at once, having to provide for his large family because his father had lost both his legs. He had been thinking like a grown-up since he was barely out of his mother's womb. I admired him, and even though I didn't always share his opinions, I knew there was sense in them, and that quality – still there underneath it all, despite centuries of failure – which the old-timers called 'dignity'. The boy had panache. Even though he was two years younger than me, I would have given anything to be his son. It was reassuring to know that he existed and that he brought a touch of loyalty to our collective defeat, which had reduced universal values to selfish needs and ancestral wisdom to an undignified survival strategy. Ramdane taught me how much more worthwhile it was to be useful than to be rich.

Next, I met Gomri, an apprentice blacksmith as squat and solid as a bollard, a touch ridiculous in his apron, which was far too big for him. With his curly red hair, pockmarked face, clear eyes and skin as white as an albino's, he made me uncomfortable at first because of an old tribal belief that redheads have evil intentions, which seep out of their hair. I was wrong. Gomri didn't have an evil thought in his head and never tried to trick anybody. In between shoeing horses, he would show up and offer Zane hammers, hoes and other implements he had made himself. As the smithy was not far from the shop, Zane ordered me to go there and check there wasn't anything fishy going on, because, in his opinion, Gomri was too young to produce such skilled work. I would watch Gomri take a piece of scrap iron, plunge it into the fire until it was red-hot, then place it on the anvil and beat it, and I would see the common metal gradually transformed, as if by magic, into an almost perfect tool.

Ramdane introduced me to Sid Roho, a fifteen-year-old black boy nicknamed the Billy Goat ever since he had been caught behind a thicket with his trousers on the ground, abusing a hairless old nanny goat. According to malicious gossip, when the nanny goat had given birth, a delegation of jokers had gone to see him and asked him what name he planned to give his offspring. But Sid Roho never lost his temper over digs and jibes. He was funny and helpful and wouldn't have hesitated to give the shirt off his back to someone in need, which didn't stop him living off the proceeds of sin. He was an out-and-out thief. No matter how closely the merchants kept their eye on him, he always managed to filch what he wanted in a flash. He was a real magician. On several occasions, I saw him steal things from stalls, slip them into the hood of a passer-by and recover them on the way out of the market. I doubt there was ever anyone more light-fingered than him in the whole world.

Ramdane, Gomri, Sid Roho and I became friends without

even realising it. We had no obvious affinities, but we got along well. After a day's work, we would meet up in the evening near an abandoned orchard to swap jokes and laugh at our disappointments until night caught up with us.

At home, things seemed to be going well. My uncle had discovered that he had a gift for business and was managing quite nicely. He had made a cart from what was left of a wheelbarrow, stuck a cast-iron cooking pot on it and, from morning to evening, he would sell soup on the main square of Graba. My mother, my aunt and Nora all redoubled their efforts, supplying him as well as delivering fresh bread to cheap cafés. I didn't feel inferior because of how hard they worked; as a result of my own job, I too was entitled to some respect and, before going to bed, to a prayer and a blessing. I felt grown up, almost as much of a man as my friend Ramdane, and could also afford to say, like the others and with some reason, that soon we would have colour in our cheeks and enough money to move to a real house with a door that locked and shutters on the windows, somewhere where the shops would be better stocked and there would be hammams on every street corner.

I was tidying the shelves when a shadowy figure slipped in behind me and headed for the back room. I only had time to glimpse a white veil disappearing through the curtain. A smile of satisfaction glimmered on Zane's face. He first checked the contents of his drawer, then, smoothing his moustache, indicated the front door out of the corner of his eye, meaning that he wanted me to keep watch.

Zane had no more scruples than a hyena, but he dreaded the idea of his female conquests being followed by jealous husbands or family members with a keen sense of honour.

'Don't let anyone in, all right?' he said. 'Any beggars, just send them away. As for customers, ask them to come back later.'

I nodded.

Zane cleared his throat and joined his prey behind the curtain. I couldn't see them, but I could hear them.

'Well, well,' he said in his overbearing voice. 'You finally saw reason ...'

'My son and I have nothing left to eat,' the woman said, stifling a sob.

'Whose fault is that? I made you an offer and you rejected it.'

'I'm a mother. I ... I don't sell myself to men.'

I was sure I knew that voice.

'So what are you doing in my shop? I thought you'd changed your mind, that you'd realised we're sometimes forced to make concessions to get what we can't afford ...'

Silence.

The woman was sobbing softly.

'In this life, it's tit for tat,' Zane said. 'Don't think you can make me feel sorry for you, pretending butter wouldn't melt in your mouth. Either you pull up your dress or you go back where you came from.'

Silence.

'So, do you want my four soldi or not?'

'My God, what will become of me afterwards?'

'That's your problem. Are you going to show me your pretty backside or not?'

Weeping.

'That's better. Now turn round, sweetheart.'

I heard Zane pin the woman up against the table. A terrible cry rang out, followed by loud, rapid creaking noises, covering the woman's moans, until Zane's triumphant groan put an end to the din.

'You see?' he said. 'It wasn't so difficult … Come back whenever you like. Now get out!'

'You promised me four soldi.'

'Yes, two today, the rest next time.'

'But —'

'Clear off, I said.'

The curtain was raised and Zane threw the woman out. She collapsed on the ground on all fours. Looking up, she saw me standing there and her red face turned as white as a shroud. Choking with embarrassment, she quickly gathered up her veil and ran out as if she had seen the devil himself.

It was our neighbour, the widow.

That evening, as I was on my way home, she intercepted me at the corner of the street. She had aged twenty years in a few hours. Hair dishevelled, wild eyed, foaming at the mouth, she looked like a witch who had just emerged from a trance. She grabbed hold of my shoulders.

'I beg you,' she said, her toneless voice sounding like a dying breath, 'don't tell anyone what you saw.'

I felt embarrassed and sorry for her at the same time. Her fingers were crushing me. I had to remove them one by one to get her off me.

'I didn't see anything,' I said.

'Yes, earlier, in the shop.'

'I don't know what shop you're talking about. Are you going to let me get home?'

'I could kill myself, my child. You don't know how much I regret giving in to hunger. I'm not a loose woman. I didn't think it would ever happen to me. But it happened. Nobody's safe. That's not an excuse, it's the facts. Nobody is to know, you understand? I would die on the spot.'

'I tell you I didn't see anything.'

She threw herself on me, kissed my head and my hands and got down on all fours to kiss my feet. I pushed her away and ran to our shack. As soon as I was far enough away, I turned and saw her huddled by a heap of scrap metal, weeping her eyes out.

The next day, she had vanished.

She had taken her son and nobody knew where she had gone.

I never saw her again.

I realised I had never even known her name, or her son's.

## 3

The disappearance of the widow and her son had shocked me. I was angry with myself for having witnessed that willing rape that had plunged our neighbour into the depths of hopelessness. How could I rid myself of the memory of that desperate woman? Her voice continued to ring in my ears and my eyes were full of her distress. It made me feel disgusted with the whole human race.

I was furious with those people who drifted from day to day as if tomorrow had no more interest than yesterday. I saw them pass through the shop, sick with hunger and despair, ready to lick the counter if there was a little sugar on it. They didn't care about their appearance or their pride; all that mattered to them was a wretched mouthful of food. I tried to make excuses for them, and for myself, but in vain. In Zane's shadow, I wallowed in bitterness and anger all day long; my sleep was filled with beggars, louts, thieves, fallen women, wild-haired witches and beaming tyrants whose mouths spat swirling flames. I would wake up dripping with sweat and as sick as a dog, run outside and throw up. I felt hatred for Zane. Had he ever been a child? If so, would I be like him when I grew up? Or would I be like one of those confused spectres who dragged their damnation around with them like a ball and chain, the dirt so thick on their skin you could have stuck a knife into it without hurting them? No, I told myself, Zane was never a child. He was born like that, with his twirled moustache and his sewer-like mouth. He was corruption in human form and stank like carrion in the sun, except that, horror of horrors, he was alive and well.

Zane noticed how sad and distracted I was and threatened to fire me. I would have left of my own accord if he had paid me what he owed me.

Worried by my low spirits, my friends plied me with questions, but I kept my secret to myself. How could I tell them what went on in the back room of the shop without being complicit in it? How could I explain the widow's disappearance without being guilty?

Zane fired me in the end and I felt a little better. He had been the cause of my depression. Nobody can live in close proximity to perversion without being soiled by it in one way or another. Zane's actions hadn't simply spattered me; I was infected by them.

Even now, my silences are disturbed by the creaking of the table in the back room and the weeping of the women he sodomised to his heart's content. *I have enough mouths to feed without burdening myself with bastards*, the loathsome Zane would tell them.

My uncle almost fell over backwards when he heard I'd been dismissed. When he discovered that Zane hadn't paid me a penny after months of slavery, he grabbed his nail-studded club and set off to have a word with him. He returned in a terrible state, lying on a cart, thoroughly beaten. *This is your fault again!* my mother yelled at me, sententiously.

Left to my own devices once again, I joined Gomri in his smithy. His boss chased me away after a few days, claiming that my presence slowed down production. Then Ramdane suggested I give him a hand in the market. We were prepared to take on any task without worrying about how much it brought in as long as we were hired again the next day. Ramdane had no concept of rest, or how to choose between horrible jobs. At the end of the month, I threw in the towel, much preferring to loaf around in the fields or go to the souk to see Sid Roho cleverly robbing his victims. Sid was a wizard. Once, he even stole Laweto's marmoset under everyone's nose. Laweto was a curious old fellow who sold miracle potions at the entrance to the market. Whenever customers he'd fleeced brought back his poison, calling him a quack, he would come back at them with, *What do you have against quacks? They've made more discoveries in medicine than scientists have.* To draw his audience in, he would get his monkey to perform obscene acrobatic tricks that made us double up with laughter. That day, as he was trumpeting the far-fetched qualities of a scorpion's sting that he was passing off as the thorn of an aphrodisiac plant, he noticed that his marmoset was no longer on his shoulder. In an instant, the scene descended into chaos. Laweto screamed and ran into the crowd, knocking people over, looking into baskets, under stalls, behind shacks, shouting at suspects and tearing his hair out in handfuls. Such was his agitation that even the thieves and pickpockets rallied round, suspending their activities to lend us a hand. But there was no trace of the marmoset. Laweto was sick with worry. He confessed through hot tears that he wouldn't survive without his monkey and that he would die if it wasn't brought back to him before nightfall.

Night fell, and there was still no news of the marmoset.

'Has anyone seen the Billy Goat?' Gomri asked. As it happened, nobody had seen Sid Roho all day, either in the souk or during the search. Gomri was suspicious. He asked Ramdane and me to follow him, and we immediately set off for the Billy Goat's place.

Gomri was right: there was Sid Roho lying on what was left of a stretcher picked up from a rubbish dump, his heel resting on his knee, chewing on a stick of liquorice, like a young dignitary taking a cure, and ... tied to a beam, Laweto's monkey, scared to death, wondering what it was doing there with a crazy boy it didn't know from Adam.

'I knew it was you,' Gomri cried, beside himself. 'I thought you had some respect for poor Laweto.'

'It was just for a laugh,' Sid Roho said, completely unaware of the panic his theft had caused in Graba.

'Laweto is about to have a heart attack,' Ramdane protested. 'Give him back his monkey straight away, or I swear I won't talk to you again as long as I live.'

The next day, with his marmoset on his shoulder, Laweto was roaming the streets like a sleepwalker, proclaiming a miracle and telling all and sundry that a winged angel had freed his monkey from a spell and brought it back in a dream.

My young uncle was tired of seeing me come back in the evening without a penny. He found me a job as a *moutcho* in an ancient hammam in Kasdir, an old douar where night arrived faster than day. It was an Arab quarter grafted onto the southern part of Sidi Bel Abbès, with whitewashed houses and foul-smelling drains in the middle of the streets. The people were suspicious, mistrusting everything from Graba – child, animal, fruit or dust. I have no idea what Mekki did to persuade the owner to take me on. It was clean, honest work. I would carry the bathers' towels, wring out their loincloths and scrub their children clean. As far as tips went, I could whistle for them, but I made seventeen douros a week, and that helped boost the family coffers. Everything went well until the evening a customer who was broke and couldn't pay his bill accused me of robbing him.

I was dismissed immediately.

*

I didn't think it was a good idea to tell my uncle that I'd lost my job. During the day, I would hide in the scrub to avoid running into him. When the sun went down, I'd join my gang in the orchard. My friends knew about my bad luck and they all had suggestions for me. Sid Roho proposed I steal for him. He needed an accomplice to expand his business. I declined the offer. Categorically.

'I don't want to end up in prison,' I said.

'Some people get away with it.'

'Maybe, but it's haram.'

'Don't talk rubbish, Turambo. It's not having any money that's haram. How do you think people survive around here? When you have nothing, it doesn't matter what you turn your hand to.'

'Nobody's ever stolen anything in my family. My uncle would throw me out if he discovered I was stealing.'

Sid Roho tapped his temple with his finger, but didn't insist.

Two days later, he came back to see me with a box slung over his shoulder.

'So you want to earn your living by the honest sweat of your brow? All right. I'm going to teach you my old trade of shoeshine boy. There's only money to be made from it in the city, in the European quarters. How would you like to come with me to Sidi Bel Abbès?'

'Oh, no, not the city. We'd get lost.'

'There's no reason we should. I go there all the time.'

'My uncle says people get run over by cars there every day.'

'Your uncle knows nothing about the city. He's never walked on a pavement in his life ... Come on. Sidi Bel Abbès is quite something, you'll see. It isn't meant for the likes of us, but there's nothing to say we can't go there.'

'No, those big places scare me.'

'My grandfather used to say: a man born in hell doesn't fear volcanoes. Trust me. I'll show you things you could never imagine. You can speak a bit of French, can't you?'

'Of course. I grew up on a colonial farm. My father worked in the stables and my mother did the housework. Xavier let me play with his kids. I can do arithmetic too. Division's difficult, but as far as addition and subtraction go, all I need is a blackboard and a piece of chalk.'

'All right, all right, no need to go on about it,' he cut in, sounding jealous. 'Will you come with me to the city, yes or no?'

I still hesitated.

'Learn to make up your own mind, Turambo,' he went on. 'Someone once said: if you want to get to the moon, start climbing now.'

Sid Roho managed to convince me and we ran off to wash our faces in a drinking trough where a mule was quenching its thirst. Then Sid Roho took me to his place to try on a shirt, a pair of trousers that reached down to my calves and sandals with hemp soles.

'In your country clothes, they'd put you in the dog pound before you got to town.'

Sidi Bel Abbès was a real shock to me.

My universe had been limited to Turambo and the colonial estate. As far as I was concerned, the Xaviers' farm had been the height of affluence, comfort and modernity. I'd never seen anything as opulent. I'd spend hours gazing at the big house with its tiled roof, its wide front steps bordered by balustrades, its big front door of carved wood opening onto a light-flooded reception room, its French windows painted green looking out on a vast flowery veranda where, on Sunday, the owner and his guests ate grilled meat and drank ice-cold orangeade. That, I had thought, was the pinnacle of fine living, the acme of success, a privilege so rare that only those blessed by the gods could enjoy it.

I had never set foot in a city before and had only a vague notion of Europeans, confusing them with sultans from the stories Aunt Rokaya told Nora and me when we were hungry or had a fever.

For a boy with limited horizons like me, there were only two, diametrically opposed worlds: the world of the colonial Xavier, a tall, strapping man who had orchards, a carriage drawn by a magnificent thoroughbred, and obsequious servants, and who ate *méchoui* on every public holiday; and the world of Turambo, where time seemed to have stood still, a sad, joyless, deadly place, without prospects, where people went to ground like moles.

And now here was Sidi Bel Abbès, which swept away my points of reference with a lordly hand by revealing a world I had never suspected, made up of paved streets, proper street lighting instead of the old-fashioned gas lamps we had, pavements lined with trees, shop windows displaying fine lingerie that would have frozen me with embarrassment just imagining it on Nora's body, bistros with sun-drenched terraces and people in their best clothes puffing contentedly on their pipes.

I stood there open-mouthed for a long time, watching the carriages coming and going at a syncopated rhythm; the cars parked here and there when they weren't backfiring along the boulevard; the women in colourful, figure-hugging dresses, some on the arms of distinguished gentlemen, others sheltering beneath pretty hats, all breathtakingly beautiful; the officers striding with a martial air in their freshly pressed uniforms, chests thrown out; and the children in short trousers running about like will-o'-the-wisps on the square which was bedecked with flags.

This discovery would remain engraved in my memory, like a prophetic revelation.

For me, Sidi Bel Abbès wasn't so much a chance encounter as proof that a different life, poles apart from mine, was possible. I think it was that day that I started dreaming – I certainly couldn't remember having done so before. I would even say that dreams, like hopes, were barely familiar to me, so convinced was I that everyone's role was determined in advance, that there were those who had been born to strut in the limelight and those who were condemned to fade away in the wings until they disappeared. I was bewildered, charmed and frustrated all at once …

Sidi Bel Abbès awoke feelings in me I had never suspected. I was faced with a challenge. To be or not to be. To make a choice or give up. The city wasn't rejecting me, it was opening my eyes, removing my blinkers, showing me new prospects; I already knew what I no longer wanted. Well before it was time to go back home, I was certain I couldn't settle for Graba. I was determined to do anything, even commit a sin, in order to rebuild my life elsewhere, in a city where sounds had their own music and the people and the streets smelt of luck and hope.

While Sid Roho set to work shining shoes, I couldn't help lingering over my discoveries, absorbing everything down to the smallest detail, like a dried-up sponge thrown suddenly into a stream. That neat church regally watching over the square, those shop windows reflecting back at me my own bad fortune, and those dazzling girls who seemed to dance as they walked, and those avenues so clean that no dirt dared land on them, and those grassy verges strewn with roses, and those children, the same age as me, who had everything they needed, in their sailor suits and caps, with socks up to their knees and their feet in soft shoes, and who passed me without seeing me, racing around like streaks of pure happiness! Watching those children moving about in such a carefree way, I told myself, without wishing to offend the saints, that their God was more considerate than ours and that, if paradise was indeed promised to us rather than to them, a semblance of decency in our lives wouldn't have gone amiss.

'Hey, don't just stand there gawping, come back down to earth. This is real life, Turambo. Watch how I handle the brush if you want to learn the trade.'

Sid Roho was putting the finishing touches to a soldier's leather boots. After polishing them, he went over them with a cloth, his wrists moving as fast as pistons. The soldier ignored us. With his hands in his pockets and a lopsided smile on his face, he was ogling two young girls on the opposite pavement.

'There you are, Monsieur. Your boots are as good as new.'

The soldier dropped a coin on the ground and crossed the road, whistling.

'Do you think I'll ever live in a city like this?' I asked, my eyes full of all the colourful details.

'Who knows? My grandfather used to say that what's difficult isn't necessarily impossible.'

'What did your grandfather do?'

'He made children. One after the other … Well,' he added, making a large circle with his arm, 'do you believe me now? Sidi Bel Abbès is magical, isn't it?'

'I can't believe there are so many wonderful houses in a single place.'

'And you haven't seen what they're like inside. The people all have their own rooms, separated by corridors. Their lamps don't use wicks. They have lots of mirrors, and prints in gold frames. And carpets on the floor so they don't hurt their feet. And they have beds. Not straw mattresses, not mats, but iron beds with springs that cradle them to sleep. And sometimes pianos. These people don't have to go to the well to fetch water. Water comes to them in pipes. They have it in the room where they cook and in the room where they relieve themselves. While we have to look in every direction before we pull our trousers down behind a bush, they just have to kick open the toilet door. And you know what? Apparently, they read the newspaper while they're doing their important business.'

'I saw some of these things on the Xaviers' farm, except that for water they had a pump in the yard.'

'Not the same thing at all. You're in the city, my poor Turambo. Here, the streets and squares have names and the doors have numbers. In these houses, you don't live, you take it easy. You're the luckiest of lucky devils and the gods eat out of your hands. And that's not all. Tomorrow is Sunday, when high society throngs the square after mass. Sometimes there are bands playing in the open air, and the women powder their noses to make themselves more beautiful than their daughters.'

'Will we come back tomorrow?'

'You can't learn everything in a day.'

And he hurried off to offer his services to a fashionably dressed man.

By the time I got back to Graba, my head was filled with stars. I was so obsessed by Sidi Bel Abbès I didn't sleep a wink. I recalled the extraordinary neighbourhoods and the refined people who walked in them as if they had nothing else to do. In the morning, I ran and woke Sid Roho, eager to go back to the city and draw from its sun the light that was lacking in my life. We found a few shoes to shine, then went to a park and watched the young lovers whispering sweet nothings to each other on the benches. We quite forgot that we were hungry.

Sid Roho taught me how to rub the shoes to get the dust off, then how to polish them without getting the laces dirty and, finally, how to go over them with a cloth to make the leather shine. At the end of the day, he entrusted two pairs of shoes to me that were difficult at first, but which I managed to clean acceptably. Then he went and sat on a low wall to rest for a while and left me to get on with it by myself.

'Well?' he asked when he returned.

'I've no complaints.'

'That's you set up, then. Now give everything back to me,' he said, seeing a policeman approach. 'I need to make some real money today.'

The policeman immediately stuck out his foot, raising the hem of his trouser leg so as not to get it dirty. Sid Roho displayed his skills with unusual dexterity, as if the uniform inspired a particular enthusiasm in him. At the end, the policeman grunted with satisfaction and went on his way without putting his hand in his pocket.

'He didn't pay you.'

'He doesn't have to, I suppose,' Sid Roho said, putting his equipment back in the box. 'Only, he's made a big mistake.'

When we were some distance away, he took a whistle from his pocket.

'That copper thought he could get away with anything,' he said, excited. 'Well, so do I, my friend. I pinched that stingy bastard's whistle.'

'How did you do that?'

'The ways of the Lord are unfathomable.'

He was really impressive.

That evening, we didn't go straight back to Graba. Sid Roho was determined to show me the extent of his daring. When night had fallen on the city, he took me to a neighbourhood lit by gas lamps. No sooner did he start blowing the whistle than other whistles sounded in the surrounding area and we saw two policemen run past. Sid Roho was doubled up with laughter, his hand pressed to his mouth. 'I'm going to drive them crazy all night long, those uniformed skinflints who won't pay a penniless shoeshine boy.' Thinking the alarm had been raised, the policemen inspected the area thoroughly before withdrawing. Sid Roho took me to another neighbourhood and repeated the performance. Again, other whistles answered him. Again, we had a good laugh and moved on to a different area. The poor cops sped past us, holding their kepis down with one hand while clutching their truncheons with the other, bumping into each other as they turned corners, yelling orders at each other, running back the way they had come, before finally, panting, driven to distraction by the fact that they couldn't understand what was going on, they went morosely back to their station. Huddled in the shadows, Sid Roho and I laughed until we cried, our feet pedalling in the air, our throats tight with the effort to keep as quiet as possible. This practical joke of ours gave us goose pimples, it was so wonderful and at the same time so scary. A few streets further on, Sid Roho took out his whistle once more and started all over again. The poor policemen emerged from the darkness, looked around like disorientated spaniels, and set off again on their wild goose chase. One of them, out of breath, wheezing like a dying animal, came close to our hiding place and threw up. It was an amazing sight, which almost made me throw up too. I was laughing so much I could barely stay upright and had to beg Sid Roho to give it a rest. Towards midnight, absolutely delighted by our prank, we got back to Graba to enjoy a well-earned sleep.

In the morning, the ghetto was like a punch in the face.

Now that I had seen Sidi Bel Abbès, I didn't want to see anything else.

In Graba, there were no shop windows, no bandstands, no esplanades lined with verdant hedges, no dance halls. There was only the stench that gnawed at our eyes and throat; the shacks blackened with use and overgrown with weeds; the dogs trailing their colonies of fleas from one end of the shanty town to the other, so skinny you could have played the zither on their ribs; the beggars huddled in their own shadows and the bare-bottomed brats running in all directions like mad things.

I could no longer bear this hell that fried our brains and dried our veins without leaving us a drop for our tears. One moonless night, I vowed, I would set fire to it and watch the flames destroy these dishevelled slums that wanted me to believe they were my graveyard and I was a ghost.

'What's the matter?' Mekki asked, catching me talking to myself on the doorstep of our shack.

'I want us to leave here.'

'On what? A flying carpet? We can't afford it. Why don't you get back to the hammam instead of talking nonsense?'

'The owner fired me.'

He almost choked. 'When was this?'

'A week ago.'

'Why didn't you say anything?'

'You get angry about a lot less.'

'What did you do this time?'

'It wasn't my fault.'

'Whose was it – mine? If you can't even hold down a job, how do you plan to leave here? You should follow Nora's example. She works so hard, she's almost worn her fingers to the bone. And she doesn't complain. And what about your mother? And your aunt? As for me, I've forgotten what having a rest means, while you don't seem to care that we have no money.'

'I couldn't force him to keep me.'

'He's a reasonable man. But you just do whatever comes into your head, if you still have one, that is. I'm fed up with you being under my feet.'

'I'm going to work for myself.'

Mekki gave a brief, dry laugh, a kind of irritable hiccup. 'For yourself? Are you planning to start a business? With what, may I ask? With your fingers up your nose?'

'I'm going to be a shoeshine boy.'

Mekki staggered as if the sky had fallen on his head. He frowned to make sure he had heard correctly, then, his face ashen and his nostrils dilated with anger, he grabbed me by the throat and pushed me up against the wall with the clear intention of seeing me disappear through it.

'A shoeshine boy? Nobody in our family has ever kissed the feet of a master. Our houses may be nothing but ruins, our fields may have been confiscated, but we still have our honour. When are you going to get that into your head, you mangy dog?'

I pushed him away angrily. 'Don't insult me.'

'Is there a worse insult than lowering yourself to polish the shoes of your fellow men?'

'It's a living, like any other. And I don't want you ever to raise your hand to me again. You're not my father.'

'I'd tear your heart out with my bare hands if I was your father. And since I'm the one who gives the orders here, I forbid you to dishonour the name of our family. A shoeshine boy! That's all we need. What'll you do when your brush is worn out – shine shoes with your tongue?'

I didn't know any more whether to laugh or cry. Mekki dared to talk to me about honour and abstract, solemn duties while I sniffed shame with every breath of air. Was he blind or stupid? Didn't he understand that I was as determined as he was to flee this backwater of canvas and zinc, where people kept their rotten luck like an ember still smouldering beneath the ashes and refusing to die? Didn't he understand that I had just become aware of a reality other than the one I'd always thought was our lot, that at the very moment I was confronting him I was becoming someone else, that it was Sunday, a Sunday unlike any other, no longer just the day of the Lord and Roumis, but a crucial day that would stand out for me and that there are some dates that matter more than others, in which you are born again? I didn't yet have the words to express these things, but I felt them deep inside. It was a strange feeling, nagging and confused, like the one you feel when you have a name on the tip of your tongue and you just can't find it. And I was determined to find it.

Sid Roho advanced me the money to buy a box, brushes and polish, and I set off in search of shoes to shine. I soon realised that I wasn't the only one who'd had that idea. I needed to negotiate according to the current rules, because competition was tough and supply was limited. The Arab kids who did the same job as me were quick with their fists and didn't hold back once they'd got the intruder on the ground. But I held firm and defended my territory.

What mattered to me was to make as much money as possible to allow Mekki to find us a house in stone on a real street, in a real neighbourhood with street lighting that came on at night and shops with window displays. I wanted to see high society pass beneath my window, take a moment's rest on a public bench and – why not? – believe that I was a man of my time, capable of making the most of it. To do that, I had to earn the right to dream and the right to hope. I didn't deceive myself that I would ever achieve the same status as a Roumi: it wasn't my territory; but it wasn't unreasonable for a poor boy to find another way, another destiny, and, with a bit of luck, to escape once and for all those disaster areas where songs echoed like curses, and where tomorrows were inspired by yesterdays as dark as night. I had seen a few Arabs who'd apparently done well for themselves. They wore neat suits and there wasn't the slightest stain on their fezzes. They walked among Roumis without tripping up and lived in whitewashed houses with doors that could be locked and shutters at the windows – the kind of houses I dreamt about. And that had given me confidence.

I'd get to the main square of Sidi Bel Abbès early in the morning, my box slung over my shoulder and my brush openly displayed, watching out for someone clicking his fingers or nodding his head, at which point I'd throw myself at their shoes and not let go of them until I could see my reflection in the leather. The kicks in the side that I received taught me the tricks of the trade; the customers' anger made me more skilful; I took care not to go beyond the shoe itself, the one great sin of the profession, and when they threw me a coin, I'd catch it and pocket it, already imagining myself on my balcony waving to friends in the street.

Alas, there weren't that many customers. There were days when I returned home empty-handed, with nothing in my belly. Not all Europeans were eager for my services: many wore shoes as worn-out as mine. That didn't discourage me. I prowled endlessly around the cafés, the church, the town hall – and the brothel, because, according to Sid Roho, some boys about to lose their virginity were anxious to look presentable for their sexual baptism. My box seemed to grow heavier every day, but didn't slow me down. Years later, I could still feel the straps of that box digging into the back of my neck and the slap an outraged client gave me. I clearly remember that particular man, who almost lynched me because of an unfortunate mark on his sock. Huge, his face crimson with sun, he wore a colonial helmet, a spotlessly white suit and a fob watch on his waistcoat. He was coming out of the barber's when he hailed me. As I set to work putting a shine back in his shoes, he began ogling a girl who was hanging out washing on a balcony. I don't know how my brush slipped. The man almost fainted when he saw his soiled sock. His big, bear-like hand came down on my cheek with such violence that I saw the night stars appear in broad daylight. It didn't put me off. Blows were part of life; they were the price of perseverance, the price I had to pay in order to believe and to dream. And I believed and dreamt so much, my head was almost bursting. I told myself that what was allowed to some was allowed to all, and that although there might be people who gave up, there was no reason for me to do so. According to an old saying, the man who hopes is worth more than the man who waits, and the man who waits is less to be pitied than the man who gives up. My ambition was as great as my hunger and as raw as my nakedness. I wanted one day to wear nice clean clothes and braces over my shirt, to soap my body until it vanished beneath the suds, to comb my hair and live it up on the streets ... Between customers, I would sit on the pavement and imagine myself coming out of a pastry shop arms laden with cakes, or leaving a butcher's with thick slabs of meat in a nice parcel, or sitting on a bench, smoking my cigarette like that gentleman over there studying his newspaper. When a bus passed, I saw myself inside it, just behind the driver, watching his every move because – who knows? – I too might find myself behind a wheel one day. When a young couple came along arm in arm, I would feel a frail, tender hand taking me by the waist ... I would hear Sid Roho's grandfather whisper to me, 'What's difficult is not necessarily impossible ... What's difficult is not necessarily impossible ... not necessarily impossible ... possible, possible, possible,' and I would nod with conviction as if the old man was right there in front of me.

## 4

Dreams are a poor man's guardian, and his destruction. They take us by the hand, walk us through a thousand promises, then leave us whenever they want. Dreams are clever; dreams understand psychology: they accept our feelings just as we take an inveterate liar at his word, but when we entrust our hearts and minds to them, they give us the slip just when things are going badly, and we find ourselves with a void in our head and a hole in our chest – all we have left is eyes to weep.

What can I say of my own dream? Like all dreams, it was captivating. It cradled my soul with such tenderness that I would have preferred it to my mother with my eyes closed. And my eyes were indeed closed, because I saw things only through my dream. But a dream isn't brave and doesn't think things through. It runs away when the hour of reckoning arrives; its principles crumble, and we come back down to earth as stupid as we were before we flew up to the sky, with, in addition, the annoyance of returning to square one and finding it even more unbearable than before. All at once, dusk seems like the smothering of our illusions, and the colour of night recalls the ashes of our vain passions, because none of our so-called wishes have been granted.

My mother used to say that the gods are only great because we see them from below. That is true of dreams too. Lifting my head from the shoes I was polishing, I would realise how small I was. My brush wasn't a magic lamp, and no genie would choose a worn shoe to hide in. After six months of hard graft, I still didn't have enough to buy myself a pair of trousers; the stone-houses-with-numbers-on-streets-with-names were receding like ships leaving for the land of plenty, while I was falling to pieces on my desert island with nothing but sand filtering through my fingers. Even if my fingers were green, had anyone ever seen flowers grow on sand dunes?

All it took was a little boy pointing at me for my dream to burst like an abscess. I was getting ready to have a bite to eat under a tree, sitting on my box, when I heard, 'That's him, officer!' He was a European kid, dressed like a prince, the summer in his hair and the sea in his eyes. I had never seen him before and didn't know what he wanted with me. But misfortune can never rest. It waits for you – then, tired of hanging about, comes looking for you. The policeman didn't waste any time. His truncheon came down instinctively on my head. An Arab is guilty by nature. If you don't know what he's actually guilty of, there's no point asking him. I had no idea what the little Roumi was accusing me of. I don't suppose there was any point asking him either. My piece of bread stuck in my throat; the blood that spurted in my mouth didn't help it go down. The policeman hit me several times with his truncheon and kicked me in the side. 'You vermin!' he cried. 'You lousy piece of filth! Get a move on! Go back to your kennel and stay there. If I catch you prowling around this area again, I'll put you in a cell until the rats have finished gnawing your bones.'

Dazed, my legs like jelly and my face split open, I set off at a run and left the city, forgetting my shoeshine box, my stupid daydreams and a whole lot of other things that only a peasant my age would have been naive enough to think possible.

I never set foot in Sidi Bel Abbès again.

*

Our stay in Graba continued.

Two years had passed and we were still there. Mekki would take me to work with him in order to keep his eye on me. He had made a counter out of wooden boards and we would stand side by side, selling not only soup but also hard-boiled eggs and tomatoes with onion.

I was seeing less of my friends now. We would meet in the same place, the abandoned orchard, but we were seldom all there at the same time; we would each take turns at skipping our evenings together.

Ramdane had developed a nasty swelling in the middle of his stomach. The healer had assured him that it was because of the loads he was carrying all day long. Ramdane refused to take the healer's recommendations seriously. He wrapped a bandage around his waist to contain his hernia and resumed work. He was wasting away before our eyes. As for Gomri, he had found himself a 'fiancée' and was starting to neglect us so that he could meet up with her behind the wooded hillocks. Sid Roho and I followed him one evening to see her for ourselves. The fiancée was a girl from Kasdir, either a runaway or an orphan, because in those days a girl had to be one or the other to be out at night and go around with boys. She had a long, thin face tightly wrapped in a scarf, narrow shoulders, a flat chest and disproportionately long and spindly legs. She looked like a grasshopper. She kept laughing for no reason. Gomri, his hands between his thighs as if struggling to hold back an urge to pee, couldn't take his eyes off her, even for a moment. It has to be said, the girl was quite a tease, a hot flame straight from the fires of hell. She would squirm in simulated embarrassment, her fingers in her mouth, cooing, showing more and more of her undeveloped breasts and going so far as to pull her dress up above her thighs to get Gomri even more excited. Hidden in the bushes, we watched this little performance in perfect silence, Sid Roho massaging his rod and me thinking about Nora.

The winter of 1925 was terrible. It hadn't been so cold in the region in living memory. After the torrential rains that flooded our shacks, the ground was covered in ice, turning Graba into a skating rink. It snowed three days running, without stopping. People were up to their waists in the snow, and children stayed at home. Many straw huts had collapsed beneath the rain and some had burnt down because of the logs lit inside. For two weeks, the stalls remained closed and the market empty. Dozens died of hunger, dozens more of cold. When the snow melted, the place turned into a mud bath, causing more deaths and the collapse of homes. When the first provisions reached us, people went mad; Ramdane's crippled father was trampled in the stampede.

My family didn't escape unscathed. Nora caught a bad cold and almost died. Then Mekki and my mother were sick for a whole week, throwing up even the rancid water they drank, which was the only thing we could put in our mouths anyway. As for me, I had a high fever and my body was covered in boils. At night, I had visions of cockroaches crawling around me. Then, one by one, we came back to life. All except Aunt Rokaya, whose knees had stiffened. She couldn't bend her legs or sit properly. We thought she was going to die, and it was almost as if she had. Her lower limbs no longer responded. She lay on her mat, as stiff as a piece of wood. Seeing Nora and my mother drag her behind the thicket to help her relieve herself, I realised the full extent of human misery.

Many families had gathered their meagre belongings and set off to some new hell. They no longer had a roof over their heads and didn't see any hope of rebuilding their lives in Graba. Ramdane was among those who left. He piled his mother and siblings onto a cart and went off to bury his father in his native douar. He would never return.

Sid Roho mourned the loss of both his parents, carried off by hunger and illness. He made sure he said goodbye to me before leaving.

'Sorry about your parents,' I said.

'It's the survivors you should feel sorry for, Turambo. My parents' act has finished and the curtain has come down. I'm the one still up on stage like an idiot, not knowing what to do with my grief.'

'It is written,' I said, unable to think what else to say.

'Yes, but who by? My grandfather used to say that fate only strikes those who've tried everything and failed. If you have a broken arm, nothing can help you accept that. I don't think my parents ever tried anything. They died because all they did was endure what they should have fought against.'

'And where do you plan to go?'

He shrugged. 'I don't care. When I'm tired of travelling, I'll stop. The world is vast, and anyone who's known Graba can go anywhere he wants, knowing the worst is always behind him.'

I walked with him to the 'Arab' road and watched him limp off in search of his destiny, a bundle on his head and his shoeshine box over his shoulder.

It was a dark, ugly morning and even the birds had stopped singing.

In turn, Mekki admitted that the time had come for us to reinvent ourselves elsewhere. He gathered us together in our shack, whose sheet-metal roof had been demolished by the snow.

'I think we have enough money to try our luck far from here,' he said, emptying our savings onto a scarf. 'There's nothing for us in this dump any more anyway.'

That was true. Half the ghetto had been devastated by the bad weather and the few vendors who had tried to cling on had given up one after the other, for lack of customers or supplies. The suppliers preferred to sell to Kasdir and run. The track leading to Graba was impassable and the paths were overrun by robbers. The most alarming thing of all was that epidemics were breaking out here and there. There was talk of typhoid and cholera. The deaths continued. The makeshift graveyard behind the military dumping ground bore witness to the extent of the disaster.

'If you hadn't already made up your mind, I'd have left of my own accord,' my mother declared. 'From the start, I've been telling myself you'd realise there was nothing for us here. But I suppose men are slower on the uptake than mules.'

My mother's anger astonished us. She had always concealed her sorrows, like a hen sitting on her eggs, and now here she was expressing her discontent without pulling her punches. Her unexpected outburst was proof that we had reached rock bottom.

My mother shifted a pile of packages in a corner of the room, extracted a tightly bound cloth and untied it as we watched. A wonderfully carved solid gold *kholkhal* rolled across to our feet, with the head of a roaring lion at each end and calligraphic inscriptions of exceptional delicacy on the edges; a genuine work of art from a lost era when our women were all cherished sultanas.

'Take it,' she said to her brother.

Mekki shook his head. 'I have no right to touch it. This jewel belonged to your great-grandmother.'

'She doesn't need it any more.'

'It belongs to you now.'

'I'm hungry, and I can't eat it.'

'No, I can't ... It's all we have left of our history.'

'Don't be a fool. The only history is the present, and we're dying. If it's written that this jewel will stay in our family, it'll come back to us ... I'm sick of this shanty town. Find us somewhere to go where people are like people, so that we too can be what we were.'

She seized Mekki's hand, put the impressive jewel in his palm and closed his fingers over it. With that, she left the room and got down to work putting some kind of order in her belongings.

I had often wondered what my mother really expected of life. I'm sure she expected nothing, any more than she expected something of death, except perhaps the relief at having finished with everything, absolutely everything, provided there was no heaven or hell afterwards.

Mekki set off the next day in search of somewhere to go. He hadn't decided on anywhere, but was planning to ask the advice of people he met on the road. Ten days went by without any news of the head of our family. We couldn't digest the crop we brought back from the scrub and we couldn't sleep. Whenever a man passed our shack, we prayed it was Mekki. But it wasn't. The waiting was even more agonising when the sun went down and we started to fear the worst.

One morning, Rokaya woke bathed in sweat, her eyes popping out of their sockets.

'I had a bad dream, I shudder to think of it. I'm sure something has happened to Mekki.'

'Since when have your dreams been premonitions?' my mother said curtly.

'What did you see?' Nora asked Rokaya.

Rokaya shifted painfully on her mat. 'Even if Mekki went to the ends of the earth, he'd have been back by now.'

'He'll be back,' my mother cut in. 'He promised us a quiet place, and quiet places aren't so easy to find.'

'I have a bad feeling about this, Taos. My heart has turned to jelly. You shouldn't have given him your bracelet. With all those scoundrels on the roads —'

'Shut up! You'll bring him bad luck.'

'It may already have happened. Mekki may be dead by now. Your jewel has caused his downfall, and ours.'

'Shut your mouth, you witch. God can't do that to us. He has no right.'

'God has every right, Taos. Why are you blaspheming?'

My mother went out into the yard. She was furious and didn't know what to reply.

I had never before heard her raise her voice or show a lack of respect to her elder sister.

Mekki did come back, exhausted but radiant. From a distance, I saw him waving to me enthusiastically and I realised our connection with Graba was coming to an end. We greeted Mekki like a gift from heaven. He begged us to let him eat first, then, having savoured our impatience, he announced that we were leaving for Oran. My mother remarked that Rokaya wouldn't be able to stand such a journey in her state. Mekki reassured us: a haulier from Kasdir who had a delivery to make in Oran had agreed to take us on his lorry for a few francs.

We gathered together our knick-knacks and our utensils, our clothes and our prayers, and at dawn climbed into the back of the vehicle and closed our eyes in order not to see Graba recede into the distance; we were already elsewhere.


Mekki had found us a place to live on the north side of Medina Jedida – a Muslim quarter the city council called the 'Village Nègre' – a stone outhouse inside a courtyard, with a balcony and shutters on the windows, located on the corner of Rue du Général-Cérez and Boulevard Andrieu, opposite an artillery barracks.

The dwelling was spacious, consisting of two large connecting bedrooms, one of which looked out onto the street and the other onto a beaten-earth esplanade, and a narrow room for cooking; the toilets were in the courtyard, which we shared with the landlady, a Turkish widow, and a Kabyle family who ran a Moorish bath. We were very pleased with our new accommodation. Nora shed a few tears to bless the place.

It took me a while to familiarise myself with city life: the straight pavements, the roads that might prove fatal to the distracted, the panic instilled in me by the cars with their blaring horns. But I was in seventh heaven. Our house had a door with a lock and a number above it. As far as I was concerned, it was the best I could have hoped for.

My dreams were coming true.

The first few days, I enjoyed leaning with one foot against the wall and staying like that for hours so that the residents would know I lived in that beautiful residence with glass in the windows; that seemed to me as important as the fact that we were no longer obliged to fetch water from springs miles away but could draw it from the well in the courtyard. And at night, from my balcony, I would gaze out at the Moorish houses adorned with street lights, at their white slanting façades, the *mashrabiyas* behind which shadows moved in the light of gas lamps and, on the esplanade, quiet now, passers-by strolling here and there, carrying lanterns like giant fireflies borne on the wind. Spray from the sea, which I had never before seen in my life, was carried from the harbour and dampened my face with thousands of cooling droplets. I would breathe in the air until my lungs almost burst and catch myself humming unknown tunes, as if they had long been buried deep in my subconscious and now my joy had freed them all at once and launched them into the sky.

Disorientated by the forest of identical houses and the inextricable web of avenues, I undertook to walk up and down my street from end to end several times, in order to memorise the landmarks. When I had learnt how to find my door with my eyes closed, I extended my curiosity to the neighbouring streets, then to the surrounding boulevards, and within a week I knew Medina Jedida by heart.

My uncle went into partnership with a herbalist, a Mozabite, and set up shop in the Arab market. I would take him his meal at midday and the rest of the time I would wander.

Oran was a breathless adventure, a crossroads where every era came together, each in its own finery. Modernity offered up its lures, to which the old reflexes responded only reluctantly, as if tasting a suspicious fruit. The native population understood that a new era was under way and wondered what it had to offer them, and at what price. Frenzied and intimidating, the European city flaunted its ambitions, but something in its gorging didn't tally with their own frugality, and they were too uncertain of their place to claim a slice of the cake. Things were not distributed equally, and chances did not come to everyone. The cards had been unfairly dealt. The gulf between the haves and have-nots was too wide to bridge; segregation, which reduced the unknown other to abstraction or cliché, kept the communities in a state of heightened mistrust. At that time, Oran was stewing in a mixture of doubt and confusion, fuelled by prejudice and insularity. You wouldn't be mad enough to entrust your mother to your neighbour.

I walked for hours and hours without noticing, engrossed in the mysteries of the various neighbourhoods, which slowly revealed themselves. My search for work took me from one end to the other of the southern plateau of the city, which was strewn with the tents of nomads from the desert. Beyond the Jewish cemetery, in a kind of no man's land trapped between Sananes and the parade ground, was a little patch of countryside disfigured by urban life,

reducing its rustic charms to hollowed-out building sites; amid
the skeletal orchards, a handful of houses still dripping with wattle
and daub and covered in sheet metal laid the foundations for a
soon-to-be village. A little further on was Lamur, a vast stretch
of purple clay laid out in rudimentary courtyards. Muslim city
dwellers did not look kindly on the shacks the peasants arriving
from the hinterland erected around their territory in a hotchpotch
of rotting tarpaulins and wooden beams; squabbles erupted daily
between the locals and the newcomers, which forced the latter,
who were becoming intrusive, to fall back on Jenane Jato, a
dangerous area where you wouldn't want to venture at night. To
the west, the neighbourhood of Eckmühl descended as far as the
ravine of Ras el-Aïn with its garland of market gardens, its tiered
houses, its shaded alleys and its thrilling bullrings. The majority
of the inhabitants were Spaniards, mostly humble people and
settled gypsies who somehow eked out a living, always hoping
for something like a miracle to get them through their rough
patch. Their women, among them many fortune tellers, went
from door to door selling faded lace or reading unlikely futures in
the occupants' palms. They had a gift for spotting a sucker from
a long way away; when a customer hesitated, they would end up
telling them all kinds of nonsense, but never letting go. Amazing,
combative women, who didn't take no for an answer and could
smooth-talk even the devil. To the north-east of Medina Jedida,
below Magenta, you came to the Derb, a Sephardic quarter
where men in black skullcaps bustled about their shops, making
sure their women were securely behind locked doors. Just like us.
Apart from little girls with plaited hair playing jacks with little
boys on the pavement, there were no young people to enliven
the streets. It was a poor neighbourhood, although it refused to
admit it. And in the evening, to prove that there was some joy,

the cafés filled the streets with music in a fusion of styles which made the virgins sigh behind their shutters ...

It was the same everywhere.

Each community had nothing but its own talent to survive the ups and downs of life. A matter of self-respect and survival. Music was a weapon, an absolute refusal to surrender. In Médioni and Delmonte and Saint-Eugène, from the pine grove of Les Planteurs to the heights of Santa Cruz, people sang in order not to disappear. The Bedouin flute gave the cue to the tambourine and, when the accordion breathed its last in some hidden courtyard, the gypsy guitar took over. It was important for the inhabitants never to stop hearing the sound of their own lives. In Oran, poverty was a state of mind, not a condition. I saw people bundled up in clothes that had been mended a hundred times, shuffling along in old shoes that gaped open, but walking with their heads held high. In Oran, you could tolerate being at the bottom of the ladder, but never at someone else's feet. From Chollet to Ras el-Aïn, where I would watch the washerwomen wringing out their washing on the bank of the *oued*, from La Scalera, shared by Spaniards and Muslims worn out by three hundred years of wars and reprisals, to Victor-Hugo, where the inexorable spread of the shanty town was forcing the kitchen gardens to recede, each area had its own character, and each group jealously guarded its own honour. Of course, I would sometimes turn a corner and be waylaid by packs of kids anxious to defend their fiefdom and punish intruders, but there was invariably a grown-up around to bring them to heel.

Oran also had its seedy spots where it grew dark early, slums haunted by pimps and other shady characters, brothels that smelt of the clap and stairwells where people fornicated in a rush, standing up. The inhabitants of Oran denied any knowledge of these places of ill repute; everyone acted as if they didn't exist. Anyone who had been spotted there once was shamed for life.

The only people you saw there were strangers to the city, randy soldiers and boatmen from distant horizons.

Coming back up from the Casbah, you came out onto Place d'Armes, surrounded by centuries-old trees as big as baobabs: this was the exact spot where the different communities met without really meeting, tacitly divided by a virtual line of demarcation. It was a beautiful square radiant with sunlight, with its tram station, its cafés and terraces, its hurrying women and its pomaded pick-up artists, its flashy automobiles overtaking the carriages just to impress them, flanked to the south by the city hall with its two bronze lions guarding the entrance, to the west by the theatre and to the north by the Military Club. Then, all at once, looking down on the upper part of Boulevard Seguin, there was the plateau of Karguentah! Another world, stretching as far as Miramar, beautiful, sumptuous and self-centred. This was the other side of the mirror, where ethereal souls faded away of their own accord in order not to blight the scenery; the exclusive world of the rich, those who had the right to believe and to possess, to reign and to endure, for whom the sun rose purely to salute them and night only veiled its face to protect them from the evil eye: the famous European city with its pavements adorned with street lamps, its gleaming shop windows, its neon signs, its Haussmann-style apartment buildings bedecked with statues that seemed to rise from the walls, its verdant parks, its wrought-iron benches and its marbled lobbies where people in white suits and dark glasses resisted the good humour so dear to the southern districts and were deeply hostile to beggars and street vendors; taciturn, arrogant people, so sophisticated that they all reminded me of that fat pig who had beaten me in Sidi Bel Abbès over a tiny spot of polish on his sock.

For my part, I was only myself and proud to be so in Medina Jedida, my home port, my refuge, my country. I never tired of breathing it in, taking its pulse, being aware of its slightest spasm. Medina Jedida had an air of endurance and survival. The aroma of spices competed with incense and the stench of the tanneries, mingled with the smells of the bazaars, caught the fragrance of mint from the Moorish cafés and the scent of the kebabs being braised outside them, and all these odours merged in an alchemy that compacted the air and held the dust in suspense. The lights of the day bounced off the walls and the horse-drawn carriages in a succession of dazzling flashes, searing the eyes like razor blades. Rascally kids with their heads shaven Zouave-fashion, ran barefoot, overturning stalls in their flight, mimicking the vendors; it was pointless yelling at them – neither threats nor thrashings could calm them. The streets swarmed with a disparate and feverish collection of people, their heads covered with fezzes, chechias, turbans and sometimes even colonial helmets. The booming cries of the merchants were enough to give the crowds a splitting headache. With the garish colours and the deliciously absurd atmosphere, it was like being at a fair. I loved Medina Jedida from the moment I looked at its people – my people, but so different from those of Graba. In Medina Jedida, there was still poverty, but it had a certain reserve. Cripples didn't cling to the coat-tails of passers-by and beggars restrained their whining. The natives, mostly Araberbers,[1] burnouses over their shoulders and canes in their hands, were as dignified as in the days when their ancestors could look at the ground without lowering their heads. Here, there were no curses, no obscene remarks; politeness was all. Old men wore their white beards with nobility. They didn't sit on the ground, but on padded stools or small wicker chairs or in groups on rattan benches, telling their prayer beads with translucent hands and offering the young their skulls to kiss. In the crowded cafés, where nasal phonographs

1 Word coined by the author to indicate the unity of the Arab and Berber peoples.

endlessly played Egyptian music, the waiters in spotless aprons weaved in and out among the tables, bearing teapots on trays. It wasn't unusual to see women turn up in their flouncy veils, and out of politeness the men would turn away as they passed. And in the evening, when the heat at last consented to die down, crowds would gather on the beaten-earth esplanade to be treated to all kinds of entertainments. The *lalaoui* dancers would take out their tambourines and sticks; snake charmers would lift the lids of their baskets and cast their lascivious vipers at the feet of horrified children; other men held the crowd spellbound with virtuoso displays of fighting with clubs. Further on, a troubadour enchanted the spectators with far-fetched stories interspersed with tear-jerking songs he seemed to have made up on the spot, while a monkey trainer clearly took himself for a magician. The folklore of Medina Jedida conjured all demons away.

This was my world finding its bearings again, my people as they were before misfortune threw them off track. After so many exiles, so many shipwrecks, I was back in my element.

I was moved, reinvigorated and relieved, convinced that I could now grow up normally, safe from the Zanes and the perversity of the shanty towns, even though I was still hungry and had no nice clothes to wear.

## 5

In spite of Mekki's disapproval, my mother had found a job. She had seen how the flats of the old Turkish woman and the Kabyle family were furnished and she too wanted mattresses, low tables for eating on, tableware, woollen blankets, eiderdowns, even a sideboard with a huge mirror in the middle. My uncle earned just enough to provide food and pay the rent. My mother was ambitious. She wanted a decent house where she could receive her neighbours without making them feel uncomfortable, a bed for her elder sister, whose health was deteriorating, and nice dresses for Nora, who was growing up. Yes, Nora had grown quickly, her features had become more defined and she was blossoming as her big black eyes opened to the world. I didn't have the courage to admit it, but Nora had been occupying my thoughts a lot since I had caught her washing herself. Her adolescent body was starting to take shape and her white breasts adorned her chest like two twin suns. I had certainly seen her naked before, without it having much effect on me, but, since this last time, she'd just had to look at me to arouse me, and I was always the one who turned my head away first.

My mother did the cleaning and other housework for a widow who lived on Boulevard Mascara, not far from our house. I had to walk her there in the morning and bring her back in the evening because she got the houses and streets muddled up and was incapable of finding her way back once she had crossed the road. I would lead her to the door in question, knock and leave when the door was opened. Towards the end of the afternoon, I would pick her up from the same place. The day she got her wages, we would do the rounds of the bazaars and return home laden with iron buckets, funnels, samovars, braziers with bellows and all kinds of other items, sometimes of little use.

I was waiting for her on Boulevard Mascara when a fair-haired boy my age, neat and tidy without being dapper, stopped in front of me.

'Can I help you?' he asked me in Arabic.

There was no aggressiveness in his blue eyes. He seemed friendly, but the only memory I had of young Roumis was of that boy who had burst my dream like an abscess by pointing me out to the policeman in Sidi Bel Abbès. Instinctively, I checked to see if there was any uniform in the vicinity.

'I didn't ask you for anything,' I grunted.

'You're sitting in our doorway,' he said calmly.

'I'm waiting for my mother. She's cleaning in there.'

'Do you want me to go up and see how far she's got?'

His kindness made me uncomfortable. Was he softening me up before kicking me in the face?

'I'd like that,' I said cautiously. 'I'm starting to get a headache because of the sun.'

The boy stepped over me, ran up a staircase and returned after a few minutes.

'She'll be another hour or so.'

'What's she doing in there? Redecorating the house or what?'

'My name's Gino, Gino Ramoun,' he said, holding out his hand. 'My mother has a lot of good things to say about yours. It's the first time she's got along with a cleaner. We've had lots. Some cheated us and others stole things, not just food.'

'We're respectable people. Just because my mother works for yours doesn't mean —'

'No, no, I wasn't implying anything like that. We're not rich. My mother's disabled. She never leaves her bed. She needs help, that's all.'

I waved away his apologies.

He sat down next to me on the doorstep. I could see he was trying to redeem himself, but I didn't encourage him. I'd had enough of polishing my backside on the step and watching others go about their business.

'I'm a bit peckish,' the Roumi said. 'How about going for a bite to eat?'

I didn't reply. I was broke.

'It's on me,' he insisted. 'Come on. If your mother can be friends with mine, why can't we?'

I don't know if it was out of boredom or hunger, but I accepted the invitation.

'Do you like boiled chickpeas with cumin?'

'Anything's fine when you're hungry.'

'Well, then, what are we waiting for?'

Gino was a straightforward, uncomplicated, guileless boy. He seemed awkward and my company was a comfort to him. He didn't mix with the other boys in the neighbourhood; they scared him. I got used to him, and within a few weeks we were as thick as thieves. There was something reassuring about him. His voice was soft and his eyes clear and wholesome. He worked in a garage on Place Sébastopol. We would meet up in the evenings on Boulevard Mascara. Sometimes, he'd walk with us to our house and, after dropping my mother off, we'd go and eat doughnuts in the Arab market or test our teeth on the *torraicos* that the Spaniards sold us in paper cones.

One day, he invited me to his home. He was determined to

give me something. Gino's flat was above a haberdasher's. You reached it by a steep staircase that went straight up to the first floor. We climbed the stairs to a short L-shaped corridor that led to two large rooms on the right and a courtyard on the left. As we reached the hall, a voice cried out, 'Open the windows. I'm melting.'

The voice had come in a weary breath from the bedroom. I looked in, but couldn't see anything. Then something moved on the bed. Squinting, I made out a red-faced mass beneath a white sheet transparent with sweat. Actually, it wasn't a sheet, but a huge blouse designed to look smart in spite of its size, with embroidery along the bottom and flowered braid on the collar. There was a blonde head on the pillow with a beautiful face trapped in a crimson mass of flesh too large to be considered a neck, above a body made up of disjointed slabs furrowed with deep, winding folds. The sight took my breath away. It took me a while to distinguish breasts of supernatural volume from arms so heavy they could barely move. Her stomach undulated with rolls of fat cascading onto her sides, and her elephantine legs rested on cushions like two marble columns. Never in my wildest dreams had I imagined that human bodies of that size could exist. It wasn't so much a woman's body as a phenomenal heap of flesh that covered almost the entire mattress, a mass of flabbiness scarlet with the heat, threatening to spread through the room in a gelatinous stream.

This was Gino's mother, so monumentally obese, so suffocated by her own weight that she had difficulty breathing.

'*Sei Gino?*'

'Yes, Mother.'

'*Dove eri finito, angelo mio?*'

'You know perfectly well, Mother. I was at the garage.'

'*Hai mangiato?*'

'Yes, Mother, I've eaten.'

A silence, then his mother's voice returned, calm now. '*Chi è il ragazzo con te?*'

'This is Turambo, the son of Taos … of Madame Taos.'

She tried to turn towards us, but succeeded only in setting in motion an avalanche of shudders that went through her body like wavelets on the surface of a pond.

'*Digli di avvicinarsi, così posso vederlo più da vicino.*'

Gino pushed me towards the bed.

His mother stared at me with her blue eyes. She had lovely dimples on her cheeks, and her smile was touchingly gentle. 'Come a little closer.'

Embarrassed, I did as she said.

She tried to raise her hand to my face, but her arm remained stuck in the mass of flesh. 'You look like a good boy, Turambo.'

I said nothing. I was still in a state of shock.

'Your mother takes care of me like a sister … Gino has told me a lot about you. I think the two of you are going to get along well. Come closer still, right next to me.'

Gino noticed my growing unease and came to my rescue, grabbing me by the wrist. 'I'm taking him to my room, Mother. I have things to show him.'

'*Povero figlio, ha solo stracci addosso. Devi sicuramente avere degli abiti che non indossi più, Gino. Daglieli.*'

'That's what I was planning to do, Mother.'

Gino led me to his room. There was a bed that could be taken apart, a table with a chair in a corner, a little wardrobe that was falling to pieces, and that was all. The walls were peeling and there were greenish stains on the cracked ceiling crossed by beams. It was a sad room, with a broken window looking out onto the façade of a repulsively ugly building.

'What language does your mother speak?' I asked Gino.

'Italian.'

'Is that a Berber language?'

'No. Italy's a country on the other side of the sea, not far from France.'

'Aren't you Algerian?'

'Oh, yes. My father was born here. So were his parents. His ancestors had been here for centuries. My mother's from Florence. She met my father on a liner. They got married and my mother followed him here. She speaks Arabic and French, but when she and I are together we speak Italian. So that I don't lose the language of my uncles, you know? Italians are very proud of their origins. They're quite temperamental.'

What he was trying to explain was beyond me. All I knew of the world was what everyday life and its vileness showed me. When I was small, standing on a rock in the hills above Turambo, I'd thought the horizon was a precipice, that the earth stopped at its feet, and that there was nothing beyond it.

Gino opened the wardrobe and took a packet of photographs from a drawer. He selected one to show me. The photograph, taken on a terrace overlooking the sea, showed a woman laughing, her siren-like body held snugly in a pretty bathing suit. She was as beautiful as the actresses you saw on posters outside cinemas.

'Who is she?'

Gino gave a sullen pout. His eyes glistened as he pointed over his shoulder with his thumb. 'The lady rising like dough in the next room.'

'I don't believe it.'

'I swear to you it's my mother in the photograph. She used to turn heads in the street. She was offered a part in a film, but my father didn't want an actress in his house. He said you never know when an actress is being sincere and when she's acting. A real macho man, my father, from what I've been told. He left us to fight in the war in Europe. I don't remember him very well. He died in the trenches, gassed. My mother went mad when she found out. She even had to be committed. When she recovered her senses, she started putting on weight. She hasn't stopped since. She's been prescribed all kinds of treatments, but neither the hospital doctors nor the Arab healers have been able to control her obesity.'

I took the photograph from his hands to get a better look at it. 'How beautiful she was!'

'She still is. Did you see her face? It's like an angel's. It's the only part of her body that's been spared. As if to save her soul.'

'To save her soul?'

'I'm sorry, I don't know why I'm talking this way. When I see what's become of her, I say all sorts of nonsense. She can't even sit up any more. She weighs as much as a cow on the scales. And a cow doesn't need anybody to help it relieve itself.'

'Don't talk like that about your mother.'

'I don't blame her. But I can't help it, it makes me bitter. My mother's a generous woman. She's never harmed anybody. She gives her money away and expects nothing in return. People have often robbed her, but not once has she held it against them. She's even turned a blind eye when she's caught them red-handed. It isn't fair, that's all. I don't think she deserves to end up like this.'

He took the photograph from me and put it away in a cardboard box.

He wiped his forehead with the back of his hand and looked at me warily. Then he cleared his throat to summon up courage and said, 'I have a few shirts, one or two sweaters, and a pair of trousers I don't wear any more. Would you be offended if I gave them to you? I'd be very happy to. I don't want you to take it badly. I'd really like it if you said yes.'

85

There was a mixture of sadness and fear in his eyes. He was awaiting my reaction as if it were a verdict.

'My bottom is almost showing through the seat of my trousers,' I said.

He gave a little laugh and, relieved, started rummaging through the shelves, throwing me a quick glance to make sure I wasn't offended.

Later, several years later, I asked him why he'd been so defensive when he was only trying to help a friend. Gino replied that it was because Arabs were sensitive and had a sense of honour so excessive they would be suspicious even of a good deed.

Returning home that day, proud of my bundle of almost new clothes, I surprised Mekki and my mother talking about my father. They fell silent when they saw me come in. Their faces were twisted with anger. My mother seemed on the point of imploding. Her face was trembling with indignation and there were tears in her eyes. I asked what was going on. Mekki told me it was none of my business and shut the door of his room in my face. I listened carefully, hoping to catch a few scraps of their conversation, but neither my uncle nor my mother carried on speaking. I shrugged my shoulders and went to the other room to try on the clothes Gino had given me.

Mekki joined me a few moments later, his cheek twitching.

'Has my father been found dead?' I asked.

'After all these years?' he retorted, annoyed at my naivety, then changed the subject. 'You have to find a job. Rokaya's sick. She needs care. Your mother and I don't earn enough.'

'I look for one every day.'

'But you don't knock on *the right doors*. I don't want to see you hanging around the streets any more.'

*

I set off again in search of a livelihood, but didn't change my habits; I didn't know where *the right doors* were. In any case, whether I turned up before or after they had employed someone, it was always the same old story: either the job was already taken or I didn't look suitable.

I was sitting on a low wall, longing for a piece of the goat's cheese wrapped in vine leaves that a child was trying to sell to passers-by, when a boy approached me. He must have been about fifteen or sixteen. He was tall for his age and quite thin; his glasses made him look like one of those educated boys who were good at picking up girls outside school. He was wearing a check shirt and smart, neatly ironed trousers. His brown hair was cut short at the sides and his hands were spotlessly clean.

'Don't you live opposite the artillery barracks?' he said.

'Yes.'

'I live quite near to you. My name's Pierre.' He didn't hold out his hand. 'I heard you asking about a job at the warehouse earlier. I can arrange it. I have contacts. Neighbours should stick together, don't you think?'

'Sure.'

'It isn't easy to sway an employer these days. You don't have any experience and *of course* you don't have any education. If you let me recommend you for jobs, you can start earning your living tomorrow.'

'All right then.'

'What about this then: I find you work and whatever you make we split fifty-fifty. How does that sound?'

'It sounds fine.'

'You do understand the deal, don't you? What *you* make we share fifty-fifty. I don't want you to try and short-change me later. Is that understood? Fifty-fifty on what *you* make?'

'Yes, I got that.'

He held out his hand. 'Let's shake on it. Giving your word of honour is better than any contract.'

I shook his hand enthusiastically. 'When do I start?'

'You do live in the house with the balcony over the esplanade, the one with the door opposite the barracks?'

'That's right.'

'Wait for me outside your house at five tomorrow morning. But let's get this straight once again, it'll be fifty-fifty. And don't try to double-cross me, because I'm the one who's going to negotiate your wages.'

'I'm not a cheat.'

He looked at me thoughtfully, then relaxed. 'What's your name?'

'Turambo.'

'Well, Turambo, God has put me in your path. If you do exactly what I ask and you're as honest as you claim to be, in less than a year we'll be doing a lot of business together.'

Pierre kept his word. At dawn the next day, he came for me and took me to a huge depot where I had to carry crates of fruit and vegetables. I thought I was going to drop dead with all the kicks I got from a fat lump who kept yelling at me. In the evening, Pierre was waiting for me at the corner of Rue du Général-Cérez. He counted out my money, pocketed half and handed me the rest. It was the same ritual each time. He didn't find me work every day, but whenever a job fell vacant, it was mine. Pierre was the son of a court clerk who spent his money on prostitutes. He pointed him out to me one night, coming out of a brothel. He was a smart-looking man in a good suit, his hat pulled down over his face in order to remain incognito in such a seedy place. Pierre didn't mince his words when he talked about him. He told me that arguments were common at home. His mother knew what kept her husband out so late at night and that made her hysterical because, in addition to his shameful sexual relations, his father had no qualms about drawing on the family savings. The reason Pierre, who was still at school, skipped classes was to help his mother make ends meet. And he was counting on me to save his family from bankruptcy. In a way, I was his golden goose. I didn't see any disadvantage in that. As long as I didn't return home empty-handed, I was prepared to do anything he suggested. Although the work tired me out, I wasn't discouraged. But Pierre wanted me for himself. He kept an eye on me, noted who I mixed with, ordered me to go to bed early, in order to save my energy for work; in short, he ruled me with a rod of iron. He was particularly unhappy if I hung around with Gino in the evenings and made it quite clear what he thought about it.

'Get rid of that fellow, Turambo. He's not good for you. Plus, he's a Yid.'

'What's a Yid?'

'A Jew. Come on, what planet are you from?'

'How do you know that Gino's a Jew?'

'I saw him having a pee.' Pierre grabbed me by the shoulders and looked me in the eye. 'Haven't I been straight with you? We've always split things fifty-fifty. If you want to carry on as my partner, keep away from that queer. The two of us are going to make a ton of money, and in a few years, we'll start a business and drive around in a car like nabobs. Have you seen how well connected I am? I can get you as many jobs as you like. Well? Do you trust me?'

'Gino's my friend.'

'No sentiment in business, Turambo. That's for little girls and mummy's boys. When you were going round in circles, starving hungry, did anybody care? Yes, I did. Without you asking me. Because I have your best interests at heart. Forget that camp idiot. He's earning his own living. Nice and safe there in his garage, polishing rich people's cars. Did he ever suggest you work with him? Did he ever talk to his boss about you?'

He fell silent, waiting for a sign from me that didn't come. He puffed out his cheeks and let his arms drop to his sides.

'Well,' he went on, irritably, 'it's up to you. If you think that *mariquita* matters more than your career, that's up to you. Just don't come and tell me I didn't warn you.'

I didn't know what was so wrong with being a Jew or what I risked by associating with one. But Pierre's warning and his covert blackmail threw me. When I next saw Gino, as we were sitting on the pavement watching two carters having an argument, I asked him if he was a Jew. Gino frowned oddly; I realised that my question wasn't so much a surprise as a shock. He stared at me as if he couldn't place me. His lips were quivering. He took a deep breath, then sighed sadly and said, 'Would that change anything between us?'

I told him it wouldn't.

'Then why did you ask me such a stupid question?' He stood up, leaving me sitting there, and went back home.

He was very angry.

Over the next few days, he avoided me, and I realised how tactless I'd been.

Pierre had got his gold mine back and he was delighted that I was now his, and his alone. 'You see?' he said. 'As soon as you pointed out his little secret, he dropped you. He's not honest, your Gino.'

I tried to make it up with Gino, but in vain; he was giving me the cold shoulder. I realised how much I'd hurt him, however inadvertently. I hated seeing him angry with me, and doubly so because I'd never meant to cause him any pain. As far as I was concerned, it had been just a casual question. I didn't care if he was black or white, a believer or an atheist. He was my friend, and his company mattered to me. He'd often taken me to his home, where we would spend hours chatting away in his room. He was a devoted, obedient son. He read to his mother every evening. He would sit down next to her, on the edge of the bed, open a book, and the silence of the house would be filled with magical characters and stories of adventure. Gino's mother couldn't get to sleep without this little excursion into the world of books. She would ask her son to continue with such and such a chapter, or reread such and such a poem, and Gino would go back over the pages with an enthusiasm that gave me food for thought. I couldn't read, but I loved to sit on a stool and listen to him. He had a soft, spellbinding voice which would transport me from one setting to another.

There was a book that his mother loved more than any other. It was called *The Miracle Man*, written by a parish priest named Edmond Bourg. At first, I thought it was a prayer book. It was all about forgiveness, charity and solidarity, and Gino's mother would cry over certain passages. It was so moving, my heart contracted like a fist as I listened. I wanted to find out more about the author: was he a prophet or a saint? Gino told me the story of Edmond Bourg, who had apparently hit the headlines in the previous century. Before becoming a priest, Edmond Bourg had been a railway engineer. He was an ordinary man, a bit of a lone wolf, but amiable and considerate. One evening, he caught his wife having torrid sex with one of his colleagues in his own bed. He killed both of them and cut them up into little pieces. The police found the pieces scattered in the woods. Every day, the newspapers would announce the discovery of a piece of flesh or an organ, as if the killer was deliberately trying to traumatise everyone. This macabre story fascinated and horrified the public to such an extent that the trial had to be adjourned several times because of the crowds wanting to attend. Edmond Bourg's lawyers pleaded that he was insane when he committed the crime. The people demanded blood, and the court sentenced the murderer to death. But on the day of the execution, the blade of the guillotine jammed. As the penal code demanded that the operation continue until the head was separated from the body, the executioner pulled the lever again, without success. Curiously, when the condemned man was removed from the block, the mechanism worked, and when his head was once more placed on the blosk, the blade again refused to fall. The chaplain claimed it was a sign from heaven; Edmond Bourg's sentence was commuted to hard labour for life. He was sent to Devil's Island, a penal colony not far from Cayenne, in Guyana, where he was a model prisoner. Some twenty years after he was sentenced, a famous journalist revived the story of Edmond Bourg, and a national debate ensued, with articles and petitions, which resulted in his being pardoned. Edmond Bourg became a priest and spent the rest of his life doing good, spreading the word and helping people come to terms with their own demons. His book was a huge success when it came out in 1903. Souls in torment drew a great deal of comfort from it, and Gino's mother always kept it on her bedside table, next to the Bible.

The story of Bourg had impressed me so much that I had asked Gino to teach me to read and write, just as Rémi and Lucette, Xavier's children, had once taught me arithmetic … And then there had been that one mistake and everything had come crashing down. Since my *stupid question*, I didn't know what to do with my evenings. Sometimes, without realising it, I caught myself walking up and down Boulevard Maṣcara. I would see the light on in Gino's room and wonder if he too was thinking of me, if he missed me as much as I missed him. Sometimes, driven by an irresistible urge, I would stop outside the door of his house, on the verge of knocking on it, but didn't dare go further. I was afraid he would close his heart to me once and for all.

Pierre could see how unhappy I was. To keep my mind off Gino, he undertook to wear me out with jobs as exhausting as they were badly paid. In the next few months, he made me do all kinds of things. I was in turn a shop assistant, a stable boy, an upholsterer, a wafer seller, a delivery boy and a coalman. I never did the same job two weeks in a row. Pierre would negotiate my wages without any concern for the trials he was inflicting on me. He would pick me up from my home, leave me at work, pick me up at the end of the day and relieve me of half my pay. When he had nothing for me, he would abandon me. I could knock at his door but he wouldn't open. If I insisted, he would come out onto the balcony and yell at me. After quarrelling with Gino, I hated him for treating me like that. My pride was hurt, and I decided I wouldn't take the bait any more. After a few instances of 'insubordination', he was the one who started running after me. Now I didn't open my door to him. I'd look at him from the balcony and ignore his efforts to tempt me. He'd scratch his head, pretending to think, then offer me all kinds of benefits. He'd promise me the moon, but I'd just shake my head.

'Be reasonable, Turambo. I'm your lucky star. Without me, you won't go far. I know it's hard, but we have to stick together. One day, thanks to me, you'll stand on your own two feet.'

'I can already stand, thank you.'

'No, really, what is it you want from me?'

'A real job. I don't care what it is as long as it's steady,' I said in a firm tone. 'I'm tired of going all over town for peanuts.'

He shook his head, unable to think of any more interesting propositions. 'Can we still share everything fifty-fifty?'

'That depends.'

*

Pierre introduced me to Toto La Goinche, who owned a shabby café nestling at the foot of Santa Cruz, below an old Spanish fortification. Toto was an unassuming man in his forties. When we arrived, he was carving up a pig in the courtyard of his establishment, a butcher's apron over his naked chest. He asked me if I knew how to keep a register and I told him I didn't. He asked me if I could hold my tongue and I told him I could. Those were the right answers.

He agreed to give me a week's trial, without pay.

Then a second week to make sure he hadn't backed the wrong horse; still without pay.

At last, he welcomed me into *his* fraternity.

In truth, the café wasn't really a café, the kind you found dozens of on the outskirts of the city, but a clandestine brothel, a seedy inn stinking of adulterated hooch where elephantine whores lured sailors with strange accents and skilfully fleeced them after a botched attempt at lovemaking.

The first few days, the place gave me the shivers. It was in a dead-end alley overflowing with rubbish where, miraculously, cats and dogs amicably shared the contents of the dustbins and drunks got into fights over nothing. The owner, who believed in a certain decorum, wouldn't stand for arguments under his roof, but was happy for disputes to be settled behind the courtyard, on a strip of earth leading to a precipice. Whenever things looked like ending in bloodshed, Toto would call on the services of Babaye, a huge ex-convict from the Sahara, a man so black you could barely make out the tattoos on his body. Babaye didn't have an ounce of patience and didn't bother to reason with the warring parties, who'd be yelling at each other and brandishing their knives; he would grab them both by the scruff of the neck, knock their heads together and dump them on the ground, certain they wouldn't be heard from again before daybreak.

It wasn't the fights that bothered me – I'd seen enough of them in Graba. The urban animals I feared were the women who worked there, like crocodiles in troubled waters; they were terrifying with their hair in curlers, their faces marked by degradation, dripping with cheap make-up, their eyes black with bad kohl and their mouths so red they might have been dipped in a bowl of fresh blood. They were strange, disturbing, syphilitic creatures, with their bare breasts and their hemstitched basques pulled up over their buttocks; they smoked like chimneys and belched and farted constantly; they were fierce and vulgar, misshapen by the age of thirty but still reigning supreme over the bestial desires of men. They smelt of rancid butter by day and cold sweat as soon as night fell. When they weren't pleased, they would hit out at random, even throwing their clients out of the window and then drawing the curtains without a second thought.

I was determined not to go anywhere near them.

I slogged away in the basement while they were hard at work upstairs, and that was fine by me.

My work consisted of clearing the tables, emptying the chamber pots, washing the dishes, taking out the dustbins and holding my tongue – because strange things went on in that place. It wasn't just girls in distress who were picked up in doorways, dying of hunger, and brought to the brothel: there were boys too.

At first, I didn't pay any attention to what went on in slow motion in the damp and the dark. While the staff were busy assessing the vulnerability of the fools they were about to fleece, I would shut myself away in the basement among the bowls and the wine racks to avoid seeing anything. I was isolated and ignored, and I was starting to get bored repeating the same actions and tramping the same stretch of floor. Even Babaye only appeared occasionally. He must have hidden in a cupboard like a jinn, only emerging when his master blew the whistle. Then, little by little, I started to realise just how far into the mire Pierre had got me. That café wasn't for me. I wanted only one thing: to take my wages, get out of that part of the city as quickly as possible and never see it again. Toto pointed out that a contract was a contract, even if nothing had been signed; I would only get what was due to me at the end of the month. So, in addition to the two weeks' trial, I had to endure four more weeks, holding my breath, rinsing the glasses and turning a blind eye to the horrors around me.

One night, a dishevelled sailor came down to my hideout. He was holding a bottle of red wine in his hand and swaying all over the place. He was in tears. 'I could walk on water and no priest would notice,' he moaned to himself. 'I could spend my life doing good and nobody would take me seriously. Because nobody ever takes me seriously. "If you went to sea, you'd find it had run dry" – that was what my saintly mother, who I loved so much, said to me once.' When he saw me bent over the glasses in a corner, he tumbled down the few steps that separated us and, still swaying, took a wad of banknotes from his pocket and stuffed them under my sweater. 'Fat Bertha, who claims the wart under her nose is a beauty spot, turned it down. She told me she didn't want my money, I might as well wipe my arse with it ... Can you imagine? Even when you earn money by the sweat of your brow, you can't get laid these days ... Do you want it? Well, I'm giving it to you. Gladly. I don't want it any more. I have bundles of it at home. I make mattresses with it. You need it. It's written all over your face. You must have a sick relative. Think of my money as a gift from heaven. I'm a good Christian, I am. I may not be taken seriously, but I'm a generous person.' He fiddled with his flies and tried to stroke my cheek ...

Miraculously, Babaye emerged from his cupboard and threw the drunk out.

## 6

Mekki looked reluctantly at the money the sailor at the café had given me. He wouldn't even touch it. We were in his room. He had just finished his prayers when I held out the banknotes.

'Where did you get this?' he said, refraining from holding his nose.

'I earned it.'

'You mean you won it gambling?'

'I worked for it.'

'Even a bellboy at the Bastrana Casino wouldn't earn as much as this.'

'Do I ask you how you make your money?'

'You're perfectly entitled to know. The Mozabite keeps our accounts and you can check them. Not a penny that's haram comes into this house. And now you hand me a wad of paper money from somewhere or other and ask me to believe you have a rich man's salary. I won't take your money. It doesn't smell right.'

Disappointed, I grudgingly put the notes back in my pocket.

I was about to go to my mat to sleep when Mekki said, 'Not so fast. You're not sleeping here until you tell me what trouble you're in.'

'I wash dishes in a café.'

'Not a luxury hotel? That's the only place you can make that kind of money, and even then it's not the right season.'

I shrugged my shoulders and walked out.

Mekki followed me out into the street and ordered me to explain myself. I hurried on, deaf to his summons, then, relieved I could no longer hear him grunting behind me, I slowed down. I was furious. I was working hard and I would have liked a little respect. It wasn't fair.

After wandering around the alleys, cursing everything and kicking stones, I slept in the open air, on a bench in a park, the haunt of tramps risking the uncertainties of the night. It struck me that they and I were all practising the same self-denial.

It didn't take Mekki long to solve the mystery. He must have followed me. A week later, I got home to find the family council on a war footing. There was Rokaya, confined to her bed, Nora, sitting apart but in agreement, and my mother and Mekki glaring at me. They were waiting stiffly for me in the main room, nostrils trembling with indignation.

'You bring shame on our family, both the living and the dead,' Mekki decreed, his switch firmly clasped in his hand. 'First you choose to polish boots and, now, you wash dishes in a brothel. Well, if you have so little self-respect, I'm going to treat you like a dog until you learn to honour our absent ones.'

He raised his switch and brought it down on my shoulder. The pain made me see red. I didn't care if he was the head of the family, I grabbed my uncle by the throat and pushed him up against the wall, while my mother looked on aghast.

'You dare to raise your hand to me?' my uncle thundered, stunned by this sacrilege.

'I'm not a dog and you're not my father.'

'Your father? You talk to me about your father? He's the one feeding you, is he? He's the one sweating blood for this family?

That wretch, your father? All right, let's talk about your father while we're about it!'

'Mekki!' my mother implored him.

'He has to know,' he retorted, his mouth glistening with flecks of foam. 'Come on, you little brat, come with me. I'm going to show you what filth your pride is based on, my poor, vain, idiot nephew.'

He seized me by the neck and pushed me outside.

I followed him, curious to discover what lay behind his insinuations. The streets were baking in the sun. The air smelt of drains and overheated asphalt. Mekki kept walking straight ahead, bad-temperedly. He was inwardly seething with rage. I hurried behind him. We crossed Medina Jedida in the crushing heat, pushed our way through the crowds in the market, which no weather, however unbearable, ever seemed to discourage, came out on the avenue that led to Porte de Valmy and the grazing park before stopping outside the Jewish cemetery.

Mekki gave me a spiteful grin, pointed to the open gate leading to the rows of graves and motioned me with his head to precede him. 'After you, as the Roumis say,' he said with a cruel gleam in his eyes.

I had never seen my uncle, that twenty-year-old sage who had always been so pious, in such a state of contempt or so pleased at the harm he was about to inflict on me – I'd guessed that he hadn't brought me here to remind me of my duties, but to punish me in such a way that the consequences would stay with me until the end of my days.

'Why have you brought me here?'

'You just have to go inside and you'll know.'

'Do you think my father is buried with the Jews?'

'No, he just keeps an eye on their dead.'

Mekki pushed me into the cemetery, looked around and finally pointed to a man sitting cross-legged on the threshold of a sentry box, stuffing a piece of bread with slices of onion and tomato. Just as he was about to bite into his sandwich, he noticed our presence. I recognised him immediately. It was my broken-faced father, thinner than a scarecrow and in mismatched clothes. My heart beat so strongly in my chest that I shook from head to foot. The earth and the sky merged into one around me and I had to clutch my uncle's arm to remain upright, my Adam's apple stuck in my throat like a stone.

'He should have died in his trench,' my uncle said. 'At least we would have had a medal to add some kind of pride to our loss.'

The caretaker stared at us with his rodent-like eyes. When he in turn recognised us, he bent low over his food. As if nothing had happened. As if we weren't there. As if he didn't know us from Adam.

If the ground had given way beneath my feet at that moment, I would have gladly let it swallow me up.

'I hope you won't go on about your father any more,' Mekki said. 'He's alive and well, as you can see. He's just a pathetic character who prefers to weed graves rather than sweep his own doorway. He chose the Jewish cemetery so as not to be found. He must have thought no Muslim would ever see him here. Let alone the family he abandoned.'

He took me by the arm and pushed me towards the gate. I couldn't take my eyes off the man who was eating on the threshold of the sentry box. An unfathomable feeling spread through me like molten lead. I had a mad desire to burst into tears but managed neither to cry out nor to moan. I simply looked at that man who had been my father and my idol and was now a complete stranger to me. He was still ignoring us, intent on his food. The only thing that seemed to matter to him was his piece of bread, which he was eating with gusto. I hadn't spotted either surprise or the slightest trace of emotion on his face. After that fleeting glimmer of recognition, his whole face had closed like a pool over a paving stone. I felt really sorry for him, even though I was very aware that of all the children on earth, I was to be pitied the most.

'Let's go,' Mekki said. 'You've had enough for today.'

My strength had given way. My uncle was almost dragging me.

We left the cemetery and I saw my father close the gate behind us. Without a glance. Without a shred of embarrassment ...

A world had just ended, though I didn't know which.


I turned round several times in the hope of seeing the cemetery gate open and my father come running out after me.

The gate was still closed.

I realised I had to go, to get away, to disappear.

My uncle was speaking to me. His voce faded before it reached me. All I could hear was the blood throbbing in my temples. The houses went by on either side in a haze. It was daytime and yet it seemed dark. My feet sank into the soft ground. My stomach felt tight with nausea and I was shivering in the sun.

I walked straight ahead like a sleepwalker, carried along by my pain. My uncle fell silent, then faded into the background. I reached Boulevard National without realising it and came out on Place d'Armes. There were too many people in the square, too many carriages, too many shoeshine boys yelling, too many pick-up artists, too many women with their pushchairs; there was too much agitation and too much noise. I needed space and silence. I carried on towards the seafront. There was a party in full swing at the Military Club. I skirted Château-Neuf, where the Zouaves were confined, and went down an embankment to the promenade of Létang. Here, loving couples talked in low voices all along the avenues, holding hands like children, elegant women wandered peacefully, their heads full of dreams beneath their parasols, and children frolicked on the lawn. Where did I fit in to all that? I didn't, I was irrelevant, out of the picture.

I climbed onto a promontory to gaze at the ships in the harbour. Four freighters were moored at the quays, filled to the brim with corn; their funnels, as red as a clown's nose, belched clouds of black smoke into the air. A few months earlier, I had come to this place to gaze at the sea; I had found it as fascinating and mysterious as the sky and had wondered which took its inspiration from the other. I had stood on this same rocky outcrop, my eyes open wide, astonished at the blue plain stretching off into the distance. It was the first time I had seen the sea. A painter who was reproducing on his canvas the potbellied freighters and the little steamboats that seemed as tiny as fleas beside them had said to me: The sea is a font where all the prayers that don't reach the Lord fall as tears, and have done for millions of years. Of course, that painter was trying to be witty. Yet this time, on the same promontory, where nobody had set up an easel, those words came back to me as I once again saw, going round and round in slow motion, the image of my father closing the cemetery gate behind me, and those stupid, beautiful words broke my heart.

I remained on the promontory until nightfall. I was overwhelmed by grief, and I was sinking into it. I didn't want to go home. I couldn't have stood the looks I'd get from my mother and uncle. I hated them. They *had known* and hadn't said anything. The monsters! … I needed a culprit, and I wasn't big enough for the role. I was the victim, more to be pitied than to be charged. I needed somebody to point a finger at. My father? He was the misdeed. Not the exhibit, but the act itself, the crime, the murder. I saw only my mother and Mekki in the dock. At last I understood why they had fallen silent that time when I had caught them talking about my father. They should have taken me into their confidence. I would have been able to bear the blow. They hadn't done so. And now I held them responsible for all the misfortunes of the world.

That night, I didn't go home.

I went and knocked on Gino's door.

As soon as he saw the expression on my face, Gino guessed that if he didn't let me in, I would throw myself into the abyss and never come back up again.

His mother was asleep with her mouth open.

He led me to the little courtyard, which was lit by a lantern. The sky was glittering with constellations. In the distance, you could hear people quarrelling. Gino took me by the wrist and I told him everything, all in one go, without pausing to catch my breath. He listened right to the end, without interrupting me and without letting go of my hand.

When I had finished, he said, 'A lot of people came back from the war hardly knowing themselves any more, Turambo. They went off in one piece and returned having left a part of their souls in the trenches.'

'It would have been better if the whole of him had stayed there.'

'Don't be hard on him. He's still your father, and you don't know what he suffered over there. I'm sure he's suffering even now. You don't flee your family when you survive the war.'

'He did.'

'That proves that he no longer knows where he is.'

'I would have preferred him to be dead. What memory am I going to have of him now? A cemetery gate shutting in my face?'

His fingers closed a little more over mine. 'I'd give anything to believe that my father was still alive somewhere,' he said sadly.

'A living man can always come home eventually, but not a dead man.'

Gino said other things too, but I'd stopped listening to him. Only the creaking of the gate continued to echo in my head. However much my father tried to retreat behind it, I could clearly distinguish him as if in a one-way mirror, ghostly, shabby and grotesque. He disgusted me. I would close my eyes and there he was; I would open them and he was still there, in his scarecrow's suit, as inexpressive as a wooden skeleton. What had happened to him? Was it really him? What was war? An afterlife from which you returned deprived of your soul, your heart and your memory? These questions were eating me alive. I would have liked them to finish me off or else help me understand. But there was nothing. I endured them and that was all. I was sick of not finding a semblance of an answer to them, or any kind of meaning.

Gino suggested I sleep in his room. I told him I wouldn't be able to breathe, that I preferred the courtyard. He brought me an esparto mat and a blanket and lay down next to me on a piece of carpet. We stared up at the sky and listened out for the noises of the city. When the streets grew quiet, Gino started snoring. I waited to doze off in my turn, but anger caught up with me and I didn't sleep a wink.

Gino got up early. He made coffee for his mother, made sure she had everything she needed and told me I could stay in the apartment if I wanted. I declined the offer because I had no desire to meet my mother, who would be arriving soon. She came at seven every day to do the housework for the Ramouns. Gino didn't have any other suggestion to make. He had to go to work. I walked with him to Place Sébastopol. He promised to see me at the end of the day and took his leave. I stood there on the pavement, not knowing what to do with myself. I felt ill at ease and ached all over. The thought of going home repelled me.

I went up onto the heights of Létang to look at the sea. It was as wild as the din in my head. Then I went to Boulevard Marceau to watch the trams with their passengers clinging to the guardrails like strings of garlic. At the station, I listened to the trains arriving in a screech of whistles and pouring their contingents of travellers out onto the platforms. From time to time, an idea would cross my mind and I would imagine myself getting on a train and going somewhere, anywhere, far from this feeling of disgust I was dragging around like a ball and chain. I wanted to hit everything that moved. If anybody looked at me, I was ready to charge.

I only felt a little calmer when Gino returned.

Gino was my stability, my crutch. Every evening, he would take me to the cinema to see Max Linder, Charlie Chaplin, *The Three Musketeers*, *Tarzan of the Apes*, *King Kong* and horror films. Then we would go to a cabaret in Rue d'Austerlitz in the Derb to hear Messaoud Médioni sing. I would then start to feel a little better. But in the morning, when Gino went to work, my unease would return and I would try and shake it off in the bustle of the streets.

Pierre came looking for me. I told him it was all over between us. He called me an idiot and told me that the 'Yid' was brainwashing me. I couldn't control what my fist did next. I felt my 'pimp's' nose give at the end of my arm. Surprised by my action, Pierre fell backwards, half stunned. He lifted his hand to his face and looked incredulously at his bloodstained fingers. 'I should have expected that,' he grunted in a voice shaking with bile. 'I try to help you and this is how you thank me. Well, what can you expect of an Arab? No loyalty or gratitude.'

He stood up, gave me a black eye and finally left me alone.

## 7

We were supposed to be going to Ras el-Aïn for a walk, but Gino suddenly changed his mind. 'I have things to sort out at home,' he said by way of excuse. I walked home with him. And my mother was there, on Boulevard Mascara, a glove in one hand and a bowl of water beside her; she was just finishing washing my friend's mother. What was the meaning of this strange coincidence? I asked Gino. He replied that I was wrong to avoid my family. I hadn't set foot in Rue du Général-Cérez for nine months, not since the incident in the Jewish cemetery. I asked Gino if this was a roundabout way of getting rid of me. He told me his home was mine and that I could stay there as long as I wanted, but that my family needed me, and that it wasn't a good idea to fall out with them.

I was getting ready to leave when my mother grabbed me by the wrist. 'I have to talk to you,' she said. She put on her veil and motioned me to follow her. We did not exchange a word in the street. She walked ahead and I trailed behind, wondering what new revelation awaited me round the corner.

When we got home, my mother said, 'We're not hard on you, it's life that's hard on all of us.' I asked her why she hadn't told me the truth about my father, and she replied that there was nothing to say about him. And that was all. My mother went into the kitchen to make dinner.

Nora joined me in the next room. She was even more beautiful than before and her big eyes threw me into disarray.

'We missed you,' she admitted, turning away in embarrassment.

She's growing up too fast, I thought. She was almost a woman now. Her body had blossomed; it demanded celebration.

'I'm back, that's all that matters,' I said.

Nora smelt good, like a meadow in spring. Her black hair fell over her round shoulders and her chest carried the promise of maturity.

We could think of nothing further to say.

Our silence spoke for us.

I was in love with her ...

Aunt Rokaya opened her emaciated arms to me. 'Silly fool!' she scolded me affectionately. 'You should never be angry with your family. How could you live with your friend so close to here and ignore us?' She undid a scarf hanging from her blouse and handed me the silver ring that was in it. 'This belonged to your grandfather. The day he died, he took it off his finger and made me promise to give it to my son. I never had a son of my own. And you're more than a nephew to me.'

Aunt Rokaya had grown thinner. In addition to the paralysis of the lower limbs that confined her to her straw mattress, she complained of whistling in her ears and terrible headaches. The amulets the quacks prescribed for her had no effect. She was nothing now but a ghost with blurred features, her skin grey, her eyes full of stoic suffering.

Rokaya had the sickness of masterless people. She had contracted it in Turambo, when her home was a patched-up tent. At that time, the cauldron on the wooden fire only gurgled to stave off hunger. The flavourless crops grew once a year; the rest of the time we lived on roots and bitter acorns. By the age of five, Rokaya was looking after her grandfather's one goat. One night, the goat's throat had been torn out by a jackal because the pen hadn't been properly closed. She had felt guilty about that all her life. Whenever misfortune struck us, she would say it was her fault – it was pointless to tell her that she was not to blame. At the age of fourteen, she was married off to a club-footed shepherd who beat her to make her submit to him. He knew he was the lowest of the low and had married her to make himself feel important. So when she so much as looked at him, he considered it an outrage. He died, killed by a bolt of lightning, and the villagers saw the hand of God in that thunderbolt from heaven. A widow at nineteen, she was remarried to another peasant who was just as bad. Her body would forever bear the marks of the mistreatment meted out to her during her second marriage. Rejected at the age of twenty-six, she was handed over for the third time to a pedlar who set off one morning to sell samovars and never came back, leaving his wife eight months pregnant. Rokaya gave birth to Nora in a barn, pushing with all her might, a cloth in her mouth to stifle her screams. At the age of forty-five, she was at the end of her tether. She looked twice her age. Her sickness had eaten her up inside with all the methodical greed of a colony of termites. I had always felt sorry for her. Her face bore the traces of an old sorrow that refused to vanish. It was through Rokaya that I had thought I understood that there are tragedies that obstinately remain on the surface, like ugly scars, in order not to fall into oblivion and thus be absolved of the harm they have caused ... Because the damage returns as soon as it is forgiven, convinced it has been rehabilitated, and then it can no longer stop. Rokaya kept her wounds as open as her eyes, in order not to lose sight of even the slightest pain she had suffered for fear of not recognising it if it had the nerve to knock at her door again. Her face, in a sense, was a mirror where every ordeal displayed its duly paid bills. And the ordeals strove to make an inextricable parchment of her facial lines, all of which led back to the same original crime, that of a child of five who had neglected to close the pen where her family's one goat was kept.

We had dinner in the main room, all four of us gathered round a low table, Rokaya lying a little further away in a corner. Mekki had merely given a little smile when he came home. He didn't say a word to me. His status as head of the family spared him certain obligations. But he was pleased with my return to the fold. Nora had difficulty swallowing her spoonfuls of soup. My presence disturbed her. Or rather my gaze. I couldn't stop glancing at her out of the corner of my eye, seeing nothing but her full mouth, which strove to silence what her eyes demanded. I too had grown up. I was nearly seventeen and well built, and whenever I smiled at my reflection in the mirror, my face displayed a kind of fleeting charm. Nora harboured feelings for me that went beyond pure innocence. Those nine months of separation had revealed us to ourselves. Our silence betrayed an inner feverishness that was too much for us. In our traditions, we didn't know how to deal with those kinds of feeling. We let them simmer in secret and sometimes completely stifled them. They were feelings which were hard to bear and too dangerous to be brought out into the open. Words, in that platonic but intense debate, would have seemed indecently crude, since with us the senses were expressed in darkness. In that place, touch was more eloquent than poetry.

After dinner, Mekki claimed to have an appointment with his Mozabite partner and left; my mother cleared the table. Rokaya was already asleep. And it was that evening, taking advantage of a moment's inattention, that I put my hand on Nora's breasts. For the first time in my life, I touched the pulse of a fraction of eternity. Never would my fingers know a stronger sensation. Nora leapt back, startled by my gesture, but I could see in her wide eyes that she was flattered. She hastened to join my mother, while I retreated to the balcony, my heart racing, with the feeling that I held at the tips of my bold fingers, still heavy with Nora's flesh, all the euphoria of the world.

In the morning, I had the impression that Medina Jedida was celebrating something. Faces were radiant and the sun-drenched streets seemed to have awoken to better days. In reality, it was I who was exultant. I had dreamt about Nora, and in my dream I had kissed her on the lips; as far as I was concerned, I had really kissed her. My mouth was anointed with an exquisite nectar. My chest was filled with joy, and my heart soared. Drained of all my venom, I had forgiven everything'. I even went to my uncle's shop to show him I bore him no grudge. His partner, a Mozabite short in stature but enormously erudite, invited me to a café and we drank two pots of tea without realising it. He knew all the herbs and their qualities. I would listen to him for a few seconds then, between the names of flowers or aphrodisiac plants, the quivering image of Nora would catapult me through a thousand potential acts of daring.

It was after midday when the Mozabite took his leave of me.

I went back to Rue du Général-Cérez.

My mother was at the Ramouns'. Rokaya was dozing on her straw mattress. Nora was in the kitchen watching the cooking pot. I looked in all directions to make sure there was nobody else in the house. My cousin guessed what was going on in my head. She immediately became defensive. I approached her, my eyes riveted on her lips. She brandished her spatula. Her eyes did not reject mine, but it was a question of integrity. With us, love wasn't paramount; it was subject to all kinds of proprieties and thus became almost a trial of strength. Nevertheless, I felt capable of climbing the sacred mountains and walking all over them, twisting the neck of convention, mocking the devil in his den. My body was in a frenzy. Nora backed into the wall, her spatula raised in front of her like a shield. I could see neither the barriers nor the wrong of it; I saw only her, and nothing else around us mattered. My face was an inch from hers, my mouth offering itself to her. I prayed with all my might that Nora would do the same and I waited for her lips to meet mine. Her breath mingled with mine but Nora did not yield. A tear rolled down her cheek and abruptly quenched the fire devouring me. 'If you have any consideration for me, don't do that,' Nora said ... I became aware of the extent of my selfishness. You don't stamp on the sacred mountains. With my finger, I wiped the tears from my cousin's cheek. 'I think I came back earlier than expected,' I said to save face. She looked down and nodded. I ran to rejoin the bustle of the streets. I was happy, and proud of my cousin. Her attitude had made her grow a hundredfold in my heart and in my mind.

I don't know where I went that day, or how I managed to stay upright until Gino returned.

'I'm seriously in love,' I confided in him while he was changing in his room.

'Nothing is serious about love,' Madame Ramoun said from her bed.

Gino frowned. He gestured to me to lower my voice. We both laughed up our sleeves like two impudent children caught in the act. I glanced over my shoulder. Madame Ramoun had a broad smile on her sweat-streaked face.

'I need a job,' I said to Gino. 'To become a man.'

'Is that the condition your lady love has set you?' he teased me, laughing.

'It's my condition for being worthy of her. I want to have a life, don't you understand? Up until now all I've done is drift.'

'I can see you've got it bad.'

'I have! I don't even know where I am any more.'

'You lucky dog.'

'Couldn't you have a word with your boss?'

'You don't know anything about motor mechanics, and old Bébert is a bit of a stickler about things like that.'

'I'll learn.'

Gino pursed his lips in embarrassment, but promised to see what he could do.

He managed to persuade his boss to take me on as an apprentice.

Old Bébert told me straight away that I was to watch the others at work and not touch anything. He first asked me a lot of questions about the jobs I had done, about my family, whether I was ill and whether I had a criminal record. Next, he showed me the barrels for storing used oil, the broom cupboard and the cleaning materials and immediately put me to the test. As Gino was busy working on the innards of a large car, half buried under the bonnet, I had to get on with it by myself and familiarise myself as quickly as possible with the different sections of the garage. Old Bébert watched me from his booth, one eye on his registers, the other on what I was doing.

At about one o'clock, Gino took me to a kiosk where you could sit at a table and order sandwiches. I wasn't hungry; instead I was wondering if the stale air of the garage suited me. I felt a bit out of my depth among those stubborn mechanics. Gino sensed I was disorientated and talked about all kinds of things just to lighten the atmosphere.

Three young Roumis were lounging on the terrace. The fair-haired one stopped stirring his coffee when he saw us take our seats at the next table.

'Arabs aren't allowed here,' he said.

'He's with me,' Gino said.

'And who are you?'

'We're not looking for trouble. We just want a bite to eat.'

His two companions looked us up and down. They didn't seem inclined to leave us alone.

'They should put a sign up over the door,' the youngest of the three said. 'Dogs and Arabs not allowed.'

'What'd be the point? They can't read.'

'In that case, why don't they stay in their own pen?'

'They can't keep still either. God created Arabs to piss everyone off.'

Gino hailed the waiter, a dark-skinned adolescent, and gave him our order.

The fair-haired Roumi was looking at my clothes and sniggering. 'What's the difference between an Arab and a potato?' he said. After looking around the table with an affected air, he cried, 'A potato can be cultivated.'

His two companions laughed sardonically.

'I didn't quite get that,' I said to the fair-haired one, ignoring Gino's hand under the table trying to restrain me.

'There's no point even trying. You've been playing with yourself so much, you've addled your brains.'

'Are you insulting me?'

'Let it go,' Gino said.

'He's not showing respect.'

'No kidding!' the fair-haired one retorted, leaving his table. He towered over me. 'Do you even know what respect is?'

'Let's get out of here,' Gino begged me, already on his feet.

I heaved a sigh and was getting ready to leave when the Roumi caught hold of the collar of my shirt. 'Where do you think you're going, you Arab scum? I haven't finished with you yet.'

'Listen,' Gino said, trying to reason with him, 'we don't want any trouble.'

'I'm not talking to you. Watch your step, okay?' He turned back to me. 'Well, Arab, cat got your tongue? Apart from playing with yourself, what else can you do with your hands, you little —?'

He didn't finish his sentence. My fist catapulted him over the table. He span round amid the cups and bottles and collapsed to the ground in a clatter of breaking glass and crockery, his nose smashed and his arms outstretched.

'I can punch,' I said in reply to his last question.

The other two clowns raised their hands in surrender. Gino pulled me firmly by the wrist and we walked back up the boulevard to the garage.

Gino was angry with me. 'Bébert doesn't want any trouble in the neighbourhood. I moved heaven and earth to get him to agree to try you out.'

'What did you want me to do? Let that idiot wipe the floor with me?'

'He was just a layabout. I admit he was asking for it, but it wasn't necessary. You have to learn when it's best just to leave it, Turambo. If you start dwelling on the things that make you angry, you won't get far. You have a trade to learn, with a possible job at the end of it. So be patient and, above all, be reasonable. There are pests like that on every street corner. You could spend your life knocking them out, but they'd only keep coming. They annoy me too; I may not make a big deal out of it, but it's not for lack of self-respect.'

Old Bébert virtually worshipped his customers' cars. He handled them as if they were made of nitroglycerine or porcelain. He even sometimes polished them in places with the end of his apron. His customers came from the city's nouveaux riches, people who cared about appearances and displayed their social status like war veterans displaying their medals, proud of the struggle that had led them from the gutter to the heights when nobody would have given them much chance of survival.

You had to see these toffs leaving their cars with us. So many detailed instructions, insistent recommendations, adamant warnings. They wouldn't leave the garage until they had made sure that their 'gem' was in good hands, promising large tips to the deserving and a thunderbolt from heaven for the slightest scratch on the bodywork.

Bébert kept an eye on things. He had surrounded himself with a team of four hand-picked specialist mechanics whom he ruled with a rod of iron and pushed hard. He had given me simple jobs to do: changing the wheels, cleaning the seats and the floors, polishing the bodywork and other safe little things, which didn't stop me watching the others working because I wanted to learn the trade.

The team ended up adopting me. There were two old mechanics who had worked in factories, a young Corsican named Filippi who knew engines like the back of his hand, and Gino. The atmosphere was good and we worked relentlessly, telling each other a load of gossip about such and such a nabob and jokes that kept us human among the scrap iron and the smells of fuel.

After a few months, Bébert put me together with Gino. At last I had the right to touch the innards beneath the bonnets. I could connect a hose, replace a coil, clean a carburettor, adjust a headlight.

I was earning decent money, and not once had I been lectured by the boss.

But this respite was not to last.

It was about four in the afternoon. We were on schedule to deliver a superb vehicle which a customer had entrusted to us for a complete overhaul, a Citroën B14 touring car that looked as if it had come straight off the assembly line. Its owner, a red-headed muscle man with a broken nose, was crazy about it. He couldn't stop running his finger over the bonnet to wipe away imperceptible specks of dust. When he came back for it and saw it waiting for him, all shiny and new, in the middle of the garage, he put his hands on his hips and stood there gazing at it for a while, then turned to his companion to see if he was as impressed as he was. 'Lovely, isn't she, my old crock? Girls won't be able to resist me.' Then he opened the door and his face suddenly turned dark red. 'What's this shit?' he roared, pointing to a grease stain on the white leather seat. Gino came running to have a look. The customer took him by the throat and lifted him off the floor. 'Do you know how much my old crock cost? You could spend your whole life forging banknotes and you wouldn't be able to afford her, you slob.' I grabbed a cloth and rushed over to wipe the seat, but all that did was to spread the grease further on the leather. Horrified by my clumsiness, the customer uttered a fierce curse and, letting go of Gino, gave me a slap that made me spin round. Gino didn't have time to grab me round the waist. My arm threw a lightning hook and the customer collapsed like a house of cards. He writhed weakly on the floor, shuddered two or three times and went stiff. His companion stood there petrified, leaning back as if about to retreat. The mechanics stopped what they were doing and looked at us open-mouthed. Gino lifted his hands to his temples, devastated; I guessed that I had just committed a capital crime. Old Bébert burst out of his booth, white-faced with panic. He pushed me aside and bent over the customer. In the icy silence of the garage, all that could be heard was the heavy breathing of old Bébert, who didn't know which to tear out: his hair or my eyes. 'Have you gone mad?' he screamed at me, rising again to his full height, shaking from head to foot. 'You dare raise your hand to a customer, you toerag, you maggot? Is that how you repay me? I give you a job and you attack my customers? I don't want to see you again. Get out of here. Go back to your cave until the police come for you. Because, trust me, you're going to pay for this.' I threw the cloth on the ground and went to get changed. Bébert ran after me, continuing to insult me while I took off my overalls and put my street clothes back on. His salivating mouth sprayed me with spittle and his eyes had a murderous look in them. He went back and helped the customer to his feet. The man was still dazed and couldn't stand up straight. They put him in his car as best they could and his companion immediately started the engine. When the car left the garage, Bébert laid into Gino. He blamed him for my behaviour, held him responsible for the consequences of my attack and told him that he too was fired.

We trudged back to Boulevard Mascara. Gino walked silently, stricken, his head down. I was devastated, but I couldn't find the words to apologise for the wrong I had done him. When we got to his place, he asked me to leave him, which I did.

Sitting on the doorstep of our courtyard, I was waiting for the promised Black Maria. I imagined myself at the police station, subject to the wrath of the cops. I had hit a European, they weren't going to treat me with kid gloves. I knew Arabs who had found themselves in jail on a hunch, sometimes simply to be made an example of. And the fellow I had knocked out couldn't have been just anybody, judging by his big car and Bébert's panic.

The sun was starting to go down, but there was still no sign of the police. Were they waiting for nightfall to surprise me in my bed? I was sick to my stomach. I didn't know what to do with my hands, which were sticky with tension. I remembered all the horrible stories I'd been told about prisons and the inhuman treatment meted out to prisoners. I panicked every time I heard a screech of tyres ...

Instead of the police, it was three Europeans who came to see me: a stocky old man with a paunch, a straw boater pulled down over his head, and two other men, one stocky and bald, the other tall and thin – I'd seen this one at the local cinema, where he worked as a pianist, accompanying silent films.

'Are you Turambo?' the old man asked me.

'Why do you want to know?'

'You work at Bébert's garage?'

'Yes.'

He held out his hand, but I didn't take it, afraid he would hit me with the other hand.

'My name's De Stefano. The fellow with glasses is Francis, and this is Salvo. I run a gym in Rue Wagram, just opposite the Porte du Ravin. Everyone's talking about you, son. Filippi, who works with you, told me you knocked out Left-Hand with a single blow. I can't get over it. Actually, nobody can get over it.'

'Do you know who Left-Hand is?' the bald man asked me.

'No.'

'He's the only boxer in the Oran region to have stood up to Georges Carpentier. Three fights, and he never went down. You do know who Georges Carpentier is?'

'No.'

'He's North African champion and world champion. He beat Battling Levinsky. Do you know who Battling Levinsky is?'

'Stop,' the pianist said. 'You're confusing him with your "Do you know who this man is?" and "Do you know who that man is?" He probably doesn't even know who his own father is.'

The old man told his companions to keep quiet, then said to me, 'Listen, son. What would you say to joining my gym?'

'The police will be coming for me.'

'They won't. A boxer doesn't lodge a complaint when he gets beaten outside the ring. It's a matter of honour. Either he demands a return match or he throws in the towel. Left-Hand won't be going to any police station to report you, I guarantee it. You have nothing to fear from that quarter … So, will you accept my offer? Who knows? You may be a champion and you don't even know it. We're one big happy family in Rue Wagram. We know how to make a top boxer, all we need is the boy. According to Filippi, you like to use your fists, and that's already the mark of a champion.'

'I don't like fighting. I just defend myself.'

'You don't seem in a fit state to think clearly right now,' the pianist said, wiping his dark glasses on his sweater. 'We don't want to force your hand. These things are too serious to be taken lightly. We'll come back tomorrow and talk it over with a clear head. Is that all right with you?'

'Or you could come and see us at the gym,' the old man suggested. 'Then you'll be able to see for yourself what it's all about. Allow me to insist on this, my boy. You really look like a champion. You're well built and you look people straight in the eye. I've been in this business for twenty years and I've learnt to recognise a rare bird when I see one. We'll wait for you tomorrow morning. If you don't show up, we'll come back here and find you. Will you promise to wait for us, just in case?'

'I don't know, Monsieur.'

The old man nodded. He pushed his hat back on the top of his head without taking his eyes off me. Again, he held out his hand, and this time I took it.

'So, Turambo, can I count on you?'

'I'm not that keen on fighting, Monsieur.'

'We're not talking about a street brawl, son. Boxing is a skill. It'll open lots of doors for you. You can earn a heap of money and privileges, and everyone's respect. Respect is important for someone from the gutter. In fact it's one of the few opportunities an Arab gets to rise in the world and he shouldn't miss it. I don't know why, but something tells me you won't miss your opportunity. Think about it tonight. Tomorrow we'll talk.'

All three of them said goodbye and left.

They came back the next day, and the days after that. Sometimes together, sometimes separately. The old man promised me the earth. He told me his intuition had never let him down and that I was a real centaur. It was as if his future depended on my decision. He was so friendly I was afraid to disappoint him. I promised him I'd think about it. He told me that was the one thing I'd been doing for two weeks now, and that it all boiled down to one question: should I become a boxer or continue to roast in the sun?

Gino found the offer interesting. 'All you ever do is fight,' he remarked in a slightly reproachful tone. 'Boxing is a job like any other. The guy you knocked out in the garage was nothing but a roughneck before he got in the ring. You saw the car he drove, the clothes he wore. If you learn quickly, you can climb the ladder and be rich and famous.'

Encouraged by Gino, I asked my uncle for advice. Mekki utterly disapproved of my wish to join the gym in Rue Wagram. 'It's a sin,' he decreed. 'You don't dip your bread in other people's blood. If you want to bless your food, water it with the sweat of your brow. Any profession that throws two people into a ring like animals isn't a profession, it's a perversion. I forbid you to raise your hand to your fellow man to earn a crust. We're believers, and no faith condones violence.'

When De Stefano came back the next time, I informed him that the family council had made its decision and that I wouldn't be a boxer. He was so upset, he didn't know what to say. He took off his hat, wiped his head with a handkerchief and stared at the toes of his shoes for five or six minutes before withdrawing with a heavy heart.

Back to square one.

A wholesale merchant hired me for his ironmonger's in Rue d'Arzew. From morning to evening, I pushed a cart laden with all kinds of tools which I had to deliver to the different shops in the neighbourhood. My employer, an old Maltese riddled with rheumatism, was kind, but his customers would always find something to blame me for and would yell at me for any fault in the merchandise as if I was the one who had made it. I was ill at ease in those well-to-do neighbourhoods where the rattle of trams and the shrill blare of car horns drowned out the murmur of simple things. I held out for a few months, but after a while I'd had enough.

I was no longer the hungry kid ready to take on any cheap task, and employers were suspicious of hardened labourers. The foremen on building sites would shake their heads at me from a distance. The warehouse owners would pretend to look elsewhere. I was firmly rejected everywhere. In the harbour, there were lots of people willing to work for peanuts. The fights that broke out among the men jostling for work quickly sorted the wheat from the chaff. When the gate closed behind the lucky ones, the rejects immediately looked for scapegoats to take it out on. Poverty had reduced the unemployed to a state lower than that of wolves, and woe betide the man who succumbed. On one occasion, I almost didn't escape with my life either. A big brute had caught his hand between the two halves of the gate. The recruiter ordered him to move away. The brute couldn't obey because of his trapped hand. The recruiter started beating him with his club until the poor fellow's face was streaming with blood. I threw myself at the recruiter and his big arms descended on me like vultures. Nobody came to my rescue. Not even the brute himself, who, in order to be noticed by the recruiter and show him how loyal he was in spite of the attack, took the liberty of finishing off the job after the thugs had left. He kicked me in the back, yelling that nobody raised his hand to Monsieur Créon. He yelled louder and louder so that the recruiter could still hear him as he walked away. The brute didn't get hired that day, but he was convinced he had scored a point. After he'd finished with me, he knelt down next to me and said, 'I'm sorry. I have twelve mouths to feed and no other way out. I'd sell my soul to the devil for peanuts …'

Gino had found a job at a printing works in Rue de Tlemcen. He no longer bore me a grudge for the incident at the garage. 'I wasn't planning to work there for the rest of my life anyway,' he admitted. On the evenings when a neighbour volunteered to keep his mother company, Gino took me to *cafés-concerts* to hear musicians and singers. My uncle's partner the Mozabite, who was a lyric writer in his spare time, used to say: *Music is the proof that we are capable of continuing to love despite everything, of sharing the same emotion, of being ourselves a wonderful, healthy emotion, as beautiful as a dream emerging in the dead of night … What is an angel without his harp but a sad, naked demon, and what would paradise be for him but an exile full of boredom?* Gino was absolutely of the same opinion. He loved music. Unlike me. I only liked the Kabyle songs my mother hummed while going about her household chores, but, going around with Gino, I was starting to discover new worlds. Before him, I didn't know anything about films or different kinds of music. Gradually, my senses had opened to other people's joys, and I wanted more.

A good-natured rivalry forced the musicians to excel. From Medina Jedida to the Casbah by way of the Derb, the singers warded off ill fortune just by clearing their throats. For my part, I started showing Gino what my own people could do. I took him to a Moorish café down a dead-end street in Sidi Blel, frequented by those in the know. There was a highly experienced violinist, a lute player, a derbouka, and a singer with vocal cords as solid as ropes. Gino fell in love with the group. He promised me that one day he would write a book about the music of the different neighbourhoods of Oran.

Times were hard, especially for the people of my community. My people could still cling to the flotsam, but they weren't allowed on board the ship. The greater the poverty, though, the less the people of Oran gave in to it. Anger and humiliation might have been rife in the streets, but the wounds healed by themselves whenever the sound of the mandolin replaced the cacophony of men. In any case, we had no choice: either we listened to music or we gave in to our frustrations. These cafés were warm, welcoming places where the poor could find some respite and even, for a few hours, imagine that they were privileged. They sat on rickety chairs, their fezzes or tarbooshes tilted ostentatiously over their temples, some in suits, others in fine traditional robes. The better off among them smoked nargileh and sipped mint tea while on a makeshift stage legendary tenors took turns, men nourished by their native soil. By taking refuge in the music, I was leaving my furies behind. It was my way of hearing the sound of another bell, of feeling lucky for as long as the singing lasted, of drowning my sorrows in the sorrows of the lyric writers. It was only a brief reprieve, but for a lost soul like me it was almost a moment of grace.

Whenever Gino took his leave of me, I didn't dare go back

home immediately. I would continue to wander the dark alleys until morning, the songs still echoing in my head. In order to be left in peace, I told my family that I was a nightwatchman.

It was a Friday.

My mother had come home later than usual, tottering with exhaustion. I asked her what was wrong.

'She made me brush her hair three times in a row,' she sighed, throwing her veil into a corner. 'I think she's losing her mind.'

My mother was talking about Madame Ramoun.

'She's been raving since midday,' she went on once she had quenched her thirst. 'I didn't know if I should listen to her or finish the housework. The poor woman's not acting normally. She kept reciting something in a language which wasn't Spanish, French, Arabic or Kabyle. I think she's possessed.'

'It must have been Italian,' I said. 'Did she fire you?'

My mother told me to let her catch her breath. She lay down on a sheepskin rug and slid her arm under her head as a pillow. 'She's asking for you, my son. She wants to see you. She won't take no for an answer.'

I went to get a box of Pernot biscuits, which Gino's mother was particularly fond of, and proceeded to Boulevard Mascara.

The door wasn't locked.

I called to my friend and he came out onto the balcony and signalled to me to come up. I didn't like the darkness on the stairs. A vague sense of foreboding clutched at my heart.

Gino was sitting on his mother's bed with a defeated look on his face. Madame Ramoun lay spread over the mattress, gasping for air, a Bible on her chest. She slowly turned her head towards me. Her eyes lit up when she recognised me. She gave me a sad smile and motioned to me to come closer. Gino gave up his seat for me and stood by his mother's bedside. I sat down on the edge of the bed, with a pang in my heart.

'I was waiting just for you, Turambo. I can't move my arm. Put your hand on mine, please. I have to talk to you.'

Whenever I saw her, I felt just as sorry for her. To have to lie down day and night, every day and every night, year in, year out, to depend on other people even for your most private needs: nobody deserved such indignity. Madame Ramoun was nothing but a crucified soul beneath a heap of wild flesh, like an unhappy saint trapped in her own contrition, and I could see no rhyme or reason to her suffering.

'I love you like my son, Turambo. You're more than a friend to Gino, more than a brother. From the first time I saw you, I knew you were the twin my son never had. Gino is a good person. He never harms anyone, and we live in unforgiving times. You're younger than him, but I see you as older. And that reassures me. I want you to take care of Gino.'

'Mother, please,' Gino said.

'Why do you say that, Madame Ramoun?'

'Because I'm going. And I want to go in peace. I have nothing on my conscience, but I'm leaving an orphan behind me. I want to be sure he'll be in good hands.'

'Is she sick?' I asked Gino.

'She's rambling. She's been like this since midday. I called the doctor; he said there's nothing wrong. I don't understand why she thinks she's dying. I've been trying to reason with her, but she won't listen to me.'

'There are things a doctor doesn't see,' his mother said. 'Things only those who are going feel. My feet are freezing and the cold is spreading to the rest of my body.'

'No, Mother, you're imagining things.'

'Put your hand on mine again, Turambo, and swear to me that you'll take care of my son.'

Gino signalled to me to agree.

I swallowed, my throat tight with emotion.

'Will you take care of him as you take care of yourself?'

'Yes, Madame Ramoun.'

'I don't want anything to come between you, not money, not women, not your careers, not temptation.'

'Nothing will come between us.'

'I'll be looking down on you, Turambo.'

'I'll look after Gino and won't let any serpents come between us.'

'Do you promise?'

'I swear.'

She turned to Gino and said to him in Italian, 'Fetch me your father.'

'Mother ...'

'Please, Gino.'

Gino went to his room and came back with a framed photograph of a turbaned infantryman smiling at the camera and puffing at a cigarette. He was young, handsome, fine-featured and dark-skinned. The photograph had turned yellow in places and had scratches which, fortunately, had spared the soldier's face.

'Was he an Arab?' I asked Gino.

'He was my father, that's all,' he replied, irritated by my stupid question.

He placed the photograph on the chair next to the bedside table, so that his mother had it facing her. Madame Ramoun gazed for a long time at her husband's picture. She smiled, sighed, smiled again, and raised her eyebrows in an expression of tenderness while a thousand memories flashed before her eyes. Everything in her was asking for forgiveness. She'd had enough of being confined to her sarcophagus of flesh. Without her faith, she would doubtless have put an end to her life ages ago, but there was that fear of the Last Judgement, that horrible deadline that raises its finger to warn you against yourself, that keeps you in purgatory while promising you hell if you try to get out of it. I had often asked myself what I would do in her position; not once had I come up with an answer. I had simply watched the poor woman sink into the quicksand of her body, like someone watching the misery of the world making a spectacle of itself on every street corner. There was nothing else to do.

'And now, read to me a little, Gino ... No, not the Bible,' she said, clasping the holy book tighter to her chest. 'I prefer Edmond Bourg. Reread Chapter thirteen to me, the passage where he talks about his wife ...'

Madame Ramoun closed her eyes and let her son's penetrating voice lull her. Gino read Chapter thirteen to her. As his mother didn't react, he went on to the next chapter. Madame Ramoun shifted in her sleep and moved her finger, begging her son to go back and reread, over and over, the same chapter that the author devotes to his wife. It was a moving passage in which Edmond Bourg asked his wife for forgiveness.

Madame Ramoun died a few hours later, the Bible over her heart and her eyes filled with a serene light. First, she heaved a sigh, opened her eyes to take one last look at her son and smiled at him, then, happy, freed from the chains of her body, as light as the first thrill of her romance, she turned to the photograph propped up on the chair and said, 'You took your time coming for me, my love.'

Gino and I looked for a carpenter to make us a coffin; those offered by the undertakers were no match for the dead woman's size. It was hot and we had to be quick about it to avoid the corpse decomposing.

Gino's worst fears were realised. More than the mourning itself, it was the removal of the body that was a particularly gruelling ordeal for my friend. It was impossible to get the corpse out through the main door. She was too obese, and too heavy for the bearers.

Volunteers from the neighbourhood came to help. There was such a crowd that the tram couldn't get through. What's going on? the passengers asked, leaning over the guardrail. Apparently a woman died ... Did the building collapse on her? No, they're knocking down the wall to get her out ... Are you joking? Everyone stared at the men making a big hole in the wall around the window of the dead woman's room.

Gino was devastated at the spectacle afforded by his mother's funeral. He always preferred to be discreet and now he was on display to all and sundry like some kind of circus freak.

After knocking down the front of the house, the volunteers started erecting scaffolding with the help of ropes, pulleys and beams. A stonemason with a stitched forehead cupped his hands around his mouth and shouted instructions. The coffin, as big as a Norman dresser, was tied firmly and, to cries of Now hoist!, some dozen men starting pulling on the ropes while others, on the balcony, guided the load to avoid it crashing into the wall.

The chaos that day was unbelievable.

When the coffin emerged through the hole in the wall and swayed over everyone's heads, the crowd held their breath. In the general silence, the only sound was the creaking of the pulleys. The coffin was lowered with extreme caution and laid on a cart. The funeral cortège set off immediately, drawing dozens of onlookers in its wake.

In the streets, people stopped as the hearse went by; some took off their hats, others, sitting at café tables, rose obsequiously to their feet. Boys emerged from the thickets and trees where they were playing hide and seek, stopped their games of pignols or put off till later the errands they had been given and came to swell the cortège, suddenly silent and solemn, while housewives jostled one another on the balconies and rooftops, their children clinging to their skirts. An old madman who looked like Rasputin came and placed himself at the front of the cortège, foaming at the mouth, eyes popping out of their sockets. He pointed at the hearse, then at the sky, and shook his unruly hair from side to side, crying, 'This is a warning. We'll all die one day. What we think we possess is only an illusion. We're merely the fleeting links in a chain dragged by a ghost named Time heading straight for nothingness.' He was in a trance. Policemen had to step in and get him out of the way.

Gino kept his head down.

I took his hand; he pulled it away quickly and hurried on, wanting to be alone.

We buried Madame Ramoun in the Christian cemetery.

It was a terribly sad day.


Misfortunes never come singly. When one rears its head, a whole tribe appears in its wake, and the descent into hell begins in earnest.

It was a religious holiday and I was just getting ready to go with Gino to the beach at Kristel, where my friend had got into the habit of taking refuge since his mother's death, when a gleaming car, driven by an Arab driver, stopped outside our house in Rue du Général-Cérez. In no time at all, kids appeared from the nearby alleys and started swarming around that gem on four wheels, fascinated by so much technology and refinement.

Who was that fat lady who looked like a sultana, being helped out of the car by two servants? Who were those women glittering with jewels and silk, and where were they taking those trays loaded with gifts and beribboned cakes? What was the meaning of those loud ululations, the excitement that had gripped our courtyard?

Nobody had told me, and I hadn't seen it coming.

It was like a guillotine blade falling without any warning.

Nora's a wonderful girl, my mother would tell me. She deserves all the happiness in the world, and you don't have much to give her, my son. You have to face facts. Nora will be pampered. She'll live in a big house and eat her fill every day. Don't be selfish. Leave her to her destiny, and try to find one for yourself ...

My cousin Nora, the love I had thought was mine for sure, my reason for living, had been handed over to a rich landowner from Frenda.

How had a country bumpkin who lived hundreds of miles from Oran heard about her? Nora almost never left the house, never saw anybody.

'The matchmakers!' the Mozabite enlightened me. 'They're professionals who frequent the hammam. And there's no more propitious place to evaluate the merchandise than a hammam. The matchmakers know their business. They come and take a bath, settle in the hot room and choose from among the naked virgins those who have high breasts, shapely thighs, full hips, nice round buttocks, slender necks and pretty faces. After setting their sights on the one they prefer, they follow her from a distance, find out where she lives and gather as much information about her as they can from the neighbours. Once they're sure they've got their hands on the right girl, they inform the family that hired them and, within a week, ladies loaded with gifts appear as if out of the blue to make their offer to the beauty's parents ... It's an old practice. How else can you explain, when a virgin has been confined within four walls, that someone always comes to ask for her hand? The matchmakers are the best detectives in the country, and probably the best paid. They'd track down the Queen of Sheba without any problem.'

I was devastated.

I didn't go to Kristel that day.

No sea would have been big enough to drown my sorrows in.

No sooner requested than wrapped and delivered. Within three weeks, everything was arranged and the marriage procession was begun. I didn't have time to feel sorry for myself. My blue-bird had gone to her cage and her chirping was drowned out by the noises of the city.

In Oran, winter arrives like a thief and leaves the same way. What does it take with it in its shameful retreat? Everything the inhabitants hate – greyness, cold, short days, bad moods – in other words, what they gladly give up to it.

That winter was the worst of all winters; it had stolen the sun from me. When spring returned with its lights and its joys, it merely made my nights all the colder and sadder. With Nora gone, my people and my streets were unfamiliar to me. I had been betrayed. My aunt was not unaware of the feelings I had for her daughter. How could she have trampled on them? And why hadn't my mother tried to dissuade her? I hated the whole earth, the angels and the demons, and every star in the sky. I had the feeling I had lost sight of the one point of reference that mattered to me. Suddenly, I didn't know where I was. Deprived of my certainties and a little of my soul, I began cursing everything in my path.

My mother tried to reason with me. Love is the privilege of the rich, she said. *The poor don't have access to it. Their world is too wretched to accommodate a dream; their romance is a sham.*

I didn't agree. I refused to admit that everything could be

bought and sold, including one's own offspring. As far as I was concerned, Nora had been sold. To an old country bumpkin from Frenda, rich enough to afford a houri, but too miserly and obtuse to offer her paradise. Nora would be nothing but a kind of odalisque trapped in a hostile harem. The others would resent her for being the youngest, the most idolised by the master, and they would plot against her until she ended up as less than a shadow. Then the master would find himself a new virgin, and Nora would be relegated to the rank of occasional concubine ...

At night, I would lie on the balcony, unable to get to sleep. On my back, my hands behind my neck, I would look up at the sky as if it were some undesirable I was looking up and down. I would imagine Nora in the arms of her repulsive ogre, who probably smelt of mouldy hay beneath his satin robe; it was as if a machine had got out of control and was crushing me. It was no longer Nora suffering the advances of her lover, but me. I clearly felt that bastard's sticky hands soil my flesh, his rutting animal breath on my face, and my lungs filled with his fetid exhalations.

Never had fate seemed so unjust as it did on those nights.

I had loved in silence a cousin of my own rank and blood, and an ageing stranger had appeared from nowhere to steal her from me like a big arm taking from a child the only dream that would console him for everything he would never possess!

'Can I ask you a question?' I said to Gino.

'Of course.'

'And will you answer me honestly?'

'I'll try.'

'Am I cursed?'

'I don't think so.'

'Then why do bad things always happen to me?'

'What's happening to you, Turambo, is something everyone goes through. You're no more to be pitied than a workman who falls off a ladder. That's what happens in life. With a bit of patience, this bad patch will be nothing but a vague memory.'

'You think so?'

'Don't you?'

I waited for the bad patch to turn into a vague memory, but every morning, when I awoke, there it was, omnipresent, stinking up the air I breathed and contaminating my thoughts.

I could no longer sleep.

By day, I would keep close to the walls like a crab. Oran had become a circus of horrors. I was a curious beast on display for the neighbours to mock. None of them had ever dared look up at Nora when she hung the washing out on the balcony. They *knew* she was mine, and they were jealous. Some were delighted at my disappointment now and made little attempt to hide it. Others had no qualms about making hurtful insinuations. Even when I responded with my fists, they continued to make fun of me ... To escape these unpleasant remarks, which often led to nasty fights, I would retreat to the Cueva del Agua, a cliff to the east of the city, far from the bustle and the misunderstandings. It was a sinister spot where a few ragged fishermen would pretend to be watching their lines while getting blind drunk and having arguments. Looking at them, I felt like getting drunk too, as if there was no tomorrow, so drunk I would take a wave for a flood. I felt like proclaiming my sorrow in order to drown out the noise of the waves, insulting all the patron saints of the city one by one, cursing the rich and the poor until I'd got rid of all of them.

What difference would it have made?

I contented myself with gazing at the sea. I would sit down on a big rock, put my chin on my knees, wrap my arms round my legs to warm them and stare at the horizon. The ships in the harbour proved to me that there were other places to go, other shores, where you could have fabulous chance encounters, meet people who spoke strange languages. I dreamt of jumping on a boat and setting sail for some mirage. With Nora gone, I had lost my moorings. I was unhappy every time a voice, a figure, a rustle brought her memory back to me. Leave her to her destiny, my mother had said, and try to find one for yourself ... How could I imagine a whole destiny when a mere blow of fate was enough to disqualify me?

I spent hours questioning the sea, feeling the breeze swell my shirt without soothing my soul. I longed to become a bubble of air, to fly above the storms and the malice of men, to put myself out of reach of my grief. I felt confined in my body, disorientated in my own mind, as empty of interest as of meaning.

I saw Nora again six months after she got married. She had come back to see her mother.

I returned one day from my wanderings and there she was, in shimmering silk, like a young princess, more beautiful than ever. The sight took my breath away. But she wasn't alone. Two sisters-in-law and a reptilian maid watched over her; she was the apple of their eye and they wouldn't let her out of their sight. As soon as they heard my footsteps in the corridor leading to the inner courtyard, they hurriedly lowered the curtain in the doorway to shelter their protégée. For three days, I tried to approach Nora, but in vain. I kept clearing my throat and coughing into my fist to let her know that I was in the next room, waiting for her, but Nora didn't appear. On the fourth day, I managed to outwit her guards. Nora almost fainted when she saw me looming over her. She wouldn't have been so scared if she'd seen a ghost. Are you mad? she choked, turning pale. What is it you want? To ruin me? I'm married now. Please go.

She pushed me unceremoniously out of the room, out of her sight, out of her life ...

I meant nothing to her any more, except perhaps a potential source of scandal.

That was when I remembered De Stefano's offer, and I found myself knocking at the door of his gym in Rue Wagram.

If you wanted to beat yourself up, there was no better place to do it than in a boxing ring.

# II
# Aïda

1

Rue Wagram echoed to the yells of kids kicking a rag ball. It was one in the afternoon and the sun was beating down. De Stefano's gym was below street level, facing Porte du Ravin, with the date 1847 – the year it was built – above the door. It was a huge, ugly building, its walls full of cracks, and had once been a stable for thoroughbred horses before being transformed into a makhzan towards the end of the last century. Threatened by a landslide, it was evacuated by the military, padlocked and abandoned to the ravages of time and rats before being taken over in the 1910s by lovers of boxing. The area smelt of horseshit and of the drains that ran off into the wild grass of the gully.

Overcome by the heat, a wafer vendor was dozing in the shade of a basket shaped like an African drum. Facing him, two scrawny brats sat on the pavement, swathed in moth-eaten rags, their eyes as empty as their bellies, like two puppies staring at a piece of sugar. Not far off, a housewife was emptying dishwater outside her front door, her dress pulled up above her knees. Further down, a gang of urchins were harassing an alley cat while an amused old drunk looked on impassively.

The wafer vendor woke when he heard me approach and immediately became defensive. I gestured to him to calm down.

The doors of the gym were open. I walked into a large, depressing-looking sports hall. Light filtered in through the holes in the roof and the shutterless windows and bounced off the filthy tiled floor. To the right of the door stood a small table littered with the remains of food, a dirty glass and a Paloma bottle filled with water. To the left were a few crinkled posters of boxers on the walls. An old boxing ring was just about holding up on a platform, its ropes hanging loose. Behind, a shapeless punch bag hung from its gallows. At the far end, a dilapidated cubicle could be made out through the gloom. I could hear two men arguing, one angry, the other conciliatory.

I took an instant dislike to the place. It stank of mould and defeat.

Just as I was about to leave, a tall, thin man emerged from the toilets, hopping on a wooden leg. 'Who are you looking for?' he asked, walking back to the table near the door.

'De Stefano.'

'He's busy. What's it about?'

'He asked me to come by.'

'Was it De Stefano who asked for you and not somebody else?'

I didn't reply. Doormen often grant themselves an authority they don't have and shamelessly abuse it. He waved me to a bench.

'You chose the wrong time, son. At this hour of the day, they're either eating or sleeping.'

He collapsed onto his chair and started biting into his sandwich.

The two men in the cubicle were still arguing.

'Why does he call me a monkey?' one of them said excitedly. 'Did he pick me off a tree?'

I recognised De Stefano's voice saying, 'You know what they're like at *Le Petit Oranais*. They aren't journalists, they're madmen and racists. They hate wops. Plus, they're jealous.'

'Are you sure it's because they're jealous, and not because I'm Portuguese?'

'Absolutely. That's the way the world is: there are those who become legends and those who make lots of noise because that's all they can do.'

The doorman swallowed his last mouthful, washed it down with a gulp of water, let out a formidable belch, wiped his mouth with the back of his hand and said to me in a low voice, 'Rodrigo's a nutcase. He's never been in a ring in his life. He's made up this idea that he's a champion and he believes it totally. When he's having one of his attacks, he comes here and drives us all up the wall. He tells everyone the press are giving him a hard time, that he's had enough, and so on and so on, and De Stefano likes to tell him he sympathises and tries to encourage him ...'

I nodded out of politeness.

'I think De Stefano gets a kick out of it,' the doorman went on. 'He thinks he's really encouraging a champion and that makes him feel he's important. He used to be big. He had a whole lot of promising fighters in his stable. Then it all fizzled out, and all he's left with is nostalgia. So he keeps Rodrigo around in order not to lose the thread, and waits for the good old days to come back ...'

The little door of the cubicle opened and a gangling, pale-eyed individual in a threadbare jacquard pullover and a pair of crumpled trousers came out, strutted across the room, saluting the poster of a champion as he passed it, and went out into the street without taking any notice of us.

De Stefano opened his arms wide to greet me. 'So you made your mind up at last ...'

In the street, Rodrigo started shouting abuse at us.

'That's Rodrigo,' De Stefano said. 'A former champion.'

Behind him, the tall, thin man wagged his finger to deny this.

'Well, Turambo? To what do I owe the pleasure?'

'You asked me to come by, so here I am.'

'Congratulations! I promise you won't regret it.'

'I don't see anyone here …'

'It isn't time yet. Most of our boxers have to work to make ends meet. But in the evening, it's bedlam, I can assure you …' Then, turning to the doorman, 'Did you deliver the package, Tobias?'

'Not yet. There's nobody to mind the shop.'

'Go now. You know how Toni is. He doesn't like being neglected. Take Turambo with you. That way, he'll find a few boys in the ring when he gets back. And tell the baker to send me a snack. I'll take over; try not to dawdle, please.'

Tobias started to clear the table, but De Stefano told him he'd take care of it and pointed to a package in the corner.

'Can you carry it for me?' Tobias asked me. 'It isn't heavy, but with my wooden leg …'

'No problem,' I said, picking up the package.

Tobias walked fast; his wooden leg banged on the road surface and made him lurch to the side.

'Did you lose your leg in an accident?'

'In a garden,' he said sarcastically. 'I stepped on a seed, the seed got embedded in the sole of my foot, and in the morning, when I woke up, a wooden leg had grown under my thigh.'

We walked in silence for a while. Tobias was very well known. Everywhere we went, people greeted him. He would trade insults with some, jokes with others, and throw his head back in a shrill laugh. He was a handsome man, very clean beneath his old clothes; without his disability, he could have passed for a commercial traveller or a postman.

'I left my leg on a battlefield, at Verdun,' he admitted suddenly.

'You were in the war?'

'Like millions of other fools.'

'And what's it like?'

He wiped his forehead on his forearm and asked me to pause

because of his wooden leg, which was starting to torment him. He sat down on a low wall to catch his breath. 'You want to know what war is like?'

'Yes,' I said, in the hope of understanding a little of what had happened to my father.

'I can't make any comparison. It isn't like anything else. It's a bit like every nightmare, and no nightmare could describe it. You're simultaneously in a slaughterhouse, a bullring, a chamber of horrors, down the bottom of a toilet and in hell, except that your pains never end.'

'Do you have children?'

'I had two. I don't know where they are. Their mother walked out on me while I was trying to survive in that abattoir.'

'Haven't you tried to find them?'

'I'm too tired.'

'I had a father. He was a good man. When he came back from the war, he deserted his family. He left us one night and abandoned us in the mud.'

'Yes, that kind of reaction is common. War is a strange kind of excursion. You go to it to the sound of bugles, and you come back in the skin of a ghost, your head full of noises, and don't know what to do with your shitty life afterwards.'

He pointed to a monument behind us and an equestrian statue in a little park at the corner of the street.

'All those statues tell us about the madness of men. When we put flowers on them on Remembrance Day, all we're doing is hiding our faces and lying to ourselves. We don't honour the dead, we disturb them. Look at that statue of a general over there. What is it saying? Just that however much we fight and burn towns and fields, slaughter people while proclaiming victory, and make the tears of widows flow, the heroes end up on marble pedestals for pigeons to shit on ...'

He pulled up his trouser leg and adjusted his prosthesis. His brow furrowed.

'I've never understood how each generation can allow itself to be deceived. I suppose the nation is more important than the family. Well, I don't agree. You can have as many nations as you like, but if you don't have a family, you're nobody.'

He pulled down his trouser leg with an abrupt gesture. The furrow on his forehead deepened.

'Amazing, isn't it? You carry on with your daily routine, calmly, you cultivate your garden, you put your meagre savings away in a safe place, and in a corner of your head you make plans, modest plans, as small as a wisp of straw. You look after your kids, convinced it's going to be that way till death do us part. Then, all at once, some high-ranking strangers you've never met decide your fate. They take away your little dreams and land you in the middle of their crazy scheme. That's war. You don't know why it's there, but you fall into it like a hair into soup. By the time you realise what's going on, the storm has passed. When the light comes back on, you no longer recognise what was there.'

He hauled himself up.

'War is only an adventure for those fools who believe a medal is worth a life. I wasn't the king of the world before, but I didn't complain. I was a railway worker; I had a home and reasons to hope. Then something got into me and I left everything to wave a flag and march to the sound of drums. Obviously, that threw my life off course. I don't blame anyone. That's the way it is, and that's that. If I had to do it all over again, I'd pour wax in my ears so that I couldn't hear the bugles, or the orders, or the cannon fire … Nothing is worth a life, my boy, neither glory nor a page in the history books, and no field of honour can equal a woman's bed.'

\*

By the time we got back, the gym was looking a bit livelier. A few young men in shorts were doing body-building exercises. De Stefano was talking to a thickset young man whom he dismissed when we arrived. He asked Tobias if Toni had had any objections. Tobias told him that the fellow in question had grumbled a fair amount, but that the misunderstanding had been resolved. De Stefano grunted something, then took me aside.

'Get in the ring,' he said.

'I don't have the right clothes, or gloves.'

'It doesn't matter. Get in as you are; don't take your shoes off.'

I did as he asked. The thickset young man joined me on the platform. He had put on gloves and sports shoes. He came and stood in front of me, cracked his neck, did a few knee bends and took two steps back. I was expecting to be given instructions. There weren't any. Without warning, the boy started punching me in the face. I lost my bearings, unsure if I was supposed to respond or just take it. My opponent kept pummelling my body. I felt as if a piston was trying to crush my sides. The floor gave way beneath my feet. While I was down, the boy continued jumping up and down on the spot.

'Get up!' De Stefano cried. 'Defend yourself!'

No sooner was I on my feet than I had to shelter behind my arms to withstand my opponent's frantic assault. My few counterattacks went nowhere. The boy was quick on his feet, elusive; he dodged my punches, pushed me away whenever I tried to hold on to him; he would feint at me, his head never in the same place for more than a second.

He knocked me down again.

De Stefano ordered the boy to leave, and me to get down from the ring.

'Now you know that boxing is nothing like street fighting,' he said. 'On the ground, you're a single person, a nobody. In the ring, you're asked to be a god. Boxing is a science, an art and an ambition ... I'd like you to remember this day, my boy. That way, you'll realise how far you've come the evening you score your first victory. There's a whole programme to get through, and you'll have to follow it to the letter. Buy yourself a duffle bag, a pair of shorts, a vest and some sports shoes. The gloves are on the house. Tobias will explain the training schedule. As of tomorrow, I want to see you here every day.'

'I have to look for a job.'

'That's what I mean by training schedule. There are three timetables, just choose the one that suits you. The members of my club also work. You have to have something to sink your teeth into before you can think of breaking other people's teeth.'

For the first few weeks, I wasn't allowed in the ring. De Stefano was waiting for me to earn that privilege. He had to clear away the cobwebs first, and so he started by testing my stamina: I had to go up and down the hills of the Ravin, run as far as the pine grove at Les Planteurs, climb the sides of Murdjadjo clinging to the bushes, listen to my body, push it to the limit, control my breathing, adjust my stride to the uneven terrain and end with a sprint. By the time I got home, I'd be all in, with my tongue hanging out and my throat burning. Mekki, who didn't look kindly on this self-imposed ordeal, tried to discover what I was up to, suspecting I was in some kind of trouble. As I couldn't admit to him that I'd chosen to be a boxer, our conversation ended very badly, and Gino, to put an end to my rebellion, suggested I stay with him. I accepted without hesitation.

I felt much better on Boulevard Mascara. Not having to give any account of myself to anyone, I devoted myself fully to my new vocation.

On Sundays, Gino would come with me to the gym, where we would see Filippi, the mechanic who'd worked with us at

Bébert's garage. Whenever he had time off, Filippi would come to De Stefano's to keep fit. He had boxed in his younger days, without much success, and continued to go to the gym and train his athlete's body. He was enthusiastic, a bit of a show-off, and he was good at motivating me. The three of us would set off together to tackle the hills and paths. Gino often gave up halfway, unable to maintain the pace we set ourselves, but Filippi, in spite of his age, excelled and really inspired me.

At home, on Boulevard Mascara, Gino and I made body-building equipment from bits of scrap iron and cemented metal cans; we were proud to display our pectorals to the girls hanging out their washing on the neighbouring rooftops.

Sport proved to be excellent therapy for Gino and me. My friend was mourning his mother and I was mourning my love ... Ah, Nora, how beautiful she was! She was as dainty, graceful and frail as a poppy, and when she smiled, the world glittered with promise. Our hearts had beat as one, I had thought. I had believed she was mine, believed it so firmly that I'd never even thought of a future without her ... Alas, our future is determined in spite of us. We have no hold or rights over it, and it will still be there when we've gone.

In the evening, after a good sweat and a hot bath, we'd go out on the town, looking for fun. There's nothing better than the bustle of the city to drown out nasty voices calling from the depth of torment, and nothing better than crowds to shake off missing loved ones.

Oran's nights absorbed our anxieties like blotting paper. We couldn't afford much, but we could still have a good time; we just had to go where our steps led us. Everything was worth looking at in Oran, the carriages and the cars, the drunks and the entertainers, and everything was there to be seen without any obligation to touch it, window shopping. The cinemas, lit up as bright as day, attracted as many night owls as a lantern attracts insects. The neon signs outside the nightclubs splashed colours on the façades opposite. The bistros never emptied and were always filled with noise and tobacco smoke.

Gino and I were the valiant surveyors of the night. After doing the rounds of the open-air dance halls or coming out of the cinema, we would go to the seafront to look at the lights of the harbour and watch the dockers bustling around the freighters. The sea breeze cradled our silences; we sometimes even daydreamed, our elbows on the parapet and our cheeks resting in the palm of our hands. Once we were tired of counting the boats, we would sit down on a terrace, eat lemon ices and watch the girls swaying their hips on the esplanade, looking wonderful in their guipure dresses. Whenever a pick-up artist made a teasing comment to them, the girls would turn to him, laugh and walk away like wreaths of smoke. The man would then flick away his cigarette end and swagger along behind them, before eventually returning to his post, empty-handed but determined to try his luck again and again until there was nobody left in the streets.

They were strange people, these pick-up artists. Gino was certain that they were more interested in the chase than the catch, that their happiness lay not in conquest, but in the process of picking up. We once watched one of them closely; as far as smooth talking went, he had no equal, but whenever a girl took the bait, he would realise that he was out of ideas and would stand there dumbly, not knowing what to suggest.

As there was no chance we'd find soul mates for the evening, Gino and I made do with going to the rough end of town and watching the prostitutes. They would emerge from the shadows like hallucinations, show us their big breasts, swollen by anonymous mouths, make dirty remarks and snap the elastic on their knickers. It made us laugh, and our laughter was a way of overcoming our fears and silencing those rasping voices that echoed inside us like warnings.

It was the days that were difficult. Once Gino had gone to work, I was back on the scrapheap again. Nothing interested me. Nora had given me back my heart, but I didn't know what to do with it. It had been beating only for her. The sun would turf me out of bed like someone unclean, the streets made me go round in circles until I was seeing things and, when the time came for taking stock, I was convinced I had once again taken a wrong turn.

I needed a task to assuage my hunger.

After running all over town, I'd end up at De Stefano's gym, exhausted and angry. I would train hard to rise above my fate, impatient to get into the ring. De Stefano deliberately kept me on the ground. The honour of stepping into the ring had to be deserved. For two months, I limited myself to physical exercises, jogging, controlling my breathing, the basics of boxing. I had to learn the different positions of my arms and fists, coordinate my reflexes and my thoughts, feint and punch in the air, smash the punch bag. De Stefano paid me more attention than the others. I could see an excitement in his eyes that he found hard to conceal. Although in his opinion, I still had some way to go to develop the right aggressiveness, he acknowledged that I was making progress, that my moves and flexibility had something, that my attacks and retreats were elegant.

I had a champion's instincts, he would say.

Rodrigo sometimes came back, playing the victim, brandishing an 'enemy' newspaper, inventing deadly conspiracies. He wasn't just eccentric, he was insane. Some people at the gym didn't rule out the possibility that one of these days the poor devil would end up killing someone or setting fire to a newspaper office. Tobias was convinced this case of split personality would end badly. Sometimes, in sheer exasperation, he would take it upon himself to throw the Portuguese kid out. Rodrigo would continue his performance in the street, rousing the kids and the dogs, in the hope of seeing De Stefano come out to calm him down, except that De Stefano no longer needed to encourage anyone now that he believed the good old days were back.

When at last, after months of waiting, I was allowed to get in the ring and face a sparring partner, it was as if all at once I was reborn, discovering a secret faith buried in my unconscious. I was on a pedestal, noisily demanding laurel wreaths a thousand times bigger than my head. I knew immediately, as my opponent tried in vain to dodge my punches, that I was made for boxing. People were already talking about my left hook and I hadn't even had my first fight.

## 2

My first fight was on the third Sunday of February in 1932.

I remember there wasn't a wisp of cloud in the sky.

We took the bus for Aïn Témouchent very early in the morning: De Stefano, Francis the pianist, who handled the gym's paperwork, Salvo the second, Tobias and me. De Stefano hadn't given permission for Gino to come with us.

I was nervous. I was shivering a little, probably because of the four days of hammam I'd imposed on myself to make weight. On the seat in front of me, a veiled old woman was trying to calm two unruly chickens in a basket. A few peasants in turbans were also on the bus, silent and morose. Some Roumis sat at the front, one of them smoking a pipe that made the atmosphere, which already smelt of petrol fumes, stink even more.

I opened the window to let in some air and watched the landscape drift past.

The countryside was green, glittering with dew in the rising sun like millions of sparks. On either side, the orange groves of Misserghin looked like Christmas trees.

De Stefano was leafing through a magazine. He was trying to appear confident, but I sensed how tense he was, clinging to his magazine, stooped, his face inscrutable. His silence spoke for him. For two years he'd been waiting to finally see one of his protégés in a ring that mattered. He was only a believer when he was forced to be, and I'd seen him cross himself before he got on the bus.

We were a few miles from Lourmel when I saw *her* …

A beauty, on horseback, her hair blowing in the wind; she was galloping flat out on the ridge of a hill, as if she had emerged from the blazing dawn to seize the day. As if drawn in Indian ink, her slender silhouette stood out clearly against the pale-blue horizon, like a magic pattern on a screen.

'That's Irène,' De Stefano whispered in my ear. 'She's the daughter of Alarcon Ventabren, a former champion who's now confined to a wheelchair. They have a farm behind the grove over there. Some really good boxers sometimes go there to recharge their batteries before big fights … Beautiful, isn't she?'

'She's too far away to get a proper idea.'

'Oh, I assure you she's dynamite, is Irène. As pretty and wild as a freshwater pearl.'

The horsewoman climbed a hillock and disappeared behind a line of cypresses.

It was as if all at once the countryside had lost its beauty spot.

Long after she had gone, her image stayed in my head, giving rise to a strange feeling. I knew nothing about her, apart from a name whispered by De Stefano over the rumble of the bus. Was she young, blonde or brunette, tall or short, married or single? Why had she taken over the countryside, replacing the daylight and everything else? Why did that fleeting apparition refuse to go away? If I'd crossed her path, if I'd had her face directly in front of me, I would have attributed the quiver that went through me to a kind of love at first sight and thus found an explanation for the dizziness that followed. But she was only a remote, elusive figure speeding to some unknown destination.

Later, I would understand why an unknown horsewoman had, for no apparent reason, raised so many questions for me.

But that day, on the morning of that third Sunday in February 1932, I was a long way from guessing that I had just met my destiny.

The ring had been set up in the middle of a cleared stretch of waste ground at the entrance to the town. The scaffolding left a lot to be desired, but the organisers had transformed the place into a party zone. Hundreds of pennants and tricolour flags flapped on ropes and around poles erected for the occasion. From the bus, you could see workmen hurrying to put up the last garlands before the match, which was due to start at one in the afternoon. A little welcoming committee greeted us as we got off the bus. We were quickly shown to an isolated policeman's hut, not far from the stadium. De Stefano wasn't happy. He had been promised a hotel, photographers and journalists, as well as a good meal before the match, and now it looked almost as if they were hiding us. A large man in a severe suit tried to explain to us that the mayor's instructions were clear and he was merely carrying them out. De Stefano refused to be fobbed off and threatened to return to Oran immediately. Someone ran off to fetch one of the organisers. He appeared, a broad smile on his face, took De Stefano aside, put his arm round his shoulders and spoke into his ear. De Stefano demonstrated his anger, stamping on the ground to underline his threats, then, when the man slipped an envelope into his pocket, he lowered his voice and his gestures grew less brusque.

'More funny business,' sighed Francis the pianist, who hadn't missed a thing.

De Stefano came back to us, pretending to be indignant. He ordered us to go into the hut and get ready, then went back to the organiser.

The hut smelt like a putrid coffin. There was a thin metal

wardrobe in a corner, a school desk with a fitted bench and a corroded inkwell on the rim, two stools and a ramshackle camp bed. The paneless window looked out onto a path that led to a bare hillock where an old dog was looking in all directions, its tongue hanging out. For a historic day, it was depressing.

'You'd better get changed,' Salvo said. 'And please try to knock the bastard out in the first round. I don't want to be gathering dust here.'

Salvo had also been expecting a warm welcome. As a native of Oran, he couldn't stand being treated this way by provincials.

Tobias wasn't exactly delighted either. Something was bothering him. He hadn't liked the way De Stefano had become less forceful because of an envelope he hadn't even opened.

For his part, De Stefano pretended to take exception to everything, but he was totally unconvincing. The organiser, aware that he had the upper hand, was more relaxed; he spoke with an affected air, his hands in his pockets, and, at the slightest thing, he would throw his head back and let out a neighing laugh, pleased to see the first spectators converging on the stadium in their best clothes and straw boaters.

I opened my bag and started to change.

Tobias began fidgeting on the camp bed. He leant over to Salvo and said, 'I have more and more problems with women.'

'What kind of problems?' Salvo said, scratching behind his ear.

'You know what I mean.'

'I don't live in your head.'

Tobias leant closer and said in a low voice, 'Before going to the brothel, I'm on heat, and, as soon as I'm in the room with a whore, it's like I've taken a cold shower.'

'You don't have to take just any of them.'

'I've tried with several and it still hasn't worked.'

'What do you want me to do about it, Tobias? If you can't manage with your cock, use your wooden leg, that'll be a real thrill.'

'I'm not joking. It's serious ... You're good at healing things. I thought maybe you had some tricks, potions, something like that. I've tried all kinds of methods, but I'm getting nowhere.'

Salvo assumed a solemn air and put his hands together under his nose to think. After meditating like a Buddhist monk, he looked up at Tobias. 'Have you tried the Hindu method?'

'I don't know it.'

Salvo nodded sagely and said, 'Well, according to a revered fakir, to obtain the ideal erection, what you have to do is sit down on your finger.'

'Ha-ha. I suppose you think you're funny?'

Angry now, Tobias went out into the yard, pursued by Salvo's sardonic laughter.

A little boy in short trousers arrived on his bicycle, with a basket full of fruit, bottles of pop and sandwiches. Before leaving again, he asked me if I was the boxer and wished me good luck. De Stefano thanked him on my behalf and pushed him gently towards the exit. We ate in silence. Outside, we could hear the roar of the crowd around the ring.

Salvo bandaged my fists, tied my gloves and realised he had forgotten my gum shield. De Stefano shrugged his shoulders and asked everyone else to leave except me.

'You have to take it easy, son,' he said, embarrassed, when we were alone. 'This is a friendly match.'

'Meaning what?'

'Meaning there are no bets. It's the show that matters, not the result. People are here to have a good time. So don't get too excited and make the pleasure last. Keep your left hook for next time.'

'What is all this? I thought this was going to be a serious match.'

'I thought so too. The mayor of Aïn Témouchent lied to me.'

'In that case, why not cancel and go home?'

'I don't want any problems with the council, Turambo. And besides, it's not the end of the world. It's still a fight. You'll get a chance to see what it's like to have a hostile audience. You have eight rounds. The organisers decided on that. Try and see it through to the end. You don't have to finish off your opponent before that. In fact, you shouldn't. It'd spoil the party.'

'The party?'

'I'll explain later.'

He wiped his face with a handkerchief and asked me to follow him outside. He was so sad for me that I stopped complaining.

The stadium was divided in two by wire fencing. Inside, the stony part of the waste ground had vanished beneath the crowd. There were only men in suits and white hats, some with their children on their shoulders. Behind the fence were a few Araberbers in burnouses and Arab kids perched at the height of the barbed wire to see over the heads of the crowd.

I waited a good twenty minutes in the ring before my opponent arrived. And what an arrival! The town hero appeared in a horse-drawn carriage, preceded by a blaring brass band. Cheering wildly, the crowd stood back as the procession passed. Standing on his seat, my opponent raised his arms to greet his fans. He was a tall, strapping, fair-haired fellow, his head shaven over his temples, with a long thick lock of hair falling over his face. He was hamming it up, shadow-boxing, flattered by the pennants frantically waving around him. Servants helped him out of his carriage and into the ring. The clamour grew even louder when he again brandished his gloves. He gave me just a quick glance before once again offering himself up to the crowd.

De Stefano avoided my eyes in embarrassment.

The referee motioned my opponent and me to approach. He gave us our instructions and sent us back to our corners. As soon as the bell rang, that huge mass of muscle, who was a whole head taller than me, rushed at me and started to grind me down, galvanised by the lively yells of the crowd. He had no technique, he was banking on his strength. His aim was rough; he simply lashed out. I let the squall pass and managed to push him away. My first left hook made him take several steps back. Shaken, he stood there for a few seconds in bewilderment before coming back to his senses. He hadn't been expecting my counter. After moving around me, sizing me up, he got me in a corner and covered me with his hulking body. De Stefano yelled at me to use my right, just to remind me of his instruction to 'make the pleasure last'. I was disgusted. My opponent kept letting his guard down; I could have knocked him out any time I wanted. At the end of the third round, he started to tire. I begged De Stefano to let me finish him off. I couldn't stand being just a punchbag for a conceited idiot any longer. But De Stefano wouldn't yield. He admitted to me, while Salvo was cooling me down, how much he regretted the way things had turned out, and promised me it wouldn't happen again. Just this once, he said, I had to play the game through to the end because he'd given his word to the organisers.

The rottenness of it stuck in my throat. I tried as best I could to dismiss my black thoughts, but anger kept gaining the upper hand. I was punching now to hurt. My opponent reacted in a surprising way. When my blows hit home, he deliberately staggered from one rope to the other or else bent double, waggling his behind and pretending to throw up over the referee. Clearly he was just playing to the gallery. There was no tension in his face, no doubt in his eyes, just a theatrical, grotesque, ridiculous aggressiveness.

Only one thing mattered to me: I wanted this nonsense to stop! This wasn't my day; there was nothing historic about this damned Sunday. And to think that the night before, I had been so worried about my first fight that I hadn't slept a wink! I was so incensed that I found myself popping out my left, which stopped my opponent's clownish kicks dead in their tracks. He again had a few seconds of confusion, as if he suddenly couldn't place me, then resumed his attacks, hitting any old how before retreating, pleased with himself, and monkeying around for the audience. He was playing the clown, concerned more about the amusement of the crowd than my retaliation.

This farce went on until the sixth round. Against all expectation, the referee decided to stop the match and officially declare my opponent the winner. The crowd went wild. I looked for De Stefano. He had retreated behind our corner. My opponent swaggered around the ring, arms raised, eyes popping out of his head in childish joy … It was only on the way back, on the bus, that I learnt that the hero of the day was called Gaston, that he was the eldest son of the mayor of Aïn Témouchent, and that he wasn't a boxer at all but had fought this, his first fight, as a way of celebrating his father's birthday. Next year, he might pay for a swimming contest, or else a football match during which his teammates would make sure that he scored the winning goal after the referee had rejected those of the opposing team.

De Stefano tried to talk me round. I changed seats every time he came and sat down next to me. Tiring of it, he went and sat at the back of the bus. I felt his eyes on the back of my neck all the way to Oran.

'I told you I'm sorry, damn it!' he exploded when we got off the bus. 'You want me to go down on my knees or what? I swear I didn't know. I genuinely thought the boxer was a local champion. The organisers assured me he was.'

'Boxing isn't a church service,' Francis the pianist said, anxious to see De Stefano take out the envelope the official had slipped into his pocket. 'The paths of glory are paved with trapdoors and banana skins. When money's involved, the devil is never very far away. There are sponsored fights, fixed fights, fights lost in advance, and when you're an Arab, the only way to deal with biased referees is to drop your opponent so that he doesn't get up again.'

'This is between me and my champion,' De Stefano cut in. 'We don't need an interpreter.'

'Understood,' Francis said, looking significantly at De Stefano's pocket.

De Stefano took out the envelope, extracted a wad of banknotes, counted it and gave each person his share. Tobias and Salvo took theirs and left, pleased that they hadn't come back empty-handed in spite of my 'defeat'. Francis remained where he was, not happy with his cut.

'What do you want, my photograph?' De Stefano said.

Francis immediately beat a retreat.

'His eyes are bigger than his belly, that Francis,' De Stefano grunted. 'I've divided it equally, but because he knows how to sort out the paperwork and do the typing, he thinks he deserves more than the rest of us.'

'I don't want your money, De Stefano. You can give it to Francis.'

'Why? It's fifty francs, damn it. Some people would sell their mother-in-law for less than that.'

'Not me. I don't want money that's haram.'

'What do you mean, haram? You didn't steal it.'

'I didn't earn it either. I'm a boxer, not a comedian.'

I left him standing there in the middle of the street and ran to join Gino on Boulevard Mascara.

Gino wasn't in a good mood. He didn't look up when he heard me come in. He was sitting barefoot at the table in the kitchen in his vest, dipping a piece of bread into an omelette he had just taken off the stove. Since the death of his mother, he had been unusually moody and no longer turned a deaf ear when he was provoked. His language had grown harsher, and so had his look. At times, I had the feeling I was disturbing him, that he didn't want me in his home. Whenever I slammed the door to go back to my mother's, he wouldn't try to run after me. The next day, he would waylay me on my way out of the gym. He wouldn't apologise for his behaviour the day before and would act as if nothing had happened.

'Aren't you going to ask me how it went in Aïn Témouchent?'

Gino shrugged.

'The only things missing were Buster Keaton and a pianist in the hall.'

'I don't care,' he said, wiping his mouth with a napkin.

'Are you angry with me?'

He pounded furiously on the table. 'How dare you let that imbecile treat me that way? I'm not a dog. You should have shut his mouth and demanded that I go with you.'

'He's the boss, Gino. What could I do? You saw I wasn't pleased.'

'I didn't see anything of the sort. That shit stood in my way and you just stared at your feet. You should have insisted he let me go with you to Aïn Témouchent.'

'I didn't know how these things work. It was the first time I've had a fight. I thought De Stefano was within his rights.'

Gino was about to protest, but changed his mind and pushed away his plate.

I was sufficiently angry not to put up with Gino's complaints.

I turned on my heel and ran down the stairs. I needed to clean myself at the hammam and put my thoughts in order. I spent that night at my mother's.

I skipped training for three days running.

De Stefano gave Tobias the job of reasoning with me, but Tobias didn't really need to do much; on the contrary, I was glad of the opportunity not to lose face, because I was starting to find the days long and monotonous. I went to the gym and got back in the ring like a dunce approaching the blackboard, not really applying myself, out of revenge for the dirty trick played on me in Aïn Témouchent. De Stefano realised how much his casual attitude had hurt me. He didn't like the fact that I was behaving like an idiot but, not wanting to complicate things, he kept quiet about his feelings. To redeem himself, he did a lot of negotiating and managed to find me a serious opponent, a guy from Saint-Cloud who was starting to make a name for himself. The fight took place in a little town, in the middle of a stony field. It was such a hot day that there wasn't much of a crowd, but my opponent had brought most of his home village with him. His name was Gomez and he knocked me out in the third round. When the referee finished the count, De Stefano threw his straw boater on the ground and stamped on it. It was Tobias who offered to give me a talking-to. He came and found me in the hut where Gino was helping me get dressed.

'Are you happy now?' he said, his hands on his hips. 'That's what happens when you skip training. De Stefano paid you more attention than you deserve. If he'd set his sights on Mario, we wouldn't be in this position.'

'What has Mario got that I haven't?'

'Self-control. Humility. He's someone who thinks, is Mario. He knows his business. He has ideas. Ideas so big that when he has two of them at the same time, one has to kill the other so they can both stay in his skull.'

'Why, don't you think I have ideas?'

'Yes, but they're so feeble, they dissolve on their own in your pea-sized brain. You think you're punishing De Stefano by losing a match? You're making a big mistake, my young friend. You're ruining your prospects. If you want to go back to your souk and watch the donkeys being eaten by flies, no problem. You can do what you like provided you don't come back and complain about the flies, which'll be after you this time. De Stefano will get his hands on a champion in the end. There'll only be one loser, and it won't be him.'

Gino said much the same thing to me when I got back to the flat. 'There's no shame in losing,' he said. 'The shame is in not doing anything to win.'

I knew I'd been wrong, but every cloud has a silver lining. Losing so painfully to Gomez was the moment I woke up. With my pride hurt, I vowed to redeem myself. It was no longer De Stefano running after me, but the other way round. I trained twice a day. On Sundays, Gino would take me to the beach and make me run on the sand until I was dizzy.

Around mid-July, a military boxer from the naval base at Mers el-Kébir agreed to fight me. A ring was set up on one of the quays, in the shadow of a huge warship. The area was packed with sailors. Officers in their dress uniforms occupied the front rows. When night fell, floodlights illuminated the quay as if it was broad daylight. Corporal Roger appeared in a white robe, a tricolour scarf around his neck. His arrival set off a wave of hysteria. He was a close-cropped, hefty-looking man with bulging muscles, his right shoulder adorned with a romantic tattoo. He danced around a bit, waving to the human tide, which waved back. The bell hadn't stopped ringing when an avalanche of blows landed on me. The corporal was trying to knock me out from the start. His comrades cupped their hands around their mouths and yelled at him to kill me. There was a terrible silence when my left hit him in the temple. Cut short in his frenzy, the corporal staggered, his eyes suddenly empty. He didn't see my right coming and fell backwards. After a moment of stunned silence, cries of 'Get up' were heard, and spread through the base. In pride of place among his fellow officers, the commander was on the verge of eating his cap. Much to the joy of the sailors, the corporal braced himself against the floor of the ring and managed to get up. The bell stopped me from finishing him off.

Salvo slipped a stool under my backside and began to cool me down. The minute's break went on and on. There were people in the opposite corner and the referee was deliberately not disturbing them; he was letting the corporal recover. De Stefano was ostentatiously looking at his watch to remind the man in charge of the bell of his duty. The fight resumed when the corporal at last deigned to tear himself away from his seat.

Apart from his buffalo charge, which sent him flying into the ropes, the corporal was no firebrand. His right was weak and his left was just hot air. He'd realised he was out of his league and was trying to gain time by subjecting me to exhausting clinches. I knocked him out at the end of the fourth round.

As good losers, the officers invited us to the mess, where a banquet awaited us. The banquet had been intended for the victory of the local champion, which they had thought was a foregone conclusion, and the band that were supposed to have appeared that night left their instruments where they were and didn't turn up at all. It was a grim party.

De Stefano was on cloud nine. Our clash of egos was nothing more now than a distant bad memory. I resumed my training with ferocious determination and had two successful fights in the space of forty days, the first in Medioni, with an obscure celebrity, the second with Bébé Rose, a handsome guy from Sananas who collapsed in the third round from an attack of appendicitis.

In Rue Wagram, the local kids were starting to make me their hero; they would wait for me outside the gym to cheer me when I came out. The shopkeepers would raise their hands to their temples in greeting. I still hadn't had my picture in the newspaper, but in Medina Jedida, a legend was spreading through the alleyways, embellished as it passed from mouth to mouth until it verged on the supernatural.

## 3

Gino told me that a group of gypsies from Alicante were appearing in La Scalera and that he wouldn't miss them for the world. He lent me a light suit for the evening and we set off for Old Oran. The coopers were going back to their cellars and the street vendors were putting away their gear. Night had taken the city by surprise while the people on the street were still living their daytime lives. It was always like that in winter. The people of Oran were used to the long days of summer, and when these grew shorter without warning, they went a little crazy. Some automatically went home, others lingered in the watering holes for want of anything better to do, until night brought out its own, and the few shadowy figures who still dawdled here and there were suspicious.

We strode across the Derb and took a few short cuts to get to the Casbah. Gino was really excited.

'You'll see, it's a brilliant group, with the best flamenco dancers in the world.'

We climbed several stepped alleys. In this part of the city, there were no street lamps. Apart from the wailing of babies that could be heard every now and again, the quarter seemed dead. Then at last, at the end of the tunnel, a semblance of light: a lantern hanging as if crucified over the door of a stunted shack. We climbed more stepped alleys. From time to time, in the gaps between the houses, we glimpsed the lights of the harbour. A dog barked as we passed and was yelled at by its master. Further on, a blind accordionist tormented his instrument under an awning, standing there in his wretched state like a statue. Beside him, watching over his whores huddled in the shadows, a potbellied pimp, his loose-fitting jacket open to display his flick knife, was dancing a polka. Gradually, in places, life resumed. We came to a kind of disused barn where whole families had piled in to watch the gypsy show. The performance had begun. The group of musicians occupied a stage at the end of the room. A stunning beauty in a tight-fitting black and red dress, castanets on her fingers and her hair in a tight bun, hammered boldly on the floor with her heels. There were no free seats and the few benches in front of the stage were collapsing under the weight of the people on them. Gino and I sat down on a hump to see over people's heads and … What did I see, on a patch of beaten earth, aping the dancer? I had to rub my eyes several times to make sure I wasn't hallucinating. Yes, it was him, stamping his heels on the ground frenetically, moving his hips and buttocks in grotesque contortions, drunk but still lucid, his shirt open on his ebony torso and his tartan cap pulled down over his face … Sid Roho! Sid Roho in the flesh, still delightedly making a spectacle of himself! He couldn't believe his eyes when he saw me waving at him. We threw our arms round each other. The noise of our reunion made the spectators turn to look at us; they frowned and raised their fingers to their lips to silence us.

Sid Roho pulled me outside and we hugged each other again.

'What are you doing around here?' he asked.

'I live in Medina Jedida. And you?'

'I have a place in Jenane Jato. For the moment.'

'And how are you managing?'

'I'm always in two places at the same time; sometimes I'm in a mess, but I get by.'

'Do you like it in Jenane Jato?'

'Of course not! It's a dangerous place. A big-city version of Graba. Lots of fights and the occasional murder.'

He was speaking far too quickly. His words jostled in his mouth.

'It wasn't so bad when I arrived,' he continued, in a sharper tone. 'But ever since this ex-convict has been parading around with his gang of wild dogs, life's become hell. El Moro, he's called. With his scars, he's the ugliest bastard you've ever seen. Always making trouble. If you aren't happy, he kills you with his knife.'

Suddenly, he perked up.

'I've made a name for myself. Oh, yes! Your brother's no slouch. He has to leave his mark. He's the Blue Jinn ... What about you, what are you up to? You're looking good. Big and strong. Do you work in a butcher's?'

'I do a bit of everything. Do you still hear from Ramdane and Gomri?'

'I haven't heard from Ramdane at all. He went back to his douar and has not been seen since. As for Gomri, I left before you did. I have no idea where he is ... Do you remember his "fiancée"? He was the only one who thought she was pretty. A mouse hypnotised by a snake, was Gomri. If you'd stabbed him, he wouldn't have woken up. Maybe he married her after all.'

After a silence, we again embraced. Tall and gaunt-faced, Sid Roho was as thin as a skeleton, and his wine-reeking breath betrayed how far he'd fallen. Although he laughed heartily, there was no laughter in his eyes. He was like a stray animal exposed to the blows of everyday life. With no family and no points of reference, he trusted his instincts and nothing else, like those wild-eyed thugs who haunted the dark alleys.

I asked him if he had plans and what he wanted to do with his life. He laughed for a moment, then said that someone like him didn't have any more of a future than a sacrificial lamb and that, if he drifted from season to season, it was because he was a bit like a tree that loses its leaves in winter, only putting on its finery in the spring to play to the gallery instead of advancing in life.

'You dream you're a king,' he said, bitterly. 'In the morning, when you come back down to earth, the first thing you see shatters your crown to pieces. Your palace is nothing but a slum where the rats pass themselves off as fabulous animals. You ask yourself if it's worth getting up, because the only thing waiting for you outside is what was there yesterday, but you have no choice. You can't stay where you are. So you go out and lose yourself in all that crap.'

'You used to be thicker-skinned than that.'

'Maybe. As time goes on, the only person you can still deceive is yourself. The God who created me wasn't too sure about me. He stuffed me in a cupboard and I can't stand to be gathering dust any more.'

'You always landed on your feet, didn't you?'

'Yes, but I'm not a child any more. I've reached the age where you have to face facts, and the facts aren't good. I met a girl,' he said abruptly. 'A girl from Tlemcen, as blonde as a ray of sunshine. I was ready to settle down, I swear. Her name was Rachida. She said to her cousin, "Sid brings light into my life." Her cousin laughed and said, "And when you switch off the lights, how do you find that Negro of yours in the dark? Especially when he closes his eyes?" ... I decided never to see Rachida again.'

'You were wrong.'

'It's words that ruin everything, Turambo.'

'I thought you were stronger than that.'

'Only beasts of burden are strong. Because they don't know how to complain.'

He admitted that he expected nothing of the future, that the die was cast and that, if he pretended to enjoy himself as he had this evening, it was simply to make the best of a bad job.

'Chawala used to say, "Life is nothing at all; it's up to us to make something of it,"' I reminded him.

'Chawala was crazy; he didn't even have his own life.'

His tone was full of sadness and disappointment, and he punctuated his words with sharp gestures.

A drunkard we hadn't noticed in the darkness moved the tip of his nose into a beam of light and said to Sid in a thick voice, 'Excuse me, son. I haven't been eavesdropping, but I couldn't help hearing what you said. I feel sorry for you, with your stories, except that you have an ace up your sleeve: youth. Believe me, it's those who go through hell when they're young who get tougher as they grow old. When I was thirty, I was rolling in money. Today, at sixty, I'm wading through shit. Nothing can be taken for granted, and no misery is insurmountable. The good life is all bluster. You laugh as you lie to yourself, you take it easy as you sink, you don't give a damn about other people and you don't give a damn about yourself. But poverty, now that's serious. You take it on the chin and that keeps you alert. Whatever you say, nobody hears you. You learn to count on nobody but yourself.'

Sid Roho wasn't convinced. 'I've seen how the rich live,' he grumbled. 'From a distance, it's true, but I've seen them stuff their pockets and have a good time. Well, with all due respect, I'd give all of my youth for a single one of their nights.'

We sat for a long time on a flagstone, hopping from one subject to another. Behind us, the group of gypsies were bringing the house down. We heard cheers and applause, but something was stopping Sid and me from enjoying the celebration.

Some time later, Gino joined us. When I hadn't come back into the hall, he had imagined the worst. He was relieved to find me safe and sound. I introduced him to Sid. The three of us decided it was time to go home.

On the way, Sid teased a few whores before taking up the offer of a big woman with overflowing breasts. Naked under her green tulle, she merely had to flash her enormous behind for Sid to abandon us on the spot, but not before he and I had agreed to meet in the Haj Ammar café, at the entrance to the Arab market.

I saw Sid again the next day, and over the following few weeks. We spent our days wandering around different neighbourhoods or scouring flea markets. Sometimes, he would come with me to De Stefano's gym, although he'd always be gone by the time I finished my training. Nor did he come to my match with Sollet, whose trainer was forced to throw in the towel in the fifth round. De Stefano had invited quite a lot of people to celebrate my sixth victory in a row and Sid refused to join us, claiming that he had some urgent business to deal with. In reality, he didn't much like the fact that I was mixing with Roumis. He didn't dare reproach me openly and waited until he was drunk one night to tell me: A man who tries to sit between two chairs ends up with a crack up his arse. I had no idea he was referring to me.

At first, Sid gave the impression he hadn't changed a jot. He was funny, a bit scatterbrained, but engaging, even fascinating ... It didn't take me long to become disillusioned. Sid wasn't the same as before. Oran had made him even crazier. He reminded me less and less of the kid I had loved in Graba, the famous Billy Goat who laughed about everything, even his own disappointments, who knew just what to say to cheer me up when I was down and had a head start on all of us. That was ancient history. The new Sid was randy, wild-eyed and foul-mouthed. I wasn't sure if he'd matured or if he'd gone bad; either way, he worried me.

'Why did you start drinking?' I yelled at him one night as he staggered out of some shady dive, his shirt open.

'To have the courage to look at myself in the mirror,' he replied immediately. 'When my head's clear, I turn away quickly.'

I didn't agree with what he was becoming. I reminded him he was a Muslim and that a man had to remain sober if he didn't want to lose control.

Sid railed against me as he walked through an Arab neighbourhood, crying out, 'God would do better to take a look at all the lousy things that happen in this world instead of spying on a failure who drowns his sorrows in a glass.'

I had to put both hands over his mouth to muzzle him, because words like that were capable of starting a riot in our neighbourhoods. Sid bit me to break free and continued blaspheming at the top of his voice, while passers-by looked at him menacingly. I really thought we were going to be lynched on the spot.

I pushed him up against a wall and said, 'Find a job and get on the right path in life.'

'You think I haven't tried? The last time, I applied to a wholesaler. You know how that son of a bitch greeted me? Do you have the slightest idea how that fat, red-faced pig greeted me? He made the sign of the cross! He made the sign of the cross like an old woman who sees a black cat run across her path at night! Can you imagine, Turambo? Before I'd even come into his shop, he made the sign of the cross. And when I offered my services, he dismissed them with a wave of his hand and told me I was lucky not to have chains on my feet and a bone through my nose. Can you imagine? I told him I was the son of an imam and a child of my country. He laughed and said, "What does your black father know how to do apart from knocking up your mother and wiping the arses of his masters' dogs?" He added he had no maids to marry off and no dogs in his house. He was proud of his words. The find of the century! Where does he know my father from, eh? My father would have dropped dead on the spot if he'd heard that, he was so pious and had such respect for my mother. You see, Turambo? We aren't worth anything these days. They insult us and then they're surprised that we're hurt, as if we didn't have the right to an ounce of pride. Rather than put up with insults like that, I prefer to keep my distance. There's nothing for me, Turambo. Not on earth and not in heaven. So I take what belongs to other people.'

'Some of our people have succeeded. Doctors, lawyers, businessmen ...'

'Oh, my God, why don't you take off your blinkers, boy? Look at the masses begging around you. Your heroes aren't even allowed to be citizens. This is our country, the land of our ancestors, and we're treated like foreigners, like slaves from the savannahs. You can't even go to a beach without them sticking a notice in your face telling you Arabs aren't allowed. I saw a kaïd revered in his tribe called a lousy Arab by a mere white ticket seller. You have to think about these things, Turambo. The facts are there in front of you. You might try to disguise them, but the truth shines through ... I refuse to be nothing but suffering. An Arab doesn't work, he gets fucked up the arse, and I don't have an arse that's big enough. Since nobody's handing me anything on a plate, I grab a good time for myself where I can. Hunger and deprivation have instilled this philosophy in me: live life as it comes, and if it doesn't come, go looking for it!'

I had the feeling I was dealing with a pyromaniac.

Sid had chosen a path that wasn't mine. He scared me. One evening, he actually dressed up as a girl (he had put on a haïk) and slipped into a hammam to ogle the naked women. After getting his fill of that, he started running round the building, looking for a virgin to lay in the laundry room. It was pure madness. He could have been killed in a stairwell. In Medina Jedida, you could get yourself killed for even minor sins. But Sid Roho refused to calm down. The air of the city had gone to his head like a blast of opium, except that he never sobered up. He saw everything from the point of view of his 'exploits', thus putting the theft of a piece of fruit and the honour of races on the same level. His morbid self-confidence blinded him to the point where the closer he came to disaster, the more he clamoured for it. He drank where he shouldn't, which was an offence according to Muslim custom, stole in full view and full knowledge of everyone, and dared to go hunting for women in neighbourhoods where they didn't take kindly to strangers. He was bitter and suicidal, and was constantly putting himself in danger. I wondered if Rachida, her cousin and the wholesaler were merely excuses he'd made up, big stones he'd tied to his feet so as to sink as deep as possible and never come up again. He seemed comfortable in his descent into hell, as if he felt a wicked pleasure in taking revenge on himself and bringing about his own misfortune. Obviously, he had plenty of reasons to behave the way he did, but what is a reason if not, sometimes, a wrong that suits us?

Not wanting to be a witness to his eventual lynching, certain that sooner or later he'd fall into his own trap, I started declining his 'invitations' and saw him less often.

It didn't take him long to notice.

One morning, he waylaid me near the girls' school. I'd have bet anything that he wasn't there by chance.

'Well, well, Turambo!' he said, pretending to be surprised. 'I was just thinking about you.'

'I have an appointment with the boss of a warehouse. He's going to give me a trial. Gino is already there to introduce me.'

'Mind if I walk with you?'

'As long as you don't slow me down. I'm late.'

We hurried to Place de la Synagogue. Sid Roho was looking

at me out of the corner of his eye. My pace and my silence were bothering him.

Just outside a haberdasher's on Place Hoche, he stopped me with his hand. 'Are you upset with me about something, Turambo?'

'Why do you ask me that?'

'You've been doing your best to avoid me for weeks now.'

'You're imagining things,' I lied. 'I've been looking for work, that's all.'

'That's no reason. We're friends, aren't we?'

'You'll always be my friend, Sid. But I have a family and I'm ashamed to be sponging off them. I'm nearly twenty-two, don't you see?'

'I see.'

'I'm late.'

He nodded and took his hand off my shoulder.

Under the statue of the general, a blind man was playing a barrel organ. His music made my friend's distress seem somehow irreversible.

A little further on, again bothered by my silence, Sid said, 'I'm sure you're upset with me, Turambo. I want to know why.'

I looked him straight in the eye. He seemed disconcerted. 'You want the truth, Sid? You're really not with it these days.'

'I've always been like this.'

'Precisely. You don't seem to realise.'

'Realise what?'

'That it's time for you to settle down.'

'Why work when you can help yourself, Turambo? I have everything I need. I just have to reach out my hand.'

'Someone will cut it off in the end.'

'I'll get an artificial one.'

'I see you have an answer for everything.'

'You just have to ask.'

'My mother says that when we have an answer for everything, we might as well die.'

'My father said more or less the same thing, except that he died without finding an answer for anything.'

'Apparently, I'm wasting my breath. You won't listen. I really have to meet Gino now.'

'Gino, Gino ... What's so interesting about this Gino? The bastard isn't even funny, and he blushes when he accidentally looks at a whore's arse.'

'Gino's a good person.'

'That doesn't stop him being a bore.'

'Drop it, Sid. A friend doesn't have to act like an idiot to earn the right to be considered a friend.'

'You think that's why I'm acting like an idiot?'

'I didn't say that. Gino has helped me a lot. Friends like him are a rare commodity and I want to keep him.'

'Hey, I'm not setting you against him!'

'I don't doubt that for a second, Sid, not for a single second. Nobody could set me against Gino.'

He stopped dead.

I went on my way, without turning round. I was far from suspecting that this would be the last time I saw him.

I suddenly felt uneasy. In trying to reason with Sid, I had hurt him. I realised it as I walked away. I caught myself slowing down every ten metres, then stopping at the corner of the street. We shouldn't have parted on a sour note, I told myself. Sid had never refused me anything; he'd always been there for me.

I ran back to where we'd parted company ...

The Blue Jinn had vanished into thin air.

\*

I looked for Sid in Jenane Jato and Medina Jedida, in the bars where he was a regular, but without success.

After a week, I gave up. Sid Roho must have been playing the fool somewhere, in no way affected by what I'd said. He couldn't bear a grudge against anyone, let alone a friend. He'd show up eventually, and even if it wasn't what he would have wanted, I'd ask him to forgive me. He'd brush aside my apologies with a sweep of his hand and, still unrepentant, drag me with him on a thousand dreadful escapades.

But things didn't work out that way.

I learnt later that I wasn't the cause of his disappearance. Someone had challenged him and Sid had taken up the challenge. He had vowed to steal El Moro's dagger in broad daylight, right there in the middle of the souk. The former convict loved to strut around in public with his dagger under his belt, flaunting it like a trophy. And Sid dreamt of getting it off him.

He was caught with his hand on the hilt.

He was first beaten to within an inch of his life, then dragged behind a thicket and raped in turn by El Moro and three of his henchmen.

At that time, a man's honour was like a girl's virginity: once you lost it, you couldn't get it back.

Nobody ever saw Sid again.

## 4

We were in the cubicle, talking about my next fight, when Tobias opened the little door. He didn't have time to announce the visitors before they pushed him aside and came in. There were two of them, both dressed to the nines.

'Are you De Stefano?' the taller of the two asked.

De Stefano took his feet off the desk to look more businesslike. The visitors said nothing, but it was clear they weren't just anybody. The tall man must have been in his fifties. He was thin, with a face like a knife blade and cold eyes. The other, who was short, seemed on the verge of bursting out of his grand suit; he wore a huge signet ring on his finger and was puffing at an impressive cigar.

'What can I do for you?' De Stefano asked.

'Forget it,' grunted the man with the cigar. 'It's usually me being asked for help.'

'And you're Monsieur … ?'

'You can call me God if you want to. I fear that may not be enough to absolve you of your sins.'

'God is merciful.'

'Only the Muslim God.'

He looked us all up and down – Francis, De Stefano and me, Tobias having left – one after the other, in a silence like the lull before a storm. It was hard to know whom we were dealing with, gangsters or bankers. De Stefano couldn't keep still on his chair. He stood up slowly, eyes alert.

The man with the cigar abruptly took his hand from his pocket and held it out to De Stefano. Startled, De Stefano took a step back before realising that he didn't have a gun pointed at him.

'My name's Michel Bollocq.'

'And what do you do for a living, Monsieur Bollocq?'

'He calls the shots,' the thin man said, visibly annoyed that his companion's name meant nothing to us.

'That's quite something,' De Stefano said ironically.

'You're telling me,' Michel Bollocq said. 'I have an appointment and I'm in a hurry. Let's get down to business: I'm here to make a deal with you. I saw the last match and your boy made an excellent impression on me. I've never seen such a strong, quick left. A real torpedo.'

'Are you involved in boxing, Monsieur?'

'Among other things.' He gave me a sidelong look, chewed his cigar and came up to me. 'I see you're more interested in my clothes than my words, Turambo.'

'You look very smart, Monsieur.'

'Just the coat costs an arm and a leg, my boy. But you'll be able to afford one just like it one of these days. It all depends on you. You may even be able to afford several, in different colours, made to measure by the best tailor in Oran, or in Paris, if you prefer, although our suits are just as good … Would you prefer a tailor from Oran or Paris?'

'I don't know, Monsieur. I've never been to Paris.'

'Well, I can give you Paris on a silver platter, however big Paris is. And you could walk around in a coat and a suit like this, with a red flower in your buttonhole matching your silk tie, diamond-studded gold cufflinks, a hundred-gram signet ring on your finger, and snakeskin shoes so classy that any arse-licker would be happy to wipe his tongue on them.'

He went to the window and gazed out at the backyard, his hands behind his back, his cigar in his mouth.

The second visitor bent over De Stefano and said in such a way as to be heard by all of us, 'Monsieur Bollocq is the Duke.'

De Stefano turned pale. His Adam's apple bobbed up and down in his throat. 'I'm truly sorry, Monsieur,' he stammered, his voice barely audible, almost obsequious. 'I didn't mean to show you any disrespect.'

'That would have been very stupid,' the man said threateningly, without turning. 'Can I speak frankly? From what I've seen, things aren't exactly going well around here. Even a fugitive with a price on his head wouldn't want to hide out in this fucking circus. Your gym's on the skids, your safe's clearly full of cobwebs, and your ring leaves a lot to be desired.'

'We lack funds, Monsieur,' Francis cut in, 'but we have ambition by the barrel.'

'That certainly makes up for a lot of difficulties,' the man admitted, puffing his smoke out over the fly-blown window pane. 'I like fools who wade through shit while keeping their head in the clouds.'

'I don't doubt it, Monsieur,' De Stefano said, glaring at Francis.

'Shall we talk business now?'

'I'm all ears!' De Stefano almost cried out, pushing a chair of chrome tubing in the man's direction.

I'd heard of the Duke. It was the kind of name you didn't have to remember since he moved in high circles, in other words, in a world beyond the reality of people in our situation, but which, once you were aware of it, became imprinted on your subconscious, remaining lodged there in dormant form, so that the first time it was mentioned, the memory of it came flooding back. In boxing circles, people instinctively lowered their voices when the name came up in conversation. The Duke was a real bigwig; he had a stake in everything lucrative in Oran and aroused as much fear as admiration. Nobody was sure of the exact nature of his business, his stamping grounds, the people he rubbed shoulders with. For many people, the Duke was someone to be mentioned fleetingly in idle talk, like the prefect, the governor or the Pope, a kind of fictitious character who was the subject of rumours or news items and whom you were never likely to run into. Seeing him in the flesh had a strange effect on me. The top dogs you hear about are seldom like the image you have of them. When they come down off their clouds and land at your feet, they disappoint you a little. Stocky, with stooped shoulders and a paunch, the Duke reminded me of the Buddha I had glimpsed in a second-hand shop on Place Sébastopol. He had the same solemn, morose air. His round, shiny face formed flabby jowls at the sides before ending in a resolute chin that was almost out of place in that mass of fat. His hairy hands were like tarantulas waiting for their prey as they lay on the armrests, and the gleam in his eyes, barely perceptible above his excessively high cheekbones, went through you like darts from a blowpipe. In spite of all that, seeing him sitting in a worn armchair in our dilapidated cubbyhole in Rue Wagram, where respectable people seldom ventured, was a huge privilege for us. Our gym wasn't highly regarded. It hadn't produced any champions for ages, and lovers of boxing cold-shouldered it, calling it a 'factory for failures'. The fact that an important man like the Duke should honour it with his presence was a rehabilitation in itself.

The Duke puffed on his cigar and sent the smoke swirling up to the ceiling. His stern eyes came to rest on me. 'What exactly does Turambo mean? It isn't a local name. I've asked educated friends and nobody could explain it.'

'It's the name of my native village, Monsieur.'

'Never heard of it. Is it in Algeria?'

'Yes, Monsieur. Near Sidi Bel Abbès, on the Xaviers' hill. But it's vanished since. A rise in the water level swept it away seven or eight years ago.'

The other visitor, who hadn't moved from his place since he'd come in, pursed his lips and scratched his chin. 'I think I know where it is, Michel. I'm sure he means Arthur-Rimbaud, a village that was buried in a landslide at the beginning of the twenties near Tessala, not far from Sidi Bel Abbès. The press reported it at the time.'

The Duke looked at his cigar, turning it between his thumb and index finger, a grin at the corner of his mouth. 'Arthur-Rimbaud, Turambo. What an abbreviation! Now I understand why, when you're dealing with Arabs, you can never find the right address.' He turned to De Stefano. 'I saw your boy's last three fights When he knocked out Luc in the second round, I said Luc was getting old and it was time for him to hang up his gloves. Then your boy polished off Miccellino in one minute twenty. I couldn't figure that out at all. Miccellino's a tough customer. He'd won his last seven fights. Had he been caught unprepared? Maybe ... But I admit I was impressed. I wanted to be certain in my own mind, so I made sure I attended the match with the Stammerer. And again, your boy took my breath away. The Stammerer didn't last three rounds. That's quite something. True, he's thirty-three, he boozes and runs after whores, and he skips training sessions, but your boy made short work of him, and I was staggered. So my adviser Frédéric Pau here' – he gestured reverently to his companion – 'suggested I sponsor your boy, De Stefano. He's convinced he's a good investment.'

'He's right, Monsieur.'

'The problem is that I hate buying the wrong merchandise and I hate losing.'

'Quite rightly, Monsieur.'

'This is what I propose. I believe your champion's meeting Rojo in Perrégaux in three weeks' time. Rojo's young, strong and dedicated. He has his eye on the title of North African champion, which is no easy task. He's already seen off Dida, Bernard Holé, Félix and that bruiser Sidibba the Moroccan. I was on the verge of sponsoring him, but Turambo's really come on in the past few months and I told myself the next match will clinch it for me. If Turambo wins, he'll be my protégé. If not, it'll be Rojo. Have I made myself clear, De Stefano?'

'I'll be delighted to work for you, Monsieur.'

'Not so fast, my friend. The ring still has to decide.'

The Duke threw his cigar on the floor, stood up and left, with his adviser hard on his heels.

We were speechless for two whole minutes before De Stefano started mopping himself with a handkerchief.

'You know what you have to do,' he said to me. 'If the Duke takes us under his wing, nothing can harm us. The man is manna from heaven. When he bets on a cat, he turns it into a tiger. How would you like to dress like a nabob, Turambo?'

'It'd make a change. Right now, my clothes are falling apart.'

'Then go and kick the arse of that cocky Rojo.'

'Just watch me! Luck only smiles on you once, and I have no intention of letting it slip through my fingers.'

'That's the wisest resolution I've heard in my whole damned life,' he said, taking me in his arms.


Gino found me on a café terrace in Medina Jedida, a pot of mint tea on the table. He sat down next to me, poured himself three fingers of tea in my glass and casually lifted it to his lips. Opposite us, on the esplanade, Moroccan acrobats in shorts were performing amazing feats.

'Guess who came to see us today.'

'I have a bit of a headache,' he said wearily.

'The Duke.'

That woke him up. 'Wow!'

'Do you know him? They say he's rolling in it.'

'No doubt about that. He's so rich he hires people to shit for him.'

'He came and said that if I beat Rojo, he'll take me under his wing.'

'Then you have to win … But watch out, if he offers you a contract, don't sign anything if I'm not there. You're not educated and he might put a leash round your neck that even a dog wouldn't want.'

'I won't sign anything without you, I promise.'

'If things work out for you, I'll leave the printing works and take care of your affairs. You're starting to make a name for yourself. Would you like me to be your manager?'

'I'll hire you right now. We'll share everything fifty-fifty.'

'A normal salary would be fine … Let's say ten per cent.'

We shook hands to seal the deal and burst out laughing, amused by our own fantasies.

The Duke wanted to make sure we got to Perrégaux feeling fresh and on good form, so he sent a taxi to pick us up from Rue Wagram. The five of us bundled in, Francis and Salvo on the fold-up seats, Gino, De Stefano and I on the back seat. The driver was a tense little fellow, his cap pulled down as far as his ears, so tiny behind the wheel that we wondered if he could see the road. He drove slowly, in a stiff and sinister way, as if he was going to a funeral. Whenever Salvo tried to lighten the atmosphere by telling dirty jokes, the driver would turn to him with an icy look and ask him to show some restraint. Unsure if he was the Duke's official driver or an ordinary cabman, De Stefano didn't want to take any risks, but he didn't like the idea of this obscure celebrity teaching us good manners.

It was a fine May day. Summer had come early, and although it wasn't yet quite at its height, the hills were carpeted in yellow and the farms glittered in the sun. The luxuriant fields and orchards meant that the cows would be nice and fat this year. We took the road to Saint-Denis-du-Sig by way of Sidi Chami, much to the dismay of Francis, who couldn't understand why we had to make so many detours when the railway led straight there from Valmy. The driver told us this was the route decided on by the Duke himself ... It was nine in the morning. A horde of veiled women were climbing a goat path in the direction of a saint's tomb, their children limping along far behind in single file. I looked up at the tomb, which was at the top of a hillock, and made a solemn vow. I hadn't slept well in spite of my mother's herbal teas. My sleep had been disturbed by tortured dreams and heavy sweating; by the time I woke up, my head was burning hot.

Opposite me, Francis was excited, his eyes shining. Discreetly, he rubbed his thumb against his index finger and batted his eyelids to amuse me. All he thought about was money, but seeing him like that made me less anxious. Gino gazed out at the landscape, fists clenched. I was sure he was praying for me. As for De Stefano, he just kept staring at the back of the driver's furrowed neck as if trying to melt it with his eyes.

Perrégaux appeared after a bend in the road. It was a small town in the middle of a plain dotted with orchards. Here and there in the distance, patches of swamp shimmered like pearls. At the side of the road, amid the fig trees, Arab carters offered their harvest, while kids, their containers filled with snails, waited patiently for buyers. In a field, a thermal spring gurgled, shrouded in white steam. A fat colonist with a guard dog was watching a male donkey circle a female donkey on heat. I had the feeling I was seeing scenes from my native countryside.

The taxi slowed down at the entrance to the town, jolting over the railway track so cautiously that it almost stalled.

De Stefano looked at his watch; we were an hour late.

Frédéric Pau, the Duke's adviser, was waiting for us on the steps of the town hall. He took his watch from the pocket of his waistcoat and looked at it meaningfully when he recognised our taxi. He was angry and at the same time relieved that we'd arrived at last. The pavement was packed with cars all the way to the post office. The driver chose to park under the palm trees on Place de France, near the covered market. Curious people came to take a look at us. Someone cried, 'That's him, that's the boxer from Oran. Our Rojo will polish him off in no time at all.' Two policemen, sent by someone or other, held back the hordes of kids who had started to scream when we got out of the car.

'I was starting to get worried,' Frédéric Pau cried. 'Where did you get to, damn it? We've been waiting for you for more than an hour.'

'It's the driver's fault,' De Stefano said, gesturing with his thumb over his shoulder. 'Where did you get him from? An undertaker's?'

'It was the boss who insisted he get you here in one piece, but I think he overdid it. Now let's get a move on, they're getting impatient inside.'

The Duke was lounging in an armchair, facing the mayor's desk, his cigar clamped in the corner of his mouth. He was wearing a white linen suit, with a hat and moccasins of the same colour. He didn't stand to greet us and simply gestured with his arm at the man sitting behind the desk.

'Let me introduce Monsieur Tordjman, the patron saint of the town.'

185

'Let's not exaggerate, Michel,' the mayor said without moving from his seat. 'I'm just a humble servant of this place. Now how about some food?'

'Provided you give us a taster you can vouch for,' the Duke said, heaving himself up. 'I don't want any cook with bad intentions laying my champion low before the fight.'

'Our Rojo doesn't need that kind of help, Michel. He'll make short work of your little town mouse.'

'We'll see, Maklouf, we'll see.'

The mayor was offering a 'light meal' on a colonial estate; it was actually a mammoth feast. The banqueting table stretched for several metres, covered in white tablecloths and bristling with an assortment of trays and baskets of fruit. There were about forty guests sitting on either side, mostly colonists and civil servants as well as dignitaries from Sig; the mayor sat in the middle, opposite the Duke. There were no women anywhere to be seen, just men with thick moustaches and bulging bellies, their cheeks scarlet and their mouths dripping with gravy, who laughed at anything and greeted every remark of the mayor's as if it were the word of a prophet. Salvo dug in, sucking in his cheeks, his eyes darting greedily from dish to dish. Francis kept kicking him under the table, trying to restrain him, but he just grunted like an animal being disturbed and ate twice as much, completely unconcerned. As for De Stefano, he was sizing up Rojo, who was sitting next to the mayor. The local champion was eating calmly, heedless of the commotion around him. He was as tall and broad as an advertising hoarding, his face copper-coloured, his jaw square, his nose so flat you could have ironed a shirt on it. Not once did he look up at me. Cheers went up when servants in djellabas appeared with the *méchoui*, whole roast lambs served on large dishes strewn with lettuce leaves and onion slices. At that moment, Rojo raised his head; he gave me an enigmatic pout and took advantage of the scramble to leave discreetly.

The match took place in the open air, on a cleared area of the town's park. A cheerful crowd jostled around the ring. As I was getting ready to step up and join the referee, an Araberber in a gandoura whispered in my ear in a Kabyle accent: 'Show them we're not just shepherds.' Cheers rang out when Rojo stepped over the ropes. He greeted his fans simply and walked slowly to his corner. His robe was taken off. He braced himself against the ropes, did a few knee bends then straightened up, his muscles tense and his face inscrutable. The first three rounds were well balanced. Rojo hit straight and hard and took my punches with Olympian calm. He was correct and polite, a real gentleman, following the referee's instructions to the letter; conscious of his skill, he was managing the fight like the good technician he was. His feints and dodges delighted the crowd. De Stefano yelled at me to keep my distance, to avoid exposing myself to my opponent's sudden jabs. Every time I hit home, he would bang his fist on the floor of the ring hard enough to dislocate his wrist. 'Put him under pressure!' he would cry out. 'Keep your guard up! ... Don't cling to him! ... Watch his right! ... Back up, back up fast! ...' Rojo kept his composure. He had a plan and was trying to make me fall in with it, as if he knew me by heart – as soon as I prepared my 'torpedo', he would make sure he veered to the opposite side to throw me off balance. In the fourth round, as I trying to avoid being forced into a corner, he surprised me with his left. My gum shield shot out of my mouth and I saw the sky and earth merge. The floor of the ring fell away beneath me. De Stefano's voice reached me as if through a series of walls. 'Get up! ... On your feet! ...' Salvo's grimacing face looked like a carnival mask. I couldn't quite figure out what was happening. The referee was counting, his arm coming down like a machete. The yells of the crowd made me lose my bearings. I managed to grab hold of a rope and pull myself to my feet, my calves wobbling. The bell saved me ... 'What the hell got into you?' De Stefano cursed while Salvo rubbed my face and neck with a towel soaked in water. 'I told you to keep your distance. Don't let him get you in a corner. It isn't his right you should watch out for, it's his left. Work on the body. I don't think he likes it. As soon as he moves back, go in with all guns blazing ... He was starting to hesitate, damn it! He's yours for the taking ...' The fifth round was an ordeal for me. I hadn't recovered and Rojo didn't give me any respite. I sheltered behind my gloves and stoically withstood his onslaught; De Stefano was almost apoplectic. The minutes dragged on. The blows echoed inside me like explosions. I was choking, dehydrated and thirsty. Between two dodges, I looked for Gino in the crowd as if the smallest sign from him could save me; all I could see was the Duke's disapproving pout as the mayor teased him mercilessly. In the seventh round, exasperated by my stamina, Rojo started to lower his guard. His punches became less and less precise and his moves had lost their spring. I took advantage of a badly managed clinch to land a series of punches that catapulted him onto the ropes. Just as he charged, I hit him with my left cut on the tip of his chin. He slumped and collapsed on his stomach. Silence fell over the park. The referee started counting. 'Stay down!' someone yelled at Rojo. 'Get your strength back!' On the count of eight, Rojo stood up. His eyes were blurred and his guard was weak. He tried to retreat and lean on the ropes, but I pursued him with a shower of blows that took him aback. He'd had enough of dodging; he punched in the air and clung to me, literally thrown off balance. By the time the bell came to his rescue, the champion of Perrégaux didn't even know where his corner was. De Stefano was jubilant; he was yelling things in my ear, but I couldn't understand a word he was saying. I had my eyes fixed on my opponent. He was at the end of his tether and so was I. I had to find a flaw in his apparatus, a fatal flaw. I was shaken, exhausted, certain I couldn't hold out much longer. Rojo handled the next two rounds bravely. I was leading on points; he knew it and was trying to catch up. In the eleventh round, just as my strength was about to give out, my left hook set off from deep inside me, drawing on the last ounce of its effectiveness, and split the air. I thought I could hear the bones in Rojo's neck crack. My fist smashed into his temple with such power that I felt a terrible pain explode in my wrist; its shock wave went through my arm and inflamed my shoulder. Rojo whirled around and fell, throwing dust up from the floor. He didn't get up. De Stefano, Salvo, Francis and Gino climbed into the ring and threw themselves on me, mad with joy. I had the vague feeling I was weightless.

The Duke came to see us in the changing rooms as we were packing up our things. He shook my hand without taking his cigar out of his mouth.

'Congratulations, son. It was hard, but you held out.'

'Thank you, Monsieur. It's the first time I've fought a real champion.'

'Yes, I like his technique a lot.' This was said to the whole team. 'To be quite honest with you, I'd have preferred Rojo to win. He's a great artist.' There was regret in his voice.

De Stefano scratched his head under his straw boater, puzzled by the Duke's attitude. 'Turambo didn't let you down, Monsieur.'

'I didn't say that. He was perfect.'

'But you don't seem pleased, Monsieur.'

The Duke threw his cigar to the floor and crushed it with the tip of his shoe. 'I still have to think about it. Turambo can take the blows, but Rojo's more agile, more elegant and more technical.'

De Stefano grabbed his handkerchief and mopped his face. His

Adam's apple stuck in his throat and he had to swallow several times to dislodge it. 'What is there to think about, Monsieur?'

'Let's just say your boy didn't convince me.'

'But, Monsieur,' Francis said in a panic, 'Turambo's only just starting out. At this stage of his career, Rojo was spending most of his fights clinging to his opponents like an octopus.'

'I said I'll think about it,' the Duke said resolutely. 'I'm the one who's going to invest heavily, not you. This is my money we're talking about, and money doesn't grow on trees. I want my own champion and I'm prepared to spare no expense to have him. But I need guarantees. Turambo didn't give them to me today, not all of them. I found him less good than before. He was variable and lacked determination.'

That wasn't how De Stefano saw things. He felt betrayed. His flushed face looked as if it was about to fall apart. He took his courage in both hands and dared stand up to the Duke. 'Turambo won, didn't he? That was your condition, Monsieur. Rojo has had sixteen professional fights and this was the first time he was knocked out.'

De Stefano could use all the arguments in the world, the Duke wouldn't budge. He motioned to Frédéric Pau to follow him and left us standing there in the changing room.

We weren't allowed a taxi on the way back.

We returned to Oran by bus, surrounded by rough peasants, baskets filled with cackling poultry and bundles smelling of manure.

## 5

De Stefano had cherished a lot of dreams since the Duke had dangled the prospect of financial help in front of him. He thought he might renovate the gym, install a new ring, along with punch bags and all the other paraphernalia that went with it, recruit potential champions and relaunch his career. It was too good to be true, but he had to believe in it after so many pious wishes. For years now he'd been asking luck for a helping hand, without ever giving up. Did he have any choice? The gym was his whole life; he'd fallen into it before he'd learnt to stand. He'd known highs and lows, gone from the peaks to the gutter, and not once had he considered throwing in the towel. For him, there was nothing after boxing, no income, no relaxation, just a total blank. With the Duke as his sponsor, he was sure he could force the hand of fate. Already, in boxing circles, people had started to be jealous of him. He himself had no qualms about telling everyone that the Duke had come to see him to discuss business and lay the groundwork for a fame that would mark entire generations. At night, in the bars, he would gather around his table a cluster of friends and make their heads spin with his staggering plans. To prove to them it wasn't just wishful thinking, he'd buy rounds; his slate looked like a complicated maths puzzle, but the barman didn't need to be asked twice, convinced as he was that the gym in Rue Wagram was getting a new lease of life.

Every day for a week after we got back from Perrégaux, De Stefano would go through the press, hoping to come across an article praising my victory over Rojo, one that might make the Duke see reason. But neither *L'Écho d'Oran* nor the evening paper *Le Petit Oranais* said anything about my fight. Not even a short item. De Stefano was outraged. It was as if the gods were conspiring against him.

I didn't really grasp what was at stake. I'd go so far as to say that De Stefano's dismay didn't affect me. I knew that the Roumis had a strange mentality, that they complicated their lives because they didn't really believe that 'everything is written'. As far as I was concerned, things obeyed imperatives that were outside my control; I just had to make the best of it. To rebel against fate, far from averting it, might bring even greater misfortunes down on your head, pursuing you even to your grave ... I trained morning and evening, with growing flair, certain that fortune was smiling on me and that my salvation was at the end of my gloves. The press might have ignored me, but the Arab bush telegraph was buzzing to its heart's content, spicing up my matches and building statues to me on every street corner. In Medina Jedida, not a single café owner would allow me to pay for what I consumed. The children cheered me and old men stopped telling their prayer beads when I passed and called down blessings on my head.

I invited Gino to dinner at my mother's. My latest victories having brought me a small fortune, I wanted to celebrate that with the family. Mekki joined us reluctantly. He didn't like the fact that I'd become a boxer, but he didn't hold it against me too much. I wasn't a child any more.

My mother made us a wonderful dinner of *chorba* with chickpeas, roast chicken stuffed with Jerusalem artichokes, grilled liver kebabs, seasonal fruits and two large bottles of Hamoud Boualem pop bought from an Algiers grocer.

Before we sat down to eat, I begged her not to rekindle Gino's grief. My mother had a tendency to lament the dead woman every time he came to share our meals, which rather spoilt our get-togethers. My mother gave a maraboutic sign and promised to avoid painful subjects. She kept her word. At the end of the meal, as she was getting ready to clear the table so that she could serve tea, I took a box wrapped in a kaftan from my bag and gave it to her.

'What is it?' she asked.

'Open it and see.'

She took the gift cautiously and undid the ribbons. Her eyes opened wide at the sight of the solid gold *kholkhal* in its casket.

'It's not as beautiful as yours, but it's heavy. I looked in all the Arab jewellers' and it was the best one I could find.'

My mother was stunned. 'It must have cost you an arm and a leg,' she panted.

In his turn, Mekki stood up, went to his room and came back with a cloth tightly wrapped with string, knelt in front of my mother and undid it. On the table, he placed the *kholkhal* with the lions' heads.

'I didn't dare sell it or pawn it,' he said. 'I kept it for you because it's yours. I wouldn't have let another person have it for anything in the world.'

Moved, shaking all over, my mother put her arms around him, then around me. She kissed me. I felt her heart beating against my chest and her tears sliding down my neck. Embarrassed by Gino's presence, she hid her face with her scarf and ran to take refuge in the kitchen.

I walked Gino home. It was a magnificent night, fragrant with amber and mint. The sky glittered with millions of constellations. A group of young men were laughing their heads off under a street lamp. We walked in silence to Boulevard Mascara. An empty tram passed us. I felt light, fresh; an honest joy filled my lungs. I was proud of myself.

'I'm sleeping at my mother's tonight,' I said to Gino when we got to his door. 'I'll just go up and drop my bag.'

Gino put on the stair light and went up ahead of me.

When he reached his mother's room, transformed into a living room, he gave a start. On the chest of drawers stood a brand-new horn gramophone and a pile of records in their sleeves.

'It's my gift to you,' I said.

'You shouldn't have,' he said with a lump in his throat.

'Do you like it?'

'Of course I do!'

'And I got you all the Jewish-Andalusian music I could find. This way, you won't have to venture out into dangerous areas at ridiculous hours.'

Gino looked through the pile of records. 'Where did you buy these?'

'In a very smart shop in the centre of town.'

Gino burst out laughing. 'Well, smart or not, they took you for a ride. These are all military band records.'

'No!' I said in astonishment.

'They definitely are. Look, it's even written on the sleeves.'

'The crook! How did he know I couldn't read? I was all dressed up like a matinee idol, with brilliantine in my hair. I swear I insisted on records of Jewish-Andalusian music. I told him it was for someone who loves that kind of thing ... The bastard! Plus, they cost me a fortune. I'm going to have a word with him tomorrow morning.'

Touched by my disappointment, Gino let out another boyish laugh. 'Come on, it's not that bad. Now I won't need to go to the bandstand to hear this kind of music, that's all.' He gave me a big hug. 'Thank you from the bottom of my heart.'

Two weeks later, De Stefano stopped me in the doorway of the gym. His face was radiant with a joy he couldn't contain. The Duke had *thought it over*! 'It's in the bag,' Francis said, rubbing his hands. Frédéric Pau was perched on the edge of the ring, his legs crossed, his thumbs in his braces, smiling from ear to ear. 'Put it there, son,' he said, holding out his hand. 'From now on, we're partners.' He told me that his boss was inviting De Stefano and me to his house to seal the deal. I told him I wouldn't sign anything without Gino, much to the dismay of Francis, whose face immediately darkened. Frédéric told me we hadn't got to that point yet, that this was just a friendly meeting. In the afternoon, a gleaming car pulled up outside the haberdasher's on Boulevard Mascara. Gino and I were on the balcony, sipping orangeade. Filippi got out of the car in a tight-fitting bellboy's tunic, a cap jammed on his head. He stood to attention and gave us a military salute.

'Did Bébert fire you from his garage?' Gino shouted down to him.

'No.'

'Then what are you doing in that uniform? You look like a soldier in his Sunday best.'

'I'm a chauffeur. The Duke was looking for a driver. De Stefano told him about me, and the Duke hired me immediately. He has a good business head, the Duke. For the price of one employee, he's got himself a chauffeur and a mechanic ... I have something for Turambo.'

'Come up, it's open.'

Filippi carefully took a package from the back seat and joined us upstairs. There were two suits in their wrapping, one black and the other white, two shirts and two ties.

'They're from the boss,' he said. 'He wants to see you looking handsome tonight. Go to the hammam and get yourself cleaned up. I'll pick you up at seven thirty. Make sure you're ready; the Duke's a stickler for punctuality.'

Filippi came back at sunset. I'd had my bath and put on the black suit, and Gino had helped me knot my tie. I stood in front of the wardrobe mirror, combed, scented ... and barefoot. I didn't have any suitable shoes. Filippi offered me his own shoes, not the ones he was wearing, but the ones he had at home, in Delmonte. It was on our way. We made a detour to pick up De Stefano and, at eight on the dot, we were at the Duke's door.

The Duke lived in a big villa in the south of Saint-Eugène, or to be more accurate a magnificent manor house surrounded by a huge, luxuriant garden. An Arab guard opened the gate, which had a gold thistle on it. We had to go a good thirty metres along a gravel drive lined on either side with hydrangeas and small bushes pruned into cubes before we reached the canopied front steps of the house.

Frédéric Pau was waiting for us on the top step in a charcoal-grey frock coat that made him look like a heron. He adjusted De Stefano's tie, asked him to take off his straw boater, then looked me over and adjusted a few things, a crease in my jacket, a hair out of place.

Members of polite society were chatting in a big, high-ceilinged room, beneath a massive chandelier. There were elegant ladies with elbow-length gloves, accompanied by distinguished-looking gentlemen with outlandish moustaches. When he saw me, the Duke opened his arms wide and cried, 'Ah, there's our hero!' He didn't embrace me, or even hold out his hand; he merely introduced me briefly to his guests, who looked me up and down, some with interest, others with curiosity, before turning away from me and returning to the sophisticated hubbub. They were all of a certain age, women and men, probably married couples, reeking of successful business and high positions. De Stefano whispered in my ear that the fat man with the swollen nose was the mayor and the skinny gentleman with the greying temples was the prefect. Out on the veranda, a Parisian dignitary in a tailcoat and top hat was pretending to take the air in order to distance himself from the locals and enhance his metropolitan aura.

A servant passed between the guests with a tray of glasses. De Stefano eagerly accepted a glass of champagne; I didn't take anything, intimidated by the luxury around me, the ladies' sophisticated clothes, their companions' regal disdain.

A neat, bouncy young girl approached me, hands twisted behind her back, her face red with embarrassment and curiosity.

She was cute, with her blonde plaits and her big blue eyes.

'I'm Louise, Monsieur Bollocq's daughter.'

I didn't know what to say in reply. In the distance, De Stefano winked at me, which annoyed me for some reason.

'Papa's convinced you're going to be world champion.'

'The world's a big place.'

'When Papa says something, it always happens.'

'...'

'I love boxing. Papa won't take me to see matches, so I listen to them on the radio. Georges Carpentier's fights are amazing. But I won't cheer him on the way I used to now that Papa has his own champion ...'

Shyly she went up on tiptoe. Her tongue moved back and forth over her thin lips.

'How can you take the blows round after round? The announcer almost fainted when he described the flurry of blows you exchanged in the ring.'

'You train a lot to keep going.'

'And does it hurt when you box?'

'Not as much as a toothache.'

A refined lady came along and cut short our conversation. She must have been in her forties and was very grand and aggressive. Barely glancing at me, she seized the girl by the arm and led her away from me.

'Louise, my dear, you should leave this young man alone. We'll be sitting down to eat soon.'

She was Madame Bollocq.

Louise turned several times and gave me a sad smile before disappearing among the guests.

At the table, the Duke delivered a solemn speech in which he promised that Oran would soon have its North African champion – me, of course. This fine city deserved to have idols it could flaunt in the faces of those snobs in Algiers, and it was imperative that we all work together, politicians, businessmen and sponsors, to restore the lustre of the most emancipated city in Algeria. He spent a long while boasting of my potential and my achievements, insisted on the need to stay with me until I reached the top, and warmly thanked the mayor, the prefect and the other dignitaries who had agreed to join him and make this evening the beginning of a new era crowned with trophies, sensational titles and outstanding sportsmen. At the end of his speech, he raised his glass to all those who, in a large or small way, out of self-interest or loyalty, with their money or simply with their hearts, were contributing to the rise of the wonderful city of the two lions.

All through the dinner, while the ladies and gentlemen stuffed their faces and laughed at the Duke's anecdotes – he was on truly entertaining form – Louise kept looking at me and sending me friendly signs from the end of the banqueting table.

*

Gino came to my room, curious as to why I hadn't switched the light off, or why I was lying fully clothed on my bed, staring up at the ceiling. He sat down on a chair next to me, lit a cigarette and blew the smoke in my direction.

'What's wrong?'

'Do I look like something's wrong?'

'No, but you're up to something. Your silence worries me, and your insomnia too. Have you signed something behind my back?'

'I've already agreed with De Stefano. It's you, and you alone, who'll handle my business affairs.'

'So why aren't you asleep? You have two training sessions tomorrow and your next fight's in three weeks.'

I was silent for a while before confessing, 'I think I'm in love.'

'So soon?'

'I guess you'd call it love at first sight.'

'Is it serious?'

'Yes, seeing that I can't sleep.'

'And who's the lucky girl?'

'Her name's Louise. She's the Duke's daughter. The problem is that she's only fourteen or fifteen.'

'Are you sure that's the only problem?'

'I'm a man now. I need a wife and children.'

'Stop putting a spoke in your own wheels. You really don't need to complicate your life with all that. You're too young to have a noose round your neck. Get that idea out of your head, and fast. A champion needs a good punch bag and his freedom. And anyway, the Duke would give you a beating if he found out you had a crush on his daughter.'

'What do you know anyway?'

The next day, halfway to the gym, I turned round and hopped on the first tram that came along. In a florist's in Saint-Eugène, I bought a pretty bunch of pink peonies and found myself ringing at the Bollocqs' gate. The Arab asked me what I wanted. I showed him my flowers. He asked me to follow him to the front steps of the manor and await Madame's instructions. Madame Bollocq didn't seem pleased to see me. I told her I'd brought a gift for her daughter. She told me that was kind of me, but that there was no need, and asked the guard to walk me back to the gate. I didn't have a chance to catch a glimpse of Louise.

Towards midday, Frédéric Pau informed me that the Duke wanted to talk to me. Immediately. I got down from the ring and went to change. Frédéric was waiting impatiently in the car. He drove me straight to the Duke's office, which was on the seafront.

The Duke dismissed his adviser and closed the door behind him. We were alone in a big room adorned with old paintings and figurines.

'It seems you came to the house,' he said, taking a big cigar from a gold case on a chest of drawers.

'That's right, Monsieur. I was in the area and I thought —'

'I have an office, Turambo,' he cut in, putting the cigar down and glaring at me.

'I wanted to give Louise flowers.'

'She has a whole garden full of them or didn't you notice?'

I'd been expecting to sign papers or talk about matches, and the Duke's remark threw me. I had no idea where he was going with this, but it was clear he blamed me for something.

With his finger, he motioned to me to follow him. We crossed his wood-panelled office and went out onto the balcony, which overlooked an inner courtyard in the middle of which stood a huge plane tree. The Duke leant on the wrought-iron balustrade, sniffed the air, moved his face into the sun's rays then, without turning to me, pointed to the tree.

'You see that tree, Turambo? It was here long before my great-grandmother. Probably before the first civilised people even settled in this barbaric country. It's survived invasions and a whole lot of battles. Often, when I look at it, I wonder how many love affairs started beneath it, how many confidences were exchanged in its shade, how many plots were hatched under its branches. It's seen generations pass and yet there it is, imperturbable, almost taciturn, as if nothing had ever happened … Do you know why it's survived the centuries and why it'll survive us? Because it's stayed stubbornly in its place. It's never going to trample on the roots of other trees. And it's right. The reason it's fine where it is, relaxed, well-behaved, is so that no other tree can come and overshadow it.'

'I don't understand, Monsieur.'

'You should know this, young man. To me, you're just an investment. You're not a member of my family, you're not a friend. You're a racehorse on which I've bet a lot of money. I may indulge you and spoil you, but that has nothing to do with affection: it's so that you don't disappoint me or short-change me. But whatever the satisfaction you give me, you'll always be the little Arab from the souk who'd do better not to take for granted the favours people do for him. Do you follow me?'

'Not really, Monsieur.'

'I thought as much. I'm going to try and be clearer.' He tapped on the balustrade with his finger. 'I don't want you to ring my doorbell without being invited, and I forbid you to go anywhere near my daughter. We aren't of the same class, let alone the same race. So stay in your place, like that tree, and nobody will step on you … Have I made myself understood, Turambo?'

My hands had left damp patches on the edge of the balustrade. The sun was burning my eyes. A cold shower would have been less of a shock.

'I have to go and train, Monsieur,' I heard myself stammer.

'An excellent idea.'

I wiped my moist hands on the front of my trousers and walked back to the main door.

'Turambo!' he called.

I stopped in the middle of the room, without turning round.

'In life, as in boxing,' he said, 'there are rules.'

I nodded and went on my way.

That day, I let myself go on the punch bag until my arms were almost pushed back into their sockets.

## 6

'The Duke would give you the moon if you asked him,' Frédéric Pau said to me, 'but you can't even swat a fly without his permission. He's strict with everyone. He and I have known each other since we were barefoot boys in the gutter. We stole fruit from the same orchard and bathed in the same trough. And yet I'm at his beck and call. Because he's the boss ... I acknowledge he's been hard on you. He admits it himself. But don't make a big deal of it. He just wanted you to know that there are lines that mustn't be crossed. I assure you he has an enormous amount of esteem for you. He wants to make you a legend. He'll get you to the top, I guarantee it. Only, he insists on certain principles, do you follow me? Otherwise, how can he get people to respect him?'

It was after midnight. Gino and I had been sleeping when there was a knock at the door. Going down to open up, I'd been surprised to see Frédéric Pau standing in the street, puffing on a cigarette. He'd apologised for disturbing us. It was obvious he wasn't there by chance. The way he was smoking betrayed a nervousness I'd never seen in him before. I'd stood aside to let him come up. It occurred to me the Duke might have fired him; I was wrong. Monsieur Pau had come to lecture me ...

Gino joined us in his pants in the living room, which was dimly lit by an old oil lamp because of an electricity blackout. As soon as he was seated, Monsieur Pau got straight to the point. He'd been given the task of clearing up that afternoon's misunderstanding, following the words the Duke had said to me in his office. Gino, still half asleep, couldn't follow much of the discussion. His eyes darted from my tense mouth to Frédéric Pau's conciliatory hands, trying in vain to grasp what it was all about. I hadn't told him about the incident in question. The Duke had wounded me deeply and I had preferred to save my resentment for Sigli, my next opponent, an arrogant fellow who was constantly shouting from the rooftops that he would polish me off in the first round. So I was furious with Pau. He was revealing everything without realising the embarrassing situation he was putting me in. However many pained looks I gave him, in the hope of making him aware of his indiscretion, he just kept on talking.

A sound reached us from the end of the corridor. Much to my relief, Pau at last fell silent. He asked Gino what the noise meant. Gino reassured him it wasn't a poltergeist but might have been a rat overturning something in the kitchen.

I took advantage of this unexpected interruption to divert the conversation. 'When are we going to sign the contract, Monsieur Pau?'

'What contract?'

'What do you mean, what contract? I work for your boss now, don't I?'

'The Duke never said anything about a contract.'

'Well, it's time we sat down round a table and clarified things. In three weeks, I'm meeting Sigli. I'm not getting in that ring without first sorting out the details of my career. The Duke wants me to follow the rules. Let him do the same. And please note, it isn't Francis who manages my affairs now, but Gino here. From today, you'll have to negotiate with him.'

'All right. I'll see what I can do.'

'And now, go home, Monsieur. Tomorrow, very early, De

Stefano is picking me up to go to Kristel.'

Pau took his hat off the table. His hand was shaking. 'What should I tell the Duke?'

'About what?'

'About what happened in his office this afternoon.'

'Nothing happened in his office this afternoon.'

Pau was confused. He didn't know how to interpret my attitude. I pushed him gently outside, making sure he didn't trip on the dark staircase, and slammed the door behind him.

'What was all that about?' Gino asked.

'All what?' I said, going back to my room.

The next day, when I got back from Kristel, Gino told me that Filippi had come to fetch him and take him to see the Duke and that, although he hadn't signed any papers, the situation was looking better than he'd hoped. He informed me that Monsieur Pau would be coming round that evening to bury the 'misunderstanding' once and for all and that, in order to do that, I needed to have a good bath and put on my formal suit.

'Will you come with me?'

'Not this time. The situation has changed. From now on, whenever you're invited, you're not expected to bring your tribe with you. You just do what you're told, full stop. But don't worry, I'm looking after your interests whether I'm there or not.'

That evening, the car driven by Filippi pulled up outside the haberdasher's. Frédéric Pau opened the door for me in person. From the balcony, Gino gave me a little wave and mouthed something I read as *Have fun*.

The seafront was swarming with people in loose shirts, and the ice-cream parlours overflowed with holidaymakers. Ladies were strolling on the esplanade, their hair blowing in the wind. Leaning on the railing overlooking the harbour, young people were gazing at the setting sun, its fire in marked contrast to the silhouette of Murdjadjo. From the top of the mountain, Santa Cruz watched over the city, hands joined and wings outstretched. In Oran, summer was a party, and the neon signs were conjuring tricks.

The car turned off from the bustle of the streets and glided slowly into the thick silence of the countryside. A strip of asphalt climbed to the heights of the Cueva del Agua. On this side of the city, you turned your back on the wonders of nature. Now wasn't the time for contemplation. Poverty was born out of misfortune, and both were accepted as a given, like a curse handed down as punishment for an unknown crime. Huts of hessian flapped in the dust-laden breeze. On a mound of rubbish, ragged children, watched by a sad, rheumy-eyed old dog, were learning to overcome their sorrows ... Further on, a sign announced the entrance to the village of Canastel. Filippi turned onto a track and plunged into a thicket filled with the sound of cicadas. We passed little cabins hidden behind reed trellises, crossed a deserted clearing, and finally came to the gate of a comfortable-looking residence perched on a belvedere overlooking the sea.

Filippi parked in a little courtyard and rushed to open the door for Monsieur Pau. Pau waited for me to get out first before getting out himself.

'Where are we?' I asked him.

'Somewhere between heaven and hell.'

I looked up at the big house with its tiled roof. Tall windows with austere curtains cast their subdued light on the surrounding area. Pau motioned to me to climb the three front steps.

'Isn't Filippi coming with us?' I said, a little disorientated.

'Filippi's a chauffeur. He's fine where he is.'

An Arab dressed like an Abbasid eunuch – turban pinned at

the front, a shimmering kameez above a baggy *sirwal*, horned slippers and a broad sash around his waist – bowed when he saw Pau on the steps.

'Larbi, tell Madame Camélia that Monsieur Pau is here.'

'Right away, *sidi*,' the man whispered before disappearing down a hidden passageway.

The main room, which had a faint odour of perfume and tobacco, was twice as large as that of the Bollocq house. At the time, I couldn't have put a name to the gargantuan furniture in it. The walls, hung with cold materials, were adorned with dark frescoes, paintings of naked odalisques, sophisticated lamps, bevelled mirrors and hunting trophies. On potbellied chests, bronze statuettes rubbed shoulders with porcelain figurines and hieratic candelabra. Opposite the cloakroom, presided over by a pale-faced old lady, was a wood-panelled counter, blood red in colour, above a silver cabinet filled with crystal objects. A smartly dressed young man in a bow tie was working the lever of a chrome-plated machine with all his might. He greeted us with a slight nod before being hailed by a client who seemed about to fall into a drunken coma. Couples kissed on sofas in alcoves covered in Florentine mosaics, not at all disturbed by prying eyes. Their casualness shocked me more than the brazenness of their embraces. I had thought that kind of shameless display only happened in shady bars where whores fleeced sailors and fights were always breaking out; seeing it in these hushed, opulent surroundings, practised with the most disgusting audacity by men in white collars and dance-hall starlets, was a great surprise to me. I had thought that distinguished people cared about appearances ...

A red-carpeted marble staircase led to the upper floor, where an old harridan with exposed breasts sat on guard duty, smoking a cigarette in a long holder. She watched over an assortment of young girls in suspenders, with arched backs and plump buttocks, perched on high stools at the counter, glasses in their hands. All around, on padded and brocaded banquettes, other slightly drunk women chatted with smartly dressed gentlemen, some of them sitting on their knees, others letting themselves be boldly groped.

'Come, let me introduce you to a future champion of the world,' Frédéric Pau said, bringing me back down to earth. He led me to the far end of the room where a tall black man in a three-piece suit was lounging on a sofa, with two barely pubescent girls all over him. The man was a force of nature. He was drinking a glass of brandy, knees crossed, crushing one of the girls, a blonde, with his free arm, while she writhed with pleasure. Both girls were carefully made up and wore satin lingerie through which their firm breasts and frilly knickers could be seen. They seemed captivated by the man.

'Is it true you hit Jacquot?' asked the other girl, a brunette with short hair, eyes half hidden by her curly fringe.

'It was a misunderstanding,' the man grunted in a lazy voice.

'I saw him at the casino,' the brunette went on, 'and didn't recognise him. What did you hit him with? His nose was completely flattened. The poor man's profile was ruined.'

'I'd rather not talk about it.'

'Please tell us why you hit him,' the blonde said excitedly, cuddling up closer to the man.

The tall black man put his glass down on a table in front of him, buried the blonde beneath his armpit and let his other hand run over the brunette's thighs. 'I was training hard when Jacquot said to Gustave, "What a stud, your boy." So I punched him in the face.'

'But that's not an insult,' the blonde cried, 'in fact it's a compliment. It means you're in great shape.'

'Yeah,' the black man sighed, 'except I'd never heard the expression before. Gustave explained it to me later. I told him Jacquot could have found another way to flatter me ...'

The two girls fell silent when they saw us standing over them. Intrigued by his companions' sudden silence, the tall man turned his head, frowning.

He drew his lips back displaying a row of gold teeth. 'Are you listening at doors now, Frédo?'

'Not at all,' Frédéric Pau reassured him. 'I wanted to introduce our new champion.'

The black man looked me up and down.

I held out my hand; he looked at it scornfully.

'I haven't got my white gloves on, boy,' he grunted rudely.

'I have a feeling we've met before,' I said.

'In your dreams, kid,' he said, turning his back on me.

Frédéric took me by the arm and dragged me away.

'Who is that brute?'

'His name's Mouss,' he said in a low voice. 'He's a heavyweight. It's hardly surprising you thought you knew him. You'll have seen his posters on walls and his picture in the papers.'

'Did you see how he treated us?'

'He has a bad attitude. He's very full of himself. One day, someone asked him, "Who are you?" He replied, "I'm Me." "Don't you have a name?" And Mouss replied, "I don't need one because I'm unique." See what I mean? I thought he'd be delighted to make the acquaintance of a promising colleague from his own community. I was wrong. But we shouldn't let that stupid megalomaniac spoil our evening.'

A woman looking like a priestess, an artificial beauty spot on her cheek and her blue eyes adorned with false eyelashes, came towards us. With her hair swept back into a large bun and her haughty bearing, she carried her sixty years as if carrying a sceptre. She was beautiful, with an indefinable but impressive charm, but her hardness and arrogance immediately intimidated me.

'How wonderful to see you again, Monsieur Pau,' she said, wearily dismissing the servant scurrying behind her.

'No happiness is complete if it isn't shared, my dear Camélia.'

She briefly glanced at me with a regal eye. 'Is this the young man Monsieur Bollocq told me about this morning?'

'That's right.'

In a hurry to get rid of me, she sent a coded sign to the old harridan sitting upstairs and told me to go up and join her. As I hesitated, not understanding what was expected of me, Frédéric Pau said encouragingly, 'What are you waiting for? Go on.'

The woman passed her gloved hand under my companion's arm and drew him over to the bar. 'Let's have a drink, dear Frédéric. People as polite as you are becoming increasingly rare around here. Tell me, how's your lovely wife? Still a slave driver?'

They abandoned me on the spot.

I climbed the stairs unsteadily. I had an unpleasant feeling in my stomach. The harridan, clearly some kind of maid, stubbed out her cigarette in an ashtray and seized a fan, which she waved over her garishly made-up face, her blouse open on the bulges of her belly, her navel as big as the barrel of a musket. She led me down a maze-like corridor with a polished floor. On either side there were doors. Through them, bursts of laughter, noises of lovemaking and orgasmic moans could be heard. My unease increased as I advanced. The old harridan opened a door at the end of the corridor and I found myself looking into a cosy room where a young woman sat at a pretty dressing table, brushing her long black hair, which fell all the way down her back. She threw me a look that made me freeze.

'Aïda,' the maid announced before withdrawing, 'here's the young man you were expecting.'

Aïda smiled at me. With her finger, she motioned me to enter. As I stood stunned in the doorway, she got up, gently drew me inside and closed the door. She smelt good. Her big doe-like eyes enveloped me with an intensity that choked me. My heart was pounding in my chest, I had a lump in my throat, and I was sweating profusely.

'Is something wrong?' she asked.

I couldn't swallow.

She examined me, amused by my embarrassment, then went over to a low table covered with bottles. 'Would you like a drink?'

I shook my head.

She came back to me, a little disconcerted this time. 'I assume preliminaries are a waste of time for young Arabs.'

With a mystical gesture, she undid the braid of her shirt and the thin muslin veil that covered her slid silently to the floor, revealing a perfect body, with high breasts, full hips and slender legs. The woman's sudden nakedness threw me completely. I turned on my heel and almost ran out of the room. I got lost several times on the way back.

The maid frowned when she saw me beating a retreat.

Once in the little courtyard, I braced myself against my knees and breathed deeply to shake off my dizzy spell, which was now turning to nausea. The breeze outside refreshed me a little.

Filippi got out of the car. 'Are you all right?'

With my hand, I motioned him away.

I needed to snap out of it. Frédéric Pau joined me, completely taken aback by my reaction. I demanded that he take me home immediately. He asked me to calm down and tell him what had happened.

'You should have told me,' I said.

'Told you what?'

'That we were going to a brothel.'

'Why?'

'I wasn't prepared.'

'It isn't a boxing match, Turambo. Don't tell me you've never slept with a girl ...'

Filippi guffawed. 'Is that why you're so upset?'

'Filippi!' Frédéric snapped. 'Get back behind the wheel and start the engine.'

'I can't believe it,' Filippi exclaimed. 'The giant slayer collapses at the sight of a nice frizzy pussy. *I wasn't prepared*,' he aped me in a grating voice. 'I suppose you should have got some training in first in the toilets.'

Frédéric put his arm round my shoulders and moved me away from Filippi. 'Sorry. I didn't know you were a virgin. It was the Duke's idea. Camélia's is the most prestigious brothel in the region. Only important people go there. The girls are healthy, they know how to hold a conversation and they get regular medical checks. Plus, you don't have to spend any money. It's all on Monsieur Bollocq.'

He turned me towards him and looked me in the eye.

'You're still young, Turambo. At your age, starting out on what looks like being a fabulous career, the only thing you should think about is victory in the ring. I know that in your community, people marry very young. But you don't belong to your tribe now. You have a legend to build. Everyone in Oran, from the dignitaries to the flunkies, the ladies to the harlots, is behind you, the Duke at the head of them. You want a wife? We can offer you concubines by the shovelful. At Camélia's, no scenes, no worries, no judges and no dowries. Just a bit of well-earned relaxation. You come, you have a good time, and it's thank you and goodbye ... Imagine you have an important fight and your wife is ready

212

to go into labour, imagine you have a title fight the night your kid complains of appendicitis, imagine that as you get in the ring you're told your daughter has fallen down the stairs, what would you do? Do you put your gloves on or do you jump in a taxi and rush home? ... So, girlfriends, marriage, all that mess, forget about it. You have mountains to climb, titles and trophies to win. To get there, the first thing you have to do is get rid of anything that could slow you down or distract you.'

It was clear that Gino was behind this 'trap'. He had said the same kind of thing the other day when I had told him about Louise. Angrily, I pulled Frédéric's hands off my shoulders and said, 'I want to go home now.'

Gino was waiting for me calmly in the kitchen, eating a sandwich of kosher sausage, a napkin round his neck, his braces undone. A lock of hair dangled over his forehead, adding an unusual serenity to his charm. The way I slammed the door behind me and climbed the stairs four steps at a time, cursing, didn't disturb his mocking, slightly distant smile. He seemed more interested in the gramophone droning in the living room than my bad mood.

'What are you playing at?' I screamed.

He cut me off before I'd finished giving vent to my temper. 'You chose me to run your affairs,' he reminded me, 'so do as I say and shut up.'

The following evening, he himself went with me to Madame Camélia's. The fact was, I wanted to go back. I was angry at myself for not having kept a cool head and dodged things honourably. Filippi's sarcastic laughter was still ringing in my ears. I had to make amends for my self-inflicted insult ...

Aïda received me with exaggerated solicitude. In spite of her efforts to put me at ease, I couldn't relax. She told me about herself, asked me questions about my life, my plans, told me innocent jokes that barely raised the ghost of a smile, then took my jacket off, laid me on the bed and began *touching* me very carefully and whispering in my ear, 'Let me see to it.'

I was in a kind of stupor when I got back in the car, where Gino and Filippi were waiting for me and sniggering. Filippi suppressed his giggling and ran out to crank up the car. Gino joined me in the back seat.

'How was it?' he asked.

'Fantastic!' I cried, drained of all my toxins.

Three days before my fight, not quite sure if it was to overcome the pressure Sigli was putting me under with his thunderous declarations or simply to rediscover a corner of paradise in Aïda's arms, I took my courage in both hands and went back to Madame Camélia's. All by myself, like a grown-up. With the private conviction that I had reached a turning point and was now in a position to decide my own fate. I was determined to take control. I stopped Aïda from undressing me, anxious to prove to her that I was capable of doing it myself. Aïda had no objection.

I undid her bodice, gazed admiringly at the undulation of her hips, followed the voluptuous swelling of her breasts with my finger, kissed her lips, which quivered with desire, then, after switching the light off in the room to make my senses fully alert and reduce the world to nothing but my sense of touch, I carried her in my arms and put her down on the bed as if placing a wreath at the foot of a monument. All I could see were her eyes shining in the darkness, but that was all I asked.

And so I discovered the sweet, irrepressible torments of the flesh.

The Duke was determined to put his own stamp on the event. He called on the best photographers and drummed up support from a whole lot of journalists to make my match the fight of the year. His photograph had been appearing on the front page of

*L'Écho d'Oran* for several days. To ensure the greatest impact, he hired a huge hall in the centre of town used by the city council for big occasions and galas. When I got there, the street outside was swarming with onlookers. Flashbulbs popped and the men of the press jostled one another to get an opinion or statement from me. Gino and Filippi had to elbow their way through the crowd to let me through. On the opposite pavement, a group of Araberbers were shouting and gesticulating in the hope of attracting my attention. They were all in their early thirties, with ties and parted hair.

'Hey, Turambo!' one of them shouted at me. 'Why won't they let us in? We have money to buy tickets.'

'It isn't fair,' another cried. 'You have to box for us too. You're the jewel in our crown.'

'You're the champion,' the first one went on. 'You can demand it. Insist that they let us watch the match. We're here to support you. Those are just your enemies around the ring.'

A big red-faced man keeping watch outside the main door of the establishment asked me to go to the changing rooms without delay.

'Why won't they let them in?' I asked him.

'They didn't provide any animal skins in the hall,' he retorted, 'and these apes don't know how to sit properly on chairs.'

Gino seized me round the waist to stop me hitting the man and pushed me into the lobby, where a welcoming committee were waiting impatiently. From the hall, the din of the audience reached us. Frédéric Pau immediately led me to the changing rooms. Salvo and De Stefano were already there, nervous and sweating.

'All the elite of the city are here,' Frédéric said. 'It's up to you to get them on your side. If you win, the sky's the limit for us.'

Frédéric wasn't exaggerating. The hall was packed and

overheated. In the front few rows sat the dignitaries, the journalists, the judges, and a restless character surrounded by microphones for a live radio broadcast. Behind, a tide of faces crimson with excitement, cooling themselves with fans and newspapers. There were just Roumis in suits here, yelling at each other, jumping up and down on their seats, or looking for each other in the chaos. Not a tarboosh or fez in sight. I suddenly felt alone in the midst of a hostile throng.

As I got in the ring, jeers rang out, soon drowned out by the clamour of a crowd getting ready to celebrate. Spotlights shone down fiercely on the ring. I thought I recognised Mouss in a corner, but the blinding lights forced me to turn away. Applause came from the left side of the hall and spread in a crescendo through the whole room. Whistles and the squeaking of chairs were added to the loud cheers. Sigli emerged from the shadows and made his way through the crowd in a white robe. He was a big, fair-haired man, his head shaven at the temples, with skinny legs. I had seen him fight two or three times and he hadn't made a particularly good impression on me. He was one metre ninety tall, which protected his head, and he used his long arms to keep his opponents at a distance, his punches being much more of a reflex than genuine aggressiveness. I knew he was only fairly good at taking blows, and there weren't many people who rated him highly. All the same, everyone was expecting a miracle and praying that someone would shut the mouth of the dirty Arab whose meteoric rise was starting to upset people. Sigli raised his arm to greet his fans and did a quick dance step before climbing over the ropes to thunderous applause. Below the ring, cigar in mouth, the Duke gave me a thumbs-up. Salvo gave me a drink and adjusted my gum shield. 'Let him come,' De Stefano whispered in my ear. 'Walk him around a bit and then get in there with your right to rile him up. He's a madman. If you hit him first, he'll try and get back at you at all costs, and that's when he'll lower his guard.' The referee asked the seconds to leave the ring and Sigli and me to approach. He began by reciting the instructions. I didn't hear him. I saw my opponent's muscles quivering, his jaws clenching in his tense face, his faltering breathing, and I sensed that he was sick to his stomach and that all his loud declarations were just a feeble attempt to help him overcome his doubts.

Sigli folded at the first blow. He fell onto one knee, his hand to his side, his mouth grimacing with pain. People stood up in the hall, stunned by my 'lightning move'. Jeers rang out across the ring. Sigli staggered to his feet. What I read in his eyes was a mixture of terror and rage. He knew that he was outclassed, but was hoping he could hold out for three or four rounds. He charged at me in a desperate surge. My left caught him on the tip of his chin. He collapsed to the floor, determined to stay there to the end of the count. The fight had lasted less than a minute. The audience showed its annoyance and started leaving the hall, overturning chairs and whistling in anger. Even the Duke was disappointed. 'You should have made their pleasure last,' he said to me in the changing rooms. 'When a whole lot of people take the trouble to attend a show, they want their money's worth. Especially when the seats are so expensive. You were too quick. The latecomers didn't even have time to sit down.'

I didn't care.

I had won and I didn't give a damn about the rest. There was only one thing I wanted to do: run and throw myself into Aïda's arms.

As soon as I had done up my bag and put on my suit, I apologised to my comrades that I couldn't celebrate my victory with them as planned, jumped into Filippi's car and went straight to Camélia's to give myself a well-earned bit of relaxation.

## 7

Place d'Armes was in jubilant mood. The trams disgorged their hordes of passengers; the carriages swayed under the weight of their occupants. The few policemen didn't know which way to turn in the carousel of cars and pedestrians. Beneath the gigantic trees around the fountain, families in their Sunday best were taking the air, the men with their jackets over their arms, the women under their parasols, the children trailing along behind like reluctant chicks. On the steps of the theatre, a throng of spectators was waiting for the box office to open, ignoring the Arab shoeshine boys fluttering around them. Soldiers in dress uniforms were vying with eccentric young men for the attentions of the girls, each using his seductive skills with the care of someone lighting fireworks. It was a gorgeous, colourful day, as only Oran could provide, softened by the breeze coming up from the harbour and fragrant with delicate scents from the gardens of the Military Club. We were sitting at a table on the terrace of a brasserie – De Stefano, Salvo, Tobias, Gino and I – some of us drinking anisette, others iced lemonade. Gino was telling me about the party the previous evening, to which many local personalities had been invited. Salvo was praising in great detail the succulence of the dishes served at the banquet.

'You shouldn't have run off,' De Stefano said reproachfully. 'It was your victory we were celebrating. Lots of the guests were upset not to see you at the restaurant.'

'You're not a street pedlar any more, you're a champion,' Tobias said.

'The Duke wasn't pleased to see that you weren't there. He gave Frédéric an earful because of you.'

'I was tired,' I said.

'Tired?' Gino said. 'That's no excuse. There are conventions.'

'What conventions? I have a right to rest after a fight, don't I?'

'They were honouring you,' Tobias reminded me. 'Honours are important. The same people whose shoes you used to shine were there to shake your hand, damn it! To congratulate you. To cheer you. And you run off and throw yourself into the arms of a whore.'

'What of it?'

'It's unreasonable behaviour,' De Stefano said calmly.

'*Inadmissible*,' Tobias corrected him.

'It's time you learnt good manners, Turambo,' De Stefano went on. 'When people honour you, the least you can do is be there at the ceremony.'

'It was just a dinner,' I said. 'A big one, but a dinner. Plus, there was pork and wine on the menu.'

'Do you ever stop for two seconds and think?' Gino said angrily. 'Try to understand what we're telling you instead of listening only to yourself. You've become someone, Turambo, a hero of the city. And honours can't be negotiated. When an event is organised in your honour, things turn sour if you're not there. Do you follow me? There were highly placed people who'd come specially for you; even the mayor was on time, and you were nowhere to be seen.'

'It's not the end of the world,' I said, anxious for them to change the subject.

'Maybe not, but take care, it might be the end of everything for you. A champion mustn't snub his people, especially if he depends on them. And he mustn't do the first thing that comes into his head ...'

'Provided he even has one,' Tobias sighed.

'Why, do you?' Salvo retorted.

Tobias didn't take the bait. Since his arguments with Salvo often ended up to the latter's advantage, Tobias wasn't keen to make a spectacle of himself. The few jibes at me were mere diversionary tactics. The fact was, he was bored in his corner, and his expression was sombre. He kept staring at the jug in front of him, without touching it.

'Weren't you at the party?' I asked him, determined to move on.

'Oh, yes,' he grunted, scowling so that his eyebrows met like two hairy caterpillars.

'He's hopping mad because Félicie refused to dance with him,' Salvo said. 'Was she scared he'd stick his wooden leg in her foot?'

'Wrong. Félicie is sulking because I didn't give her a jewel for her birthday. I gave her flowers instead. That's more romantic, isn't it?'

'Maybe,' Salvo said, 'but it doesn't count.'

Tobias scratched himself behind the ear. 'Mind your own business, egghead. I don't like your insinuations.'

The two men looked stonily at each other.

'What have you done with your ring, you randy bastard? Did you leave it up the arse of some old bag?'

'Watch it, Tobias, *I* wasn't being vulgar.'

'Don't worry. It might get jammed.'

'You're on good form, pegleg. What did you eat this morning?'

'You're the one who smells bad. Your mouth's a sewer – when you open it the whole city starts to stink. Men like you can only do it up the arse.'

De Stefano laughed, making his paunch wobble.

'You're lucky I don't have my knife on me,' Salvo muttered.

'I'd gladly lend you mine,' Tobias said. 'What would you do with it? Circumcise me?'

Gino and I were convulsed with laughter.

Francis joined us, his nostrils quivering with rage and indignation. He brandished a newspaper as if it were a tomahawk. 'Have seen today's paper?'

'Not yet,' Gino said. 'Why?'

'Those bastards on *Le Petit Oranais* didn't pull their punches.'

Without taking a seat, preferring to remain standing to dominate us with his fury, Francis opened the newspaper with a peremptory gesture and spread it in front of him. 'It's the most disgusting article I've ever read in my life.'

'It's just an article, Francis,' De Stefano said, trying to calm him. 'Don't have a fit.'

'It isn't an article, it's a hatchet job.'

'Someone from the editorial board told me about it this morning,' De Stefano said calmly. 'I know pretty much what it says. Sit down and have a beer. And don't spoil our day, please. Look around you. Everything's going well.'

'What's in it?' Tobias asked.

'Crap,' De Stefano said wearily.

'Yeah, but we want to know what,' Tobias insisted.

Francis, who had just been waiting for permission to start, cleared his throat, took a deep breath and began reading so feverishly that his nostrils dilated even more.

'THE SHOCK OF EXTREMES.'

'What a headline!'

'Spare us your comments and let's hear what's in the damned article,' Tobias said.

'Here we go then!' His voice throbbing, Francis read:

'Our dear city of Oran invited us to a truly dismal spectacle at the Salle Criot yesterday. We were expecting a boxing match and we were treated to a fairground attraction in very bad taste. In a ring transformed into a Roman arena, we were forced to witness a display of absurd sacrilege. On one side there was a fine athlete who practises boxing in order to contribute to the development of our national sport and who had come to impress the audience with his technique, his panache and his talent. Opposing him was a fighter like a wild beast who should never have been released from its cage. He was devoid of ethics. What can we say about this terrible farce other than express our intense indignation at seeing two conflicting worlds confront each other in defiance of the most elementary rules of decorum? Is it right to set the noble art up against the most primitive barbarity? Is it right to apply the word "match" to the obscene confrontation of two diametrically opposed conceptions of competition, one athletic, beautiful, generous, the other animalistic, brutal and irreverent? Yesterday, in the Salle Criot, we witnessed a vile attack on our civilisation. How can we not consider it as such when a good Christian is placed at the mercy of a troglodyte barely escaped from the dawn of time? How can we not cry scandal when an Arab is allowed to raise his hand to the very person who taught him to look at the moon rather than his own finger, to come down out of his tree and walk among men? Boxing is an art reserved for the world of the enlightened. To allow a primate access to it is a grave mistake, a false move, an unnatural act ...'

'What's a troglodyte?' I asked.

'A prehistoric man,' Francis said, eager to continue reading out the article.

'Let us be under no illusion. To treat Arabs as our equals is to make them believe that we are no longer much use for anything. To allow them to face us in a boxing ring implies that they will one day be granted the opportunity to face us on a battlefield. Arabs are genetically destined for the fields, the mines, the pastures and, for those able to take advantage of our vast Christian charity, for the signal honour of serving us with loyalty and gratitude by doing our washing, sweeping our streets and looking after our houses as devoted and obedient servants ...'

'What prehistoric man are they talking about?' I asked.

'Don't you get it?' Francis cried, annoyed at being forced to interrupt his reading. 'He's talking about you.'

'Do I look as old as that?'

'Let me finish the article and I'll explain.'

'You don't have to explain anything,' Gino cut in. 'We've heard enough. That article is just like its author: only good for wiping your arse on. We know the journalists who work on *Le Petit Oranais*. Fanatical racists, with as much restraint as a bout of diarrhoea. They don't even deserve to be spat at. Remember the anti-Semitic massacre they caused in the Derb a few years ago. In my opinion, we should ignore them. They're just low-grade provocateurs who prove, through their editorial line, that the civilised world isn't always where we think it is.'

'I don't agree,' Francis yelled, spittle showing at the corner of his mouth. 'The man who wrote this rubbish has to pay for it. I know him. He used to go to the Eldorado cinema when I worked there as a pianist. He wrote film reviews for his paper. A pathetic nobody with a face like a barn owl, as thin as a pauper's wages, ugly and untrustworthy. He lives not far from here. I suggest we go and have words with the bastard.'

'Calm down, my boy,' De Stefano grunted.

'No Algerian can keep calm without forcing himself. If we give in, we lose face.'

'Shut up, Francis!' Tobias roared. 'You can't fight journalists. They'll always have the last word because they're what counts as public opinion.'

'Tobias is right,' De Stefano said. 'Remember how those bastards on *Le Petit Oranais* treated Bad-Arsed Bob, or Angel Face, or Gustave Mercier. They lifted them up only to dump them. Bob ended up in an asylum. Angel Face killed his poor wife and ended his career in jail. Gusgus works as a bouncer ... Fame is also paid in kind. What matters isn't the occasional blows we take, but the nature of the marks they leave on us.'

All eyes turned to me.

I raised my glass of lemonade to my lips. The jibes, the filthy names, the vulgar insults: I'd hear them again and again every time I climbed into a ring. They were part of the atmosphere. There is no fight without abuse. At first, the jeers and the racist remarks hurt me. With time, I learnt to handle them. The Mozabite, my uncle's partner, would say to me, 'Fame can be measured by the hatred it arouses in its detractors. Where you are praised to the skies, others trip you up; such is the balance of things. If you want to see things through to the end, don't linger over the droppings you crush beneath your feet, because there will always be some on the path of the brave.'

'Are you going to let this go?' Francis said.

'It's the only way to move on to serious things, don't you think?' I said, meeting his indignant gaze.

Francis slammed the paper down on the table and walked away, giving us the finger and telling us to go to hell. We watched him until he had disappeared round the corner. Calm returned to our table, without the open camaraderie that had prevailed a few minutes earlier. Hands grasped glasses and tankards; only Salvo had the courage to go further. De Stefano heaved a big sigh and sank into his chair, visibly annoyed by Francis's intrusion. Gino picked up the paper, opened it at the offending page and read the article to the end in an unsettling silence. To dispel the unease that was starting to affect all of us, Tobias hailed the waiter, but then didn't know what to order.

For my part, I had found Francis's anger excessive, even unlikely. He himself had no qualms about kicking the backsides of Arab boys who tried to sell us snacks. Seeing him defend my honour so ferociously made me sceptical. It really wasn't like him. I had often caught him complaining that I behaved 'like an unpredictable, narrow-minded country bumpkin'. Whenever I disagreed with him about something, he'd raise his eyes to heaven as a sign of irritation, as if I wasn't entitled to express an opinion. He had never really taken me to his heart. Even though he did his best to hide it, I knew he hated me for preferring Gino to him. According to him, I had pulled the rug out from under him … This business of the newspaper article was only a way of driving me to do something wrong, with, as a bonus, a long stay in prison that would put a definite end to my career as a boxer. Francis was quite capable of going that far; he was cunning and resentful.

A one-armed beggar approached our table. He was wearing a tattered cape over his naked, grimy torso, a rag that must once have resembled a pair of trousers, and torn canvas shoes.

'Clear off!' Salvo cried. 'You're going to attract every fly in the place.'

The beggar took no notice of him. He was examining me with a smile, his chin between his thumb and index finger. He was young but skeletal, his face withered and furrowed. His arm had been severed at the elbow, displaying a horrible bare stump.

'Aren't you the boxer in the posters?' he asked me.

'I might be.'

His face seemed familiar, but I couldn't place him.

'I knew a Turambo once, years ago,' the beggar went on, still smiling. 'In Graba, near Sidi Bel Abbès.'

A succession of faces flashed through my mind – the Daho brothers, the kids in the souk, the neighbours' children – but I couldn't place this man. And yet I was certain he was familiar to me.

'Sit down,' I said.

'Out of the question!' thundered a waiter standing in the doorway of the brasserie. 'How will I disinfect the chair afterwards?'

The beggar was already beating a retreat. He crossed the road and hastened towards the Derb, limping slightly. He quickened his pace when he heard me running after him.

'Stop, I just want to talk to you!'

He hurried on straight ahead. I caught up with him behind the theatre.

'I'm from Graba,' I said. 'Do we know each other?'

'I didn't want to upset you. It wasn't right, what I did. You were with your friends and I turned up like that and made you feel ashamed. I apologise, really, I apologise —'

'Never mind that. Who are you? I'm sure we know each other.'

'We weren't together for long,' the beggar said, impatient to go on his way. 'And besides, it's all in the past. You've become someone; I have no right to bother you. When I saw your picture on the poster with your name above it, I recognised you immediately. And then I saw you at that table and I just had to approach you. I couldn't help myself. Now I know I was wrong. I realised it when your friends were embarrassed by me.'

'Not me, I assure you. But tell me who you are, damn it!'

He looked at his stump, weighed up the pros and cons then looked up at me and said in a thin voice, 'I'm Pedro the gypsy. We used to hunt for jerboas. And you often came with me to the camp.'

'My God! Pedro. Of course, Pedro … What happened to your arm?'

'You remember I always dreamt of joining a circus.'

'Oh, yes! You could juggle, throw knives, wrap your legs round your neck …'

'Well, I did join a circus in the end. I wanted to be a trapeze artist. The owner had seen my work but didn't want to take any risks. I was too young. To keep me on, he hired me as a stable boy. I'd feed the animals. One morning, I got careless outside one of the cages, and a lion took my hand in his mouth. It's a miracle he didn't pull me in through the bars. The owner kept me on until my arm healed, then started to find excuses, and finally threw me out.'

'My God!'

'I'm hungry,' he admitted, turning towards a soup vendor.

I bought him a bowl. He crouched on the pavement and started eating very quickly. I bought him a second bowl, which he knocked back in a flash.

'Do you want another one?'

'Yes,' he said, wiping his mouth with the back of his hand. 'I haven't eaten a thing for days.'

I waited until he'd finished his fourth helping. He stuffed the food into his mouth without taking the trouble to chew. His chin was dripping with sauce and his fingers left black marks on the rim of the bowl. It was as if he was trying to fill himself up to prepare for fasts to come. Pedro was nothing but a walking scarecrow. He had lost his teeth and some of his hair; his eyes wore a veil as faded as his face. From his wheezing, I guessed that he was sick, and from his sallow complexion that he might be dying.

'Would you buy me some shoes?' he said suddenly. 'I don't have any skin left on the soles of my feet.'

'Anything you like. I don't have enough money on me now, but I'll wait for you tomorrow in Rue Wagram and we'll go shopping. Do you know where Rue Wagram is?'

'No. I don't know anyone here.'

'You see that alleyway crossing the Derb? At the end of it, there's a little square. On your right, there's a workshop. The gym where I train is opposite. Just ask the doorman and I'll be there for you. I'll buy you shoes and clothes and take you to have a bath. I'm going to take care of you, I promise.'

'I wouldn't like to take advantage.'

'Will you come?'

'Yes ...'

'Do you give me your word?'

'Yes, my word as a gypsy ... Do you remember when my father used to play the violin? It was good, wasn't it? We'd sit around the fire and listen. We didn't notice the time passing ... What was your friend's name?'

'No idea.'

'Is he still with you?'

'No.'

'He was weird, that boy ...'

'And how's your father?'

Pedro passed his good hand over his face. His gestures were jerky, his voice shaky. When he spoke, his eyes darted in all directions as if trying to escape his thoughts.

'I don't know where my people are ... I've met lots of caravan drivers, nomads, gypsies, nobody has seen my people. They may have gone to Morocco. The Mama was born there. She was determined to be buried in the place where she'd come into the world ... Thanks for the soup,' he said, getting up abruptly. 'I really needed that. I feel better now. And I'm sorry if I embarrassed you in front of your friends. I have to go ...'

'Where are you going?'

'I have to see someone. It's important.'

'Don't forget, Rue Wagram tomorrow. I'm counting on you.'

'Yes, yes ...' He stepped back to prevent me hugging him. 'I'm crawling with insects. They jump on anyone who comes close to me, and then you can't get rid of them.'

He nodded by way of goodbye, gave me a last smile and descended the steps leading to Old Oran. I waited for him to turn round so that I could wave goodbye to him, but he didn't. Something told me this was the last time I would see him. My intuition was correct. Pedro didn't come to the gym, either the next day or ever, and I never found out what happened to him.

## 8

Aïda planted her elbow on the pillow and rested her cheek in the palm of her hand to watch me getting dressed. The satin-soft sheet emphasised the harmonious curve of her hip. She was magnificent, posing there like a nymph exhausted from lovemaking and getting ready for sleep. Her long black hair flowed over her shoulders, and her breasts, which still bore the marks of my embraces, were like two sacred fruits. How old was she? She looked so young, so fragile. Her body was like porcelain, and whenever I took her in my arms, I was careful to be gentle with her. For two months now, I had been coming here to recharge my batteries in her perfumed room, and whenever I saw her, my heart beat a little faster. I think I was in love with her. Born to a great Bedouin line from the Hamada, she had been married off at the age of thirteen to the son of a provincial governor somewhere in the High Plains. Rejected after a year because she had not given birth, Aïda was disowned by her family, who considered her dismissal an insult. Now that she was known to be infertile, none of her cousins deigned to take her as a wife. One morning, she set off across the plains, walking straight ahead without turning round. Nomads dropped her at the entrance to a colonial village where she was found by a Christian family. Late at night, her employers' sons came in turn and abused her in the cellar where she had been given lodging, surrounded by spiders' webs and old junk. When the abuse turned to torture, Aïda had no choice but to run away. After weeks of wandering about, she was forced into prostitution. Passed from one pimp to another like contraband goods, she at last found herself at Madame Camélia's.

In telling me of her misfortunes, Aïda showed neither anger nor resentment. It was as if she were recounting the tribulations of a stranger. She took her misfortune with a disarming stoicism. When she realised that her misadventures made me uncomfortable, she would take my face in her hands and look deep into my eyes, a sad smile on her lips. 'You see? Don't force me to rake up what might spoil our evening. I'd hate it if I made you sad. That's not what I'm here for.' I confessed to her that it was hard for me to remain insensitive to her sorrows. She would give a little laugh and scold me. I asked her how she managed to bear these trials which clung to her like ghosts. She replied in a clear voice, 'You learn to cope. Time sees to it that things are bearable. So you forget and convince yourself that the worst is behind you. Of course, when you're alone the abyss catches up with you and you fall into it. Curiously, as you fall, you feel a kind of inner peace. You tell yourself that's the way things are, and that's all there is to it. You think about people who suffer and you compare your suffering with theirs. It's easier to bear your own after that. You have to lie to yourself. You vow to pull yourself together, not to fall back in the chasm. And if, for once, you manage to pull yourself back from the edge of the precipice, you find the strength to turn away. You look elsewhere, at something other than yourself. And life reasserts itself, with its ups and downs. After all what is life? A big dream, nothing more. We may buy, we may sell ourselves, but we're only passing through life. We don't possess much in the end. And since nothing lasts, why get upset about it? When you reach that conclusion, however stupid it is, everything becomes bearable. And so you let yourself go, and everything works.' It was the only time she really confided in me. Usually, one sentence was enough to start her talking, and then I wished she would never stop. Her voice was so soft, her words so full of sense. She gave the impression that she was strong and resolute, and that calmed me a little. I wanted so many things for her; I wanted her to be Aïda again, to draw a line under her past and start again on the right footing, hardened but triumphant. I forbade myself to think for a second that her life could end in this dead-end place, on a violated bed, at the mercy of cannibals with contaminated kisses. Aïda was beautiful, too beautiful to be nothing but an erotic object. She was young and pure, so pure that the stains of her profession disappeared on their own as soon as she was alone in her room after her clients had gone. I liked her company a lot. Sometimes, I didn't feel the need to take her; I was content just being near her, sitting face to face, she on the edge of the bed and me in the armchair. When the silence became oppressive, I would regale her with stories about my life. I told her about Sid Roho, Ramdane and Gomri, and she would laugh at their quirks as if she knew them really well. I was proud when I amused her and I loved setting off her crystalline laugh, which always started from below, like little bells, before reaching the heights, so high that it touched the sky ... But our time was limited. I had to leave at a certain time. I had to wake from my dream. Aïda had other lovers waiting in the parlour. Much as I tried to ignore them, the maid with the impassive face keeping guard on the landing was there to rebuke me. She would knock at the door and Aïda would open her arms wide as a sign of apology.

What I felt for Aïda belonged only to the two of us. I parted from her with the feeling I was leaving my own body.

How I wished we could walk together through the thicket and forget ourselves in the shade of a tree, far from the whole world!

I had suggested that she go with me to the city, but she couldn't. The rules of the house only allowed its residents to go to Oran once a month. Not to walk about, but to buy clothes. A car would take Aïda, with other prostitutes, to the same shops, closely guarded by a servant. Once they had made their purchases, they were taken directly back to the house. No prostitute was allowed to wander in the parks or even sit down on a café terrace, let alone greet a client in the street.

It was like being in prison.

The maid knocked at the door. Insistently this time. Aïda got out of bed.

'He's just getting dressed,' I heard her whisper in the corridor.

'It's not that,' the maid said in a low voice. 'Madame sent me. She wants to see the young man before he leaves.'

'All right. He'll be down in a minute.'

I tucked my shirt into my trousers. Aïda came up behind me, planted a kiss on the back of my neck and put her arms round me.

'Come back soon, my champion. I'm going to miss you.'

'I'd like to introduce you to my mother.'

'I'm not the kind of girl you introduce to your parents.'

'I'll tell her you're my girlfriend.'

'That kind of word is not part of our traditions, champion. And besides, can you imagine me turning up at your mother's house dressed and made up like the wanton woman I am?'

'You're not a wanton woman, Aïda. You're a good person.'

'That's not enough. Your mother mustn't suspect that her beloved son goes with whores. She wouldn't be able to bear it. For our people, vice is worse than sin ... Hurry up, Madame hates being kept waiting.'

The maid was lying in wait for me at the end of the corridor. She gestured to me to hurry up. At the foot of the stairs, Larbi the servant was chuckling at my tardiness. In the main room, the girls in their flimsy camisoles and lace knickers were busy bewitching their clients. At the counter, their victims were ruining themselves to impress their harem. Mouss, the tall black man, was in an alcove, with two languid beauties on his knees. Automatically, perhaps to thank him for coming to my last fight, I waved at him. He bared his gold teeth in a grin and grunted, 'Don't proclaim victory too soon, kid. Sigli's just a nobody who thinks he's the cat's whiskers. He's nothing but a lot of hot air.'

'It doesn't matter,' I retorted angrily. 'He didn't hold out for a minute.'

'I wasn't surprised. He was already scared to death before he got in the ring.'

Larbi pulled aside a curtain and pointed to a padded door at the end of a corridor. Madame Camélia sat enthroned behind a small desk, with her severe bun and her inscrutable face, a twill shawl over her shoulders. There was no window in the room, which was dimly lit by two candles on a chest of drawers. The mistress of the house seemed averse to electricity. She must have felt more comfortable in the semi-darkness, which gave her a certain mystical air.

Her eel-like smile was intended as a barrier between us.

With her hand in its white elbow-length glove, she pointed to a velvet-upholstered chair, waited for me to sit down, then pushed a piece of paper in my direction.

'What's this?'

'The address of an excellent little brothel in Oran,' she said in a falsely cheerful tone. 'Not far from the centre of town. The girls are pretty and very nice. That way, you won't have to get Monsieur Bollocq's chauffeur to bring you all the way here. You can just hop on a tram or even walk there; it'll only take you a few minutes.'

'I like it here.'

'Young man, all these girls are alike. Isn't it better to have them close at hand?'

'I'm fine here. I have no desire to look elsewhere.'

'Nobody's forcing you. Go to that address and judge for yourself. I'm sure you'll soon change your mind.'

'I don't want to change my mind.'

Madame Camélia pursed her lips in a disappointed grimace. She breathed deeply through her nose, betraying an effort on her part not to implode. Her eyes had an unhealthy gleam in the flickering light of the candles. 'Does Monsieur Bollocq know about your constant comings and goings in my house?'

'He's the one who sends me his chauffeur.'

'When charity is blind, it makes beggars greedy,' she said in a drawling voice full of disdain.

'Pardon, Madame?'

'I was talking to myself ... Don't you think you're abusing your benefactor's generosity, young man?'

'You benefit from it more than I do, don't you?'

She put her fingers together and placed both hands on the table, inwardly struggling to keep calm. 'I'm going to be honest with you, my boy. Some of my clients are complaining about your presence in my house. They are men of a certain rank, if you know what I mean. They don't like to share their private moments with strangers from a world ... how shall I put it? ... not entirely accustomed to the special features we offer. My clients are officers, financiers, businessmen, in other words, important people, and they are all married. They need to preserve their reputations and their marriages. In this kind of place, discretion is of the essence. Put yourself in their shoes ...'

'I'm not in the habit of shouting what I see from the rooftops, Madame.'

'This isn't about you. It's about their state of mind. Your presence makes them uncomfortable.'

I leapt to my feet. 'Then why don't you give them the address you just gave me?'

Before she had a chance to put things right, I left the room and slammed the door behind me. I was sure my presence didn't bother anyone and that this whole thing was merely the result of the loathing she felt for me. An Arab in her house damaged the special character she was striving to give it. Wasn't it her ambition to make her brothel the most exclusive in Oran?

Madame Camélia didn't like me. It wasn't by chance that she had 'assigned' me a Muslim girl. As far as she was concerned, I wasn't worthy of laying my hands on a European woman. I don't think she liked anybody in particular. There was too much bile in her eyes, too much venom on her lips; if she had a heart, she would have made sure nobody ever got to it ... I didn't like her either. I hadn't liked her since the first time we'd met. Her 'aura' stank of sulphur. As arrogant as only vice can be when it brings virtue to its knees, she really despised her clients, who, the second they hung up their prestige and status in the cloakroom, let themselves be debauched by a glass of vintage wine and a mechanical show of affection. Her good graces concealed deadly traps; her charisma was tinged with a cold duplicity. She wasn't made of flesh and blood: she was nothing but calculation and manipulation, the obscure priestess of a despised Olympus where the soul and the flesh were quartered on the altar of desire, having nothing but blatant contempt for one another.

I wasn't there for *her*. Or for *her* girls. I was there for Aïda, and only for Aïda. And although she also belonged to other men, Aïda was mine. At any rate, that was how I saw it. I didn't just *sleep* with Aïda, it was a kind of marriage. I had respect for her; I hated the fate that had led her to this centre of lust and vice, this den of demons and perverted angels. In that purgatory of sensuality, it was tit for tat, love reduced to a sordid commodity. Even a false smile had to be paid for; you bought the moment, you traded the sexual act, the least look was added to the bill. Only one aim prevailed: to ensure the client spent excessively and, in order to make this happen, to reduce him to his base instincts, a consenting, devoted slave in search of ecstasy, ready to lose himself in an orgasm only to be born again and again to the craziest fantasies, never satisfied, always demanding, since everything was paid for in cash, since nothing could resist the power of money when the clock on the wall turned into a money-making machine. Aïda didn't work that way. She was generous and sensitive, without malice or deceit. She was just as good as those respectable women you raised your hat to in the street. I was unhappy to see her being a receptacle for dregs and vomit, offering herself indiscriminately to perverts who, in other circumstances, wouldn't even have dared look at her. That wasn't the role of a woman who loved as she could love. Aïda had a soul, an unusual grace, a kind of nobility; she was nothing like her profession, and it was obvious she wouldn't survive it – with time, I was sure, the little humanity she had held on to would rot in her breast and she would die of it as of a cancer … But what could I do except dwell on my bitterness and clap my hands? Whenever I arrived at the brothel and was told she had a client and I would have to wait my turn, I couldn't see any light at the end of the tunnel. And when I took my leave of her so that another man could immediately replace me, I felt I was burning in a kind of hell. I would return to Oran so sad that my room welcomed night faster than usual. In the morning, when I got to the gym, the punch bag would sag under my blows and I swear I heard it moaning and begging my forgiveness.

*

My conversation with Madame Camélia had left its mark. I was asking myself questions. Did my presence really bother the clients of the brothel? Was I abusing the Duke's generosity? Strangely, Filippi started sneaking off whenever I asked for him, claiming he had urgent business to attend to or an errand to run for the boss. At the gym, my training left a lot to be desired; I listened only absently to De Stefano's entreaties. My lack of concentration almost cost me dear. At the end of the month, I had a great deal of difficulty finishing off my opponent, a tough fellow from Boufarik, who was ahead of me on points until the seventh round. My left hook saved me at the last moment. Disgusted by my performance, the Duke gave me a dressing-down in the changing rooms. We returned to Oran by train, each racked by his own anxieties.

At night, when I switched off the light in my room, I would slide my hands behind my head and let darkness overcome my thoughts. Aïda occupied my mind. I would wonder who she was sleeping with at that moment, what impure hands were crushing her. I was jealous, and I was unhappy for her. What future was there for a prostitute? One evening, they would realise that she was no longer as young and fresh as she had been. Her lovers would prefer other courtesans. They would start to desert her, then mock her. The priestess would ask her to pack her bags and give back the key to the room. Aïda would go and stagnate in some rooming house in the outlying districts where the beds were cold and the sheets rank. When she didn't have enough to pay the rent, she would wander from dive to low bordello, from mezzanine to stairwell, before going back on the streets and using up her last resources walking the pavements. She would pass from a docker to a penniless carpenter, so common and drab now that no pimp would deign to take her on. Then, after hitting rock bottom and absorbing every insult, she would end up in some insalubrious bolthole, defeated, sick, hungry, worn to the bone, coughing blood and longing for death.

I had nobody to share my distress with. Gino was too busy buying himself suits and mixing with polite society to worry about my moods. We hardly ever saw each other. While he strove to become the Duke's shadow, the Duke having promised him an office in his establishment, I wondered how to overcome the doubts that Madame Camélia had sown in me. I had to come to a decision. I missed Aïda. Confiding in Gino struck me as wasted breath. He would try to dissuade me, would laugh at the feelings I harboured for a prostitute. Wasn't he against lasting relationships? He would find words to disarm me, and I had no desire to agree with him. I needed to listen to my heart. Lots of boxers were husbands and fathers; they didn't seem to suffer because of it.

I asked my uncle's partner the Mozabite for advice. Of course, I dreaded his verdict. In order not to arouse his suspicions, I told him that a friend of mine was in love with a girl of easy virtue and was planning to marry her. The Mozabite, whose wisdom I appreciated, didn't know what to reply. He wasn't keen. He told me that my friend might regret it one day. Then I asked him what the attitude of our religion was to that kind of thing. He told me Islam wasn't against it, and that it was even honourable for a believer to rescue a lost soul from prostitution. He advised me to send my 'friend' to see the imam of the Great Mosque, the only person qualified to pronounce on the subject. The imam received me with consideration. He asked me questions about my 'friend', if he was a Muslim, if he was married, if he had children. I told him he was a bachelor, healthy in body and mind. The imam wanted to be sure that the prostitute could be trusted, that she hadn't bewitched her lover and wasn't interested only in his money. I told him that she didn't even know of my 'friend's' intentions. The imam opened his arms wide and said, 'Restoring her honour to a poor woman robbed of her soul is equal to a thousand prayers.'

I was relieved.

A week later, after thinking about it until my brain was exhausted, I bought a ring and asked Filippi to drive me immediately to Canastel.

Aïda wasn't free. I had to wait downstairs for an eternity, unceremoniously repelling the other girls' diligent advances. It was after eight; night brooded at the windows. An excited client was torturing an upright piano by the bay window. His erratic playing interspersed with bum notes got on my nerves. I was hoping that someone would say something to him or that a girl would entice him to the counter, but nobody seemed interested in him. I concentrated on the first-floor landing, where the maid was keeping her eye open. Every time a client appeared at the top of the stairs, she would look down at me and shake her head. Every passing moment was wearing down my patience. My hands were damp from so much fidgeting. At last, a fat, bald, red-faced, shifty-looking man appeared. This was the one. I ran up the stairs, deaf to the protests of another client, who was waiting on a sofa. The maid tried to run after me; the glare I gave her stopped her in her tracks.

Aïda was finishing powdering herself at the mirror. Her hair was still loose and the sheets on the bed were rumpled. I stood there in front of her, trembling from head to foot. I found her more beautiful than ever, with her big doe-like eyes *smiling* at me.

'I wasn't expecting you,' she said, mechanically unfastening her corset.

'That's not what I came for.'

'Have you found someone better elsewhere?'

'No woman could distract me from you.'

She gave me a sidelong glance, eyebrows slightly raised, then reknotted the braid round her neck and turned to face me. 'What's the matter? You seem agitated.'

I took her hands firmly enough to break them and placed them on my chest. My heart was pounding. 'I have great news for you,' I said.

'Great news? Great in what way?'

'I want to marry you.'

'What?' she cried, pulling her hands away abruptly.

I'd been expecting that reaction. A lady of the night doesn't imagine she will hear such declarations. In her mind, she wouldn't be worthy. I was so happy for her, so proud to be rehabilitating her, to be giving her back her dignity and her soul. I took her hand again. Her eyes went through me like shafts of light that a branch deflects in the wind. I understood her emotion. In her place, I would have leapt in the air.

'The imam assured me that, for a believer, to save a woman from dishonour is equal to a thousand prayers.'

She took a step back, more and more incredulous. 'What imam? What dishonour?'

'I want to give you a roof, a family, some respect.'

'I had all that before.'

Something was eluding me.

Aïda's face had turned white and I couldn't understand why. 'Who says I want to get married?' she said. 'I'm fine where I am. I live in a beautiful house, I'm fed, protected, I want for nothing.'

'Are you serious?'

'Why wouldn't I be?'

'Do you realise what I'm offering you?'

'What are you offering me?'

'To make you my wife.'

'I haven't asked anything of you.'

My temples tensed.

Thrown off balance, I tried again. 'I don't think you understand. I want to make you my wife and take you away from this indecent life.'

'But I have no desire to depend on a man,' she exclaimed, with a brief, nervous laugh. 'I have lots of men and they all treat me like a queen. Why do you want to shut me up in a slum, burden me with kids and make me work hard? And besides, where do you see the indecency here? I work. I have a job and I love it.'

'You call that a job, selling your body?'

'Don't workers sell their hands, don't miners risk their lives in deadly tunnels, don't bearers sell their backs for next to nothing? I find the struggle of a poor devil killing himself with work from morning till night for pennies a lot less decent than the exhilaration of a whore who takes pleasure in making more money in a month than a track-layer in ten years. And what about you? Do you find it decent to have your face smashed in a boxing ring? Isn't that also selling your body? The difference between your profession and mine is that here, in this palace, I don't receive blows, I receive gifts. I sleep in a real bed and my room is more luxurious than anything I'd find in a home, even if my husband was a champion. Here, I'm a sultana, Turambo. I bathe in hot water and rose water, my toiletries are of silk and essential oils, my meals are banquets and my sleep is soft as a cloud. I have no complaints, I assure you. I was born under a lucky star, Turambo, and no honour could ever compare with my little joys here.'

My legs failing, I collapsed into the armchair and put my head in my hands; I refused to admit that Aïda could talk to me like that, so uncompromisingly, her words as final as a funeral. I found it hard to control the ideas swirling around in my mind. Sweat was spreading down my back in a tangle of shivers, freezing my body and my blood.

I didn't recognise my voice as I said, 'I thought I wasn't like the others, I thought you loved me.'

'I love *all* my clients, Turambo. All in the same way. It's my job.'

I no longer knew right from wrong. I'd thought I was doing the right thing and now I realised there were other logics, other truths a million miles from those I had been taught.

Gino burst out laughing when I told him how I had been rejected by Aïda.

'You have a problem with your emotions, Turambo. You've been very badly brought up. Aïda isn't wrong. All things considered, you owe her a lot. Don't fall in love with every woman who smiles at you. You don't have the means to maintain a harem. Just try not to shoot yourself in the foot. You can't get in the ring when you're walking on crutches.'

He struck me on the shoulder.

'We live and learn, don't we? And yet it's never enough to protect us from disappointments. Come,' he said, throwing me a jacket, 'there's a wonderful group performing in Sid el-Hasni. There's nothing better than a folk dance to get rid of evil spirits.'

# III
# Irène

# 1

Filippi asked me when I was planning to unlock my chastity belt; I told him I'd lost the key.

A year after being rejected by Aïda, I was practising abstinence and devoting myself to my training. I hadn't gone up onto the cliff of the Cueva del Agua to watch the drunks squabbling; I hadn't clung to the walls or cursed the saints; at last, I had grown up.

There is always life after failure; only death is final.

According to the Mozabite, love can't be tamed, can't be improvised, can't be imposed; it takes two to build it equally. If it were up to just one, the other would be his potential ruin. When you chase it, you scare it and it runs away, and you never catch up with it.

Love is a matter of chance and luck. You turn a corner and there it is, an offering on your path. If it's genuine, it gets better with time. And if it doesn't last, it's because you haven't understood how to handle it.

It wasn't that I hadn't understood how to handle it. I hadn't understood anything at all.

So I'd locked my heart away and listened to nothing but De Stefano's instructions.

Nine fights, nine victories.

In the souks, the troubadours spiced up my story to dazzled

audiences. The barbers of Medina Jedida adorned the front of their shops with my posters. Apparently, a famous *cheikha* sang about my victories at weddings.

One night, a carriage came for me in Rue du Général-Cérez. The coachman seemed straight out of an Eastern tale, with his red, brass-buttoned waistcoat, his smock shining with adornments and his tarboosh tilted over his ear. Some kind of pasha was with him, a man with a moustache like rams' horns. They drove me to a large farm to the south of the city. In a courtyard garlanded with lanterns, a hundred guests were waiting for me. As soon as the carriage crossed the threshold of the property, tambourines, cymbals and darbukas launched into a frenzied cacophony. Black dancers bounced about in a trance. And She came towards me, ethereal, stately, regal, the legendary Caïda Halima, who was said to be as rich as ten dowagers and as powerful as the Queen of Sheba. 'We're proud of you, Turambo,' said the woman who had subdued the Terras and was respected by prefects and powerful colonists. 'This party's for you. As well as celebrating your victories, it reminds us we're not dead and buried.'

Aïda hadn't led me astray: she had given me back to my people …

I was at my mother's, enduring her neighbour's screams. Since midday, the woman had been calling down curses on her brood of kids, who were making sleep impossible. The children would quieten for a moment then, blaming each other, resume their din. I'd had enough of putting the pillow over my face to muffle their cries. Wearily, I got dressed again and went out into the blazing heat of the city.

Gino was at home. He was waiting for Filippi, dressed like a young nabob in a shirt and tie, dark glasses on his handsome face, his forehead sporting a sophisticated fringe. Gino only ever wore made-to-measure suits from Storto and brand-name shoes. We hardly saw each other these days. Our nightly jaunts, the *cafés-concerts*, the cinema trips – all that was over. Gino had other priorities. In the street, the girls devoured him with their eyes. With his dashing looks and devastating smile, he just had to click his fingers to arouse passions. And yet nothing ever happened. Gino barely looked at them. Ever since the Duke had given him a little office on the second floor of his establishment, with a view of the plane tree, Gino had kept his tie on even on the hottest days and talked about nothing but business. Of course, he was fiercely defending my interests, but I missed him, and I didn't know what to do with myself when he was busy elsewhere.

'I suppose you have another urgent meeting to go to?' I asked as he admired himself in the mirror.

'I'm sorry, I can't put it off.'

'When will you be back?'

'No idea. We may go to dinner afterwards. These are important people. We have to cultivate them.'

'I see.'

'Don't make that face. It's your career we're working so hard for.'

'Take it easy, Gino, or the day we finally make it I'll be putting flowers on your grave.'

'Why do you say that?'

'Because I'm fed up. You're constantly shadowing the Duke, and I'm going round in circles.'

Gino adjusted his jacket collar and turned both ways to check the impeccable cut of his suit. 'Turambo, my poor Turambo, millions of young men would like to be in your shoes, and you reduce the world to these little off-days of yours. Think about what you've become. You can't go out on the street any more without a crowd mobbing you. You're bored, are you? Some people don't have that privilege. Take a look outside. People are working until they're ready to drop just for a piece of bread. Think how much they'd give for a moment's rest, instead of constantly wearing themselves out, slogging away in the hot sun, doing work even a beast of burden would refuse. Remember what you were just a few years ago and think of how far you've come. If you can't be happy with that, it isn't God's fault.'

He took my chin between his thumb and index finger and looked me up and down.

'You should sulk less and smile more, Turambo. Follow my example and do something about your image. There's nothing worse than a jaded champion. Tidy yourself up and stop moaning.'

'The Mozabite says: Only women are beautiful, men are just narcissists.'

Gino threw his head back and laughed. 'That's not so far from the truth … By the way, I almost forgot: the gym's closed for work. The Duke's planning to spend a fortune on a complete refurbishment. Now that we have a future North African champion, we can't carry on working in a disused stable. The Duke has ordered a top-quality ring. We're going to put in toilets, showers and a real office, repaint the walls, tile the floor, replace the windows. When you come back, you won't believe your eyes.'

'Come back from where?'

'Didn't De Stefano tell you?'

'No.'

'You're going to Lourmel to prepare for your next match. To the house of a man named Alarcon Ventabren. Apparently, the best boxers often go there to get a change of scenery and do a bit of training. The Duke has spent lots of money so that you can benefit from the best facilities. You're meeting Marcel Cargo in two months. And after that, with any luck, you'll be able to make a claim on the title.'

Filippi didn't look happy driving in the heat, sweating profusely in his chauffeur's tunic. The summer was surpassing itself that late July of 1934. When we lowered the windows, the air burnt our faces; when we put them up, the car turned into an oven. In front of us, the road broke up into an endless chain of mirages. Not a bird ventured into the white-hot sky, not a leaf moved in the trees.

In the seat next to Filippi, Frédéric Pau sat brooding over old resentments. From time to time, he would make an exasperated gesture with his hand. Four of us watched him from the back seat: Gino, Salvo, De Stefano and me.

'The Duke's been giving him a hard time,' Gino whispered in my ear.

On either side of the road, farms were bleached by the mother-of-pearl glare of the afternoon. The fields and orchards were deserted. Only a donkey with its forelegs tied was sliding down a steep path beneath its burden.

Frédéric at last stopped muttering to himself. He pointed to a fruit seller's hut at the end of the road and asked Filippi to take the path just after it.

'We can't go to a person's house empty-handed,' I said.

We pulled up on the roadside next to the hut. The fruit seller was sleeping the sleep of the just, surrounded by piles of melons. He jumped up when he heard us slamming the doors, wound a moth-eaten turban round his head and apologised for having dozed off.

'What's your name?' Frédéric asked.

'Larbi, Monsieur.'

'Another one!' Frédéric cried, thinking of Madame Camélia's

servant. 'Why do you all give yourselves the same name? Are you afraid you'll be confused with the Turks or the Saracens?'

De Stefano didn't greatly appreciate Frédéric's rudeness. He gave me a meaningful look; I shrugged, immune to that kind of insult. The fruit seller was confused, unsure if the Frenchman was teasing him or scolding him. He cleared his throat and tugged at his collar. He was a short, emaciated man with a greyish-brown complexion, wearing a tattered sweater and mud-encrusted trousers. He had a Berber tattoo on the back of his hand and almost no teeth showed when he gave his embarrassed smile. We chose two huge watermelons, three melons and a basket of figs from Bousfer, got back in the car and climbed the path that wound between the arid hills. A few miles further on, we glimpsed a large stone house flanked by an outhouse and a stable. The car went through a gate, passed a trough and stopped at the foot of a tree. A pregnant woman ran to inform the master of the house of our arrival.

A plump man in his fifties came out in a wheelchair.

Frédéric took off his hat to greet him. 'Pleased to see you again, Monsieur Ventabren. You know De Stefano ...'

'Of course, who doesn't know De Stefano?'

'The egghead next to him is Salvo, our second. At night, he turns into a ferret, and if you don't have a padlock on your pantry, you won't have a pantry left in the morning.'

Salvo attempted an ingratiating smile.

'This handsome young man in shirt and tie is our accountant Gino. And last but not least, Turambo, a walking legend.'

'And I'm Filippi!' cried the Corsican, who was still in the car.

'Well, gentlemen, you've arrived just in time for an aperitif,' the man in the wheelchair said.

'In this heat? Cold water would suffice.'

'Fatma has made lemonade. Please come in.'

It felt good inside. We entered a drawing room furnished with a rustic table, a very old sideboard and a padded bench seat. On a badly proportioned mantelpiece, framed photographs showed a young boxer posing for posterity.

'The good old days,' our host sighed.

He invited us to sit down at the table. Fatma, the pregnant woman, served us glasses of lemonade and withdrew. Ventabren let us quench our thirst before announcing that his daughter would be there soon and that she would be in charge of showing us our 'quarters'.

Frédéric noticed some paintings stacked in a corner. He stood up to examine them closely.

'I paint in my spare time,' Ventabren said, coming up behind Frédéric in his wheelchair.

'You have talent,' Frédéric admitted after glancing at the canvases.

'One has to earn a living. My hands dream of brushes but my fists demand gloves. The defeated warrior who wants to eat his fill, even if he has the soul of an artist, chooses to be a brigand.'

'You're not a brigand, Monsieur Ventabren. You have a way of capturing the sea that absol— '

'It isn't the sea, it's the sky,' came a woman's voice from behind us. 'You're holding the canvas upside down.'

A young woman was standing in the entrance hall. She was wearing a red scarf around her neck, a shirt with a low neckline, riding trousers that emphasised the curve of her hips and knee-length boots. In her hand she held a plaited riding crop.

'If you're interested in the painting, we can give you a good price,' she went on.

'It's just …' Frédéric stammered, taken aback, '… Monsieur Bollocq likes this kind of painting.'

'It's called a gouache.'

'Of course, a gouache. I'm convinced Monsieur Bollocq will love it.'

'I don't suppose he's very knowledgeable.'

'But he has good taste, I assure you.'

'In that case, it's sold. His price will be ours.'

The young woman gave off a strong sense of authority that immediately intimidated us. She didn't so much speak as machine-gun the words out of her mouth. Every time her remarks hit home, she would flick her thigh with her riding crop and raise her voice even more as if she were trying to drive Frédéric into a corner. His growing embarrassment inspired in her an arrogance that verged on aggressiveness. But my God, how beautiful she was, with a rebellious, almost wild beauty, with her black hair gathered in a ponytail and her piercing eyes.

At a loss, Frédéric didn't know whether to put the painting down or hold in to it.

Ventabren came to his rescue. 'Gentlemen, this charming young lady is my daughter Irène. She has no fear of lightning or sunstroke. At an hour when not even a lizard would venture outside, she rides all over the estate on her horse.'

'My mare, Papa ... I'll change and then I'm all yours,' she said to us as she went upstairs.

Alarcon Ventabren watched us out of the corner of his eye, flattered by our heavy silence. De Stefano leant over to me and asked me in a whisper if I remembered the girl galloping flat out over the hill on the morning of my very first fight at Aïn Témouchent. I didn't reply, my eyes fixed on the place where the young woman had been standing a few moments earlier. In reality, I wasn't seeing the hall, but that white dawn stretched like a screen across which a beautiful horsewoman had ridden to seize the day.

She joined us in the drawing room. She had freshened up,

changed her shirt and replaced her boots with hemp-soled sandals. Although she was young, she seemed so mature that it was hard to estimate her age. In her hardened gaze, which kept everything it touched at a distance, you sensed an inflexible strength of character. She wasn't the kind of woman to blush at flattery or overlook an inappropriate remark. I was impressed.

She led us to the outhouse, where there were tidy bunk beds for four people. The sheets were new and the pillows covered in embroidered percale. There was a table with an indigo tablecloth on it, four wooden chairs, a jug on an enamelled tray, a basket of fruit, and a rug on the floor. A crude painting of a boxing match occupied much of one of the walls; it was signed *A. Ventabren*. Two oil lamps hung from the ceiling beams, their glass clean and the wicks new.

After the 'dormitory', Irène showed us into a large adjoining room equipped with a punch bag, a punching ball, wall bars and other bodybuilding tools.

'Where are the toilets?' Salvo asked.

'We say lavatories, Monsieur,' the young woman shouted at him. 'They're outside, behind the carob tree. As for the bath, we don't have running water, but we do have a well.'

Frédéric asked me if that was all right with me and I said it was.

Alarcon Ventabren insisted that we stay for dinner. Oran being only some twenty-five miles away, we accepted the invitation. While waiting for night to fall, he showed us around the property. Apart from mastic trees, nothing grew in that stony earth stripped bare by the winds from the sea. Ventabren told us that he had chosen to settle here for only one reason: he loved listening to the wind whistle past his window at night. Above all, he had a stunning view over the plain; from the top of his hill, he was 'closer to God than men'. He told us he had never wanted to become a farmer. He didn't care for it and certainly had no vocation. After his career as a boxer had ended, he had come here for a well-earned rest. In order to make ends meet, he had built a little gym where a few stars of the ring came to train. The purity of the air, the isolation of the farm and the surrounding calm, he insisted, ensured that a fighter could prepare mentally and physically in the best possible conditions.

The sun was going down. Gino, Filippi and Frédéric stood round the former champion at the foot of a tree; Salvo was tormenting a Barbary fig in search of a ripe fruit. Below the hill, Fatma was going back to her douar, astride a donkey, escorted by a little boy. As for Irène, she had left after showing us our quarters.

I sat on the edge of the well, savouring the shade the setting sun had brought to a countryside severely afflicted by the heatwave. A breeze came up from the coast, as light and gentle as a caress. From my makeshift observation post, I could see everything, capture everything, even the creaking of the stones imploring the evening to relieve them of their burns. Screwing up my eyes, I could make out the steeple of a church in the heart of a little town fading into the twilight. You could sense the sea just behind the mountains, mocking the heat now struggling for breath. I had the impression I was leaving the hullabaloo of the city and its pollution far behind and recovering my senses, now wiped clean of their detritus and totally calm.

Dinner was served in the main hall. As the maid had gone home, Irène took over. She came and went from the kitchen to the table, her arms laden with trays, carafes and baskets of fruit, paying no attention to our chatter. Her father told us about his various fights in Algeria, France and elsewhere, praising some of his opponents, cursing others. Carried away, he would almost rise in his chair, shadow-box and dodge imaginary attacks to show us that he was still skilful and flexible. He was a fascinating character: he would describe the fights as if we were watching them live, which was incredibly exciting. He was so amazingly vivacious, we wouldn't have noticed if he'd got up and started walking. I found it hard to accept that such a strong man could ever resign himself to being trapped in a wheelchair.

'I've been told you lost the use of your legs in the ring, Monsieur,' I said.

Irène stiffened at the end of the table. For a fraction of a second, there was a kind of flicker in her impassive eyes. 'My father doesn't like to talk about that,' she said, glaring at me and gathering up the soup tureen.

'I don't mind, sweetheart.'

'But I do.'

'It doesn't matter,' I said to avoid any further upset.

'Our guest is a boxer,' Ventabren said in a placatory tone. 'He has to know these things so as to watch out for them.'

Irène turned and stormed out.

'I'm sorry, Monsieur Ventabren,' I said, no longer knowing what to do with my spoon.

'It's all right. Irène is still upset about the whole thing. That's how women are. As far as they're concerned, no wound ever heals completely.'

He poured himself a drink.

'It did happen in a ring,' he went on. 'In Minneapolis, on 17 April 1916. I was almost thirty-five and I wanted to retire in style. I was twice North African champion, French champion and ranked second in the whole world. A friend of mine, an influential English businessman, suggested I end on a high note with a gala match. I was booked to meet James Eastwalker, a black American, a former light heavyweight who'd become a wrestler. Not knowing the man, I thought I was being offered a chance for a last stand. It wasn't like that at all. I was being put on display like a circus animal. I was so disappointed, I refused to get in the ring. Then someone said I was chickening out and my Algerian blood was roused. It was a real bloodbath. The black man punched like a blacksmith. And me like Vulcan. It was obvious that one of us would not make it out of there. But I lost my temper and, in a match between two madmen, losing your temper is unforgivable. I tell you that because you have to get it into your head. When you lose your temper, you don't think. You hit out and you lose sight of the basics. I don't know how I left my sides unprotected. An anvil came down on my pelvis, compressing my stomach. I fell to one knee just as the bell rang, but the black man pretended not to have heard, and his other fist, the stronger one, smashed into my chin while I was trying to recover my senses and get my breath back. I went over the ropes and fell on the corner of the judges' table. I heard my back crack and I blacked out.'

'What happened then?'

'In boxing, son, it's when you think you've made it that everything goes wrong. I'd gone to America in triumph and I came back home in a wheelchair.'

After dinner, Frédéric and Gino got in the car and begged Filippi to drive them back to Oran. De Stefano, Salvo and I continued talking to Ventabren late into the night, sitting on the porch round a lantern bombarded by insects. It felt good. An invigorating coolness bathed the countryside. From time to time, you could hear the howl of a jackal, immediately answered by stray dogs in the darkness.

Ventabren talked a lot. It was as if he was sweeping away the cobwebs from a century of silence. He could talk for hours on end without letting anyone else get a word in edgeways. He was aware of it, but how to stop? Confined to his chair, he spent most of his time gazing out at the plain and confronting his memories. His nearest neighbour was miles away, below the hills, too busy taking care of his vines to pay him a visit.

De Stefano was getting bored. However many times he took out his pocket watch to indicate to our host that it was getting late, it was impossible to stop the flow of words. It was Salvo who put an end to Ventabren's chatter. He told our host that if we wanted to get up at dawn and take full advantage of the time for training, we should go to bed now. Even then, Ventabren felt he had to tell us one last anecdote before letting us go.

We lit the two oil lamps in the outhouse. De Stefano undressed in front of us; he took off his pants without any embarrassment and lay down on the sheets. He was hairy from head to foot, with clumps of thick hair on his shoulders and a horrible curly fleece on his chest. Salvo thought his backside was like an orang-utan's and advised him to 'give his left posterior a trim' if he didn't want a colony of creepy-crawlies to invade it. 'I'd happily offer you my right posterior so that you can show me the extent of your expertise,' De Stefano retorted. We laughed a lot before turning out the lights.

Through the skylight next to my bunk, I could see the upstairs window of the main house. The light was on and it cast Irène's silhouette on the red curtain as she undressed. She too went to bed in the nude. When she switched off the light, the night was at last able to reclaim the whole of the countryside.

## 2

The Duke had chosen the right place for me to recharge my batteries. What a joy it was to wake up in the morning far from the din of the souks and the fish markets! No dumping carts, no motor horns, no iron shutters being raised with a terrifying racket. The calm of the countryside was so perfect that the dream continued long after I got out of bed. I washed my face in the trough, breathed in the smells of the uncultivated fields and the orchards that reached us from the bottom of the plain, put my hands on my hips and let my gaze become one with the landscape. Emerging out of nowhere, the braying of a donkey gave me back the authenticity of the world, while the sight of a shrew running wildly in the dry grass aroused in me a sublime sense of simplicity. It was magical. I saw myself as a child standing on a large rock, wondering what there was behind the horizon. I wanted to stay there for all eternity, my peasant streak awakening in me.

We had been at the farm for a week. At dawn, De Stefano, Salvo and I would set off to conquer the ridges, not to return until lunchtime, sweating, tongues hanging out, but happy. Once we had eaten, we resumed training. After working on the punch bag and practising my feints and dodges, I'd give myself over to Salvo's restorative massage. In the evening, we joined Ventabren under a tree and drifted through more of his inexhaustible supply of stories. Apart from the spluttering van of the milkman, who appeared every day at nine, we might have been cut off from civilisation.

Whenever the milkman showed up, he shattered the peace of the countryside. He was a man in his early fifties who didn't look anyone in the face, but was useful for passing on the juicy gossip he had picked up in the surrounding villages. I didn't pay much attention to his indiscretions. I'd go so far as to say I didn't like him. He was a strange, shady character, furtive and lecherous, with crafty eyes, and he was also a pervert – I had surprised him with his nose pressed to the window, spying on Fatma in the kitchen and masturbating. He really disgusted me. Seeing him jumping into his van and leaving the farm was, for me, a moment of deliverance, like the sudden disappearance of a splitting headache.

De Stefano, Salvo and I enjoyed ourselves a lot. One morning, we set off to see the sea. We hoisted bags filled with food and drink on our shoulders and climbed the mountain. It took us four hours to reach the dome of a saint's tomb at the summit. There, we halted and gazed at the sea until we felt as if we were drowning in it.

Irène seldom had lunch with us. I had the impression she didn't feel comfortable at the farm. Her relationship with her father left a lot to be desired. They hardly spoke to each other. Whenever Alarcon Ventabren started to talk about his life as a champion, Irène would ostentatiously slip away. Something wasn't right between father and daughter. They lived together as if bound by a moral contract – he clinging to his bygone exploits, she glued to her saddle – but showed no real affection for each other.

Salvo asked if Ventabren was a widower or divorced, but Ventabren preferred to talk about his father. 'I don't miss him,' he told me one evening between two glasses of Phénix anisette. 'My old man was always either hanging around the seedy parts of town or in prison. When he was young, fascinated by easy money and the shenanigans that go with it, his ambition was to become a gang boss, except that he really wasn't cut out for it. He hoped to pimp a herd of prostitutes, surround himself with a gang of crooks with scarred faces and live on his income until a rival unseated him. Having fleeced a few lonely old biddies and extorted money from one or two small shopkeepers, he could already see himself swaggering down the boulevards, a beret pulled down low, his fingers covered in huge rings. He'd get into fights at the drop of a hat, in the hope of creating a legend for himself, and never stopped getting his face smashed in by lowlifes on every street corner. The fact was, nobody took him seriously. They all knew he was a loudmouth, full of hot air, and they knew he'd never amount to anything. Coming out of a long stay in prison, my father dreamt of settling down, except that he wasn't cut out for starting a family either. He lived like an animal, with no presence of mind and no sense of responsibility. He married my mother for her jewellery. Having stripped her of her last centime and gnawed her to the bone, he kept her for practical purposes – at least, that way, he could use our house as a hideout when he had thugs after him. He never took me in his arms. People in the street might ruffle my hair, but not him. Just once, when he'd come home to choose a piece of furniture to sell off, he found me sitting in the doorway of our house and called me by the wrong name. That was the day I realised how much of a stranger he was to me. Then overnight, he vanished into thin air. Some say he stowed away on a liner leaving for the Americas, others that he'd got himself killed in Marseilles. In the 1880s, a man's life could just go up in smoke and leave no trace. No point searching for him. There were more urgent things to deal with, and not enough time.'

I couldn't help thinking about my own father every time

Ventabren dug up the ghost of his. I saw the Jewish cemetery again, that ragged man closing the gate as if closing the door on a chapter of my life, and a sense of grief again took root in me.

Irène loathed her father's stories. She'd stay as far away from us as possible in order not to hear a word. Ventabren couldn't tell a story without turning a party into a wake. He was perfectly well aware of it, but couldn't help it.

We had dinner later and later to allow our host to make the most of our presence. He was pleased to have us with him, and doubly so when he realised how receptive we were. At the age of fifty-five, Ventabren's eyes were turned to the past; ahead of him, there was nothing but a terrible blank.

Every night, when we switched off the light in the outhouse to sleep, I would look through my skylight at the lighted window on the first floor of the main house and wait to see Irène's silhouette. When it appeared on the curtain, I'd watch, unable to take my eyes off it, until the darkness stole it from me; and if it didn't appear, the shadows would creep over even my most private thoughts and I would get no sleep.

My first face-to-face encounter with Irène was a disaster. I was sitting on the edge of the well. Irène appeared with a rubber bucket, attached it to the pulley rope and flung it into the hole. I took hold of the rope to help her raise the bucket back up. Instead of thanking me, she told me to mind my own business.

'I was only trying to help, Madame.'

'I have a servant for that!' she retorted, grabbing the rope from me.

The next day, as I was finishing my morning cross-country run, our paths crossed again. There was a spring in the hollow of a *talweg* a few miles from the farm. I liked to dip my feet in it after a last sprint. The water was as cold as if it had come from a block of ice. That morning, Irène had got there ahead of me. She was squatting on a mound of earth, watching her mare drink. I turned back so as not to have to say anything to her. She rode after me and caught up with me on the hillside.

'Nobody owns that spring,' she said. 'You can use it.'

'No, thanks.'

'I don't know what was the matter with me yesterday.'

'It's not important.'

'Are you angry with me?'

'It's all forgotten.'

'Really?'

' … '

She dismounted and walked beside me. Her perfume wafted around her. She had tied her shirt around her waist, uncovering her flat belly. Her luxuriant breasts jiggled at each step, barely contained by the shirt.

'I don't like people doing things for me that I can do myself,' she said. 'It annoys me. I have the feeling they confuse me with my father, don't you see?'

'No.'

'You're right. It was stupid. I see you're still angry.'

'With good reason.'

'I was horrible, but it's not in my nature.'

I nodded.

'How old are you?'

'Twenty-three, Madame.'

'Madame? Do I look like a constipated old tart?'

'Not at all.'

'I'm only six years older than you.'

'You don't look it, Madame.'

'Stop calling me Madame. It doesn't make me feel any younger.'

I wished she would go away.

264

She stooped to pick a twig up from the ground and her shirt gaped open even more, freeing a firm white breast. She replaced it as if nothing had happened.

'In the evening, from my room, I can hear my father pestering you with his stories and I feel sorry for you. You should stop him; he could go on all night.'

'It doesn't bother us.'

'How touching! I suppose he's letting you know what awaits you when you retire. All boxers end up as mad as him.'

'Why mad?'

'You have to be mad to choose getting knocks on your head and blood on your face as a career, don't you?'

'I don't believe that.'

'What do you believe in? Glory? There's only one kind: a settled family life. That's all that matters. You can be in heaven, talking to the angels, but if, when you go home, you go back to hell, you've really missed the point. My father had everything you need to be happy, a loving wife, a healthy daughter. He never saw them. The only things he cared about were the ringing of the bell and the cheers of the crowd. He died the day he hung up his gloves. Even now, he hasn't come back to life.'

'That's how it goes,' I said, short on arguments.

'I don't agree. No career lasts. One day, you'll come up against someone stronger than you. Your fans will yell at you to get up, but you won't hear them. Because everything will be vague and blurred around you. They'll insult you and curse you, and then they'll cheer on another gladiator with fresher blood than yours. It's always been like that in the arena. The spectators have memories as short as their arms. Nobody will dream of helping you back on your feet. In boxing, the gods must have short lives for the passion to be recycled.'

'It's the risk we take.'

She got back on her mare. 'No risk is worth it, champion.'

'There's no life without risk.'

'I agree. But there are those who are subjected to it against their will and those who provoke it and even demand it as a kind of blessing.'

'Everyone has their own way of seeing things.'

'Men don't see things, they fantasise about them.'

'What about women?'

'Women don't think like men. We think the right way; you just think about yourselves. We can immediately home in on what's essential while you spread yourselves too thinly. Happiness for us is in the harmony of our surroundings. For you, happiness is in conquest and excess. You distrust what's obvious like the plague and look elsewhere for what's within your reach. That's why you end up losing sight of what was yours from the start.'

She pulled on the bridle, made an about-turn and rode off across the plain.

When Filippi came to fetch us, Irène wasn't there to say goodbye to us. She had left at dawn on her mare, giving our stay an unfinished feeling. Something in that young woman was calling out to me, but I refused to listen. I needed to keep a cool head, not let myself get drawn into any more adventures where the heart has no grip on reason. All the same, getting in the back seat of the car, I couldn't help turning in all directions in the hope of seeing her come galloping back to the house.

The little square along Rue Wagram was fluttering with pennants. Garlands of paper lanterns and paper stars intertwined in the air. The road had been swept and the paving stones and tree trunks at the crossroads had been whitewashed. The shopkeepers stood in their doorways, arms folded over their chests; kids waited impatiently at the foot of the fences, feverish and unruly; journalists were scribbling in their notepads; all eyes were on the gym with its freshly painted front. The masons and craftsmen had surpassed themselves: the window panes gleamed; the wooden door looked brand new; inside, photographs and framed posters of some of the gods of world boxing adorned the now white walls. Turkish-style toilets had been installed, with taps and showers, and instead of the cubicle there was a real office complete with metal filing cabinet, shelves and cane chairs. As for the ring, it was a magnificent piece of work lit by a spotlight.

De Stefano was smiling from ear to ear. His dream was taking shape. He had been waiting for this moment for years. Stamping nervously, he walked up and down the room, his hands clasped behind his back.

Shaved and scented, his hair washed and oiled, Tobias must have turned his attic upside down to unearth the faded but newly ironed suit he wore with pride.

'Did you have that undertaker's costume made by a stonecutter?' Salvo teased him.

'No, by your fat sow of a sister.'

'You should have put on a pair of shorts. How else are they going to admire your fabulous wooden leg?'

'You know why you're still alive, Salvo?' Tobias said, annoyed. 'Because ridicule has never killed anyone.'

'No, I mean it. A wooden leg is quite a draw.'

'Let me tell you something, egghead. I don't believe in God for a second, but when I see the mug he gave you, I almost feel like singing his praises.'

'They're coming!' someone yelled from the street.

Immediately, the kids left their fence and came and formed two lines outside the door of the gym. Six cars drew up at the crossroads. The Duke, the mayor and a delegation of dignitaries got out with great pomp and gladly posed for the frenzy of photographers. 'Oran has a fine history,' the mayor declared to the journalists. 'Now it is up to us to give her heroes. Soon, due to everyone's hard work, this establishment will produce great champions.' The journalists trooped into the gym behind the dignitaries, while the police pushed back the children. Flashbulbs exploded. A film camera was turning.

The delegation inspected the various parts of the gym and congratulated Monsieur Bollocq on the remarkable work he had carried out.

'Who are these strapping fellows on the posters, Michel?' the prefect asked.

The Duke, who couldn't answer, turned to Frédéric, who was at the back. He elbowed his way through the swarm of journalists and reverently indicated the pictures on the walls.

'These are the greatest boxers in the world, Monsieur. That one's our national hero, Georges Carpentier, middleweight champion of the world.'

'It's an old photograph,' the mayor said in a learned tone, indicating to Frédéric that it was to him, the elected head of the city, that explanations were due.

'No, Monsieur, it's quite recent.'

'I thought he was older.'

Frédéric realised that the mayor didn't know much about boxing and that his intervention was a pure formality. 'Battling Levinsky, an American our Georges knocked out in the fourth round in Jersey City on 12 October 1920,' he went on. 'To his right, Tommy Loughran, another American. This one's Mike McTigue, he's Irish. Maxie Rosenbloom, American, he's the current world champion; Jack Delaney, Canadian; Battling Siki, French ...'

De Stefano had been expecting to be invited to the ceremony, but neither he nor I nor anyone from our team were shown any consideration. The dignitaries blithely ignored us.

'If you'd put on shorts, these venerable gentlemen would have been curious enough to ask you if your wooden leg blossomed in the spring,' Salvo whispered to Tobias. 'You could have told them about your bravery in the trenches, and in less than a week a medal would have arrived in the post. And we wouldn't be here gathering dust in the shadows.'

'We don't count,' De Stefano grumbled.

'It's because of Tobias's suit,' Salvo said. 'It stinks of bad luck and these gentlemen are afraid it'll contaminate their fine clothes.'

'That's enough,' De Stefano said. 'You're bad jokes are staring to piss us off.'

His speech over, Frédéric was relegated once again to the background, and the Duke invited his guests to continue their visit.

Aggrieved, I went out in the street. The kids had gone back to their corner. Francis, who'd been giving us the cold shoulder since the biased article in *Le Petit Oranais*, was standing in a carriage entrance, puffing on a cigarette and distractedly stroking a cat with the tip of his shoe. Further back, Gino was leaning on the door of the Duke's personal car. He hadn't even taken the trouble to come and say hello to us. Elegant in his neatly fitting three-piece suit, his smile radiant and his face half hidden by dark glasses, he was flirting with Louise, the Duke's daughter, who was wriggling with pleasure in the back seat. I felt my chest tighten and I quickly turned into an adjoining alley and hurried back to Medina Jedida.


My mother was relaxing in the courtyard. Her Kabyle neighbour, who'd been keeping her company, slipped away when she heard me open the outside door. She walked through the beams of light that filtered through the gaps in the trelliswork like an optical effect. We had been living together for years, but not once had I managed to glimpse her face. She was a discreet, self-effacing woman; all we knew of her were the hoarse cries she aimed at her little devils all day long.

Wearily, my mother sat up. She had aged. Her tattooed face was like a chewed-up old parchment. Of course, with the money I was earning she was eating and dressing properly but, cut off from her sister Rokaya, she lived mechanically, disorientated in this city with its overwhelming noise and bustle. She missed her native village and the people she had once known. My gifts gave her less and less pleasure. My chosen profession worried her. Whenever I got back from a fight, my face bearing the marks of my opponents' punches, she would go to her room and pray. As far as she was concerned, I was merely a madman who got into fights all the time, and she dreaded the day when the police would throw me into prison. However much I tried to explain to her that it was a sport, all she could see in my new vocation was violence and distress.

I kissed her on the head. She put her arm round my neck. 'He's back,' she said in a toneless voice.

There was a gleam in her eyes that was impossible to decipher, but I didn't need to ask her who she meant. I headed for the main room, and there he was, sitting cross-legged on a mat, wrapped in a frayed cape, his head bowed, his shoulders hunched, barely visible beneath its shroud of misery. I stood in the doorway, waiting for him to look up. He didn't move. It was as if he had died while meditating. His hands rested in his lap like two dead crustaceans. His trousers were torn at the knees and clumsily patched on the sides. He smelt of cold sweat and the dust of remote roads, and in the way he held himself bent over his silence there was a kind of surrender that was pathetic in its despair.

Trembling, more moved than I ever thought I could be, I crouched in front of him and reached out my hand to his. At the contact, a shudder went through me. He remained quite still, not moving a muscle.

'Father,' I said, almost inaudibly.

He sniffed.

With the tip of my finger, I lifted his head. His broken face was bathed in tears. I took him in my arms and clasped the bundle of bones he had become. We both wept, stifling our sobs as if the whole world might hear us.

## 3

When something keeps turning round and round in your head, the streets do the same. I wasn't walking, I was going round in circles. I'd intended to go to the café on the corner of Boulevard Mascara and Rue de Tlemcen, but found myself at the bottom of Boulevard National. I'd passed the café without even noticing. My steps led me to the seafront. Again, leaning on the guardrail, I wondered what I was doing there. The harbour hid the sea from me, and the buildings behind me blocked my retreat. I climbed back up to Place d'Armes, only to stop at the foot of a monument and realise that I'd come the wrong way. I wasn't in the street: I was in my head. It was as if a mischievous dream were playing with my sense of direction. At first, I thought it was my father's return that had sent my head spinning, but I was wrong. My father was merely a vase abandoned in a corner, a shadow in the gloom. He didn't speak, preferred to eat alone, locked inside his shell. In comparison with him, the sideboard cut a finer figure.

A cooper stopped me outside a warehouse. 'The people in my village have clubbed together to buy a wireless so we can listen to your fights.'

His voice made my head hurt.

It was Sunday. With families having left for the beach, Oran was drained of life. The avenues were almost empty. Only a few shops were open and there weren't many people in the cafés. I had the feeling I was lost in an imaginary city stretching on all sides of me through an endless succession of elusive reflections, distorting mirrors, concealed doors and patches of quicksand. I heard voices, met people, shook hands in a kind of fog. I was drifting, not knowing what to do with myself.

I hadn't planned anything for that day. So I was surprised to end up outside the hut of Larbi the fruit seller. My shoes weren't suited to the uneven path that led to the Ventabren farm, but that wasn't a sufficient pretext to turn back. If I was here, twenty-five miles from home, on a whim, there must have been a reason.

By the time I reached the farm, my feet were inflamed. Alerted by Fatma, Alarcon Ventabren was waiting for me under the tree in the courtyard, in his wheelchair. He was pleased to see me. He told me that since our departure the silence of the countryside had been like lead. Even the air, he added, smelt of stale ashes.

'It's very kind of you to come back and keep me company,' he said in Arabic. 'I'm really touched.'

'I need your advice,' I lied.

'Well, you've come to the right place, my friend. A drink before we eat?'

'I'm a Muslim, Monsieur.'

'Do you think God is watching us at this hour? At his age, he must be fast asleep in this heat.'

'You mustn't talk like that, Monsieur Ventabren. It makes me uncomfortable.'

'How can you possibly sit through my cock-and-bull stories if I don't get you drunk beforehand?'

'I'll appreciate them more if I stay sober.'

He laughed. 'Show me your fist, son. Someone told me it's carved out of bronze.' He took my wrist, turned it over and over, weighed it up. 'Fine piece of workmanship,' he admitted. 'Try not to stick it just anywhere.'

'I'll try, Monsieur.'

After the meal, Fatma served us mint tea. A slight breeze ruffled the foliage above our heads. I helped Ventabren to sit up in his chair, straightening the cushion that protected him from the hard back.

'Your next match is soon, isn't it?'

'The end of next month, Monsieur.'

'I hear that Cargo fellow's a tough customer.'

'I don't know him.'

'That's a bad mistake. You have to know the man you're going to meet. What do your staff do? Twiddle their thumbs? In my day, we sent spies to gather as much information as possible on the opponent. I knew everything about mine: how he boxed, his technique, his strong points, his failings, his latest fights, which hand he wiped his arse with, the kind of brush he used on his hair. And even then there was always something missing. You don't climb into a ring blindly.'

He fell silent.

Irène had just come out of the house in her riding gear, her eyes more beautiful than the stars in the sky. She leant one shoulder against the pillar of the porch, arms folded over her chest. I immediately understood the reason that had led me to the farm: I needed to see her, to feel her close to me.

'Don't you have any more stories to tell each other?' she berated us.

With that, she headed for the stable. A few minutes later, she galloped away on her mare towards the plain. I was no longer prepared to listen to anyone.

With Irène gone, the farm had lost its soul.

When the heat eased off, I took my leave of Ventabren, walked back to the road and waited for the bus.

*

The next day, I *demanded* that Frédéric Pau send me back to the farm to get ready for my fight with Marcel Cargo. The Duke didn't see any reason why not. De Stefano apologised: he wouldn't be available before the end of the week because of a family problem. Only Salvo went with me. We found ourselves back in the outhouse, waking up at dawn, running up the vertiginous paths, climbing big rocks and staying up late round lanterns bombarded by insects, much to Ventabren's delight; every night, I would watch the window opposite my skylight.

Irène sometimes joined us at mealtimes. She often smiled at me, but I mistrusted her mood swings. The woman was like a rifle. She fired at point-blank range and hit home with every shot. Whenever she joined us, Ventabren would abandon his epic stories. As for Salvo, he would swallow his sarcastic remarks and keep his eyes on his plate. Put in his place on two occasions, he knew he was helpless against Irène, who didn't really like him. He had tried to outsmart her and had ended up realising that this was no fun. Irène had the insolent self-confidence of challenges won in advance. As no ulterior motive ever escaped her, she would intercept ours before they were even conceived. Nevertheless, we enjoyed her company. She brought a kind of freshness to our meals.

After my morning runs, while Salvo was walking back to the farm, I would go and cool down at the spring. In truth, I was hoping to meet Irène. The first few days, she didn't go there to water her mare, then, just as I was starting to despair, she appeared like a blessed ray of sunlight.

She dismounted, slapped her mare's rump and crouched on a stone. 'I'm exhausted.'

'You should spare your animal.'

'She's my mobile garden.' She stood up, approached her mare and caressed its coat. 'When I was little, I wanted to be a champion rider.'

'Didn't your father approve?'

'No, Jean-Louis came along. He was handsome, intelligent and funny. I was a fresh-faced seventeen-year-old. I fell into his arms like a ripe fruit. We married without waiting. I was happy, and I thought it was going to be like that all my life.'

'What happened?'

'What usually happens in marriages that are too quiet. Jean-Louis started coming home later and later. He was from the city; the calm of the countryside made him nervous. One evening, he put his hands on my shoulders, looked me in the eye and told me he was sorry. And he walked out of my life.'

'He was wrong. I'd never leave such a pretty girl.'

'That's what he said at the start.' Her smile returned. 'Do you like horses, Monsieur Turambo?'

'We had a donkey once.'

'It's not the same. Horses are noble and they're therapeutic. When I'm fed up, I jump in the saddle and gallop to the mountains. I feel so light that no anxiety can weigh me down. I love to feel the wind in my face. I love it when it rushes under my shirt and takes me by the waist like a lover … Sometimes I even have an orgasm that way.'

The crudity of her words took me aback.

She burst out laughing. 'You're blushing.'

'I'm not used to hearing women talk like that.'

'That only shows you don't spend enough time with them.'

She pulled on the bridle of her mare and started on her way. I walked beside her, embarrassed. She kept throwing me sly glances and chuckling.

'There's nothing shameful about an orgasm, Monsieur Turambo. It's a moment of grace that restores us to our cardinal senses.'

Her theory only embarrassed me even more.

'Do you have a girlfriend?'

'Our traditions don't allow it.'

'So it's either marriage or sin?'

'That's about it.'

'Are you engaged to be married, then?'

'Not yet. I have to think of my career.'

'How do you plan to hold out until you marry?'

I felt my ears burning.

She burst out laughing again. With acrobatic agility, she got back in the saddle. 'Is Turambo your real name?'

'It's my nickname.'

'What does it mean?'

'I don't know. It's the name of my village.'

'I see. What's your real name?'

'I prefer the name of my village. At least that way I know where I come from.'

'Because you don't know who your parents are?'

'It's not that. It's my choice.'

'Well, Monsieur Turambo, you may look like a brute, but you have the soul of a cherub. And though you may always lack daring, please keep your soul. I'll leave you to your exercises and go back to my ovens. You can't cook with secrets.'

She spurred her mare, then stopped after a few paces.

'There's a dance in Lourmel tomorrow night. How would you like to be my partner?'

'I can't dance.'

'We'll watch the others.'

'All right.'

She raised her hand in a salute and rode off in the direction of the farm.

I watched her until she disappeared behind the hillocks. As she galloped away, I dreamt of being the wind under her shirt. My heart was beating so loudly, I decided not to continue with my exercises. Irène had the power to elevate the basest instincts to the level of great exploits, and then to silence them just by raising a finger to her mouth.

I felt an obsession growing in me, one that would never leave me.

I had been on tenterhooks, waiting for evening to come. I sat in the drawing room, eyes turned to the staircase that led to the first floor. Irène was taking her time. I had heard her having a shower, but she was still getting ready. When at last she appeared at the top of the stairs, I thought she was like something out of a dream, in her white dress with its tight bodice and her hair down to her shoulders. She reminded me of those American actresses who burst through the screen, relegating the sets and their co-stars to the background.

We cut across the fields to get to Lourmel. In the distance, villages dotted the plain like tiny will-o'-the-wisps. It was a fine night. The full moon wanted the sky for itself, reducing the stars to tiny glimmers. Along with the sound of rodents scurrying through the undergrowth, the air smelt of coral, seaweed engorged with salt and the foam of the reef. It was as if, pining for the earth that belonged to man, the sea had disguised itself as a breeze and had come to ruffle the orchards, move up and down the inlets and tease the church steeples.

A jackal followed us as far as the asphalted road before turning back, empty-handed and disconcerted.

Irène strode on calmly in her summer dress and canvas sandals.

I had become used to seeing her in shirt and trousers, looking like a tomboy; discovering her as a radiant young girl was a delight. Her perfume filled the countryside with fragrance. A thousand times, my hand brushed against hers without catching hold of it. I was afraid she would react angrily and put me in my place. Irène was as unpredictable as lightning, capable of going from hot to cold in a fraction of a second. She was unusually sensitive, and the same words could make her laugh out loud or fly into a temper. There was a mystery about her I couldn't fathom. Distant with her father, horrible to Salvo, she aroused an unease in me that faded whenever she rewarded me with a smile. I think she was trying to prove to me that she wasn't the same with everybody. Ever since our altercation at the well, Irène had treated me with respect. At the same time, her rebellious temperament hadn't lessened in any way. She wasn't asking for my forgiveness; she enjoyed my company, nothing more. She felt at peace with herself. And I had the feeling I was privileged.

The pretty square in Lourmel glowed with a thousand lights. A festive throng danced amid tables whose white cloths were covered with food and bottles of wine. Couples old and young whirled to the sound of an inspired band. On a stage garlanded with pennants, a singer in a dark-red suit acted like a god come down from Olympus. Pomaded, seductive, glittering, he flung his stentorian voice at the sky, his gestures theatrical, his chest all-conquering, his eyes coming to rest on the ladies sitting in the front rows. He knew he had seduced them, they were already crazy for him; in order to finish them off he lowered his eyebrows over his gleaming eyes. Bewitched and floating, they swayed gently on their chairs, pressing handkerchiefs to chests heaving with emotion.

Irène found us a free bench overlooking the festive esplanade. Children in short trousers frolicked beneath the trees. Young lovers took refuge behind the low wall of the park; some were asleep on the grass. Adolescents were being initiated into the trials of their first flirtations, away from prying eyes. Here and there, a few kisses were exchanged in the darkness, as furtive as the frisson they provoked. It was nice to see, and nice to sense. My native douar was a long way away, slowly dying in a parallel world.

Irène went off to fetch me some pop and returned with a large plate. 'I brought you some barbecued meat and some lemonade. Are you sure you don't want any wine? It's the best in the region.'

'No, thanks.'

'You don't know what you're missing.'

'Well, well,' said a man, approaching us. 'Our George Sand has come down off her high horse to walk among the hoi polloi.'

Irène put the plate down next to me.

The man was in his thirties, handsome, poised, well-dressed. He wasn't especially tall, but he had a proud bearing. He took a big drag on his cigarette and flicked it away. The glowing end burst into a multitude of sparks as it hit the ground.

'Good evening, André,' Irène said in a neutral voice.

'So you still remember my name?'

'How's your wife?'

The man pointed over his shoulder with his thumb. 'She's down there, dancing like a madwoman.'

'You should join her. Someone might steal her from you.'

'He'd be doing me a favour.' He clicked his fingers at an Arab waiter who was circulating among the partygoers with a tray, grabbed two glasses of champagne and offered one to Irène. 'I'm pleased to see you again, my dear.'

'I thought you'd been transferred to Algiers.'

'Have you been spying on me?'

'I heard Jérôme the milkman tell my father.'

'No, they're keeping me in Aïn Témouchent until further notice. Tell me about yourself. What have you been up to?'

'Nothing.'

'Well, it seems to suit you. You're prettier than ever. What do you do all day long, so far from civilisation?'

'I have no complaints.'

'But I feel sorry for you. You should be having fun, not turning your back on the world ... I've bought a little boat. There are wonderful crecks and unspoilt beaches to the west of Rachgoun. They can only be reached from the sea. I can show them to you if you like.'

'I'm sure your wife would appreciate them more than I would.'

'I'm talking about you.'

'I'm not available.'

The man swallowed a gulp of champagne and smacked his lips as he searched for more persuasive arguments. Suddenly, he pretended to notice my presence. He took Irène by the elbow and led her away from the bench a little. 'Did you win your pet in a shooting gallery?'

He spoke about me so rudely that if I'd been in his way he would probably have walked straight over me. As far as he was concerned, I didn't count; I was merely a speck in his eye, which would vanish if he blinked.

'Please, André. I've only just arrived. Don't force me to go home.'

'You still haven't told me where you won your guard dog.'

'I warn you, he bites.'

'In that case,' he said, turning her to face him, 'you should put a muzzle on him.'

With a peremptory gesture, Irène asked me to keep out of what she considered a strictly personal matter.

Amused, André sneered. 'Still as wild and unconventional as ever.'

'André, I don't like what you're doing.'

'Why, do you think what you're doing is right? You come here with a dirty Arab and you think nobody's going to mind. You like showing off, don't you? Whenever you emerge from your cave, everybody has to know about it. But be careful, people have venomous tongues around here. There'll be a lot of gossip.'

'I don't give a damn.'

'I thought as much. Provocation is second nature to you. Only this time, you've gone too far. You can't come to a dance with an Arab. Arabs aren't allowed here. They can't tell a light bulb from a magic spell ... Look at him. He's only just got down from his tree.'

'Please, André.'

'Tell me, what has he got that I haven't?'

'He's polite.'

'I don't suppose that's the only thing.'

'There are others.'

'How is he in bed?'

'That's none of your business.'

'From what I've heard, their women don't have orgasms. Not surprising, when you think their men ejaculate before they even get hard.'

'I must go, André. I left my gas mask at home and there's a really nasty smell coming from you tonight.'

André again seized Irène by the arm and drew her to him. She pushed him away. As he returned to the attack, I grabbed his wrist in mid-air and forced him to move back. He glanced around; much to his relief, nobody was taking any notice of us. To save face, he shrieked, 'Never put your dirty ape hand on me, you little shit, or I swear by all that's holy I'll thrash you in this very square until you're just blood and pus … I'm a police officer. You don't want to stick around here, trust me. If you're still here in ten minutes, you'll spend the rest of the night at the station.'

For Irène and me, the party was over.

We set off back to the farm.

'I'm sorry,' I said to Irène as we passed the last orchards in the village.

'It's not your fault. I thought André had calmed down, but he's got worse.'

'Who is he?'

'Someone I used to know. Someone who thinks he can get away with anything.'

'He called you George. Isn't that a man's name?'

She burst out laughing and wagged her finger at me. 'I see through you, Monsieur Turambo. But it's not what you think.'

When we got to the farm, she walked with me to the outhouse. Salvo's snores could be heard through the walls, making the window panes shake. They sounded like a faulty engine. Even the crickets seemed intimidated by his nasal thundering, which would have kept the boldest of predators at bay.

'Are you going to be able to sleep with that din, champion?'

'I'll manage.'

'Sorry about the dance,' she said. 'I'd have liked to teach you a few steps.'

'Another time, I hope.'

'People are stupid.'

'Not all of them.'

'You think we should have stayed?'

'That wouldn't have been a good idea.'

'You're right. That idiot would have come back. I didn't want him to get you into any trouble.'

'I'd have left of my own accord. The police really scare me.'

She nodded. Just as I was about to open the door of the outhouse, she put her arms round my neck and pressed her lips to my mouth. Before I had time to realise what was happening, she was gone.

She didn't put the light on in her room.

Nor did she join us for breakfast the following morning.

I thought she had gone to seize the day, as was her habit, but her mare was in its stable.

I didn't dare ask Ventabren where his daughter had gone. That day, I ran in a void. I didn't see the paths or the rocks. I didn't even feel my legs, let alone my efforts. My stride had no rhythm. The bushes fled before me. I was a wandering obsession …

Salvo, Ventabren and I had lunch in a cathedral-like silence. The table seemed to have tripled in size. The tasteless food stuck in my throat.

The only thing that kept me on earth was the gentle touch of that kiss on my lips.

Irène …

Her absence turned the farm into a gloomy enclosure where I was running around in circles. The walls were nothing but heaps of stones, the landscape an accident, the countryside a shipwreck waiting to happen.

I waited for evening. Evening came, but not Irène. The sun had gone down, but I was still up. There was no light in the window opposite.

Early the following morning, Salvo told me he was going back to Oran. He'd got out of bed on the wrong side. He didn't know what he was doing in this godforsaken hole. 'You don't listen to me, you don't take my advice, you don't follow my programme. In the circumstances, I don't see what use I am.'

He stuffed his clothes in a bag and began walking towards the asphalted road.

I didn't try to stop him.

I set off to do some feverish sprints as far as the mountain. As if I was fleeing my own shadow.

I was getting my breath back in a clearing when I heard neighing behind the thicket. It was Irène. She tied her mare to a bush and sat down next to me. Her shirt was steaming in the sun, her forehead was red and her eyes glistened with a sort of wild intoxication. She picked up a branch, twisted it, then started breaking it into little pieces. Her breathing drowned out the rustling of the foliage. I waited for her to speak but she said nothing.

'Is it because of what happened at the dance?' I asked, to break the silence.

'Don't be silly.'

'I thought you were giving me the cold shoulder because of the incident with the policeman.'

'If only that was all.'

'Where did you go yesterday?'

'I stayed in my room.'

'All day?'

'Yes.'

'Didn't you put the light on?'

'No.'

'Were you sick?'

'In a way.' At last she turned to me and looked me straight in the eye. 'I spent the whole day and night thinking.'

'Thinking about what?'

'About that moment. I kept asking myself if it was a good idea or if I should hold back. A really difficult exercise, weighing the pros and cons. In the end, I told myself nothing ventured nothing gained.'

She grabbed me by the back of the neck and pulled me to her. Her mouth devoured mine. And it was in that clearing, where the chirping of the cicadas had conspired to silence the uproar in my chest, that Irène gave herself to me, between a bush and a praying tree, right there amid the profusion of gold coins scattered by the sun on the ground like a generous prince. No ecstasy could have equalled the thrill that went through me when our bodies became one.

# 4

Filippi had received strict orders. *If you have to tie him up, tie him up and bring him to me before midday*. Filippi didn't want any problems with the Duke. Pale and stammering, he begged me to get my things together and follow him. It was as if his fate depended on the mission that had been entrusted to him. I looked at Irène; she stood by the well, hands on hips, smiling. Out of pity for Filippi, she nodded to me to pack my bags.

'Thank you, Madame,' Filippi stammered. 'You're really helping me out.'

'I won't be so lenient next time,' she warned him.

As soon as I took my seat in the car, Filippi set off at top speed, doubtless afraid I might change my mind. I turned to wave at Irène, but she was already walking back to the stable.

Gino stopped me at the entrance to the Bollocq offices. While waiting for us to be seen by the Duke, he showed me his office on the second floor with a view of the courtyard.

'You haven't wasted any time,' I said.

'Best to strike while the iron is hot.'

'What do you actually do?'

'A bit of everything. I negotiate contracts, explore deals, check the accounts … The Duke is training me. He has plans for me.'

He was looking better, more handsome, as he got older. He just had to flash one of his smiles and he'd be forgiven any rudeness. His hair, now light chestnut, was starting to darken at the temples, adding a hint of manliness to his charm that was in marked contrast to his angelic air. I understood why nobody could resist him, why the girls sighed over him and the Duke was so generous. I think I was jealous of him. Gino didn't need to make much effort. He could have had the moon on a silver platter if he'd asked for it.

He motioned me to a chair and poured me a glass of lemonade.

'How's it going with Louise?' I asked.

He frowned. 'Who told you about that?'

'I saw you flirting with her.'

'Nothing definite for the moment,' he said, annoyed by my indiscretion.

He flopped into the chair behind his desk, every inch the young nabob. He couldn't yet put his feet up on the desk, as was appropriate for those who climb the social ladder on a flying carpet, but he took his ease with a certain detachment. His suit was impeccable, and he wore gold cufflinks and a chain bracelet on his wrist.

'Does the Duke know what you're up to?'

'What's your problem?'

'You know the Berber proverb: the hen lays an egg and the cockerel gets a pain in the arse.'

'Don't worry about me.'

'No, I don't suppose I need to.'

'That's right.'

'Did the Duke talk to you about the plane tree?'

'What plane tree?'

'The one down in the courtyard.'

'Why should he talk to me about the plane tree?'

'Forget it,' I said, aware that I was distracted. 'So, how's the fight with Cargo coming along?'

Gino stared at me for a moment or two, bewildered by the mystery of the plane tree, then, making himself even more comfortable in his padded armchair, said, 'It's coming along fine. If you win, the North African champion won't be able to wriggle out of it. He'll be forced to meet you. We're going to work twice as hard,' he said with sudden enthusiasm. 'That title belongs to us. The Duke wants it at any cost. For the city, and for all of us. You can't imagine the trouble he's going to for you, the money he's spending to make you king of the world.'

'No joy is complete if it isn't shared.'

Gino gave a start, increasingly intrigued by my insinuations. 'I don't follow you, Turambo. What are you getting at?'

'Nothing.'

'You seem bitter.'

'I felt good at the farm.'

'It was the Duke who decided to bring you back.'

'Don't you think I should have a say in the matter? I'm the one who's doing the work, aren't I?'

'Yes, but I'm the one who's spending the money,' the Duke growled, coming into Gino's office.

He was in his shirtsleeves, with big patches of sweat under his armpits, and he was frowning. Gino stood to attention. The Duke motioned him to sit down again.

'Do you think I don't know?' he yelled at me, waving his cigar under my nose. 'I sent you to the farm to work, not to fall for that prick-teaser. You have no excuse.'

Gino started wiping his forehead with a handkerchief.

'You're behaving like a spoilt child, Turambo,' the Duke went on, 'and I'm not used to indulging spoilt children. When are you going to get it into your head that you have obligations? Do you know where Marcel Cargo is right now? In Marseilles. In a camp cut off from the world. Preparing for his fight with you. Even the press can't get to him. He's working like a dog day and night. No booze, no girls, no films.'

He threw his cigar out of the window and came back to me, his mouth quivering with rage.

'As of today, as of now, as of this moment, I don't want to hear any more about your escapades. You're going to get back to work, and every evening I want to see a carafe filled to the brim with your sweat. Marcel Cargo also wants the title. For your information, Olivier, the manager of the French champion, has said he wouldn't like to see his boy fight Cargo. That shows you the level he's at. I haven't slept since I heard that.'

The Duke had settled on a drastic programme. For the next ten days, I didn't have a minute to myself. It was one training session after another, at a frantic pace. In the morning, I would run on the beach. In the afternoon, I trained constantly at the gym. At night, Gino and Frédéric watched over my sleep, double-locking me in my room. I needed their permission to go to the toilet. Once I was in bed, the lights were switched off as if we were in a barracks. But in the dark, there was nothing to stop me thinking about Irène.

One Sunday, I claimed a family emergency and took a bus to Lourmel. I'd had enough of waiting. Fatma had gone home to give birth and there was nobody to take care of Ventabren. So I was hoping to find Irène at the farm, and there she was.

She asked me to stay for lunch. Afterwards, we retired to the outhouse and made love.

The next day, after training, I refused to follow Gino and Frédéric to Boulevard Mascara. Gino protested, tried to reason with me, but I wouldn't give in. I needed them to back off. Without Irène, the night was a deadly abyss. Filippi agreed to drop me outside Larbi the fruit seller's hut, provided he didn't go back without me. Nor would he drive all the way to the farm. He didn't want to be seen there, because he might be fired. I accepted his offer.

The following nights, with or without Filippi, I saw Irène. Much to Gino's dismay. But by six in the morning, I was back in Oran, right as rain. I would train intensively to make up for having 'deserted my post' the previous night.

'If the Duke hears about our little outings,' Filippi grumbled, 'he'll hang us on his coat rack.'

I didn't care.

My nights with Irène were worth the risk.


Gino told me he was going on ahead to Bône with Frédéric and De Stefano. The Duke needed a team on the spot to supervise the preparations for the fight with Marcel Cargo. I went with them to the station to make sure it wasn't a diversion. Once the train had left, I took a taxi to join Irène. We kept Ventabren company for much of the evening, then put him to bed. There was a fair in Saint-Eugène. Irène agreed to go with me.

The fair was in full swing. Families in their Sunday best bustled around the stands, some fishing for bottles, others shooting at cardboard targets. Loud old men, their sleeves rolled up to reveal withered biceps, attempted the high striker, much to the joy of the children. Mysterious fortune tellers looked for prey in the crowds. A garishly made-up clown juggled, surrounded by a flock of laughing kids. Everyone made merry, but I only had eyes for Irène, who looked wonderful in her guipure skirt. In that crowd, she was like the Pole Star in the Milky Way. She was wearing a pretty blouse decorated with fleur-de-lys, open at the neck; her black hair, hanging loose over her shoulders, emphasised her fine features. Young men turned to look at her as she passed, wolf whistles following in her wake. Irène burst out laughing, rather flattered. A squad of tipsy Zouaves started gravitating around us. I said a few words in Arabic and immediately we were left alone. I fired at rabbits for Irène without hitting a single one. Probably because of my over-excitement. I was so happy, and so proud when she put her arm round my waist. I'll never forget that night. The lanterns and the stars in the sky all shone for us. I was rediscovering a lost world, feelings that were far from original, of course, but they were very intense. With Irène beside me, I was having the time of my life. She marvelled at everything, cheered the entertainers, happily lost at games, laughed when I too failed. It was magical. We had a snack at a stall, standing amid the throng, biting into our burning-hot sandwiches; we rode wooden horses on a merry-go-round packed with children. I don't think I'd ever laughed so much in my life. I was laughing for nothing, laughing without reason, laughing because Irène was laughing. On the dodgems, where the vehicles mercilessly crashed into each other, parents were encouraging their kids to hit harder. Irène was game for a ride. There were no women on the track, but I didn't care. Not for anything in the world could I have refused her her fun. There was a long queue in front of the ticket office. We waited our turn, jostled by soldiers who were the worse for drink and attempted to grope the women. A hand tried to touch Irène's skirt; I showed my fist and the lout beat a retreat. We got in the cars and set off to attack the other drivers. The collisions lifted us out of our seats and we laughed uproariously. Irène was enjoying herself like a schoolgirl. The lights flooded her face with contrasting colours. She was happy; just watching her, I felt more content than I had ever thought I would be.

Intoxicated with ourselves, we left Saint-Eugène towards midnight, our heads buzzing with excitement, breathless but delighted.

It was late and there were no buses for Lourmel, and no taxis either.

'I'll have to learn to drive,' I said. 'That way, when I buy a car, we won't have to keep checking the time.'

To tell the truth, I hadn't looked for a taxi. I was hoping to force Irène to spend the night with me on Boulevard Mascara. Much to my delight, she didn't see anything wrong with that.

'Is this your place?' she asked when she saw the flat.

'It's my friend Gino's. He's gone to Bône.'

'I see,' she said, giving me a knowing wink. 'Could you run me a bath?'

'Right away. I'll heat the water.'

When she had finished washing, I brought her a big beach towel. She was standing in the bath, naked, hair plastered to her face. My hand shook as I wiped her back.

'You have a mark on your buttock,' I said.

'It's a birthmark.'

'It looks like a red fruit.'

'It's a strawberry.'

She got out of the bath, took the towel from me, dropped it on the floor, took me by the hand, laid me down on the bed and covered me with her body.

Day was breaking; we hadn't slept a wink. We wanted to savour every moment, we wanted the night to belong to us. We were monarchs in a room that was too small to contain our lovemaking; we no longer had to be quick about it, to make love on the sly. It was the first time in my life I had loved without constraint or anxiety, without a maid coming and knocking at the door or a client waiting impatiently in the corridor.

I would have liked the day to forget us, the minutes to reinvent themselves so that time *could take its time*. But time can't be tamed. Day was breaking, and we had to leave a little of our dream for the future.

'I leave for Bône on Tuesday,' I said with regret.

'What for?'

'For my match with Marcel Cargo.'

'Oh ...'

'It's a very important match.'

'As far as I'm concerned, a boxing match or a cockfight, it's all the same.'

'It's my job.'

'There are others.' She moved her finger over my lips, gently, tenderly. 'What's your real name?'

'Amayas.'

'What does it mean?'

'Leopard, I think, or something like that.'

'Amayas ... I like it. It sounds like a girl's name. It's certainly better than Turambo.'

'Maybe, but there's nothing behind it. Whereas Turambo tells my life story.'

'Will you tell me your life story one day?'

'As often as you like.'

She propped herself up on one elbow and looked down at me, smiling, then again snuggled up to me. 'Do you love me?'

'Yes.'

'Then say it ... Say you love me.'

'Do you doubt it?'

'I want to hear you say it. It matters to a woman, much more than a cockfight.'

'I'm crazy about you.'

'Say *I love you* ...'

'We don't say that kind of thing in our tribes.'

'Love isn't a thing.'

'I've never heard anyone say it at home.'

'You aren't at home, you're with me. Go on, I'm listening …'

She closed her eyes and listened carefully. Little beads of sweat were glistening on her silky skin. Her smell filled my head with tiny sparks. I wanted to take her again and never let her go.

'Cat got your tongue?'

'Irène …'

'Yes?' she said, encouragingly.

'Please …'

'No, you're going to say it or I won't believe you, ever again.'

I turned towards the wall. She took my chin and turned my head so that I was facing her, although my eyes were closed. 'This is where it happens, young man.'

I took a deep breath. 'I …'

'I …?'

'I love you,' I said at last.

'You see? It's so simple …'

She opened her eyes and I drowned in them. We made love until midday.

One hour before the fight with Marcel Cargo, an electricity blackout plunged the audience into an indescribable panic. There was talk of sabotage and a possible postponement of the match. The police brought in reinforcements in order to prevent intruders from getting into the hall and spectators from getting out. Nervousness spread through the changing rooms, which were lit by pocket torches. As the team of technicians were taking a long time to restore the current, lorries were dispatched to the scene and trained their headlights on the windows of the building to calm those people who were afraid of the dark. Frédéric kept going out for news and coming back empty-handed. The atmosphere was turning nightmarish. I tried to keep calm, but

De Stefano's anxiety was contagious. He couldn't keep still, venting his anger now on the organisers, now on Salvo. Mouss came and paid us a visit in the changing room. 'It's only a power cut,' he said. 'Apparently, it's common in Bône. Everything will soon be back to normal. In my opinion, it's a diversion intended to distract the opponent. The people of Bône are famous for their loyalty to their own. They're capable of all kinds of funny business to make life hard for champions from elsewhere.' He gave me a few pieces of advice, insisted I keep a cool head and apologised that he had to go because he didn't want to lose his seat.

A great cry of relief shook the hall when the lights came back on. From the changing rooms, we could hear people calling to each other, chairs being shifted; the return to normality relaxed us and De Stefano was at last able to sit on a bench and pray.

There was a huge crowd in the hall, which was shrouded in cigarette smoke. We had to elbow our way through to the ring. When Marcel Cargo appeared, the audience went wild. He was a tall, well-built fellow, so white-skinned he looked as if he was coated in flour, his hair close-cropped, his eyes inscrutable. He was quite a good-looking man in spite of his broken nose and thick mouth. He was a few pounds lighter than me, but he had a hard body and long arms. He threw himself at me before the bell had stopped ringing. It was obvious he'd prepared well. Quick, agile, he dodged my blows only to retaliate immediately with tremendous precision. He moved easily, his impressive reach keeping me at a distance, and evaded my traps with an elegance that delighted the audience. For the first three rounds, Marcel Cargo led on points. I found it hard to place my hook. Cargo was like an eel. Whenever I tried to get him in a corner, he would push me away and, with an acrobatic move, get back to the middle of the ring, his legs elusive, his right forceful. In the fourth round, he cut open my eyebrow. The referee checked the seriousness of my wound and declared me fit to continue the fight. My affected eye swelled: I could only half see, but my faculties were intact. I was just waiting for the moment to activate my left hook. Cargo was wonderfully supple and had great technique, but I knew I could get to him. In the fifth round, he made his fatal mistake. He knocked me to the ground for the second time. The referee started the count. I pretended to be dazed. Marcel took the bait. He put all his strength into a final attack, hoping to finish me off. In his frenzy, he let his guard down and my left struck him hard. He turned full circle, arms hanging loose, head tilted over towards his shoulder. I didn't need to deliver the knockout blow; he was done for before he hit the floor. A deathly silence fell over the hall. The crowd froze in their seats, as stunned as my opponent. The only sound came from the manager, yelling at his protégé to get up. Cargo didn't move. He lay on his back, unconscious, his gum shield askew. The referee finished the count and asked the seconds up into the ring. They couldn't wake Cargo. There were more and more people on the platform. The referee sensed that things might get out of hand, climbed discreetly over the ropes and vanished into the crowd. Suddenly, the manager rushed at me, screaming, 'I want to see what he's got in his glove ... I want to see what he's got in his glove ... Nobody's ever knocked Marcel out like that ... It's not possible ... That filthy Arab has something in his glove.' Salvo repelled an assailant, received a headbutt, hit back, and the fight started. In a few minutes, the brawl spread through the hall, setting Christians against Muslims in a frenzy of flying chairs and fierce blows, accompanied by a cacophony of insults and threats. The police rushed into the hall and quickly evacuated the dignitaries and officials before rushing at the troublemakers and the Araberbers. It was a mad, insane spectacle. Screams and whistles rang out over the sound of chairs being smashed. The lights were switched off and everyone rushed to the emergency exits in total confusion.

We left Bône that same night, for fear we might be attacked in the hotel. The eight of us piled into the dilapidated van of an Arab grocer who, moved by our plight, agreed to get us out of town. He drove us to a station in the middle of nowhere, some forty miles away. We took the first train to Algiers, then from Algiers the first connection for Oran, where a delegation was waiting for us with flowers and pennants. My victory over Marcel Cargo had spread like wildfire throughout the city. *L'Écho d'Oran* devoted three whole pages to it. Even *Le Petit Oranais* got in on the act, for once praising the achievements of a 'son of the city'.


The Duke gave a magnificent reception at the Bastrana Casino. The guests were hand picked. High-ranking officials, uniformed top brass, influential businessmen and local politicians mingled in a diffuse murmur. The Bollocqs received congratulations and declarations of allegiance at the entrance to the casino. All the guests were determined to greet them. The Duke played along, with the solemnity of a monarch. He loved being the centre of attention. I wasn't the hero; he was. I hated the way he displayed me like a trophy before dismissing me a minute later so he could show off some more. What did I actually mean to him? A racket, a conjuring trick, a mere puppet? In truth, sandwiched between his shadow and mine, nobody was especially interested in me.

The Bastrana was bustling. A band played popular tunes. Gino was busy flirting with Louise, satisfying her every whim. De Stefano had disappeared. I didn't know what to do with myself or whom to talk to. I felt cramped in my overly stiff suit, hemmed in by partygoers, their wine-soaked breath going right through me. From time to time, a stranger would introduce me to another stranger, who would chuckle a vague 'So this is the champion' before abandoning me to court one of the many movers and shakers there, because this kind of get-together was above all an opportunity to establish lucrative contacts and keep one's address book up to date.

I didn't like social occasions. They bored me! Always the same fake camaraderie, the same forced laughter, the same subtly poisonous words. In the midst of these prestigious people, surrounded by warbling ladies and distinguished gentlemen, I was nothing but a fighting cock arousing more curiosity than admiration. Many merely congratulated me from a distance in order not to have to shake my hand. I had the feeling I'd got off at the wrong floor, that I was in exile. This wasn't my world. I hated this pack of social climbers, substitute snobs and time-servers. Such people made me uncomfortable. They were only interested in gain: gaining ground, gaining money, coming out on top. Careerists, industrialists, men of independent means or retired buccaneers, they were all from the same mould, thought only of making a profit and getting ahead, devoid all the while of the slightest generosity, like handsome faces without a shadow of a smile. In their view, if you had money, you were worth money. If you were broke, you were of no interest. This was a long way from Medina Jedida, Eckmühl, the Derb, Saint-Eugène, Lamur or Sidi Lahouari, where good humour defied hardship. We had our show-offs, our tough guys, our big shots, but our kind had heart and at times even restraint. For those of us in the poor neighbourhoods, putting on airs was merely a good-natured bit of fun, whereas for the elite in the centre of town it was second nature. I was conscious that the world was made that way, that there were well-off families and poor families, and that there must be a rhyme and reason for this. But with these individuals in their white collars stepping on my feet without apologising because I was so invisible to them, I didn't think I could ever get anywhere; as far as they were concerned, I was simply a goose that laid golden eggs but would go straight in the cooking pot when I stopped laying.

I went out to get some air.

There is nothing worse than an idol nobody is interested in.

Outside, an endless queue of cars waited on the avenue. The chauffeurs chatted here and there in small groups, puffing at their cigarettes; some dozed behind their wheels.

I asked Filippi to drive me to Boulevard Mascara.

'I'm waiting for Gino,' he said.

'He's enjoying himself. He'll be in there for a while.'

'I'm sorry. Those are my instructions.'

I took the tram to Place d'Armes and got back to Rue du Général-Cérez on foot. I was furious.

Alarcon Ventabren wasn't unaware of my feelings for his daughter. I was at the farm practically every day and sometimes spent the night there. Irène seemed happy with me. We loved to stroll in the woods and go shopping together. In Lourmel, people were getting used to seeing us side by side. At first, unkind comments marred our shopping expeditions, then, because Irène would give as good as she got, we were left alone.

I was learning to drive in order to buy a car. I wanted to take Irène far away, where nothing could spoil our romance. A moment with her filled me with happiness. Whenever the time came for me to get back to Oran, I grew bad-tempered.

I felt like giving it all up.

At the gym, I had become so thin-skinned that the slightest criticism seemed huge to me. I couldn't bear anyone's remarks. Gino had given up trying to lecture me. He did as he pleased when it came to Louise. If he had the right to play the seducer, why not me? De Stefano tried not to upset me, but his sentimentality got on my nerves too.

Only at the farm did I regain a little calmness.

One Sunday, on a deserted beach, as Irène let the waves lap against her legs, her dress pulled up over her knees, I started drawing geometric shapes on the sand with a piece of wood.

'What are you writing?' she called, her hair flowing in the midday breeze.

'I'm drawing.'

'What are you drawing?'

'Your face, your eyes, your mouth, your shoulders, your chest, your hips, your legs …'

'Can I see?'

'No. You might distract me.'

She emerged from the water, amused and curious, and bent to look at my childish scribble. 'Is that what I look like?'

'It's just a sketch.'

'I didn't know my legs were so thin, my head's as round as a pumpkin, and my hips, my God, how horrible! … How can you be in love with a fright like me?'

'The heart doesn't ask questions. It ploughs straight on, and that's it.' I took her in my arms. 'I'm only happy when I'm with you.'

She abandoned herself to my embrace and tenderly moved her fingers over my cheek. 'I love you, Amayas.'

A bolder wave than the others came up and licked at our ankles. As the water receded, it erased my drawing as if by magic.

Irène kissed me on the mouth.

'I want to share my life with you,' I said.

She gave a start. With all my might, I prayed she wouldn't burst out laughing. She didn't. She looked at me in silence, her lips brushing mine; she trembled against me. 'Do you mean it?'

'Very much so.'

She broke free and walked over to a rock. We sat down side by side. Between our feet, little greenish crabs were playing hide and seek, almost imperceptible in the eddying of the foam. The horizon was veiled in sea spray. The squawking of the seagulls bounced off the reef, as sharp as razor cuts.

'You've caught me off guard, Amayas.'

'We've been together for months. When I think about the future, I can't imagine it without you.'

Her eyes ran to question the sea, then returned to put me to the test. 'I'm older than you.'

'I don't care about your age.'

'But I do.'

'I love you, that's all that matters. I want to marry you.'

The lapping of the backwash sounded a hundred times louder.

'This kind of decision can't be taken lightly,' she said.

'I've been thinking about it for weeks. There isn't the slightest doubt in my mind: it's you I want.'

She put her hand on my mouth to stop me. 'Be quiet and let's listen to the sound of the sea.'

'It won't teach us anything we don't already know.'

'And what do we know, Amayas?'

'What we want with all our heart.'

'What do you know about my heart?'

Her voice was soft and measured. My heart was pounding. I dreaded rejection, dreaded the thought that she would snub me like Aïda. Irène was thinking. She looked sad. I took her hands, and she didn't remove them.

'I'd like to start a family,' she said. 'But not at any price.'

'Name your price.'

She looked me up and down, a dubious gleam in her eyes. 'I'm a country girl, Amayas. I love simple things. To have a simple husband, a simple life, no clamour, no commotion.'

'Don't you think I can give you that?'

'No, I don't. A wife can't share her husband with the crowd.'

I tried to object, but she placed her hand on my mouth again and kissed me.

'Let's not complicate things,' she whispered. 'Let's enjoy the present and let the future look after itself.'

I wasn't disappointed. Irène hadn't said no.

A young carter took us as far as the road. Sitting in the back, our hands gripping the edge of the cart and our feet hanging out, we watched the sea launch its regiments of foam onto the beach. Irène was silent. Whenever she saw me looking at her, her shoulders contracted.

We waited for the bus in silence, sitting under a tree.

In the evening after dinner, we helped Ventabren into bed and then went for a walk around the estate to clear our heads. In our part of the world, autumn is a spoilsport. Once summer is over, the cicadas fall silent and faces turn grey. We are a people of the sun; the slightest imperfection in our sky unsettles us. When the weather is fine, our thoughts are bright and any small thing excites us. But all it takes is for a cloud to blot out our sun and our soul darkens. Irène was procrastinating because of the cold, I was sure of it. We sat down on the edge of the well to gaze at the countryside. On the plain, shrouded in mystery, the lights of the village shimmered like dying fireflies. Irène had her shawl pulled tight around her, and her hands lay in her lap. She hadn't said a word since the beach. I suffered her silence like a wound. Had I been clumsy? Had I upset her? She didn't seem to be angry with me, but I couldn't understand the sadness on her face.

'No,' she said, sensing I was about to take her hand, 'leave me alone.'

'Did I hurt you?'

'You upset me.'

'I'll be a good husband.'

'You can't be. I'm the daughter of a boxer. I know what a boxer's family life is like. It's no laughing matter.'

'I know some who —'

'Please,' she cut in, 'you don't know anything about it.'

'I'm not going to be a boxer all my life.'

'Maybe, but I'll be too old for you by the time you hang up your gloves. And you'll be too damaged to make up for lost time.'

Droplets of rain started falling here and there. The wind rose a notch, cold, almost icy. A large cloud moved in front of the moon, swallowing it as it passed.

'I don't like depending on something I can't control,' she sighed. 'I want to stay mistress of my marriage, do you understand? I don't want to have to worry myself sick because my husband is gambling with our life in a boxing ring ... I love this hill. One day, I'll plant vines here and watch them grow. The sea salt will give me good grapes, which I'll gather with my own hands. I'll have a few cows too. That way, my mornings won't be disturbed by the disgusting spluttering of the milkman's van. With a bit of luck, I'll raise three or four horses. I'll spend my days watching them graze and rear in the open air. That's my dream, Amayas. As simple as that.'

She stood up and walked back to the house. She went up to her room but didn't switch the light on. She hadn't invited me to join her. She didn't come to the outhouse as she had on previous nights. I waited for her, then, unable to bear the sense of abandonment that had taken hold of my refuge, I decided to leave the farm. There was no bus for Oran at that hour, but I needed air.

I slept in the hut of Larbi the fruit seller.

# 5

My mother was beside herself. She hated people dropping in unexpectedly. She liked to make sure that her guests had the best possible reception; in other words, in a house that was clean and tidy. It was after midday when I surprised her at lunch, the low table littered with scraps of food. The look she gave me was full of reproach. Especially as I wasn't alone: Irène was with me. My mother looked her up and down, her gaze lingering on her short skirt, her red-painted mouth, her bare neck. She ordered us to stay in the courtyard until she had finished clearing up. Irène was laughing to herself, amused by this surly woman who hadn't even taken the trouble to say hello.

The neighbour's children giggled in their corner, watching us, their impish little heads arranged one on top of the other in the doorway.

I had told my mother about Irène, but she wasn't expecting to see her in her own home. In our traditions, it wasn't done. Taken by surprise, my mother had to resign herself to the situation. She began by closing the door of the room where my father was rotting away and admitted us to the living room.

Irène handed her a little package. 'Chocolate for you, Madame.'

We sat down on mats. Irène found it hard to pull her skirt down over her knees. I offered her a cushion, which she hurriedly put against her legs. My mother served us mint tea.

As we sipped it, she weighed up my companion, examining her thoroughly, ostentatiously, evaluating her age, her strength, her curves, her freshness, the way she held herself, increasing Irène's embarrassment and making her put down her glass for fear of her tea going down the wrong way.

'Does she speak Arabic?' my mother asked me in Kabyle.

'Yes.'

'Is she a Muslim?'

'She's a believer.'

'I think she's too old for you.'

'And I think she's very pretty.'

'Yes, she's pretty. But she doesn't look easy to handle, not the kind to let herself be ruled with an iron fist.'

'Maybe that's why I chose her.'

'I get the feeling she's knows a thing or two about men.'

'She's been married before.'

'I suspected as much. She's too beautiful to have been spared that.'

Irène was smiling as she listened to us. She knew we were talking about her and guessed the sense of our words. 'You have a beautiful house, Madame,' she said in Arabic.

My mother made a maraboutic sign to ward off the evil eye. She said nothing more and even allowed herself to withdraw in order to leave us alone. Mekki arrived with a shopping bag, which he put down on the ground when he discovered us in the living room. The look he gave Irène was unambiguous. He went straight back out into the street, horrified by the 'outrageous dress of that painted foreigner'.

'You don't bring a half-naked woman to the house,' he yelled at me later. 'I bet she drinks and smokes. Women who dare to look men in the eyes are not desirable. What are you hoping for by going with her? To be the same as her people? They'll reject you. To impress the people of your community? They already feel sorry for you.' He turned to my mother. 'Why don't you say something, Taos? He's your son.'

'Since when do women have an opinion?'

'He's planning to marry an unbeliever. One who's been rejected, what's more. A wreck her own people are tired of. What does she have that our virgins don't? Make-up? Her offensive dress? Her shamelessness? It's all too obvious that she's older than him.'

'I'm older than my husband.'

'Am I to understand that you approve of your son?'

'He can do what he likes. It's his life.'

Mekki smashed his fist against the wall. 'We'll be the laughing stock of the neighbours.'

'Have we ever been anything else?' my mother retorted.

'I'm still the head of this family and your husband's return doesn't change that. I shan't approve a union the saints would never bless. Your son's being corrupted. He's spent so much time with unbelievers, he's starting to be like them. If he's making money, why not benefit a girl from his own people?'

I let him curse and went out to join Gino on Boulevard Mascara.


The Duke advanced me part of the money to buy a Fiat 508 Balilla sports car. I was in seventh heaven. In Medina Jedida, the urchins ran after me, shrieking as if at a carnival. They threw their chechias into the air and almost got run over. My mother refused categorically to get in and let me take her for a ride. She didn't trust me, unable to resign herself to the idea that her son might own a car and drive it without crashing into a wall.

I loved driving along the avenue, my elbow resting on the windowsill, the wind on my face. I savoured the intoxication of a freedom I had never imagined. Irène and I went everywhere, even going as far afield as Nemours. Tlemcen was ours, as were the still-rudimentary resort at Hammam-Bouhadjar, the beaches of Cap-Blanc and picnics in the woods. Occasionally, we took Ventabren with us. We'd sit him at the foot of a tree and bustle around a campfire. Our grilled meat made us smell of smoke for the whole day. In the evening, we'd go to the cinema. I had a particular liking for swashbuckling adventures, but Irène hated violence and couldn't bear stories that ended sadly; she preferred romantic films with happy endings, where the two lovers embraced and the audience cheered.

I was living through the happiest days of my life.

Five months before the big match for the North African title – Pascal Bonnot, the reigning champion, twice postponed our match for dubious reasons – the Duke summoned me to his office. Gino, Frédéric and De Stefano were there, as were two tough-looking men I'd never seen before who could easily have been gangsters. The Duke told me his plan. As far as he and his advisers were concerned, a stay in Marseilles was essential, on the one hand to prepare in secret, and on the other hand to benefit from the help of the best trainers in France.

I accepted.

The same day, I announced to Irène that I was going across the Mediterranean for eight weeks' training. We were in the stable. Irène was grooming her mare. She didn't react, just continued brushing her animal as if she hadn't heard me. Light rain was falling on the hill.

'I'd like you to come with me to Marseilles.'

She gasped scornfully. 'You want me to go with you to France?'

'Yes.'

'What about my father?'

'We'll take him with us.'

She put away her brush and threw a blanket over the mare. Her gestures were brusque. 'My father will never want to leave here. This land is his flesh. Nothing in the world suits his soul better than these hills. What landscape could make him forget this magnificent view over the orange groves and vineyards stretching as far as Misserghin, and the scrub where the wolves howl at the moon every night?'

She pushed me aside slightly because I was standing in the light.

'Neither my father nor I will ever agree to let this land out of our sight. To us, it's the gods' most perfect creation.'

'We'll come back here afterwards.'

'After what? We'll never agree to leave here, I tell you. Not for a day, not for a minute. Even when we sleep, it's the only thing we see in our dreams.'

I followed her out into the courtyard. She was walking fast as if trying to shake me off.

'This is my career, Irène.'

'I never said it wasn't. And I'm not stopping you from going wherever you like. We aren't married yet. In fact, I don't think we ever will be. I hate boxing.'

'It's a profession like any other. It's my profession.'

She stopped abruptly and turned round to face me, her lips quivering with anger. 'What kind of profession is it where you just have to go down twice in succession for the descent into hell to start? I know about it, you know, and I'm not thrilled about it. Pipo from Algiers, Fernandez, Sidibba the Moroccan – they all trained here. They slept in the same outhouse you're sleeping in now, they ran on the same tracks. They all thought they were invincible. Girls fell into their arms and the crowds worshipped them. They had their photographs in the papers and their posters on the walls. They dreamt of money and adventure, and Pipo was even planning to build himself a palace on the heights of Kouba.

And one night, in a hall full to bursting, with the spotlights on him, bang! He was down! Shock horror. The invincible Pipo is down! And everything collapses around him. The last I heard, he has more alcohol than blood in his veins and can't even find his own way home.'

'I'm not Pipo.'

'It doesn't matter, you'll meet the same fate. It's inevitable. One day, you'll meet someone who's stronger than you and you'll find yourself on the floor. Your fans will turn away from you because their hearts only beat for new blood. You'll try to make a comeback, fighting with nonentities. You'll be displayed in a dilapidated ring like a fairground strong man. When you don't have any power left in you, you'll drown your sorrows in seedy bars and come home to ruin my nights. And if I don't like it, you'll beat me to prove to yourself that you're not the lowest of the low.'

'I'll never raise my hand to you.'

'That's what men say when they aren't dead drunk. My father always had a flower for my mother when he came home in the evening. He was attentive and affectionate, and he treated my mother with a lot of respect. She was the cherry on his cake … Like you, he climbed the ladder without slipping, sure that he'd reach the top and stay there. Like you, he won fight after fight at the beginning of his career. Everything went well for him. By the age of twenty-seven, he was champion of France and nearly became world champion. Then he met his tamer. Deprived of his title, he started doubting – and changing. Whenever he won, he reverted to being the father I knew. Whenever he lost, he turned into a monster I was just beginning to discover. When he came home, no more flowers for my mother, just complaints and excuses to cause scenes. From my bed, I'd hear him swearing like a trooper. In the morning, my mother would stay shut up in her room so that I wouldn't see the marks on her face. In the evening, when she sensed that my father was about to return, she'd tremble like a goat waiting for a hyena's approach. To overcome her fears, she started drinking. Sometimes, she'd climb out through the window and run off into the night. My father would have to look for her at the neighbours' or else in the fields. He'd bring her home, promising never again to raise his hand to her, to stop drinking, to stop choosing the wrong enemy. The respite would last a few days, a week, then, without warning, the scenes would start again.'

Her face was right up against mine, contorted with sorrow; tears flooded her lashes.

'My mother went through hell,' she continued, hammering out her words. 'She was as beautiful as an angel, but by the age of thirty-five she'd grown old. Her face reflected nothing but her ordeal. Until the night she ran away and didn't come back. She left for good and we never heard from her again … That's right, Amayas! My mother left because she was tired of being a punch bag for a boxer who'd fallen from favour … And since then, I've never stopped hating boxing. It isn't a profession; it's a vice! Deposed gods aren't forgiven. Cheers are closer to jeers than disappointment is to madness. I have no desire to share my life with someone who's damaged in body and spirit. I don't see myself growing old scraping a washed-up drunkard off the ground. That's not for me, Amayas. Fame in the ring is like a yo-yo, and I don't like its highs and lows. I'm a stupid, innocent dreamer. My happiness is in the harmony of things. I want to live with a man who'll look at my fields the same way I do and have the same contempt for wealth and show. That's my price for believing you love me. And then I'll love you too, with all my heart and strength.'

*

The Duke started tearing his hair out when he heard that I didn't want to go to Marseilles to train. According to Frédéric, he'd been positively apoplectic. His shouts rang out through the entire building. Some members of his staff had deserted their desks, while others had barricaded themselves behind their files. It didn't impress me. I refused to go to Marseilles. Gino called me all the names under the sun. 'When are you going to stop behaving like an idiot?' he cried, nervously loosening his tie. 'I've had enough of cleaning up after you.' His attempts to win me over failed. The Duke didn't beat about the bush. He just threatened to fire Gino if he couldn't make me see reason.

Francis declared it was a waste of time to reason with someone as stupid as me. 'The police say that nationalist agitators are active in the mosques, hammams and cafés. Turambo must have risen to the bait. He's easily influenced. A charlatan in a turban must have filled his head with stupid ideas.'

'I'm not interested in politics,' I cried.

'Then it's a relative or a jealous neighbour who's driven you crazy. Arabs battle for advantages. As soon as one of them manages to keep his head above water, the others try to cut it off.'

'What are you trying to insinuate, Francis?'

'I'm trying to save you from a fall. You mustn't listen to your people. They're envious. They resent you because you're less and less like them, because you're a success. They're jealous. They're not looking out for you, they want you to fail. They want you to fade away, to become a shadow of yourself so that everyone can go back to the darkness. That's why you people lag behind other nations. Always fighting each other, blowing each other apart, destroying each other with slander and betrayal.'

'My family have nothing to do with my decision.'

'Damn it, do you realise the grave you're digging for yourself?'

'Provided it's not for you.'

Francis spat on the floor. 'I always thought Arabs were blinkered. Now I know why you're their champion.'

I took a step in his direction.

He took out a flick knife. 'Lay your dirty barbarian mitts on me and I won't leave you a finger to wipe your arse with.'

His eyes burnt with a murderous flame. The most surprising thing was that neither De Stefano, nor Frédéric, nor Gino condemned Francis's attitude. We were in the manager's office. In the embarrassed expressions around me, I saw a faint aversion. Their tight jaws, their drawn features, their stiffness showed revulsion for me. I had strangers around me. These men I'd held dear, these good friends who were as important to me as my family, these fine men with whom I'd shared my joys and sorrows, were rejecting me simply because for once I didn't agree with their plans. I realised at that moment that I was nothing but a modern-day gladiator, a boxing-gala slave only there to entertain the gallery, that my kingdom was limited to an arena outside which I didn't count at all. Even Gino was acting in his own interests; he was more concerned about his privileges than my wounds. And I was wounded to the core. Wounded and disgusted.

Sick at heart, my eyes went from Gino to Frédéric, from De Stefano to the flick knife.

'You bunch of vultures,' I cried. 'What I want deep down doesn't come into your calculations. It doesn't interest you. All you care about is the trade-off: blows for me, money for you.'

'Turambo,' Gino moaned.

'Don't say a word,' I said. 'I think everything's been said.'

Francis was just putting away his knife. My right catapulted him against the wall. Surprised, he slid to the floor, his hands over his face. Seeing his bloodstained fingers, he whined, 'Shit! He broke my nose.'

'What did you expect from a barbarian?' I said.

The window pane broke clean across when I slammed the door behind me.

A few days later, I overheard Jérôme the milkman asking Alarcon Ventabren if the men who had come to see him were criminals. They were chatting behind the stable, facing the sun, Ventabren in his wheelchair and the milkman on his van. When he left, I wanted to know more about that strange visit.

Ventabren shrugged. 'Oh, it's nothing really bad,' he said. 'Your friends are desperate. They told me you're refusing to go to Marseilles to train and asked me to reason with you.'

'And?'

'I think a period of training in France is important for you.'

'Did they threaten you?'

'Why would they threaten me? I've been punished enough ... You know something, my boy? When you choose a path, however difficult it is, you should see it through to the end. Otherwise, you'll never know what it has in store for you. You're a champion. You represent a lot of challenges, and a lot of hopes are riding on you. Mood swings have no place in this kind of adventure. You do what you're told, that's all. Irène's a fine woman, but women don't know when to stop interfering in men's business. They're possessive and they exaggerate their role in life. They reduce the basics to the little things that suit them. Men are conquerors by nature. They need space, room to move about in that's as big as their hunger for success. Wars are men's obsession. Power, revolutions, expeditions, inventions, ideologies, religions, anything that moves, reforms and destroys in order to rebuild is part of the vocation of men. If it was only up to women, we'd still be chewing on mammoths' bones in the back of a cave. Because a woman is a fragile creature without real ambition. For her, the world stops with her little family and she measures time in relation to the age of her children. If you want my advice, son, go to Marseilles. Don't leave the table when the banquet is made up of honours and titles. For a man, life without glory is nothing but a slow death.'

I found his ideas questionable, but I respected his age and experience too much to ask him what he had done to his wife and what he was doing in a wheelchair, turning his back on the rest of the world. I felt too sorry for him in his decrepit state to tell him that *no field of honour can equal a woman's bed*, that no glory can make up for a lost love.

Gino was depressed. According to a neighbour, he'd been shut away at home for four days, with the door and shutters closed. His face lined, his hair dishevelled, he sat bent over the kitchen table, his head in his hands, an empty bottle of brandy next to an overturned glass. I couldn't remember ever seeing him drunk before. His braces dangled on either side of the chair and his vest was an embarrassment.

He looked up at me with a hangdog expression.

'Were you with the guys who went to bother Ventabren?'

He made a vague movement with his wrist. 'Piss off.'

'You haven't answered my question, Gino. Were you with them?'

'No.'

'What did they want?'

'Why don't you ask them?'

'Who were they?'

Gino swept the table with the back of his hand. The bottle and the glass fell to the floor and smashed. 'Wasn't that performance

315

of yours enough for you? Now you have to come and piss me off in my own home.'

'Who were they?'

'The two guys from Marseilles. You don't want to rub them up the wrong way, I warn you. When they invest a penny, they see to it that it makes them a fortune. They're counting on you and they're very bad losers.'

'Are you trying to scare me, Gino?'

'What's the point when you can't see the danger?'

'Why didn't you tell me?'

'Because you don't listen.' He pushed back his chair and got unsteadily to his feet, his mouth twisted with rage. 'You're pig-headed, Turambo. Because of you, our team is suspended and our efforts may end in failure. You struggled to get to the well, but once you got there, you spat in it. It's true, you don't see any further than the tip of your nose, but not seeing a mountain crumble, not hearing it crashing down on you, isn't short-sightedness, it isn't blindness, it's worse than irresponsibility and stupidity put together. I don't understand you and I'm afraid you don't understand yourself. Anyone else in your place would be thanking heaven day and night. You were just a down-and-out doing crummy jobs and getting his arse kicked left, right and centre.'

'You think I've gone up in the world, Gino? I'm still the same wretch I was. The only difference is that now I get my arse kicked by expensive shoes.'

'Who put that nonsense in your bird brain? That whore who can't find shoes to fit her and is trampling all over you?'

'Watch your language, Gino.'

He braced himself against the wall and launched himself at me. 'Go on, hit me. You've just floored me. Carry on. Knock me out. You'd be doing me a favour. I haven't slept a wink for three nights. Knock me senseless. That way, for a few hours I'll forget the mess you're got me into. Because of your stubbornness, I've lost my job, lost my bearings, lost my prospects.'

# 6

I left for Marseilles.

My training period was revised downwards because of my reluctance and reduced to three weeks; for me, it might as well have been months. I didn't tell Irène. I didn't have the guts. One morning, I threw my things in two duffle bags and jumped into a car with the two men from Marseilles, who were waiting for me at the corner of Rue du Général-Cérez. The Duke and his men were at the quay, getting impatient. They were relieved to see me and promised me I wouldn't regret it. The crossing was rough. I'd never been on a boat before. I was violently seasick. It took me several days and many infusions to get over it.

The only thing I remember about Marseilles is a remote camp, massive trials, days as strict as a prison regime, relentless sparring partners and cold nights howling with mistral. That was enough to develop my aggressiveness. I was treated like an animal that's starved in order to prepare it for a most gruesome slaughter. I thought more about Pascal Bonnot than Irène; I was only waiting for the moment I'd meet him in the ring and reduce him to a pulp. I hated my new trainers, their rough manners, their arrogance; they were obtuse, sinister, conceited people; they didn't speak, they yelled, convinced that anyone from the colonies was a savage picked straight from a baobab tree. From the start, I sensed that things were going to work out badly. I hated being sprayed with spittle when I was yelled at. I came to blows with a stunted, swollen-headed assistant who kept making racist remarks about Arabs. Later, I realised that these provocations and hostilities were a tactic. They were driving me mad with hatred with the clear aim of making my next opponent, Pascal Bonnot, a walkover.

I returned to Oran transformed, thin-skinned, sensitive. My interactions with my former friends in Rue Wagram were limited to good morning and good night. Nothing was the way it had been before. Apart from Tobias, all the others got me down. The laughter that had once echoed round the gym had given way to cold formality. De Stefano was unhappy. Whenever he started a conversation with me, I quickly climbed into the ring. My attitude saddened him, but he realised that it was what I wanted. I'd become embittered, unpleasant, taciturn, even arrogant. Even Irène had noticed that I almost never smiled now, that I lost my temper over nothing, that I enjoyed nights on the town and cinema trips less and less. She still didn't know where I had been during those three horrible weeks and didn't ask me. I might have changed, but I was back, and that was all that mattered to her. In truth, I was asking myself a lot of questions. At night, I would wake up with my head in a vice and go out into the courtyard to get a bit of fresh air. Irène would join me, wrapped in a sheet, and walk beside me in silence. I didn't know what to say to her.

Nestled in hills garlanded with gardens and palaces, Algiers was bathed in bright sunshine that March morning in 1935. I was discovering the city for the first time in my life. It was beautiful, its seafront lined with luxurious apartment buildings that seemed to smile at the Mediterranean. In Oran, we thought people from Algiers were very affected. We didn't like them. When they came to us, they put on airs that marked them out, proud of their sharp accent, convinced they belonged to a superior class. They had a highly developed sense of repartee which often led to arguments in our streets, since all that the people of Oran had to counter the coolness of their rivals' words was their skill with their fists. But in Medina Jedida and the Araberber quarters, you couldn't separate Algiers from politics. There was talk of ulemas, Muslim associations, in other words, groups of our fellow citizens who lived in Algiers in neighbourhoods identical to ours, but who refused to be like dumb cattle: they created ideological movements that spoke of a glorious past and claimed rights about which I understood very little. And when Muslims came from Algiers to Oran, unlike the Christians, we treated them with respect. Discussions continued long into the night, and in the morning, in our cafés, everyone talked in low voices and kept a discreet eye on the street. Informants were at work, the police increased their numbers, and the crowds in the souks were infiltrated. To be honest, I wasn't interested in this occasional unrest in our cities. For me, it was a mystery as impenetrable as the ways of the Lord. The acclaim I received made me deaf even to the call of the muezzin.

Leaning out of the window of the railway carriage, I gazed at the light-filled city, its white buildings, its cars racing along the boulevards, its hordes of pedestrians who seemed to multiply at terrifying speed. Frédéric was standing next to me, telling me about the sites, the neighbourhoods, the holy places of the capital: the Jardin d'Essai, one of the most fantastic places in the world, Notre-Dame-d'Afrique overlooking the bay, the Casbah huddled around its centuries-old courtyards, Bab el-Oued where little people saw things in a big way, Square Port-Saïd overrun with pick-up artists and poets, closely flanked by the Military Club and the municipal theatre.

'It's a city of legend,' Frédéric said. 'No passing stranger leaves it without taking something away in his suitcase. When you pass through Algiers, you go through a mirror. You arrive with one soul and leave with an entirely new, sublime one. Algiers changes a person with a click of her fingers. It was in Algiers that the Goncourt brothers, who thought they were destined for a life creating art on canvas, finally turned their backs on painting to devote themselves body and soul to literature. It was in Algiers, at an ordinary barber's shop in the Casbah, on 28 April 1882, that Karl Marx, who was famous for his beard, had it shaved off in order to be able to recognise himself in the mirror …'

'You might as well talk to him about Cervantes' five years in captivity and Guy de Maupassant's sexual exploits while you're about it,' Francis muttered, making sure he stayed as far as possible from my fists. 'He probably doesn't even know the name of the President of France.'

'Leave him alone,' De Stefano grunted.

A swarm of journalists greeted us when we got off the train, immediately drawing a crowd on the platform. A handful of policemen tried in vain to contain it. Flashbulbs went off on all sides. Frédéric agreed to answer a few questions. The photographers jostled one another to get a picture of me. They yelled at me to turn and look at the camera, to pose in front of the train carriage. I didn't listen to them.

'How many rounds do you think you'll last, Turambo?' cried a puny fellow hiding behind his notebook.

'Is it true you made a will before coming to Algiers?'

'What's in your gloves this time, Monsieur Turambo?'

'His fists, nothing but his fists,' De Stefano said irritably.

'That's not what they say in Bône.'

'The people there are bad losers. My boxer's gloves were checked by experts. We even gave them as a gift to the mayor.'

The aggressiveness of the journalists and their insinuations were exasperating. We hurried out of the station and got in the cars waiting for us on the other side of the street. The Duke had booked us rooms in the Hôtel Saint-Georges. There too, photographers and journalists lay in wait for us, including some British ones speaking French nasally and some Americans flanked by interpreters. A bellboy showed me to my room, made sure I had everything I needed and lingered in the entrance as if looking for something. I dismissed him; he left reluctantly, a disappointed pout replacing the smile that had stretched from ear to ear two minutes earlier. We had lunch in the hotel restaurant. In the afternoon, a group of Araberbers came to reception and asked to meet me. It was a small committee sent by a Muslim movement to invite me to the football match between Mouloudia of Algiers and the Christian team of Ruisseau. Frédéric firmly declined the invitation, claiming that my fight was the next day, that the streets weren't safe, and that I needed calm and rest. I curtly told him to mind his own business. Since I'd come back from Marseilles, there'd been no love lost between my staff and me. I didn't listen to anyone and made it clear I wasn't going to be bossed about. Fearing that things might turn nasty, Frédéric reluctantly agreed, but asked Tobias to go with me. In the packed stadium, Muslim dignitaries came and congratulated me on my career and assured me of their blessing. Mouloudia beat the opposing team roundly by six goals to one. The committee offered me a guided tour of the Casbah. Tobias categorically refused; I don't know if it was because of his wooden leg or because he had been given strict instructions.

A few minutes before dinner, the hotel reception informed me that someone wanted to talk to me. I changed and went down to the foyer, where a man dressed like an effendi – a three-piece suit and a fez pulled down over his temples – was waiting on a sofa. He stood up and shook my hand. He was tall, with a massive nose in a chiselled face. His piercing eyes betrayed a concealed authority, a rock-solid determination.

'My name is Ferhat Abbas.' He paused, then, realising his name meant nothing to me, went on, 'I'm an activist for our people's cause ... I assume you've heard of the Association of Muslim Students?'

'The Association of what?'

The man swallowed, surprised by my ignorance. 'You don't know the Association of Muslim Students?'

'No.'

'What planet have you been living on, my brother?'

'I never went to school, sir.'

'This has nothing to do with school, but with our nation. It's sometimes necessary to listen to what is being whispered in dark corners and behind bars ... I'm a pharmacist by profession, but I write articles in the press and organise political debates and clandestine congresses. I've come from Sétif specially to meet you, and I'm obliged to leave for the Aurès tonight, as soon as we've finished here.'

'You're not staying for the match?'

'I'd rather not.'

He unfolded a newspaper on the table and tapped a picture of an athlete running on the track of a packed stadium.

'His name's Ahmed Bouguerra el-Ouafi. Have you heard of him?'

'No.'

'He's our Olympic champion, our first and only gold medallist. He won by a long way at the Amsterdam Games in 1928, but many of our countrymen don't know him because he isn't talked about in the papers or on the radio. We're going to remedy that injustice and make sure we boast of his merits everywhere in our cities and even in our remote douars. Sport is an extraordinary political argument. No nation can hold its head up high without idols. We need our champions. They're as indispensable as air and water. That's why I've come to see you, my dear brother. Tomorrow, you *have* to win. Tomorrow, we want to have our North African champion to prove to the world that we exist ...'

He abruptly picked up his newspaper and slipped it into the inside pocket of his jacket. Two suspicious-looking individuals had just entered the foyer and were walking towards the reception desk.

'I have to go,' the activist whispered. 'Don't forget, my brother, your fight is ours; we're already claiming your victory. Tomorrow, all the Muslims in our country will be glued to their radios. Don't disappoint us.'

He walked behind a row of columns, dabbing himself with a handkerchief in order to hide his face, and quickly escaped through a service door.

A forest of spectral heads were jabbering in the huge hall. The city elite had turned out for the match. There was not a free seat or a clear aisle to be seen. It was boiling hot in spite of the subdued light streaking the corners with thin shadows. People were fanning themselves with whatever they could find.

Surrounded by a delegation of dignitaries from Oran, the Duke was lounging in one of the front boxes. Local celebrities and politicians were fidgeting with impatience near the ring. There were women too, stylish, haughty-looking women. I couldn't remember ever having seen women at a boxing match in Oran or anywhere else – was it because they had this head start that people from Algiers assumed the right to look down on us?

I watched the hundreds of people shifting in their seats, like vultures hovering before the feeding frenzy. In the midst of this human chaos, I felt as lonely as a sacrificial lamb. A bottomless fear made my stomach churn. It wasn't because of Pascal Bonnot or the thousands of Muslims I imagined glued to their radios. My anxiety had nothing to do with what was at stake that evening: it was made up of nagging questions I couldn't make sense of. I would have liked time to stop because it was already exhausting me; I would have liked the match to have taken place the day before, or the week before, or else the year before. The sense of anticipation made it hard to focus. My arms had gone numb. My temples felt as if they were being squeezed by pincers, causing shooting pain at the back of my head. I was sweating profusely and the fight hadn't started yet.

A spotlight swept over the terraces and came to rest on a tall, strapping man in a three-piece suit straight from the tailor, with a long red scarf around his neck. It was Georges Carpentier in the flesh, a victorious centurion back from the war, acclaimed by the people and praised by the gods. The world champion raised his arms to thank the audience, the spotlight surrounding him with a halo …

It was a fight to the death. Pascal Bonnot hadn't come to defend his title but to dissuade contenders from fighting for it. North African champion three years in succession, he knocked out his opponents one after the other with the clear aim never to see them back in the ring again. It wasn't by chance that he was nicknamed 'the tank'. Pascal Bonnot didn't box, he demolished. He didn't have Marcel Cargo's technique or elegance, but he was as formidable as a thunderbolt and as efficient as a howitzer. Most of the legends who had crossed his path had gone into decline. Pipo, Sidibba the Moroccan, Bernard-Bernard, all kings of the ring who had enthused the crowds and set starlets' hearts a-flutter, had endured a fight with Bonnot like a blow of fate. The sun would never again rise for them. Bonnot's blows were simply intended to remove obstacles from his path. His reputation laid low his rivals before his punches did. His fights never went past the fifth round, which suggested he might have stamina problems. That was the one likely chink in his armour, hence the intensive training I had been put through in Marseilles. My trainers were banking on my ability to wear out my opponent, while Bonnot counted on brute force to wipe out his opponents in the opening rounds. He put all his strength into that, without holding anything back. My one chance might lie in taking advantage of his carelessness. Put doubt in his mind, De Stefano kept telling me. If you hold out past the sixth round, he'll lose his nerve and start to have doubts. Every time you hit him, you'll unsettle him ...

Bonnot pounced on me like a bird of prey. He hit hard. A real blacksmith. His intentions were clear. He aimed at my shoulders to soften my guard. If he kept up the pace, he was sure to get me by the third round. His tactics were clear. I got away quickly, moved around him, dodged his traps. The audience whistled, blaming me for avoiding confrontation. Bonnot charged repeatedly. He was about the same height as me. His powerful torso was in marked contrast to his thin legs. I found his figure grotesque. He hit me twice on the head, not very effectively. In the fourth round, my left hook sent him onto the ropes. It was at that exact moment that his expression darkened. I was no longer just a common punch bag as far as he was concerned. I let him come, huddling in a corner, well protected by my gloves. Bonnot unleashed his fury on me, galvanised by the deafening clamour in the hall. As soon as his panting became feverish, I pushed him away, made him run, then I went back into a corner and invited him to use up his energy. The fight turned into a bloodbath from the seventh round on. Bonnot was starting to tire, doubt settling in his mind. He increased his attacks and his blunders. His growing irritation replaced his previous concentration, botched his feints. It was time for me to set the pace. For the first time, he retreated. My uppercut knocked him twice to the floor. In the hall, the yelling died down. People were starting to fear the impossible. Bonnot recovered quickly, and then he sent me to the floor. His right plunged me into a soundless world. Dazed, I vaguely saw the referee starting to count me out. When he moved away, Bonnot was on me again. His blows echoed through me like underground explosions. Creaking beneath me, the floor felt like the trapdoor of a gallows. I went back to my corner, swaying, too shaken to get what De Stefano was droning on about. Salvo hurt me as he tended to me. My right eye was blurred, there was blood on my cheek, the gum shield in my mouth was torturing me. The Duke approached the ring and yelled something at me. Gino was holding his head in both hands. I couldn't have looked very good.

No sooner was he released back into the ring than Bonnot pursued me with his blows, determined to finish me off. I was on one knee, literally overwhelmed. The referee began the count again. I had the feeling he was counting too quickly. I got up, clinging to the ropes. The hall was swaying around me. My calves were wobbling. I felt groggy. Bonnot pushed me. My body felt like an old building shaken by an earthquake; I was collapsing on all sides. The round ended. The water-soaked sponge that Salvo wiped my face with felt like a blowtorch. The slightest grimace was like an electric shock. Bonnot was watching me intensely, as if his stool was too hot to sit on, impatient to get on with the fight. His arms were shaking with rage. Throughout the ninth round, he went after me without catching me. I kept my distance in order to recover my senses, convinced that a blow to my head would mean the end. My tactic provoked jeers from the hall. I don't know why Bonnot turned to the referee. Perhaps to complain, annoyed by my refusal to fight. He shouldn't have taken his eyes off me. Drawing on everything I'd got left, I threw a left hook.

Bonnot's neck cracked beneath my glove. He whirled round and fell back on the ropes, which threw him onto me; I immediately gave him a series of lefts and rights, and he staggered and fell on his backside, stunned. Trying to get up again, he lost his balance, sprawled on his back, and writhed feebly like an insect caught in glue. He was saved by the bell.

'He's done for,' De Stefano yelled at me, his voice so feverish as to be unrecognisable. 'He's completely dazed. Finish him off now.' The Duke was gloating in his seat. This time, Gino's hands were clasped together in prayer. The audience held its breath. Bonnot wasn't in good shape. An hour earlier, a king had climbed into the ring as if it were a throne. A few rounds later, the monarch had been reduced to a wild-eyed torture victim on a scaffold. I could see the distress in his desperate gaze and I almost felt remorse. The tenth round was horrible. Bloodstained, his eyebrows cut and his eyes swollen, and still the thunderbolts rained down on him. Now he was the one who was huddled in a corner, waiting for the storm to pass. He collapsed after a series of lefts and rights, winded. The referee started the count. Bonnot shook his head, determined to hold out as long as he could. I worked on his sides, methodically. His body arched beneath my uppercuts, lifted, twisted with suffering. Just when I thought he was about to give up, his right made me reel. The floor creaked beneath my weight. We were both at the end of our tether, he clinging to his reputation, me to my chance of taking it from him. The audience realised that one of the two of us was going to die. The shadow of death hovered over the ring, but neither manager wanted to throw in the towel, certain that victory was within reach, but all down to a roll of the dice. Things were obviously going to end badly, but we all felt a kind of euphoria as the life was sucked out of us, hypnotised by the constant and rapid shifts in the situation. Bonnot refused to yield one inch of his kingdom and I refused to give up. We were nothing now but the expression of our intense stubbornness. I no longer felt the blows. I kept falling and getting back on my feet, tossed about from one moment of dizziness to another, driven by the single thought that I was in mortal danger. It was as if I didn't want to miss out on my own death. Snapshots of my life flashed through my mind at dizzying speed. I was certain I had come to the last stretch, a point of no return beyond which there would be only nothingness. Bonnot must have been living through the same ordeal and seeing things in the same way as me: he was swaying in his fog, collapsing, getting up again, powerless to retaliate, a pitiful puppet lurching about at the end of his strings. Exhausted, but with a bravery verging on the ridiculous. With each blow, his neck looked as though it was turning three hundred and sixty degrees. I felt his ribs crack beneath my gloves. Don't get up, I begged him, horrified by his suicidal tenacity. He was refusing to abdicate, got up grimacing with pain, disorientated, drained of all energy. In a final burst of pride, he swung his right and his wrist smashed against the wooden ring post. His wounded arm hung suddenly at his side, vulnerable and useless. It was a tragic, unbearable moment. The reigning champion was finished, delivered, feet and fists tied, to the knockout blow. I was expecting him to call it quits, but no, Bonnot threatened to eat his manager alive if he threw in the towel. He went back to his stool, swaying, holding his wounded wrist up to his stomach to show that his arm was functioning normally.

The twelfth round offered up a deeply disturbing spectacle. People were uncomfortable, held spellbound by the pathetic bravery of this champion who was risking his all, counting only on his one good arm to save face. He knew he was beaten, but he wasn't giving up. It was pure madness. As I watched him charge head down and punch indiscriminately, unbalanced by his own clumsiness, driven mad by the blood that blinded him, wandering in the middle of the ring like a desperate spectre, the pertinence of Irène's words came home to me. Bonnot was showing me my own image, the fate this life had in store for me. One day, refusing to relinquish my title, I'd behave in the same way; I'd give up my health, my life, everything that mattered to me for a hypothetical flash of pride as dizzying as a leap into the void. I would fall into a pernicious delirium, firmly convinced that death would be less painful than defeat, and I would let myself be taken apart piece by piece rather than acknowledge my opponent's clear superiority. We weren't idols, we were incapable of reason; fighting animals intoxicated by the cheers; two strange, exhausted characters cutting each other to shreds; two madmen drunk with fatigue and pain whose moans were drowned out by the uproar of the hundreds of spectators horrified, and at the same time fascinated, by the unbearable violence that defined us ...

When Bonnot at last collapsed and didn't get up again, there was general relief.

The nightmare was over.

In no time at all, the ring had been taken by storm. De Stefano and Salvo showed me off like a trophy. Gino was weeping with joy. Even Francis was dancing. The Duke climbed on his seat to make sure everyone could see him, arms open wide to receive manna from heaven.

Dazed, on the verge of passing out, I gave myself up to the jubilation of my fans, my eyes fixed on Bonnot, who they were trying in vain to revive.

## 7

The consequences of my fight with Bonnot became clear as soon as I got back to Oran. I started vomiting blood and was plagued by headaches, which would wear off only to return with greater intensity, as fierce as a toothache. At times, the ground fell away beneath my feet, pins and needles riddled my thighs and my arms, and my breathing became irregular.

I was taken to a clinic run by a doctor who was a friend of the Bollocqs. The X-rays weren't alarming: I had two cracked ribs, that was all. For three days, I was given all kinds of medication, but the pains didn't go away. My sight was sometimes blurred and whatever I ate I'd immediately throw up. The mirror showed me a poor devil with a dented face, cut eyebrows, swollen lips and cheeks covered in bruises. When my bandages were removed, skin came off with them.

Gino would come to see me from time to time. I almost hated him for his intact beauty. He looked invulnerable in his smart suit.

The news from Algiers wasn't good. Bonnot still hadn't woken up. They feared for his life. Even the most optimistic couldn't see him getting back in the ring.

I felt bad for him. He had fought like a lion and earned my respect.

The mayor held a huge reception to celebrate my victory. I

didn't go. I didn't want to display my wounds to satisfy people's curiosity.

Irène asked me where I'd been. I told her I had waited for my face to start looking more the way it had before so that she could recognise me. Her father wasn't well. Confined to bed in his untidy room, his skin sallow, the sheets stained with sweat, he summoned up the strength to hug me to him.

'Jérôme the milkman told me,' he said. 'Quite a match, it seems. The whole village followed it on the radio, biting their nails. I'm proud of you.'

Irène went away, leaving us alone, no doubt exasperated by her father's words.

'Sit down next to me,' he said. 'I want to smell your warrior smell. Do you realise? You're the new North African champion. I'd give anything to be in your shoes. I suppose you haven't quite grasped your achievement yet. It's fantastic ... What about Bonnot? They say he's hovering between life and death.'

'Who isn't, Monsieur Ventabren? Who isn't?'

I went out into the courtyard. Irène was bent over the edge of the well, staring down at the bottom as if looking into a deadly mirror.

'Do you realise what you've done?' she said. 'You've killed a man you didn't even know. Do you ever think of his family, his children if he's married?'

I didn't feel up to challenging her.

Filippi found me lying at the foot of a tree. Irène had left on her mare, abandoning me to my thoughts. Since I'd left the clinic, the same questions had been nagging at me relentlessly. I had to make a choice and I wasn't feeling my best.

'We've been looking for you everywhere,' Filippi cried, pulling up level with me.

'I've been looking for myself too, and I can't seem to get hold of me.'

'The Duke wants to see you.'

'Not today. I need to be on my own.'

He left disappointed.


Next day at the gym, I surprised everyone by announcing my decision. If a bomb had gone off in Rue Wagram, it wouldn't have caused such a shock. De Stefano almost choked. Francis, Tobias and Salvo all looked at each other, thoroughly shaken. Frédéric, who was just coming out of the office, almost fell over backwards. As for Gino, the blood completely drained from his face.

'What's this all about?' Francis cried.

'It isn't about you. I'm making a fresh start. I'm through with boxing.'

A crushing stupefied silence fell over the room. Nobody had expected me to give up. Wasn't I the centre of the world now? Wasn't my name on everyone's lips? For a long while, they just stood there, stunned.

'Have we done something wrong?' Frédéric said at last, in a toneless voice.

'No.'

'Then why are you punishing us?'

'It's not about punishment, it's my life.'

'You're the new North African champion, Turambo. Do you realise how happy your people are? You're the one topic of conversation in the streets, the cafés, the houses, the factories, the prisons. You have no right to stop when things are going so well. Your life isn't just your own any more, it's an epic tale that belongs to everybody.'

'Don't try to sidetrack me, Frédéric. I'm not listening to you.'

Gino leant against the wall. Bent double, he gave a terrible groan and threw up.

The others were still speechless.

Frédéric dabbed at his temples with a handkerchief. He was as white as his shirt collar. 'Let's not rush things,' he stammered. 'You've worked hard in the last few months. You'll feel better after you've taken a break. You certainly deserve it. It's only natural, the pressure you've been under has taken a toll on your nerves.'

'Why don't you tell the Duke?' Francis thundered, foaming at the mouth. 'Why have you come to piss us off with your mood swings? It's Monsieur Bollocq who coughs up the money for you, not us. Go and tell him to his face, if you have the balls for it.'

'Shut up!' De Stefano shouted, on the verge of jumping on him.

'It's for him to shut up,' Francis protested. 'Does he think he can get away with this? Monsieur here believes he's already made it. He thinks he can cold-shoulder us, that he can just waltz in and out as he likes. He isn't alone in the world. There are people around him, people who depend on him. He can't just allow himself to bow out as he sees fit. What are we to him? Skittles to be knocked down? We have families, we have kids to feed. This bastard is suffocating us. It's blackmail. He wants to bring us down, force us to kiss his dirty feet. He's always been like this, ungrateful and narrow-minded. I swear he's doing it deliberately.'

'Get out of here before I tear your eyes out!' De Stefano threatened him. 'Go on, clear off!'

Francis straightened his jacket and stormed outside, stopping only at the door to say, 'I knew from the start you were nothing but an out-and-out bastard. I knew you'd bite the hand that fed you one of these days. Everybody knows that if you hold out your hand to Arabs, they pull you down. The other problem is that when they get to the well, they don't drink, they piss in it. That's why they poison everything they touch and bring bad luck to anyone who goes near them.'

He spat in my direction and walked out.


Frédéric thought it was too soon to tell the Duke of my decision. He was playing for time. Two days later, he invited us to his villa near Choupot. The meal was served in the garden, in the shade of a scruffy palm tree. The whole team was there, except Francis. De Stefano looked as if he was at a funeral. Salvo and Tobias, who had stopped bickering, were like two orphans. Gino had lost weight overnight. Nervous, he went to the toilet every fifteen minutes.

When the maid came to clear the table, we realised that none of us had touched the food.

Frédéric lit cigarette after cigarette, his hand shaking. 'We all need to have had a childhood,' he said at last. 'It gives us stability. That didn't happen with you, Turambo. Hunger and poverty took yours away. It's left a gap in your life. And the first woman you met has filled it. What you think is love is nothing but a return to childhood, and children don't love with reason, they love out of instinct.'

'Who said anything about a woman?'

'It's obvious.'

'Have you been spying on me?'

'We look out for you.'

'You're backing the wrong horse, my boy,' De Stefano said. 'You won't win at that game. You have to push that mirage away if you don't want to lose control. You have a career to build, rings to conquer. Only blows are capable of waking you up to reality.

The day you raise your arms above your head to acknowledge the cheers of the crowd, the whole world will throw itself at your feet, and then you'll be able to choose the woman you want without owing anything to anyone.'

'Is it you talking to me like this, De Stefano?'

'Yes, it's me, it's really me talking to you like this. How would you live without your gloves? Doing little jobs that bring in nothing, just like before?'

'I've made enough money to start again from scratch.'

'You can never make enough money for your old age, Turambo.'

'I'll get by. I'll go back to the land. I'm a peasant.'

De Stefano shook his head sadly. 'I have a wife and kids. In the evening when I go home, I find them waiting for me. The first thing they look at is what I have in my hands. If I bring something to eat, they relax and take it off me before I've even closed the door. If my hands are empty, I become invisible to them. I don't want you to have to endure the same thing, Turambo. Love is made up of dreams and generosity; it can't survive when you're broke. You're a champion. Your destiny lies in your fists. Make yourself a pile of money and then you can do whatever you like with your life. For the moment, you're still scrambling about at the bottom of the ladder. Don't waste your energy anywhere but in the ring.'

I didn't want to hear any more. I wasn't equipped to defend my decision. I knew I was vulnerable because I was dealing with emotions. The doubt was always there. I wondered if I wasn't going off course, but at the same time hardened myself against anything that could disturb me further. As far as I was concerned, Irène was worth all the risks I'd be called upon to take. I couldn't wait to see her again, to draw confidence from her way of seeing things.

*

I didn't go with Gino to Boulevard Mascara. His sorrow would only have weakened my resolve and I wasn't going to force myself to accompany him.

At the farm, Ventabren's condition was getting worse. But Irène was there and her proximity protected me from my moments of doubt.

One Sunday, as I was just walking into a park to try and clear my head, Mouss grabbed me by the wrist. It clearly wasn't a chance encounter. Maybe he'd followed me all the way from Rue du Général-Cérez.

'Will you promise to keep your fists in your pockets if I tell you something in confidence?' he asked.

'Why do you want me to keep my fists in my pockets?'

'Because I'm a heavyweight and I wouldn't want to take you apart like an old carcass.'

'Don't you think I'm a match for you?'

'No chance.'

'In that case, let's stop this right now.'

He stood in my way. 'It's for your own good, Turambo, I promise you.'

'Have you been asked to lecture me?'

'So what if I have?'

He may have been trying to act tough, but I could tell from the look in his eyes that he was genuine. 'Why are you all so worried about me?'

'We're a family, little brother. Times are hard and we have to stick together.'

'All right. Say what you have to say and let's have done with it. I need to get some fresh air.'

'Let's go in the park. They say it's more romantic.'

Mouss was patronising me, his voice throaty and drawling as if he was trying to put me to sleep. I suppose his phenomenal strength made people look tiny to him. The journalists hated him for his arrogance, but he didn't give a damn. As long as he punched right, he didn't care about anything else. But he was generally credited with being honest, he wasn't the kind to flirt with trouble or fix matches – which was common enough in that world. I think he admired me, and even respected me. He didn't come and congratulate me after fights, but he'd watch me from a distance, stand to one side so that I could see him give me a secret sign, then stride off into the crowd. I admit I didn't like him much. He often made a fuss about nothing to draw attention to himself. His narcissism irritated me. We both came from the same terrible beginnings, from the lowest of the low, but we weren't climbing the ladder for the same reasons. In the ring, Mouss was a bulldozer. He hit to kill. His gloves were fashioned out of flesh. He didn't fight to make his career or fortune, he fought to prove to himself that he hadn't died with his family, to get his revenge for the blows he had received without being allowed to return them. He had lost his family very young. His father, a slave, had been whipped to death by an overseer and his mother had thrown herself off a cliff ... For Mouss, when the bell rang, it brought back to life the dead and the absent and awoke old demons. He saw his opponent simply as an antidote: by making mincemeat of him, he was able to cure himself.

It wasn't the same for me.

As far as I was concerned, boxing was neither a cure nor a redemption, it was just a way of making a living.

We walked to a little paved courtyard lined with wrought-iron benches and opted for the shade of a weeping willow leaning over a fountain. Mouss stretched his neck to the right and left, pushed back his tartan cap, placed his big bear-like mitts on my shoulders and looked me full in the eyes.

'De Stefano wants what's best for you,' he said. 'He's a man who knows what he's talking about. If I hadn't listened to him when I was starting out, I wouldn't be wearing these smart clothes and I wouldn't be sleeping in a bed ...'

Swaying slightly, he sniffed loudly and looked to the right and left like some pick-up artist.

'I could have taken a wife and settled down,' he went on. 'That's not enough for me, little brother. Before, I was just another Negro good for nothing except unloading carts. By boxing I've become somebody. Who even notices the colour of my skin? My gloves are my visiting card now, and they can open any door. I weigh a hundred and twenty kilos, but I feel as light as a feather. I can have all the women I want, and all the privileges, and nobody asks questions. You know why? For one reason, and one reason only: I'm alive, and I take full advantage of it ... You mustn't get things mixed up, boy. Making love is one thing. Love itself is another matter entirely; it limits you. You don't reduce the world to a woman, however wonderful she is ... Why be content with a queen when you can have a harem? That's just being stupid. You can't put a rope round your neck without condemning yourself to the leash or the gallows.'

'Is that what you have to tell me in confidence?'

'I'm coming to that. I'm a heavyweight after all, I move slowly ... Personally, I agree with De Stefano. He's not just a sage, De Stefano, he's a saint. When he tells you to throw in the towel, you throw in the towel and don't try to understand.'

'Please get to the point, my head's going to explode.'

Mouss took his hands off my shoulders and folded his arms over his chest. An enigmatic smile hovered on his lips. 'Irène isn't the right girl for you. She's playing with your innocence.'

'Oh, really? And where do you know Irène from? Did your ancestors have a word with her while you were in a trance?' I was deliberately trying to wound him.

He ignored my provocation. He merely strutted about on the

spot then said, 'Does she still have that strawberry-shaped mark on her right buttock?'

My fist flew of its own accord.

He swayed, but didn't fall. 'You promised to keep your fists in your pockets, Turambo,' he grunted, casually rubbing his jaw. 'It isn't right not to keep your word … Sorry you're taking it like this. I wasn't trying to offend you or manipulate you. I thought you had a right to know and I had a duty to tell you the truth. As far as I'm concerned, I did what I had to do. You do what you want now. It's not my problem any more.'

He lifted one finger to his temple in farewell, pulled his cap down over his eyes and strode back to the bustle of the streets.

It was dark by the time I got to the farm. Drizzle was falling on the mist-shrouded countryside. Big clouds jostled in the low sky while a cold that was unusual for the time of year was sharpening its claws. A small, dirt-encrusted car stood outside the house, its door wide open. The Ventabrens had a visitor. A young doctor dressed in black was examining Alarcon Ventabren, who lay on his bed looking pale, sweating profusely, laid low by fever, rings under his eyes, his mouth cracked and dry. Irène stood in a corner of the room, wringing her hands, overcome with anxiety.

The doctor put his gear in his bag. He looked ill at ease. 'I've given him a sedative,' he said. 'That should bring his temperature down. It isn't a chill and it isn't indigestion, and I can't explain the vomiting. It may be a virus, maybe not. If his condition doesn't improve, drive him to hospital.'

Irène walked the doctor to his car. I stayed by Alarcon's bedside, upset and useless, my mind full of Mouss's revelations. During the drive from Oran to the farm, his voice had reverberated in my head until it felt as if it would explode. I couldn't see the road winding in front of me or the mist on my windscreen. Torn between sorrow and the fear of confronting Irène, I twice almost missed a bend and nearly ended up in a ditch.

What was I doing here?

I was unhappy, buried beneath a mountain of despair, disgusted with everything.

Irène returned, looking ghostly. Was it her father or the darkness in my eyes that bothered her? She sat down on a stool near the bed, dipped a handkerchief in a pan of water beside her and began moistening her father's face. It was as if she had guessed what was making me gloomy and sad, as if someone had told her what had happened between Mouss and me.

Alarcon muttered something in his sleep. Irène listened carefully but couldn't grasp the meaning. I didn't react, stuck in a glass mould that forbade me the slightest movement. Blood pounded in my temples at regular intervals, like a leaking tap.

'I don't know what's wrong with him,' she said at last. 'He came down with it suddenly.'

I didn't know why the effect of hearing her voice took away half my fears.

She stood up and walked past me, her mind elsewhere. I followed her into the kitchen, where the dishes from lunch were waiting to be cleaned. Some of the food hadn't even been touched, suggesting that things had deteriorated without warning.

'He really scared me,' she admitted. 'I thought he was going to die. I ran to the village to fetch the doctor.'

She grabbed a plate and emptied the food into a cardboard box.

'If you'd come earlier, I wouldn't be in this state. I was lost, I didn't know where to turn. I was in a panic ...'

'Mouss mentioned the mark you have on your lower back.'

I had said it. I would have given anything to take back my words, to swallow them. Now wasn't the time, I thought, scolding myself. Too late! The burden that had been weighing me down had come out into the open, taking away all my anger and anxiety. I felt as drained as a possessed person from whom the devil has been driven out, liberated but in danger, like a bird that has left its cage and is exposed to the perils of an unknown world.

Irène froze. She stood over the sink for a few moments, speechless, the plate in her hands. Her shoulders slumped suddenly, then her neck. She let the plate drop into the water, took several deep breaths, then slowly turned, her face scarlet, her eyes glistening with tears. 'What are you trying to say?' she asked in a hollow voice.

'Is it true that he knows?'

The colour returned to her face and her eyes darkened. 'He wasn't blind, if my memory serves me well.'

'He says —'

'Shut up,' she interrupted me. She wiped her hands on her apron and leant back against the sink. When at last she had her breathing under control, she folded her arms over her chest and looked me up and down with a disdain I had never seen in her before. 'How long have we been together, Amayas?'

'Almost a year.'

'Do you think I was born that day?'

'I don't follow you.'

She leant more heavily against the sink, increasingly in control of her anger. 'I wasn't a virgin when you had me in the bushes, don't forget. That didn't seem to bother you. Worse, you decided to love me all the same. You even thought about starting a family with me.'

'Yes, but —'

'But what?' she shouted. 'There are no buts. Have I ever tried to find out about your past?'

Her lips were quivering and her eyes held me, motionless, like the double barrel of a shotgun. She was waiting for a word from me to continue. I didn't know what to say to reproach her.

'In life,' she said in a curiously calm tone, 'you don't just wipe everything out and start over again. It's more complicated than that. I'd had a few affairs before you. I'm only flesh and blood. I have a heart beating in here, and a body that demands its share of excitement. But not once did I cheat on my husband before the divorce. And not once have I looked at another man since you took me in your arms ... You have to take all these things into consideration.'

She came and stood in front of me, so close that her breath burnt my face.

'We aren't from the same class, young man. Or the same race. Or the same culture. And the world is bigger than your tribe. In your world, a woman is her husband's property. He makes her believe that he's her destiny, her salvation, her absolute master, that she's merely a rib torn from his skeleton, and she believes him. In my world, women aren't an extension of men, and virginity isn't necessarily a guarantee of good behaviour. We marry when we love each other; what happened before doesn't matter. In my world, a man doesn't renounce his wife, he divorces her, and they each go their own way. Our women have a right to live their own lives. There's no shame in that. As long as we don't harm anyone, we don't have to justify ourselves. And for us, a crime of honour is simply a crime; the law doesn't find extenuating circumstances for it, let alone give it legitimacy. If you seriously thought I was going to wait patiently for you, locked up in my room, doomed perhaps never to meet my Prince Charming, then you're even more stupid than your people.'

With that, she tore off her apron, threw it in my face and left the room, slamming the door behind her.

I jumped at the noise of the door. A jolt went right through me, as if I'd had a solid right to the jaw. The kitchen seemed as cold and dark as a cellar. I collapsed onto a chair and held my face in both hands, convinced that I had just committed the worst blunder of my life.

Alarcon Ventabren's cries roused me from the thoughts that plagued me. I ran to him, half blind in the dim light of the oil lamp. Irène was trying to stop her father's arm waving about in the grip of an attack. The poor man was choking, the corners of his mouth streaming with whitish drool. The upper part of his body was convulsing jerkily. I pushed Irène aside, put my arms round the patient, pulled him out of bed and hoisted him onto my back. His saliva dripped on the back of my neck. Irène ran to open the back door of my car, helped me put her father inside and got in next to me. I started the engine and set off before I'd even switched on the headlights.

We were alone in a grim corridor where faded paint was peeling from the walls, Irène crouching beneath a window, her hands clasped around her mouth, eyes fixed on the tiled floor, and me walking up and down from one end to the other. From time to time, a nurse would emerge from a room or a cupboard and disappear before we had time to catch up with her. The terrified cries of patients reached us intermittently, then silence would fall again on the hospital, as disturbing as a bad omen.

I found it hard to look at Irène. I hated myself for not having respected her emotion, for not having waited for the right moment to lance the boil. I felt bad for her and for me. Yet, seeing her huddled over her sorrow, there in the middle of that corridor lashed by draughts, on a night so black it seemed resistant to prayers and miracles, I was certain that my love for her was unchanged, that the misunderstanding between us had merely strengthened my feelings for her. I loved her, there was no doubt about it, I loved her with all my heart – rightly or wrongly didn't matter! My heart beat only for her and no tomorrow, no horizon would have glow or meaning without Irène. What did thunder matter when the storm was simply passing; what did an insult matter if a kiss could heal wounded lips? For me, life was starting again, with greater intensity now that a new page had been turned. Irène was the chapter I had chosen for myself in order to be me and only me, an ordinary person whom love would glorify more than any success in the ring. I didn't need any signs from my hands, I didn't need anything; it was Irène I wanted more than anything else in the world.

At last, after two hours, a doctor appeared. 'I'm Dr Jacquemin.'

'How is he?' Irène asked urgently.

'For the moment, he's asleep. Go home, there's no point waiting here.'

'Is it serious?'

'It's too soon to give a diagnosis. In my opinion, it may have been a major attack of anxiety. That sometimes happens to those who are paralysed, but it looks more serious than it is. Rest assured he's in good hands. I'm taking personal charge of him. Come back tomorrow and I'll be able to tell you more.'

He gave us an encouraging smile and apologised that he had to leave us.

The drive back to the farm was extremely uncomfortable. Irène had chosen to sit in the back seat, a sign that she was still angry with me. I found it hard to drive, looking both at the road and into the rear-view mirror. Irène was stubbornly turned to the window, staring out into the darkness. Her profile stood out in the gloom, sulking but beautiful, her features finely chiselled, bare but regal. She was even more gorgeous now that her anger had dissolved into thoughtfulness.

When we reached the farm, she got out of the car without even looking at me. I grabbed her by the wrist just as she was getting ready to go up to her room.

'Please,' she moaned, 'I want to sleep.'

I drew her to me; she resisted and tried to pull away; I forced her to turn towards me and she pushed me away without success, twisted, bit my hand; I wouldn't let go, crushed her to me; she let out little cries of rage, tried to scratch my face, drummed her fists on my chest for a long time, continued to struggle, silently but intensely, then, exhausted, abandoned herself to her sobs. I lifted her chin. Her tear-streaked face glistened as much as her eyes. I kissed her on the mouth. She turned her head away. I kissed her again, forcing her; her teeth closed on my lips; I felt the blood seeping onto my tongue. Suddenly, she wrapped her arms around my neck and started kissing me with almost savage passion. Freed of our sorrows, we gave ourselves up body and soul to the joys of our reunion. We were together again, made for each other, restored to each other. We lay down on the floor and made love as never before.

Towards midday, we lunched briefly in the kitchen, reconciled. The looks we exchanged didn't need an interpreter. Words would have been absurd, even out of place should they have misrepresented what our silence excelled in expressing. There are moments of grace when saying nothing allows you to accede fully to the quintessence of the senses. The heart then entrusts the eyes with its deepest secrets. With the truth laid bare, there is nothing to be said, or else everything will disappear. We were serene because we knew that our relationship would finally know happier days.

Irène wanted to go with me to the hospital. I told her I had urgent matters to settle in town and promised that I would be back to pick her up later.

## 8

The Duke opened his arms wide. He was in shirtsleeves behind his desk, his hairy shoulders sloping above his chest. Seeing me open the door, he leapt up and almost ran to hug me. I didn't respond to his embrace. He moved back to look at me and his ardour cooled immediately.

'What's the matter? You look strange.'

'Haven't you been told?'

'About what?'

'About my decision.'

'What decision?'

I came straight out with it. 'I'm giving up boxing.'

He froze for a moment, astounded, then threw his head back and laughed heartily. 'Oh, you really had me there … You joker, you really had me going for a minute.'

'I'm serious, Monsieur Bollocq.'

The coolness of my tone completely extinguished his enthusiasm. His face became so tense that the lines on his forehead looked as if they were about to crack. 'What's this all about? Have the blows to your head driven you crazy or what?'

'Maybe.'

With a movement of his hand, the Duke swept away the files heaped up on his desk, kicked a chair, then took his head in his hands to calm himself down. He stayed like that for several seconds, with his back to me, trying to get his thoughts in order. When he turned back, there was nothing human about his flushed face. He was shaking all over, his nostrils were dilated, and his eyes were popping out of their sockets. He started by putting his finger on my chest, then took it away and looked around, his breathing uncontrolled.

'I'm dreaming,' he grunted. 'It isn't possible.'

Suddenly, he grabbed me by the throat, but he was too short to hold on. He went back behind his desk and gazed out at the plane tree in the courtyard.

'Ginooo!' he screamed.

An alarmed secretary appeared. He sent her to fetch Gino from the second floor. Gino came running. I heard him come up the stairs four steps at a time. He was surprised to see me there, but the Duke didn't give him time to recover his composure.

'Can you explain to me what's got into your friend here?'

Gino swallowed.

'Did you know about his decision?'

'Yes, Monsieur.'

'Since when?'

'I'm sorry.'

'Why didn't you say anything?'

'I thought I could reason with him.'

'Apparently, you haven't been very convincing.'

'To be honest, we haven't had the opportunity to talk about it with a clear head.'

'It's your head that's on the line, boy,' the Duke roared, charging at Gino. 'If this stupid fake brother of yours doesn't apologise to me right now, I don't rate your chances of survival.'

'It's an unfortunate misunderstanding, Monsieur. It'll all be sorted out, I promise.'

But I was resolute. 'I've made up my mind,' I said. 'Neither Gino nor anyone will get me to change it.'

The Duke again rushed at me, his speech agitated. 'I don't think you realise the risk you're taking, you little fool. I'm not a boxer and I don't follow any rules when I cross swords with an opponent. Do you follow me? I don't know if you have a brain or motor oil in that head of yours, but if I were you, I'd be careful, very careful.' Registering that his threat didn't scare me, he assumed a less abrupt tone. 'Do you mind telling me what hasn't worked out between us? We've been with you every step of the way. So why this about-turn? If it's a question of money, let's put our cards on the table. Everything's negotiable, champ.'

'I'm really sorry, Monsieur Bollocq. It isn't a question of money and I have no gripes with anybody. You're been terrific, all of you. I haven't disappointed you. We're quits.'

'Not so fast, knucklehead. I'm trying to launch your career internationally and you bring it back to me like a dog bringing back the stick his master threw for him.'

'I'm not a dog.'

'That remains to be seen … What can't be denied is that I'm the master here. All you have, you owe to me. I've spent a fortune getting an uneducated Arab street kid without a future onto the top podiums. I told you a long time ago, you're nothing but an investment, a business proposition that's cost me a lot of money, massive negotiations, and partnerships with people who made me queasy. For your sake, I've been forced to grease palms, bribe journalists, forgive people who've betrayed me and make my peace with nobodies. And now you come here, bold as brass, to tell me you're pulling out, and you think you're within your rights?'

He turned to Gino.

'Take this native of yours and get out of here. When you come back to see me, I want you both to apologise, on your knees and in tears. Otherwise, I'll come looking for you and I'll make you rue the day your paths crossed ... Now clear off!'

Gino took me straight to his office. He was in a total panic.

'What's got into you, damn it? What quagmire are you dragging all of us into? The Duke won't let you go like that. We're both in danger. For heaven's sake, let's go back and apologise.'

'I don't owe him anything any more.'

'Don't be so sure; you owe him more than you can imagine. You were nothing but an alley cat and he made you a tiger. Without him, you'd still be drinking from ditches. I know better than you do how to recognise who's wrong and who deserves respect. Your problem is, your brain would fit on the head of a pin. You don't know what's good for you and what to avoid like the plague. You want some golden advice? Give up the woman. She's leading you astray. If you meant anything to her, she wouldn't stand in your way, she'd encourage you to keep going, to win title after title, to reach for the stars. I'm begging you, in the name of our fraternal friendship, our little dreams when we were poor kids, what we've been through and what we've built up from nothing with our own hands, I'm beseeching you, I'll kiss your hands and feet, come back to me, come back to us, and get rid of that tramp who's trying to push you back into the gutter you've only just made it out of.'

'Do you realise what you're asking of me, Gino? I care about that woman. Not a minute goes by that I don't think about her, and you're asking me to forget her. Gino, my dear Gino, can't you see that I'm happy for the first time in my life? I love Irène, don't you understand? I love her. My days only have a meaning because Irène makes each one new for me.'

He slapped me. 'You're selfish. Stupid and pig-headed and

selfish. After all I've gone through for you, you're casting me aside.'

'Don't ever raise your hand to me, Gino. I mean it.'

'Then do what I ask. You're walking all over me as if I was a doormat. How dare you throw away what we've built for you?'

'I'm really sorry. This hurts me, it really does. I have a lot of affection for De Stefano, Tobias and Salvo. And you're still a brother to me. But I'm tired of taking punches. I need to get down off my cloud, to walk among people, to live a normal life.'

'You promised my mother on her deathbed. You swore never to let a serpent come between us.'

'Irène isn't a serpent, Gino.'

'She is, Turambo, only you don't see it. You're hypnotised by her like a field mouse.'

'You'll get over it, Gino. Your friendship means a lot to me. Let's not throw it away.'

'You're the one who's throwing it away. You don't have any consideration for me, or any pity. I'm this close to having a heart attack and you don't give a damn. If that's your idea of friendship, you can keep it. I'd never have landed you in the shit. You don't know how disappointed I am in you. You're behaving like a hypocrite and a coward. You disgust me. A bastard, that's what you are, a filthy, ungrateful bastard.'

His words hurt me.

Gino had fire in his eyes and venom in his mouth. His nostrils trembled with resentment, his lips cursed me. He was choking like an asthmatic, his breath hot with the magma rising in him, terrifying in its bile, his features distorted.

'Be careful,' he breathed, wagging his finger in my face. 'You aren't the one in charge, Turambo. Don't bury us too soon. I've given too much of myself for you and I won't let you ruin my future.'

'You see? *Your* future. If you care so much about yours, why do you want me to give up mine?'

'One doesn't rule out the other. Boxing isn't incompatible with marriage. Marry that slut of yours if you really want to, but for God's sake don't sacrifice us for the sake of her lovely eyes.'

'It isn't just that, Gino. I'm fed up with licking my wounds while you lick your fingers counting your money.'

'You're making money too.'

'And losing my self-respect. I don't want to make a spectacle of myself any more.'

'I beg you, Turambo, try to think for two seconds!'

'That's all I've been doing for months. I've made my decision and it's not negotiable.'

'Really?'

'Absolutely.'

He shook his head, defeated, then recovered and looked up at me with blood-red eyes, his cheeks twitching. His mouth twisted to one side. 'I warn you,' he roared, 'I won't let you get away with this.'

A transformation was taking place before my very eyes. A mask was being ripped off a wonderful time of innocence and disinterested complicity, to reveal a new face, repulsive and obscene. Gino was giving birth, painfully, to a character whose dark side I had barely suspected. You would have sworn it emerged from the wall behind him, or from a tomb, stony-faced, eyes full of dust, veiled in shadow, no, worse, embodied in shadow. Gino had the tragic look of someone who has a knife to his throat and who'd be ready to turn it on his best friend to save his own skin. I no longer recognised him. He might well have been thinking the same thing about me, except that I wasn't asking anything of him, whereas the sacrifice he was expecting of me was tearing us apart. We were no longer on the same side.

'Are you threatening me, Gino?'

'Absolutely.'

'Well, I don't give a fuck about your threats. The Duke can fire you, lynch you, preserve you in formaldehyde, I don't care.'

'You're a laughing stock, boy. Wake up. Your muse is nothing but a slut who sleeps with the first man who comes along. She'll kick you out of her bed as soon as she tires of you. Didn't Mouss tell you?'

'So it was you who sent him to see me?'

'Damn right it was. I thought you had self-respect and a sense of honour like the men of your community. I realise now you're just a fool taken in by a prick-teaser. She'd swap you for a wad of banknotes without even bothering to count them. I'm going to prove to you that that bitch on heat can be bought like any other whore.'

'Stay away from her, Gino.'

'What are you afraid of? That I'm right?'

I pushed him away and ran down the stairs.

He ran after me, yelling, 'I won't let you sabotage my plans, Turambo, you hear? Turambo! Turambo!'


After driving around the boulevards, I went to a Moorish café near Sidi Blel. The alley was too narrow to drive down. I left my car outside a little park and walked the rest of the way to the café. A few turbaned customers were chatting over their tea. A blind singer was playing the lute on a makeshift stage. I ordered cinnamon coffee and Tunisian doughnuts. I had the feeling I was being born into a new world, leaving far behind what motivated the others more than me. The moorings that had chained me to mad promises and contracts would no longer prevent me from going out into the open air. I had always dreaded confronting the Duke; his social standing, his natural authority, his seismic rages had intimidated me. I never imagined I could stand up to him, let alone inform him openly of my decision. Yet, leaving his office, I had no longer felt a leaden weight on my shoulders; his threats hadn't worked with me. I was free of that fear inherent in my condition as a 'native' forged in the test of strength and irrational guilt. I think I whistled in the street, or maybe I laughed that nervous laugh relieving us of a terror which, in the end, turns out to be as common as it's unfounded. It was a strange feeling, so light it seemed I was floating. I remembered Sid Roho's grandfather, who had, according to my childhood friend, lived like a lord even in poverty. Dispossessed of his lands, he had retired to the mountains in order not to be beholden to anyone and spent his life sleeping, daydreaming, poaching and raising a family. Apparently, he'd said, 'There's only one choice that matters: doing what we most care about. Everything else is denial.'

I had made my choice. Podium or scaffold, I didn't really care, I was beyond any doubts. Paradoxically, my serenity took the form of a great tiredness: I felt an enormous need to lie down somewhere, anywhere, and sleep. I drank one coffee after another and stuffed myself with doughnuts without even realising.

When I asked for the bill, the owner told me that someone had settled it for me, but wouldn't tell me who. In our world, in spite of poverty, that kind of thoughtfulness was common; the main thing was not to insist on learning your benefactor's identity.

I went out into the street, thanking the people sat at tables outside at random. My heartbeat had slowed down. I felt fine.

Some old men were playing dominoes in a doorway. I stopped to exchange pleasantries with them. In the square, a gang of urchins were having fun on the bonnet of my car; when they saw me, they scattered, screaming, then came back and ran after me. The more agile of them ran level with my door, their mouths wide open, laughing triumphantly. I waved goodbye to them and accelerated.

Evening was knocking on the doors of the city. My mother was chatting with her Kabyle neighbour in the courtyard, an oil lamp placed on the edge of the well. In order not to disturb them, I went straight into our flat. My father was talking to himself in his room, his hands shaking. I kissed his forehead and sat down on a cushion facing him. He looked at me, tilting his neck to the side, a vague smile on his face. For some weeks now, he had been talking to himself, giving the impression he had entered a world of shadows and echoes.

My mother shook me. I woke with a start. I had dozed off. Remembering Alarcon Ventabren, I jumped in my car and sped to the hospital. Dr Jacquemin received me very courteously. He admitted he had recognised me the day before, but given the circumstances, hadn't dared tell me how much he admired me as a boxer. He took me to Alarcon's room. Alarcon was looking well. The doctor explained to me that there was nothing seriously wrong, that his dizzy spell had been brought on by a fleeting anxiety attack, the kind sometimes caused by paralysis and the physical and mental discomfort that came with it.

'You can take him home now, but just to be on the safe side it might be advisable for him to stay here another night. After a good sleep, he'll be able to go home singing.'

'I'd prefer to wait until tomorrow morning,' Alarcon agreed. 'I don't like travelling at night, especially not in the rain.'

The doctor went away.

Alarcon pointed with his chin to a plate on the bedside table. 'The food here is disgusting. Would it be too much trouble for you to bring me a bowl of soup from the stand on the corner?'

'They must have shut up shop by now.'

'You can't imagine how much I'd like a nice spicy chorba, with vermicelli and a pinch of cumin, a nice hot scented chorba.'

I went back to my mother's. She was fast asleep, but when I told her it was for a sick man, she got up and herself made the chorba that Alarcon gulped down later, chuckling with delight.

'I should go and tell Irène,' I said. 'She must be worried.'

'We can both surprise her tomorrow. Stay with me. I'm so glad to be alive. I really thought I'd had it. And besides, I could do with the company .'

I sat down on a metal chair near the bed and got ready to listen, certain this was going to last all night. Alarcon was still talking when I dozed off.

At about ten in the morning, Alarcon was carried to my car on a stretcher. He chose to sit in the front seat, to get a good view. He told me he hadn't set foot in Oran for ages. But the city looked grim beneath the rain-laden gusts of wind. The pavements were empty, the shop fronts gloomy and the signs above the shady dives creaked in a sinister and maddening way.

In bad weather, Oran is like a botched spell.

I bought fresh bread from a bakery, lamb chops and a string of merguez from a kosher butcher, some provisions too, and we set off for Lourmel. The trees writhed at the side of the road and a stream of mist rolled down from the mountain over the elegant village of Misserghin. Alarcon gazed out at the hills and the orchards, a dreamy smile on his face. In the sky, the dismal clouds that had pressed down on Oran were starting to disperse. In places, the daylight showed through the gaps. The further we got from the coast, the less the mist flowed across the road. It was still drizzling, but the wind was abating in the orange groves and vineyards. Alarcon started humming a military tune, beating time on the dashboard with his fist. I listened to him, lost in thought. I couldn't wait to tell Irène that I'd broken with the Duke once and for all.

The hut of Larbi the fruit seller shook in the breeze, the curtains blown back. On the path leading to the farm, amid the potholes, there were recent tyre tracks. My car skidded in the ruts.

The presence of two vans in the Ventabrens' courtyard puzzled me. When they saw us, a handful of men armed with sticks and poles regrouped near the house, surrounded by three uniformed policemen. In my suddenly dry throat, my Adam's apple leapt in panic.

One of the policemen waved his kepi, signalling me to come towards him. He was a stunted little man with a toothbrush moustache, a pointed nose and large, protruding ears. He seemed exhausted.

'Thank God you're alive, Monsieur Ventabren,' he cried, recognising my passenger. 'My men and some volunteers have been combing the area for hours looking for you. We thought someone had abducted you and thrown your body in the scrub.'

Alarcon couldn't grasp what the policeman was babbling about, but the presence of strangers on his land was a bad omen.

'How could I get to the scrub in a wheelchair? What's going on? Why are you in my house?'

'Something's happened, Monsieur Ventabren. Something terrible ...'

I jumped out of the car, ran to the house and stopped dead in the hall. The table in the drawing room had been moved, the chairs overturned, some broken, and a painting had fallen to the floor. I called out for Irène; in the bathroom, around the full tub, pools of soapy water were turning black on the tiled floor. There were signs of a violent struggle, but no blood. *Irène! Irène!* My cries echoed inside me, louder than hammer blows. In the kitchen, a metal jug lay in a pool of spilt milk. I went upstairs, then came back down again; Irène didn't reply, didn't show herself.

A policeman grabbed me by the arm. 'She isn't here. Her body's been taken to the village.'

What was he talking about?

'She's been murdered. Jérôme the milkman found her dead in the drawing room this morning.'

A sudden deafness struck me with full force. I could see the policeman's lips moving, but no sound reached me. My head started spinning and I couldn't breathe. I leant against the wall in order not to collapse, but my legs gave way under the shock. I fell on my backside, in a daze, repeating to myself: *I'm going to wake up, I'm going to wake up* ...

A policeman took my place at the wheel of the car. I was incapable of starting the engine, incapable of driving. My legs had stopped working properly.

In the village, the police took us to a clinic where Irène's body lay. I was unaware of sounds or movements; everything appeared blurred, confused, surreal.

The sergeant wouldn't let me go in with Alarcon to see his daughter's body, but ordered me to stay in the car and told a subordinate to keep an eye on me.

A crowd had gathered outside the clinic. It was moving in slow motion, silent, wild-eyed. Supported by policemen, Alarcon let himself be dragged towards his grief. When he came out again, he was pale and broken, but was trying to appear dignified.

He hadn't said a word since we'd left the farm.

The sergeant took us to the station and ordered me to sit on a bench in a narrow room, watched closely by four officers, while he went with Alarcon into an office, leaving the door open. Their voices reached me intermittently.

'It can't be him,' Alarcon sighed. 'He spent the night by my bedside in the hospital. The doctor and the nurses can confirm it.'

'Are you sure, Monsieur Ventabren?'

'I tell you it isn't him.'

'Jérôme the milkman saw a black car leaving the farm just as he was arriving this morning for his delivery. It was exactly nine o'clock. Jérôme is categorical: your daughter's body was still warm when he touched it ...'

A black car!

This revelation sobered me abruptly. There was an explosion in my head. He did it! ... As far as I was concerned, there wasn't a shadow of doubt. I knew immediately who had taken from me the person I cared most about in the world.

I heaved with nausea, but nothing came out. I felt like I was breaking into a thousand pieces.

I drove Alarcon home. A terrible stiffness had come over me and my gestures were like those of an automaton. I couldn't think. I was wandering in a fog, guided only by my instinct. Alarcon was holding up. He was breathing through his mouth, eyes fixed, his face inscrutable. But as soon as he was settled in his wheelchair in the house, all the composure he had shown so far, all the almost martial dignity he had displayed in the village crumbled and he burst into sobs, bent double over his lower limbs.

Night fell. In the flickering light of the oil lamp, the shadows had the shape of misfortune. Outside, the rain started again, heavier than ever. I could hear the wind howling in the folds of the hill. I was cold, locked in a trance-like state. I don't think I yet realised the destruction that was about to overwhelm the rest of my days. A sepulchral voice went round and round in my head: *He did it! He did it!*

We were too devastated to think of eating. I helped Alarcon

to get into bed and watched over him until he fell asleep. In the kitchen, I found a hunting knife and put it in my pocket. The mirror on the wall reflected back a spectral effigy. I looked like nothing on earth. An automaton driven by a supernatural force, I got in my car and sped back to Oran.

Boulevard Mascara was deserted and the haberdasher's was closed. The light was on in Gino's window. I climbed the stairs four steps at a time … 'Gino!' It wasn't a cry, it was no longer anything but a scream, a geyser of hatred and rage that shook the walls. Gino wasn't in his room. His bed was unmade, but warm. The gramophone I had given him was on; a record was going round and round on the turntable with a monotonous scraping that bored into my brain. On a low table, an ashtray overflowed with stubbed-out cigarette ends next to a half-eaten plateful of cooked meat and a dirty glass. A bottle of wine had smashed on the ground, sending broken glass in all directions. A strong smell of alcohol pervaded the room. On a chair by the bed hung a pair of trousers and a shirt. An overcoat lay on the eiderdown, along with a pair of shoes. With a bitter gesture, I swept away the gramophone, which broke on the floor; the horn bounced off the wall, turned over and lay still. Gino couldn't be far away. He must be hiding somewhere. I looked for him in the toilet, on the terrace, in the other rooms; he must have gone to buy something to get drunk on, hoping to drown his bad conscience. That likelihood stoked my hatred. My whole body shook. I sat down on a step in the middle of the dark staircase and waited, fire in my belly, the knife in my fist.

The thunder belched like a hydra in a trance, pouring torrential rain on the city. The howling of the wind filled the night with an apocalyptic fury. Struggling with the rage that was eating me up, I refused to think of anything, to ask myself what I was doing there. I was merely an extension of the knife gripped in my hand.

And Gino arrived. Dead drunk. A litre bottle under his arm. His pyjamas soaked through. His slippers saturated with rainwater. The lightning cast his wretched shadow on the walls. I didn't give him time to say a word. I didn't want to hear anything, forgive anything. If he'd thrown himself at my feet, begged me in tears, sworn it was an accident, that it wasn't his fault, that the Duke had made him do it; if he had reminded me of our finest memories, the vow made to his mother, it wouldn't have made any difference. Gino gave a start when the knife sank into his side. I felt his hot blood on my wrist. His breath, reeking of wine, almost made me feel drunk.

He clutched at the collar of my coat, made a gurgling sound and sagged slightly.

Another flash of lightning illuminated us.

'It's me, Gino,' he said, recognising me in the dark.

'Maybe,' I retorted, 'but not the one I knew.'

His grip weakened. He slid slowly down my body and lay at my feet. I stepped over him and went out into the street. The rain fell on me like a spell.

I went to Saint-Eugène to wait for the Duke. I was hoping he'd come back from a party or an evening meeting. His villa lay in wait behind its gardens, all its lights off. A servant in a hood was keeping guard near the gate, with a big dog at the end of a leash. Hours passed. Numb with cold in my car, I kept watch on the surrounding area. Not a single night owl appeared, not a single car. The torrents of water, reinforced by the gusts of wind, blurred my view.

I went back to the farm. In the beating rain. Dazzled by the lightning.

Alarcon was asleep.

Shivering with cold, I wrapped myself in a blanket and lay down on the padded bench seat in the drawing room without taking my shoes off.

A rattling sound woke me. Dawn had come. A woman was bustling in the kitchen. She told me she was the wife of a neighbour, who had sent her to Alarcon's house to see if she could help in any way. She was making us something to eat. At about one, her husband and other locals came to console the grieving father. Alarcon didn't have the strength to see them. He preferred to stay in bed and deal with his grief alone. The neighbours were poorly dressed peasants with rough hands, rugged swarthy faces and rumpled clothes, simple people who looked at their land in the same way they looked at their wives and felt nothing but contempt for wealth and show. They didn't know much about boxing or about what went on in the city. They asked me who I was and I replied, 'Irène's fiancé.'

Late in the afternoon, a police car pulled up. An officer told us that the sergeant wanted to see Monsieur Ventabren and that it was urgent. 'It seems there's been a development.' He didn't say any more, ignorant himself of what it was about.

At the station in Lourmel, the sergeant led Alarcon and me to a cell with bars. An unkempt man was there, squashed behind a refectory table, his face flabby, his shoulders hunched. It was Jérôme the milkman, wearing a mud-stained coat with worn elbows. He was sobbing and wiping his eyes with the back of his hand, his wrists handcuffed, his face as shrivelled as an over-ripe quince.

'The inconsistencies in his testimony set us thinking,' the sergeant said. 'He kept contradicting himself and going back on his previous statements. Then he cracked.'

A terrible silence filled the police station.

Alarcon and I were transfixed with amazement. He was the first to break the silence. Getting his breath back from somewhere deep inside him, he asked in a shaky voice, 'Why did you do it, Jérôme?'

'It wasn't me, Monsieur Ventabren,' the milkman said, kneeling in front of him imploringly. 'It was the devil. He possessed me. There was nobody in the house. I went in to deliver the milk. I put the jug on the table in the kitchen as usual. I was about to leave when I saw Irène washing herself. I didn't do it on purpose. The bathroom door was ajar, I swear it; it wasn't me who opened it. I said, Jérôme go home, what you're doing isn't right. But it wasn't me. I would have gone home, as you can imagine, Alarcon. You know me. I'm no angel, but I have a sense of modesty, I have principles. In my head, I said to myself, What's happening to you, Jérôme? Have you gone mad or what? Go away, don't look, get out of here fast, except that the devil doesn't listen to that kind of thing; he doesn't ask himself questions, not the devil.'

'You raped her, then strangled her,' the sergeant cried.

'It was the devil, not me. Why else would I have given myself up as soon as I came to my senses?'

'You didn't give yourself up, you confessed. There's a difference, you piece of shit.'

I don't know if it was my cry or the thunder that shook the station from top to bottom, if I threw myself on Jérôme or if I only imagined myself tearing him to pieces with my bare hands. I don't know if the policemen tore me off him, hitting me with their truncheons, or if I hurt myself falling. I only remember the blackness that followed. Nothing in front of me, nothing behind, nothing to right or left. The sky, the whole sky had fallen on my head with its billions of stars, its millions of prayers and its armies of demons. I cursed myself as no damned soul has ever been cursed. I had killed Gino for nothing, and killed the whole world with him. I could no longer hear myself breathe. My breath was denying me. I had aged several millennia. I was a mummy deprived of its rotten bandages, I was Cain emerged from the ashes of hell, his murder more stupid than the destiny of men. What have you done? cried a voice going round and round inside me. How are you going to live now? On what? Who for? Your sleep will be made of black holes, your days of funeral pyres. You can pray until your voice gives out, recite the incantations of all the magicians on earth, deck yourself with talismans or disappear in a wreath of incense; you can read the holy verses all day long, put thorns on your head and walk on water, you won't change the fate awaiting you one iota.

I can't remember if I took my leave of Ventabren or if the cops threw me out. It seemed to me I had gone through time in a single stride, my own cries following me like a hostile crowd. I drove, drove without knowing where I was heading. I stopped under a tree to weep. Not a sob emerged. Not a hiccup. Evening was coming; I saw nothing but my own night, that cold milky darkness taking root in my being like a slow death. I don't know how I ended up at Camélia's. I drank like a fish, I who had never lifted a glass of wine to my lips. Aïda was embarrassed. She was expecting someone. While waiting, she plunged me in a bathtub and rubbed my body as if trying to erase me. Wrapped in a towel, I sat down in the armchair and continued drinking. Shadowy figures moved in slow motion around me. I heard voices without understanding them. Camélia was asking Aïda to get rid of me. My mind was elsewhere; it was still at the station at Lourmel, leaning over Jérôme as he wept. I should have finished that lecher off, thrown myself on him and not let go until I'd crushed him. I was angry with myself for listening to his confession without reacting, even though he had thrown my life into an abyss. Aïda went to fetch more wine. An ocean wouldn't have been enough to extinguish the inferno engulfing me. The more I drank, the lighter I felt; I swam above a sea of vapours and dizziness, my heart in an eagle's talon, my eyes like spinning tops. My teeth chattered as I sat in my towel, unable to make a move without knocking something over. Aïda ignored me. Sitting on a wing chair at her dressing table, she was making herself beautiful for the evening. I saw her back as a rampart excluding me from the world of the living. 'You have to go home now,' she said when the time came. 'My client's waiting in the parlour.' 'He can go to hell!' I heard myself grunt. 'My money's as good as his.' She protested. I threatened to blow up the whole place. Camélia didn't want a rumpus or a scandal in her establishment. She offered me a room. I refused to leave my armchair. Aïda had to see her client in another room. I waited for her to come back. The walls started swaying around me. I dozed off, or maybe I'd fainted. When I woke up, dawn was filtering through the blinds. Aïda wasn't in her bed. I got up and went out to call her in the corridor. 'Aïda! Aïda!' My cries were meant as explosions. I was choking with anger, a storm of drunkenness. Obtaining no reply, I started hammering at the doors, from one end of the corridor to the other, then kicking them down. Prostitutes ran out into the corridor, terrified, some completely naked; clients appeared here and there, also woken up and furious. One of them tried to stop me. Others lent him a hand. I hit out violently to push them away, continuing to call Aïda. Arms seized me round the waist, fingers caught me round the throat, fists rained down on me. I hit out in a tornado of curses, wild, stark raving mad ... Something smashed on my skull. I just had time to see Aïda go down with me as I fell, the handle of a jug in her hand.

Coming to, I realised that I was tied up at the foot of the stairs, with blood on my body and one black eye. The prostitutes and their clients formed a circle around me in stony silence. Uniformed police officers surrounded me, truncheons at the ready. A motionless body was being laid on a stretcher. In the scuffle, I had killed a man.

I didn't remember a thing.

I didn't know my victim. Had I hit him in the wrong place, thrown him down the stairs by accident? Had he slipped on a step during the fight? What did it matter? The unknown man lay there, glassy-eyed, a streak of blood on his chin.

When a misfortune happens, there's no way out.

It was written somewhere that it had to finish this way.

Wedged between two policemen in the back seat of the car, I felt myself slipping into a parallel world from which there was no turning back. The handcuffs chafed my wrists. The rancid smell of the two policemen choked me – or maybe it was my own smell. What did it matter? I had killed a man, and that had sobered me up.

'Do you know who you killed? A national hero, one of the most decorated officers in the Great War. It's the guillotine for you, boy …'

My body shook.

'Go on, laugh,' one of the policemen said, elbowing me in the side. 'We'll see how long you laugh when your head rolls into the basket.'

I wasn't laughing: I was sobbing.

It was fully daylight now, dazzling white. A limpid sky rolled out the carpet for the rising sun. Early risers hurried along the streets, dazed with sleep. A shopkeeper raised the iron shutter of his shop with a din that shatterd the morning silence. He adjusted his smock before hanging his pole on a hook. A traffic policeman whistled at a carter whose horse was refusing to move out of the way. A group of nuns crossed the road quickly. For all of them, it would be a day like any other. For me, nothing would ever be the same again. Life was going on, supreme in its banality. Mine was escaping from me in a puff of smoke. I thought of my mother. What was she doing right now? I imagined her sitting on a mat, watching my father sink into madness. My father! Would he ever see off his ghosts? Would the noise of machine guns and bombs die down at last and allow him to listen to the furtive course of time passing? In front of me, the flabby, wrinkled neck of the driver reminded me of a broken accordion. It was as if the weight of his thoughts was pressing on his neck. The police car drove past a market, past the Douniazed cinema, which was showing a comedy film. A vendor of *torraicos* was lining up his cones on his makeshift stall. Soon, urchins would start prowling around his little cart, looking for an opportunity to rob him. The driver hooted his horn to clear a path through the pedestrians; a pointless gesture because the way was already clear. Through the windscreen, I could see the prison waiting for me, implacable; I could smell the stench of the damp gloom where cries would have no echoes, where remorse would be nothing more than a cellmate or a pet, my Siamese twin.

I thought of Edmond Bourg, the author of *The Miracle Man*, the savage way he had killed his wife and her lover, the blade that had jammed on the day of his execution, the revered priest the murderer had become ... Would I too be entitled to a miracle? I would so much like to wake up to a future washed clean of my sins. I probably wouldn't be a priest or an imam, but I would never again raise my hand to my fellow man. I would pay a lot of attention to my friends and I wouldn't respond to the provocations of my enemies. I would live without anger, generous, holding on to what was essential, and I would be able to find peace everywhere I went. Of Irène, I would have a tender memory, of Gino a fervent repentance; I promised to submit to test after test without complaint if such was the price for deserving to survive with the people who were dear to me, the people I wasn't able to keep.

Almighty God, You who are said to be merciful, make the blade jam. I wouldn't like to die as brainless as I've lived.

The car drove around Place d'Armes, and I bade farewell to everything that had mattered to me. The two lions guarding the entrance to the town hall struck me as bigger than usual; stiff in their bronze costumes, they looked down on their world. And they were right. Only creatures of flesh and blood end up rotting in the sun.

Even today, plugged into machines in my hospital room, as the erosion of the years slows my pulse, I watch the dusk steal the last light of day and I remember. All I can do is remember. I have the feeling that we never die completely until we have consumed all our memories, that death is the ultimate forgetting.

I'm already confusing names and faces. But other snapshots remain, as sharp as scratches.

Each man retains within him an indelible imprint of a sin that has marked him more than any other. He needs it. It is his way of balancing his being, of putting a little water in his Grail, without which he would take himself for a deity and no praise would satisfy his arrogance. Animals too remember their first prey. It is through it that they realise their instinct for survival. But unlike animals, it is through their first misdeed that men grasp their own insignificance. To raise themselves up a notch, they will look for excuses or attenuating circumstances and persist in trying to prove that they were right.

That's how men are; God may have created them in His image, but didn't specify which one.

On my bedside table lies the book by Edmond Bourg.

I found it in a flea market, among old things and knick-knacks no longer in use. Since then, it has become a sort of prayer book. It revealed many shadowy areas to me, illuminated them with a holy light, but didn't succeed in making me keep the vows I made on that white morning as the police car took me to prison. I didn't become an imam or a just man. I continued living without really being useful to others. Rather like my father when he came back from the war. Maybe *The Miracle Man* wasn't written for me. Out of some morbid need or other, I had looked for a message in it, a sign, a way. After much dissecting of the sentences and brooding between the lines, I ended up seeing it simply as the story of a man who was a murderer, then a priest, a man I never managed to grasp fully. In Diar Rahma, where old men rejected by their offspring or consigned to the scrapheap waited for the end of their downward spiral, reading helped me to swallow my medicines and my tasteless soup without complaint. With time, prophecies become tiresome and you no longer have a desire for anything so troublesome. Oh, time – that lazy fugitive who runs after us like a stray dog which, just when you think you've tamed it, abandons us, depriving us of our bearings. Forgiveness, remorse and sin barely matter compared with a tooth falling out, and faith becomes as uncertain as a trembling hand. Sin is not merely a wrong, it is the proof that evil is inside us, that it's organic, as necessary as anxiety or fever, since our worries are born out of what we lack, and our joys can only be evaluated in relation to our sorrows.

I closed the book, but didn't get rid of it. I waited to disappear in my turn, like Sid Roho and all those I had lost touch with.

Then two miracles happened.

First the letter from Gino I received in prison a few weeks before my trial. Recognising his handwriting on the envelope, I felt faint. I pinched myself to make sure I wasn't delirious. For some nights after that, I couldn't sleep a wink, haunted by ghosts … Gino hadn't written to me from the afterlife. He had survived the stabbing. I clasped the letter to me as if it were a talisman. Of course, I didn't open it. I was illiterate and I had no desire for

371

anyone else to read it for me. Later, much later, I learnt to read in prison. Once I could make out the meaning of the sentences without stumbling too much over the words, I took the letter out again and, although it was short, took ages to get through it: Gino forgave me; he apologised for having objected to Irène and held himself responsible for the mess that had ensued. He came to visit me several times in prison. I didn't dare go to see him in the visiting room. I was afraid of disappointing him, fearful that I would have no response to his smile but a repentant expression, and no answer to his words but a helpless silence. But his letter never left me. I wrapped it in a piece of plastic and sewed it into the lining of my convict's jacket. Today, it is tucked in the middle of my bedside book, *The Miracle Man*.

Then, on the day of my execution, my heart gave out, and they couldn't revive me. The imam apparently said that they couldn't execute a dead man. The warden didn't know whether or not to cut the head off a condemned man who was in a coma … I came to in the military hospital, after weeks of blackness. My heart attack had caused considerable damage. For months, I was nothing but a vegetable. I had lost the use of my lower limbs and my left arm, that left arm whose hook had moved mountains; half my face no longer worked; I was incontinent – a noise, a cry, and my belly evacuated everything, wherever I was. I spent more than a year in hospital, in a wheelchair. In a state of shock. Locked into my lethargy. I was fed with a spoon, washed down with a hose, and was sometimes put in a straitjacket and isolated because of my anxiety attacks. At night, when the nurse lowered the sash window, I would raise my good hand to my neck and scream until they came and sedated me. I only vaguely remember those 'parallel' months, but from them I still keep a strange smell that clings to my nostrils like an animal breath; at moments, nightmarish images go through my mind and I catch myself shaking from head to foot. A photograph of the time shows me in my decrepit state: I look like a broken puppet on a pallet, saliva drooling from my mouth, my features melted, my eyes askew, an idiotic expression on my face. They tried experimental treatments on me, potions concocted by mad scientists; I would emerge from one delirium only to plunge back into another. A doctor declared me insane, unfit to be executed. That may have been what saved me – according to some sources, the Duke may have had something to do with it …

I wasn't pardoned. I was sentenced to hard labour for life. No sooner was I back on my feet than I was sent back to prison. The guards were convinced I was faking it. They would set traps to catch me, harass me constantly, get other convicts to make my life impossible. Whenever one of my attacks came on, they would put me in solitary.

The months, the years finally returned me to the inexorable march of fate. I had again become a full-time convict. A filthy animal in a zoo of horrors. I found myself sparing the cockroaches after being accustomed to squashing them beneath my shoe; they had one advantage I didn't have: they could go where they wanted without asking permission. The rats struck me as less repulsive than the smiles of the military police. Whenever a bird came and landed in the courtyard, I envied it with all my might, and I was jealous of the grain of sand that joined the storm and went travelling around while I remained stuck in my cage, rotting like carrion. At night, whenever some poor bastard howled in his sleep, you pitied him because he would be even less happy when he woke up. In that grim exile, the days wore mourning; no light reached us. In prison, you had no more respect for yourself than you had pity for the condemned man being dragged to the scaffold.

I extorted money from queers, beat up loudmouths, pledged

allegiance to gang bosses and gave up my rations to those who were stronger than me.

There was no place for God in prison. Every reprieve had to be negotiated on the scales of survival. A misplaced look, a superfluous word, a moan louder than the others, and you were automatically buried, without distinction of colour or religion. You had to keep alert; the slightest careless mistake was paid for. I learnt to scheme, to betray, to stab in the back, not to look away when a cellmate was being raped and to look elsewhere when he was being bled dry. I wasn't proud of myself and it didn't matter. I told myself my turn would come, so there was no point in feeling sorry for the first served. I sometimes slept standing up to make the bastards think I was waiting for them, and when they came to rouse me with the tip of their boots, I played dead.

Prison was like a recurring nightmare. The hell of the sky trembled before the hell of men, and horned devils licked the boots of the guards, because nowhere on earth, neither on the battlefields nor in the arenas, did life and death know such contempt as the one in which they merged within the walls of a prison.

I was released in 1962, at a time when the jails were full to bursting with political prisoners. I was fifty-two years old.

When I came out of prison, I didn't recognise my towns or my villages; no faces looked familiar. Alarcon Ventabren had given up the ghost, his farm had fallen into disrepair, and the path that led to it had disappeared beneath the wild grass. All that remained of the Duke was a rambling fable that young gangsters spiced up to make themselves seem important. Oran was nothing like any of my memories. Rue du Général-Cérez had forgotten me. The old men shielded their eyes with their hands and looked me up and down. 'It's me, Turambo,' I would say to them, shadow-boxing. They would step out of my way, wondering if I was in my right mind.

Strangers were living in my parents' house. They informed me that after my father died, my mother had followed Mekki, who had chosen to settle near Ghardaïa where his in-laws lived. My search led me to a rudimentary graveyard. On a grave, a name half erased by sandstorms: Khammar Taos, died 13 April 1949. Judging by the state of the grave and the ugly, scrawny bush that had grown over it, nobody had visited the place in a long time.

I looked for my uncle but couldn't find any trace of him.

It was as if the earth had swallowed him up.

Back to Oran. On Boulevard Mascara, the haberdasher's was now a shop selling television sets and radios. Above the door was a sign saying Radiola. Upstairs, an Arab family were living in the Ramouns' flat. Gino had left the country without leaving a forwarding address. During my imprisonment, he had married Louise, the Duke's daughter, and run a large company making domestic appliances before a bomb attack reduced it to rubble. I never heard from him again. I myself had no fixed abode where I could be contacted. I wandered where the seasons took me, like a lost, faded, stunned spectre, incapable of situating myself in relation to people and things. There was fury in the gloom, and the burning sun couldn't supplant the inferno of my country at war. Worn down to nothing, I hated myself for being no more than my misfortunes. The world that welcomed me was totally alien to me.

The history of a nation coming to painful birth was being written, putting mine aside. A history in which the miracles had nothing to do with me.

I had left my life behind me in prison; I was reborn to something I couldn't care less about, too old to start again from scratch. With no bearings or convictions, I wasn't capable of beginning all over again. I no longer had the strength. I had survived only to learn, to my cost, that a ruined life cannot be put right.

I didn't find love again either. Did I look for it? I'm not sure. It wasn't a man who had left prison after a quarter of a century of self-denial, it was a ghost; my heart only beat to give rhythm to its fears. At first, back in the world of the living, I would be reminded of Irène's perfume by the smell of the woods. I would embrace a tree trunk and stand there in silence. In the world of the living, the dead are only entitled to prayers and silence. I didn't dare dream of another woman after Irène. Nor did any woman want to stay with a wild-eyed convict who smelt of tragedy from miles away. My face told a story of expiation; my words reassured nobody; there was nothing in my gaze but the blackness of the dungeons and I could no longer smile without giving the impression that I wanted to bite … Yes, my brother, you who give no credit to anything but redemption, who question the facts and curse genius, who jeer at the virtuous and praise imposters, you who disfigure beauty so that horror might exult, who reduce your happiness to a vulgar need to cause harm and who spit on the light so that the world may return to darkness, yes, you, my twin in the shadows, do you know why we no longer embody anything but our old demons? It is because the angels have died of our wounds.

I looked for work in order not to die of starvation; I was a ragman, a nightwatchman, a caretaker of vacant property, an exorcist without a flock and without magic. I stole fruit from the markets and chickens from remote farms; I begged for charity and the leftovers of revellers, escaping the snares of the days as best I could. My fists, which had once deposed champions, were no longer much use for anything; I had cut off three fingers to make my jailers feel sorry for me – in prison, people thought of all kinds of nonsense that might give them back their freedom.

What freedom? I had clamoured for mine, but, once released, I didn't know what to do with it. I roamed from town to douar, sleeping under bridges. Strangely, I missed my cell; my fellow convicts seemed dearer to me than my lost family. The country had changed. My era was long gone.

I was arrested on military sites and subjected to brutal interrogations, was interned in a refuge for vagrants, then went back to being a tramp. A ragged drunk, I reeled through dubious neighbourhoods, yelling at the top of my voice, dribble on my chin and my eyes rolled upwards, and I fled blindly from boys who stoned me like a mangy old dog.

I learnt to live without the people I loved, roaming from waste grounds to town squares for decades, and when my legs could no longer carry me, when my eyes started confusing shapes and colours, when the slightest cold turned my eyes to winter, I gave up my bundle and the open road and, surrounded by my absent ones, let myself be tossed from one nursing home to another like a piece of flotsam blown about by contrary winds. In time, my absent ones left, one after the other. All that remained were a few vague memories to stave off my loneliness.

In my hospital room, night is getting ready to put my memory to sleep. It's dark and the nurse forgets to switch on the light; I can't get out of bed to put it on because of the tubes that hold me captive. In the next bed, a patient who's nothing but skin and bone fiddles with his tape player. It's a ritual with him. At the same hour, every day since his admission, he listens to the singing of Lounis Aït Menguellet, whose repertoire he knows by heart. The warm voice of the Kabyle singer takes me far back into the past to a time when Gino and I used to go to *cafés-concerts* in working-class areas.

I never went back to the streets of my youth; I never again approached a stadium; I didn't see myself in any celebration and no victory made my soul quiver. Sometimes, passing a poster, I would stand there dreamily without knowing why, as if I could place the face, then I would go on my way, which never led to the same place; for me, the world was populated by strangers.

I was looking at a mirror and couldn't see myself in it.

If we look closely at our lives, we realise that we are not the heroes of our own stories. However much we feel sorry for ourselves or enjoy a fame based on fleeting talent, there will always be someone better or worse off than us. Oh, if only we could put *everything* into perspective – affectation, honour, sensitivity, faith and self-denial, falsehood as well as truth – we would doubtless find satisfaction even in frugality and realise very soon to what extent humility preserves us from insanity; there is no worse madness than thinking the world revolves around us. Every failure proves to us that we don't amount to much, but who wants to admit that? We take our dreams for challenges when they are nothing but chimeras, otherwise how to explain that in death as in birth we are poor and naked? According to logic, all that counts is what remains, but we are all destined to die one day, and what trace of us will survive in the dust of ages? The image we give of ourselves doesn't make us genuine artists but genuine fakers. We think we know where we are going, what we want, what's good for us and what isn't, and we do what we can to ensure that what doesn't work out isn't our fault. Our feeble excuses become irrefutable arguments for hiding our faces, and we elevate our hypothetical certainties to absolute truths in order to carry on speculating, even though we've got it all wrong. Isn't that the way we walk over our own bodies to coexist with what is beyond us? In the long run, what have we pursued our whole life through unsuccessfully, but ourselves?

But it's over now.

My story ends in this dark room saved from hell only by the voice of Aït Menguellet. No friend by my bed, no woman at my side – maybe it's better like this. This way, I can be sure of leaving nothing behind me.

At the age of ninety-three, what can we expect of the storm or its subsiding? I expect nothing, no redemption, no remission, no news, no reunions. I've drunk the cup to the dregs, suffered insults to the point of agony; I consider that I've been paid all that was owed to me. My breathing has grown weak, my veins no longer bleed, my pains no longer hurt …

Let no one talk of miracles; what's a miracle in a hospital room with no light? I've drawn a line under my joys and made peace with my sorrows: I'm good and ready. When memory weighs on the present, replacing the daylight being born at our window every morning, it must mean that the clock has decided that our time has come. We learn then to close our eyes on the few reflexes we still have and be alone with ourselves; in other words, with someone who becomes elusive to us as we accustom ourselves to his silences, then to his distances, until the big sleep takes us away from the chaos of all things.

# The African Equation

Yasmina Khadra
translated by Howard Curtis

Through the eyes of a kidnapped westerner, literary giant Yasmina Khadra tells a gripping story of moral conflict, cultural awakening and lasting friendship in East Africa

Kurt Krausmann, a recently bereaved Frankfurt doctor, is persuaded to join his friend Hans on a humanitarian mission to the Comoros islands. On the way, misfortune strikes again: the boat is hijacked in the Gulf of Aden and the men are taken hostage. Held in a remote hideout, the prisoners suffer harsh conditions and the brutality of their guards; self-styled warriors, ex-army captains and even poets drawn to banditry through poverty or opportunism. When the group decamps to a lawless desert region and Hans is taken away, Kurt sinks deeper into despair. But fellow inmate Bruno attempts to show him another side to the wounded yet defiant continent he loves.

ISBN: 9781908313706
e-ISBN: 9781908313829

# The Dictator's Last Night

Yasmina Khadra
translated by Julian Evans

'People say I am a megalomaniac. It is not true. I am an exceptional being, providence incarnate, envied by the gods, able to make a faith of his cause.'

In this gripping imagining of Gaddafi's last hours, Yasmina Khadra delves into the mind of one of the most complex and controversial figures of recent history.

October 2011. In the dying days of the Libyan civil war, Muammar Gaddafi is hiding out in his home town of Sirte along with his closest advisors. They await a convoy that will take them south, away from encroaching rebel forces and NATO aerial attacks. The mood is sombre. In what will be his final night, Gaddafi reflects on an extraordinary life, whilst still raging against the West, his fellow Arab nations and the ingratitude of the Libyan people.

ISBN: 9781910477137
e-ISBN: 9781910477168